OTHER BOOKS BY

JEROME CHARYN

PUBLISHED BY LIVERIGHT/NORTON

Bitter Bronx: Thirteen Stories (2015)

*I Am Abraham: A Novel of Lincoln
and the Civil War* (2014)

*The Secret Life of Emily Dickinson:
A Novel* (2010)

*Johnny One-Eye: A Tale of the
American Revolution* (2008)

"Graced with vivid, vigorous writing. . . . [Charyn] has written the rousing yarn advertised in his title and dust jacket, and he has written it well."   —Gerard Helferich, *Wall Street Journal*

"Charyn captures Roosevelt's doubts, aspirations and ebullient spirit. . . . [A] lively, warts-and-all portrait of an irrepressible man."
                        —Mary Ann Gwinn, *Newsday*

"For TR, Mr. Charyn pulls out the stops offering up the man in his own voice, a magnificent mashup of macho and aristocrat. . . . *Cowboy King* is a novel at its best: engaging, immersive and compelling."
                        —*Comics Grinder*

"In retellings of the lives and doings of grand, almost mythological figures who shaped this country, the real and fantastical commingle, overlap, become inseparable. It is this fundamental inseparability that makes Jerome Charyn's novel about the life and times of Theodore Roosevelt so much fun to read. . . . [A] surprisingly poignant assessment of smaller, more universally human moments. . . . Charyn has a gift for the unexpected, both linguistically and narratively. . . . Deftly, Charyn interweaves what is real and invented about Roosevelt's life, and the result is at once surprising and very entertaining."
                        —Omar El Akkad, *BookPage*, starred review

"A rendering of Teddy Roosevelt's early life that spotlights formative moments in colorful, entertaining episodes. . . . Charyn makes artful use of historical fact and fiction's panache to capture the man before he became one of the great U.S. presidents and a face on Mount Rushmore."   —*Kirkus Reviews*, starred review

"Marked from beginning to end by restlessness and adventure. . . . A ripping, enjoyable yarn."   —Keir Graff, *Booklist*

The
PERILOUS
ADVENTURES
of the
COWBOY
KING

A NOVEL OF
TEDDY ROOSEVELT
AND HIS TIMES

JEROME
CHARYN

LIVERIGHT PUBLISHING
CORPORATION

A Division of W. W. Norton & Company

Independent Publishers Since 1923

For information about permission to reproduce selections from this book,
write to Permissions, Liveright Publishing Corporation, a division of
W. W. Norton & Company, Inc., 500 Fifth Avenue, New York, NY 10110

For information about special discounts for bulk purchases,
please contact W. W. Norton Special Sales at
specialsales@wwnorton.com or 800-233-4830

Manufacturing by LSC Communications, Harrisonburg.
Book design by Barbara Bachman
Production manager: Anna Oler

ISBN 978-1-63149-666-0 pbk.

Liveright Publishing Corporation
500 Fifth Avenue, New York, N.Y. 10110
www.wwnorton.com

W. W. Norton & Company Ltd.
15 Carlisle Street, London W1D 3BS

1 2 3 4 5 6 7 8 9 0

FOR TING,

mistress eternal

and majestic cat

CONTENTS

DRAMATIS PERSONAE

WILLIAM WINTERS-WHITE, a war correspondent who would accompany TR to Cuba and fight alongside the Rough Riders.

THOMAS COLLIER PLATT, also known as the Easy Boss and Senator Tom. Chief of New York's Republican Party, he had mixed feelings about TR and his maverick brand of politics. Yet TR couldn't have survived if the Easy Boss hadn't meddled on his behalf.

ALICE HATHAWAY LEE ROOSEVELT, TR's first wife. Blond, vibrant, and beautiful, she would die at the age of twenty-two, after giving birth to a daughter, Alice Lee Roosevelt.

ALICE LEE ROOSEVELT, also known as Baby Lee, Little Alice, and Sissy. TR's oldest and most problematic child. She was as much of a maverick as he was and would wound him *and* delight him in her own spectacular way.

TAGGART, a Pinkerton detective who would later serve in the Rough Riders and transform himself from TR's fiercest enemy into one of his most loyal friends.

SERGEANT RADDISON, leader of the bicycle squad when TR was Police Commissioner. He would also serve in the Rough Riders.

JOSEPHINE, a cougar cub.

SECONDARY CHARACTERS

MARTHA BULLOCH ROOSEVELT, TR's mother, also known as Mittie. A Southerner who felt trapped in Manhattan, she would soon become a childlike waif.

ANNA BULLOCH, also known as Auntie Anna, was Mittie's eldest sister.

GRANDMAMMA BULLOCH, Mittie's mother.

CORINNE ROOSEVELT, also known as Connie. TR's younger sister.

HYNES, one of Brave Heart's servants. He stole from the Roosevelts' cashbox and was caught by Bamie.

QUENTIN MOSS, night watchman at the Newsboys' Lodging-House, one of the charitable institutions founded by Brave Heart.

ARTHUR HAMILTON CUTLER, TR's tutor.

MRS. VALENTINA MORRIS, Elliott Roosevelt's mistress, who would remain utterly devoted to him.

VELVET BILL HOWE AND LITTLE ABE HUMMEL, two mythical nineteenth century lawyers who were the sultans of criminal court; they rarely ever lost a case.

MISS KATIE MANN, Elliott's Bavarian chambermaid who had a love child with him, and was represented by Howe & Hummel. The two sultans realized that TR couldn't afford to have the little boy's presence revealed.

ANNA HALL ROOSEVELT, Elliott's hypnotically beautiful wife, who died of diphtheria at the age of twenty-nine.

ELEANOR ROOSEVELT, also known as Granny. TR's niece was the eldest child of Elliott and Anna Hall Roosevelt. This gawky girl, who dressed in Baby Lee's hand-me-downs, was Elliott's favorite and the future wife of President Franklin Delano Roosevelt. She would become one of the most revered women of the twentieth century.

HUMBLE JAKE HESS, leader of Morton Hall, Manhattan's Twenty-first Republican District headquarters, and an early supporter of TR.

HENRY GEORGE, prominent nineteenth century socialist who ran for Mayor of New York in 1886 on the United Labor ticket.

DON RUEBEN, leader of the Vaqueros, a band of Cuban mercenaries, during the Spanish-American War.

BUFFALO BILL CODY, frontiersman and scout, who would later become head of *Buffalo Bill's Wild West*.

NANNIE CABOT LODGE, wife of Henry Cabot Lodge, United States Senator from Massachusetts. She had an incredible charisma.

CABOT, i.e., HENRY CABOT LODGE, a fellow Harvard graduate, who was one of TR's closest political allies.

MARK HANNA, also known as Fat Marcus. Affluent United States Senator from Ohio who served as President McKinley's chief political strategist.

MINNIE G. KELLY, TR's private secretary at Police Headquarters.

DR. FERDINAND JESSUP, Manhattan's chief coroner.

ASHBEL GRIEF, chairman of the Social Reform Club in Manhattan while TR was Police Commissioner.

SERGEANT FLEISCHER, the telephone dispatcher at Police Headquarters during TR's reign.

KING CALLAHAN, owner of the King's Table, a bar on Third Avenue. He fought against Police Commissioner Roosevelt's blue laws.

WHITEY WHITMAN, a crooked deputy inspector chased off the police force by TR.

ARCHIBALD TOWNE, New York County Sheriff, a despot and a thief.

SAMUEL BRATT, a shyster lawyer who defended Sheriff Towne in front of TR's Corruption Committee.

BRYSON CARTERETT, prosecutor of a small town in Indian Territory.

LONG JOHN MCMANUS, a thug for the Republican Party who nearly ruined TR's career.

TED, KERMIT, ETHEL, ARCHIBALD, AND QUENTIN ROOSEVELT, also known as the bunnies; they were the five children that TR had with Edith.

CAPTAIN LEONARD WOOD, President's McKinley's personal physician, TR's trusted friend, and the first commander of the Rough Riders.

RUSSELL ALGER, Secretary of War in the McKinley Administration.

FIGHTIN' JOE WHEELER, a United States Army general who fought on the Confederate side during the Civil War.

GENERAL WILLIAM RUFUS SHAFTER, head of the Fifth Army Corps.

PETER ALBRIGHT, leader of the Stranglers, a group of vigilantes in the Badlands.

RED FINNEGAN, a Badlands gunslinger who would later join TR's Rough Riders.

BLACK JACK MCGRAW, a cardsharp in the Badlands who hid among the Sioux.

CORPORAL ANTONIA/ANTON LITTLE FEATHER, a female Rough Rider who disguised herself as a male and carried the regimental flag into battle.

BARDSHAR, TR's orderly in Cuba.

SERGEANT BELLOWS, TR's body-servant while both were with the Rough Riders.

LITTLE HAYNES, a cloakroom attendant at the Capitol in Albany.

DR. MARTIN FARADAY, head of the Bronx Zoo.

DR. LIONEL TRELL, chief surgeon at the Bronx Zoo.

ABEL MARTINSON, a sharpshooter among the Rough Riders who worked for *Buffalo Bill's Wild West* after the war.

YOUNG-MAN-AFRAID-OF-THE-SOUND-OF-HIS-OWN-VOICE, a Pawnee scout among the Rough Riders who later worked for Buffalo Bill.

GEORGE B. CORTELYOU, President McKinley's private secretary.

JOHN HAY, President McKinley's Secretary of State, who had mythical status, since he'd once been President Lincoln's private secretary.

IDA MCKINLEY, President McKinley's half-deranged wife.

THE PERILOUS ADVENTURES
OF THE COWBOY KING

PART ONE

CHAPTER I

BRAVE
HEART

1862–1878

FIRST THERE WAS A METALLIC AROMA, THE TASTE OF TIN in my mouth. Then the monster would appear with rusty fingernails, his yellow eyes swaying like twin lanterns in the dark, his fierce red whiskers clotted with human blood. He crouched at the foot of my bed, prepared to gobble.

"Fingers first," the werewolf muttered. I could feel the walls of my chest collapse as I began to wheeze. It was always worse at night, when I would have great, rumbling gasps, with the wolf-man's yellow eyes riveted to mine, gaze upon gaze, like some diabolic vigil. As a boy with a scientific bent, I didn't believe in monsters of any kind. Yet it was hard to reconcile rusty fingernails and red whiskers. And the wheezing wouldn't stop.

We couldn't have a doctor constantly at my call, waiting with a candle. But I did have Brave Heart. My Auntie Anna had given Father that name and it clung to him for life. She said that Father reminded her of Mr. Brave Heart, whom she confused with another character, the gallant guardian who slays wicked giants and protects women and children from lions in Bunyan's classic about Christian souls.

Our Brave Heart was a bearded man with broad shoulders. He didn't wear a helmet and a sword. He was a merchant prince who might have stepped out of Christian allegory. The unfortunate mattered as much to him as the family fortune. Father possessed a leonine look. I could have imagined him slaying giants and were-wolves in another world. He gave me my breath, willed it to me. He would carry me from room to room in the middle of the night, push air into my lungs with the forceful rhythm of his gait. I drank cups of black coffee delivered from his hand and was smoking cigars before the age of five. Each puff, Father said, would replenish me. And when nothing else worked, Father would carry me in a blanket down to the stable and have the night watchman rig up the Roosevelt high phaeton with its pair of long-tailed horses and we rode into the wind. I've never had as fine an adventure in all my years. It was like sitting in the clouds, way above the horses' heads, racing along in that sloped carriage.

We careened around other carriages and delivery cars. Father was an excellent whip. His long-tails never stumbled in their traces, never went awry. He drove us to the shanties and scorched plains of Manhattan's Upper West Side. It was so far from civilization that we called it the Badlands. Our Little Dakota was stuffed with scrap heaps and desolate shacks where the impoverished lived near river rats hiding from the law. Nothing bothered Brave Heart. We passed the campfires of one robbers' roost after another. Such desperate men learned not to tinker with our carriage. If the untutored attacked us with a pipe, a rock, or any other missile, Father would lash at these river rats with his horsewhip until they landed on their rumps and sat there in one great tangle.

"Teedie, has your breath come back?"

All that excitement among the campfires had made my lungs whistle with clean air. I did not dream of a wolf-man on that ride.

"Sir, I'm fit as a combustion machine."

Father wasn't being reckless. He hadn't dealt with the river rats to entertain me and my lungs. He had to declare his right-of-way, or we would have had to stick to a prescribed path. And on we went into the Badlands, with its shantytowns, orphanages, and insane asylum. He liked to wear his linen duster on these long treks. It had very wide pockets, and he'd always stop in his traces whenever he found an abandoned kitten on the road. He'd hop down from the carriage, scoop up the kitten, and stuff it into his pocket. Tomorrow we'd bring this stray to a pet shop on Third Avenue run by a pair of spinsters. It was an orphan, most likely, chased out of some litter. Father had a fondness for the ragged, the lonely, and the lame.

We had a little patch of bad luck on this particular early morning ride. One of our wheels fell off, and the carriage would have spun out of control if Brave Heart hadn't leaned over the long-tails and pulled on the rigging with all his might. We sat there at a terrible tilt. Father hadn't forgotten his toolbox, but first he had to chase down the missing wheel. And now every damn robbers' roost in Little Dakota had us at a disadvantage. Several lubbers arrived. They were dressed in motley gear. One had a cape and an eye patch; another had torn pajamas out of the lunatic asylum; a third had a military tunic. They were all carrying lanterns, lead pipes, and long sticks.

"Lookee here," said their leader, wrapped in his cape. "Don't make a fuss, or we'll harm the boy."

I had Brave Heart with me and shouldn't have panicked, but I did. My combustion machine went out of whack. My lungs couldn't catch a lick of air. Father cradled me in his arms.

"Are you deaf?" asked the river rat. "Pay attention, or that boy will strangle on his own snot. Give us your fancy carriage and we'll be gone."

Father pushed air into my lungs with his powerful hands and waited until the wheezing stopped. Then his touch turned delicate, as if I were a boy out of a doll hospital. The phaeton remained at a wicked angle without one wheel, and Father had to prop me against his seat, while the river rats poked him with their wanton pipes and sticks.

"This is your last chance, bub."

Father didn't say a word, and the rats smiled, thinking he was silent out of fear.

These louts hadn't taken the least measure of such a man. The roots of his beard went crimson in the lantern light. He'd left his whip on the footrest of the carriage, and he had to pounce on the river rats with his bare hands, sending them all a-scatter with a series of quick blows. Afterward I watched him suck the blood from his raw knuckles. He was still shivering with rage. He had to steady the horses, whisper to them, rub their noses.

He fixed the wheel, sullying his frock coat and lingering in the same long silence. The sun began to rise over the Bloomingdale Asylum and its somber row of black chimneys, creating a fan of light that looked like very fat fingers. I was glad, glad, that I had been born, despite the frozen fist in my lungs, despite the wolf-man at the foot of my bed, and the sudden bouts of diarrhea that we called the Roosevelt colic. I belonged to Brave Heart's company of orphans, even if I wasn't an orphan at all.

THE ROOSEVELT RESIDENCE HAD a line of black rails that swept across our little balcony like a runaway musical score. Perhaps that runaway score was a premonition, because there was pandemonium on East Twentieth Street when war broke out. Mittie, as we called Mama, was a genuine Southern belle with black hair and skin as fine and pale as porcelain. She grew up at Bulloch Hall, a plantation in old Cherokee country near the Chattahoochee River.

Mama's eldest sister, Auntie Anna, lived with us, too, together with Grandmamma Bulloch. They'd fallen on hard times after Pappy Bulloch died and couldn't make ends meet. Grandmamma wore a lace cap, and when Papa had to entertain Union generals, Grandmamma would vanish into some secret corner of the house.

Once, while the Union generals sniffed brandy and puffed on their Havanas in the parlor, Papa excused himself for a moment and went on a mission to find Grandmamma. He looked every-where. Finally he discovered her in a closet on the fifth floor, where the servants lived. Grandmamma sat in the dark by her lonesome, wrapped in a shawl, with a cat's blazing eyes. She wasn't caught in a dream. She was as coherent as a lightning bolt.

"I'm a burden to ya, Brave Heart," she said.

"You are not. You've been kind to the children."

"Kindness isn't the occasion here," she said. "I've insulted you in front of your Yankee generals. We're kin now, and I should have served the hors d'oeuvres and made pleasant chatter. But I can't. It jars upon my feelings, sir."

Papa didn't say another word. He gathered Grandmamma Bulloch in his arms and carried her downstairs to the room she shared with Auntie Anna. He pretended not to notice the Rebel flag in her room.

Father wanted to join the Union Army, but two of Mama's brothers were already with the Rebels. So how could he volunteer and compromise Mama's own people? He had to hire a substitute, an Irish lad, to fight in his place. And it cut right into his soul. He couldn't run away to war and he had to tolerate the Stars and Bars in his own house. I felt his shame, and it was my shame, too. His shoulders slumped and at times he looked like a sullen black bear. I worried that he might go on a rampage. But there were no river rats around, just Roosevelts and Bullochs, and he loved us all.

My sister Bamie—a contraction of *bambina*—must have been dropped from her cradle, because she had to wear a harness for her curved spine. Father was determined to fix her humped back. But she never did outgrow that ailment, even with the harness. My brother Elliott, or Ellie, was long and limber, like Brave Heart, while Corinne was the war baby, with blond curls. Mother marched around in white muslin like a somnambule the longer the fighting lasted. She plotted with her own sister and Grandmamma Bulloch to send contraband—handkerchiefs and sweaters—across the lines. So it was Bamie who began to look after us, curved spine and all. We loved Mama, we all did. But she suffered from palpitations and melancholy fits. Papa was passionate about her from the moment they met. He bought her trinkets and babied her; he'd laugh and call Mama his fifth child, whereas Bamie was more of a mother to us by the time she was ten. Grandmamma Bulloch died one afternoon in the middle of a sentence about Yankee pilferers and pirates; Mama and Auntie Anna both fell into a profound despair.

Meanwhile, Bamie had to boss the servants around and scrutinize the butcher bills, after Brave Heart finally went to war—in his own fashion.

Father became an Allotment Commissioner, you see. Sutlers had taken advantage of Union soldiers, getting them to buy whiskey at astronomical prices, so they didn't have a penny in their pockets. The sutlers were an army unto themselves. Half of 'em wore the Union blue, borrowed from the War Department with extravagant bribes. The other half looked like undertakers, mean and malicious in their black frocks and cavalrymen's boots, several with sabers at their side. After Father was appointed a commissioner by President Lincoln himself, he traveled from camp to camp in the dark of winter, chasing after the sutlers and convincing raw recruits to send money home to their families. The sutlers fought back, surrounding Father at one encampment, attacking him with their sabers, and he had to whack at them with a loose board from a picket fence until the sabers flew into the wind. He'd return home with frostbitten hands and feet, his collar clotted with blood; it was Bamie who nursed him, rubbing Father in hot cloths until all the numbness— and clots of blood—disappeared.

But while he was away, Bamie watched over us. She'd inherited Father's broad shoulders. The servants were terrified of her masculine air. The hump on her back couldn't diminish her. She had a swarthy complexion, like an Arabian prince. I called her our own little Atlas, who carried the weight of the Roosevelt clan on her crooked back.

"Teedie, you haven't done your breathing exercises. Papa will be disappointed in both of us."

"But Papa let me smoke a cigar," I muttered in my defense.

"You're seven years old. You can't strut around like a Mississippi gambler."

She'd dress Corinne, comb Elliott's hair, and attend to Mama, who was more and more of a recluse after Sherman's men broke through Bulloch Hall on their march to the sea and robbed every pot and pan and picture from the walls. Bamie had to treat her like a delinquent child.

"Mother, if you won't eat, I'll have to force food down your gullet like a stranded chick."

"I declare," Mittie said, "you shouldn't talk to your mother in that tone of voice. I'm far from stranded. I'm in mourning, child."

"Well, then mourn with a full mouth."

That's how Bamie got her way. And when she caught one of our servants stealing gold coins from the family strongbox, Bamie fired him on the spot. He was an out-and-out rascal, this fellow, Mr. Hynes, whom Papa had hired during the war when it was hard to find first-class help. He'd arrived with a lukewarm recommendation from one of Father's banker friends. Hynes was a dipsomaniac. He'd wander about, dancing with invisible creatures, crashing into tables, as he did his phantom waltz with a terrible lust in his eye. Seems he couldn't live without the bottle. And he tried to bully my sister.

"You don't have the authority to fire me, girl. You're ten years old."

"Eleven, Mr. Hynes. And I have all the authority in the world. Your employer, Mr. Theodore Roosevelt Sr., has bonded me."

The dipsomaniac was worried now. He might have been a crack thief, but he didn't have Bamie's iron intellect.

"What sort of bond?"

She handed him a scroll. I'm not sure it made much sense, but it did have Papa's signature. And this wayward butler was wary of written documents. Still, Hynes wouldn't leave. He'd slobber one moment, repent the next. He even proposed marriage to my eleven-year-old sister. "I'll cure that hump, Miz Bamie. I'll kiss it to death." Bamie had to fend him off with a fly swatter. Mama couldn't stop him. Nobody could. And he continued to prey upon a household whose single monitor was a child who had to wear a harness.

Bamie wrote to Papa, of course, though it was hard to track him down. He was often in the saddle ten hours a day. But Hynes ran out of luck while he lorded it over us. We could hear Father's key turn in the latch. He'd come home without warning. He remembered the last time Bamie and I had stood at the front door, waving to him, and he couldn't get that image out of his mind. I'm not sure what he felt about Mama and her devotion to the South, when he himself was an Allotment Commissioner, saving Union boys from the sutlers' avariciousness.

Still, he could read the current situation in Bamie's eyes. And Papa caught the butler wearing *his* boots.

Hynes whipped his head back and forth and hopped out of Papa's boots. I could see that Papa wanted to slap Hynes into hell. But he muffled his rage somehow. The Roosevelts did not strike their servants—it was considered vile.

"Mr. Hynes, you will return the money you stole. You will apologize to my daughter, and then you will disappear from Manhattan. Should I ever find you in someone else's employ, I will not show you the least bit of mercy."

Hynes was no better than the sutlers, taking advantage of us like that, proposing marriage to an eleven-year-old girl. Father was a pinch away from throttling him. So Hynes repaid every last dollar, and had to leave without a red cent. He bowed, called me and Ellie the little masters, slobbered over my sister's hand, kissing it again and again, and vanished into the fog, one more forgotten soul.

I WOULD WANDER ON my own while Father was away. I passed a market at Union Square, with its endless caravan of open-air stalls, and discovered a dead seal laid out on its own coffin of wood. Its whiskers were still wet. It looked like a black torpedo with flippers and webbed toes. Its belly was as pink as congealed blood. The seal had been killed in the harbor, according to the fishmongers. I wasn't quite sure if the seal's meat was ever sold. But its carcass resided there on a board day after day. The fishmongers soon became my friends. They said that the seal had been put there as a kind of circus attraction, to draw customers into the market. They could tell how devoted I was to that dead seal and they didn't discourage my visits. I measured its length and girth with a folding pocket foot rule. I drew pictures of my first specimen.

One day the seal was gone. And that vanished carcass grabbed at my heart and gave me palpitations. It was curious how much dearer it was to me dead than alive. I might not have been attracted to the same seal swimming in the harbor like a primordial creature. My poor seal had begun to putrefy, the fishmongers said, and it was pulling customers away from the market. But they had a gift for me—the seal's skull. I was startled by how tiny and delicate it was. The fishmongers had shaved off the flesh and boiled the seal's head in a pot. I could cradle the skull in my hands. I marveled at its mandible, at its jagged rows of teeth, how yellow the bones were. I put the skull in a shoe box under my bed.

I'd become a zoölogist before I was seven. I started the "Teedie Roosevelt Museum of Natural History" in my room, collecting whatever specimens I could—snails and birds and the carcasses of chipmunks. My museum stank up the house, our chambermaid said—and after she refused to clean my quarters, the entire collection was relocated to a storage bin in the back hall. Bamie was rather neutral about my endeavors, though she never discouraged me. She was much too busy hiding Mother's near-criminal devotion to Jeff Davis and the Stars and Bars and having to deal with the household budget. She barely had a minute to herself.

Given her bewilderment over Mother's peccadilloes, large and little, it was Father who took delight in my studies. He'd return from a visit to the camps with his frozen feet and watch me stooped over the seal's skull, squirrel bones, and other little treasures in the back hall. I'd outgrown that original storage bin, and Brave Heart bequeathed me another. He scrutinized all the notes I had kept and stared into my eyes.

"Teedie, what do you want to be when you grow up?"

"A scientist," I said without a lick of hesitation.

"You'll be poor as a church mouse," he said. "And you'll have to economize—Bamie will watch over all your bills. But I've made enough, son, to keep you afloat. If you're a scientist, a real scientist, you can't turn into a dilettante. I won't allow that."

"Father, I'll be as serious as serious can be—I'm seven years old."

Brave Heart smiled behind the little strands of gray in his beard. "Ah, I nearly forgot."

In the spring we went out into the wild garden in our back yard, with its lone cow and family of peacocks with clipped feathers, and we listened to birdcalls. I could warble the different tunes and mating calls. I'd become a master of birdsong. Sound was *everything* to me. I could shut my eyes and gather myself into a competing symphony of songs.

"Papa, that's *our* blue jay."

"How can you be so sure?"

"Two long notes and one short trill. That's our blue jay showing off."

I also kept track of the plumage. I drew the anatomies of bird after bird. Father found me a box of pastels with every color in creation—pastels that had come from an ornithologist's private studio, and even those colors weren't enough. Nature was far more various than human desire and human will.

We went into the woods on Long Island a few summers after the war. I mimicked every birdcall.

"Teedie, you're a darn magician."

"No, Papa, I'm a scientist. I trained my ear."

Later Father would let me study with a taxidermist, and I went everywhere with a supply of arsenical soap to preserve the skin of whatever creature I mounted. I had a special toothbrush that I kept in my kit. But the maid was careless, and she mixed up all my toothbrushes; so, like a country doctor, I had to keep my own taxidermist's bag. But no matter how successful I was with my mounts, I couldn't control the marks of woe on my father's face.

"Son, you'll have to *make* your body just like you've been making your mind," he said, looking at my pitiful arms and legs. It was Bamie who had to fight off the hooligans in our back yard. A bloody nose was bad enough, but I didn't want to lose the sketches in my notebooks to some young highwayman on the prowl.

So Father installed a gymnasium in our mezzanine. I exercised with Elliott sometimes, and sometimes alone. Ellie was taller and had much more of a natural build, but I had to labor over every little band of muscle. I had my first shotgun when I was thirteen—a silver-plated piece of French design. Ellie was a much better shot, while I had to squint at every target. That's when I realized how nearsighted I was.

Papa furnished me with a pair of spectacles that were like metallic peepers; a new landscape unfolded like a miraculous fan. For the first time, the very first, I could peer through a blurry void and distinguish light and line. I could do all my anatomical drawings inside my head, and I discovered even more colors—it was like staring at the splendor of a peacock's tail and picking at an array of feathers—real feathers, not imagined ones.

Father wouldn't allow me to fall into a taxidermist's funk, where all I could think about were my specimens and Zeus, my pet garter snake. I had to accompany him to the Newsboys' Lodging-House, a sandstone castle on West Eighteenth Street; he'd built this lodging-house with his own hands, had worked with the stonemasons, had supplied the glass. He'd sup with these boys in his silk cravat and tails, and I supped with them, too, with my pet snake in my pocket. I witnessed every spoonful, while I had a trace of arsenic on my sleeves from my little taxidermy shop at home.

The lodging-house had its own night watchman, who was also caretaker, banker, and part-time cook. His name was Quentin Moss. Papa had hired Quent and vouched for him. Quent might have been an ex-prizefighter or a jailbird, but he'd come fully bonded by my father, and nothing else mattered. He kept the newsboys' receipts, doled out petty cash, filled their bellies, and attended to their wounds—they were often pounced upon by street gangs, with the encouragement of the police.

Newsies kept arriving out of the lampless night. They were a pitiful lot, their pockets weighted down or ripped from their pants, their shoes in a shamble, their faces bloodied from some recent attack; Father had noticed that dilemma before I was ever born. He knew no legislation in the world could help these boys, not the commissioners and the judges who belonged to some political boss or corrupt administration. These were orphans and runaways who couldn't be schooled, who would have ended up in an asylum until they were vacant, soulless vessels, and so Father kept his foundlings in this sandstone castle, where they could be sheltered and fed, and have their own primitive bank accounts.

Father had six generations of Roosevelts at his rear, bankers and traders in glass, and he took nothing for granted. The Roosevelts had arrived in Manhattan as pig farmers, and Father never forgot the smell of manure that clung to the family name. He was a burly man who had helped found the Metropolitan Museum of Art and the Museum of Natural History with that financial pirate, Mr. Pierpont Morgan. But his charities, it seemed to me, captured more of him than the culture of Manhattan ever could. That's why he was here at this lodging-house.

I must have been fifteen at the time, struggling with my tutor to learn Greek, desperate to read *Philoctetes*, about a hunter with a festering foot—somehow, that hunter on his uninhabited island, abandoned by his fellow warriors, appealed to me. *No man lives here—I am but a skein of smoke.* And after a severe attack of asthma, when I must have moaned like Philoctetes, I said to Papa with all the severity of a fifteen-year-old snob, "Father, not one of these boys will ever sit for Harvard's entrance exams."

A rage built up in Brave Heart—he turned root-red, and for a moment I feared he would strike me. But he calmed himself and caressed my ear.

"They are better hunters than you are. They've been hunting all their lives. And perhaps the industrious ones, the clever ones, will own a newsstand. I've financed as many boys as I can. And others will pick up grammar and become reporters, or runners at police court. But you mustn't flaunt your privilege, Teedie."

I've been plagued by his words ever since. And perhaps that's why I have striven so much, even if I often wasn't aware of what I was striving for. We moved into a mansion on West Fifty-seventh Street, with a half mile of mullioned windows, right at the border of the Badlands. And Father rented a summerhouse in Oyster Bay, on Long Island's North Shore. He called it Tranquillity. It had white columns and a verandah that must have reminded Mittie of Bulloch Hall. Brave Heart wanted to soothe my mother, but she was beyond soothing. She'd withdrawn into her own antebellum world.

I prepared for Harvard on that wide porch, with my main tutor, Arthur Hamilton Cutler, a recent graduate who already had a mythical reputation as a molder of young men; none of the lads he tutored had ever failed Harvard's entrance exams. He was still in his twenties, an ambitious fellow with bulging eyes. He had a curled mustache, and he blinked a lot, out of excitement, I'd bet. Perhaps he only felt comfortable in the presence of tycoons and philanthropists like my father. He must have thought of me as a future benefactor. Cutler liked to hunt and fish. After our studies, we would often whistle birdcalls together. We shot quail in the woodland behind Tranquillity. My tutor was always welcome at our table. I think Bamie took a fancy to him. She fed him Brussels sprouts roasted in the finest oil. But Mr. Cutler was much more interested in Brave Heart. He talked of holding special classes at the Newsboys' Lodging-House.

"Cutler, you'd have to start from scratch."

"I might find a way, sir."

Mr. Cutler could see how unsettled Papa was. His newsboys couldn't find much purchase in *Philoctetes* and all the other classics. They had to be schooled in the wild, and Father was aware of that. He had some of their wildness. He'd never been near Harvard Yard. He'd served his apprenticeship with his own father at 94 Maiden Lane, headquarters of the family "store," Roosevelt & Son. "Plate Glass & Looking Glass Plates" was written right on the front of that nondescript building.

Father found more pleasure in his newsboys than in the family business. Plate glass wasn't much on his mind, I suppose. One night he drew me out of my little taxidermy shop and dragged me to the lodging-house. "Did you bring Zeus?"

"Of course, Papa. I wouldn't go anywhere without him. Why?"

He paused for a moment, as if he were contemplating a business deal at Roosevelt & Son. "I told the boys that you were a keeper of snakes. They'd like to meet Zeus."

"Papa," I said, "I'm a taxidermist, not an animal trainer."

"Well," he said with a shrug, "you'll have to lie."

And lie I did. I had Zeus slither into a boy's ragged trousers, then resurface near his neck, and wrap himself around another boy's arm, like a living bandage. The newsies were dee-lighted. And Papa was as full of mischief as the boys themselves. "More tricks," he said. "More tricks."

I HAD TO SUFFER through the worst case of the Roosevelt colic in creation—I lived and slept on the pot. Cutler had prepared me for Harvard as best he could. Oh, I could sing my Sophocles, how the Greeks had to swipe Philoctetes' magic bow if they wanted to take Troy. But I'd never dealt with other scholars in a classroom. I was afraid, mightily afraid, that I'd shit my pants in the middle of Harvard Yard.

It was Bamie who took the night boat up to Boston that summer; Bamie, the clever one, with a drummer's eye for detail. She hiked across Cambridge in her skirts, appealing to passersby, and picked a boardinghouse on Winthrop Street, where I would live during the next four years. She bartered with the landlady, Mrs. Richardson, and shaved down the price a notch or two. She had my rooms painted and furnished, and fitted up with coal for the winter. She was, with her deeply set dark blue eyes and sad face, our "Fearless General," as my little brother had dubbed her. Bamie was *indispensable*.

I sported a pair of side-whiskers to mask my trepidation. I was seventeen, and had my own scout. I wasn't sure how a member of the elite was supposed to behave with his scout. It was Bamie who had hired him. He was a local lad, utterly untutored, with a set of false teeth. His name was Patrick. He blacked my boots and served me coffee on a tray. A multitude of freshmen before me had abused him. He still wore their scars. He ducked every time I grabbed a book.

"I won't hurt you, Patrick," I said, as kindly as I could. "What have lads from earlier classes called you?"

"Dunderhead, kind sir."

"Well, we can't have that."

"Oh, it's customary," he insisted, like a logician.

"Then we'll break that custom."

He was quite alarmed. "But it ain't proper to call me by my Christian name. What will the other lodgers think?"

I had to deal with this, my first dilemma on Winthrop Street.

"I'll call you Scout, since you are my scout, and you may call me Roosevelt, or Mr. Ted."

He chuckled to himself. He must have thought that *I* was untutored.

I'd never been near a school, you see. I was considered too frail. So Harvard was my kindergarten. But my taxidermist's shop and my study of birdcalls and flight patterns had made a scholar of me, and I didn't need any Harvard zoölogist to tell Teddy Roosevelt about the nature of things. I studied on my own, away from the lab. But everything was interrupted in my sophomore year, after Papa was appointed Collector of Customs for the Port of New York by President Rutherford B. Hayes.

It was Father's moment of glory, his maiden voyage into the political swim. I could imagine our whole tribe sitting with Papa someday in the Governor's mansion. My classmates all congratulated me. "Roosevelt, isn't that bully for your Old Man," they said. I was invited to speak at half a dozen clubs. I was glad that Papa wouldn't have to bury himself in finance at the family "store."

The United States Custom House was a gigantic political plum. Situated on Wall Street, it had over a thousand collectors and clerks who benefited from all the booty that washed into the Port of New York. Papa assumed that Hayes had appointed him as a reward for his many years of service to New York. He hadn't realized that the President was battling with Senator Roscoe Conkling, New York's Republican boss, for control of the Party.

Conkling was a handsome giant of a man, irresistible to the ladies. He loved to box, and wasn't beneath threatening an opponent on the Senate floor. He had a pointed beard and dark red hair. He could not tolerate to be touched. He favored fawn-colored vests and gloves. And Boss Roscoe ruled his faction of the Republican Party with a simple wave of his glove. He didn't block Father's appointment at the Senate hearings. He stalled the appointment instead.

Brave Heart couldn't deal with such a devious, backhanded maneuver. He came down with stomach cramps, wailed into the night like Philoctetes. *I am but a skein of smoke.* But Papa did not have Philoctetes' magic bow to relieve his pain and let arrows fly at that devil with the pointy beard. He took to bed. I visited him that Christmas, when the cramps seemed to subside. He was ghastly pale in his silk robe. I could not recognize the man who had once knocked about river rats with his fists in the wastelands of the West Side.

"Father, I won't return to Harvard. I'll stay here and comfort you."

There wasn't the least bit of luster in his china-blue eyes.

"You'll comfort me much more if you continue with your studies."

He told me how dear I was to him, how *valuable*, how I had never given him a moment of pain or displeasure. I was his *Teedie*, he said, and he feared for my future. "We cannot have so much corruption for such a long time and still survive."

He wasn't only talking about the Collectorship that had failed to materialize. Papa could live with that. It was corruption at every level of the government. He'd gone out to Blackwell's Island to see the insane, and what he saw were sleepwalkers in filthy shrouds. They wandered about like lost billy goats. Every last one of them had gone wild, their faces and fingers covered in grime—yet how timid they were to Papa's touch. They whimpered at the least caress. Papa had to retrieve them from the island's rocks, one by one, and return them to their keepers.

"Teedie, these poor souls didn't have a single champion. The guardians they had took food from their mouths. They were wards of a city that had abandoned them. They're numbers, Teedie, in some forgotten book."

"You'll fight for them, Father, when you're feeling better."

He shut his eyes. "Whistle to me, son. I want to hear the birdcalls."

I sang the mating song of the male robin, that wavering warble that Papa loved, and the dry *chip-chip-chip* of the hairbird. His eyes fluttered and he fell asleep, his hand clutching mine. He suffered from peritonitis, a fatal inflammation of the intestinal wall, but the doctors hadn't doomed him yet. And Brave Heart rallied next day. He was up and about. Papa dressed before I did. He was wearing his great scarf, his beaver hat, and winter boots. His face was waxen. The snow had been falling for a week and covered all the windowsills. Papa was in the mood for a sleigh ride, he muttered. He wouldn't have the family coachman drive him around like an invalid. "I'm not dead, Mortimer. I can be my own whip."

I had to bundle up, with earmuffs and all. The sleigh was parked outside our door, not far from Little Dakota. We sat in the Roosevelt rocking carriage, with Papa at the reins, and went into the park.

Papa wouldn't sit still. He rose up and down in that rocking car and insisted upon his right-of-way. We could hear our runners eat into the ice with a gnawing sound. There were no birdsongs. Branches snapped in the wind, as we passed several other cars in our relentless whirl. A few members of the upper crust had come for a morning drive. Papa must have frightened them with his reckless abandon of the reins. He wasn't pale in that blinding light off the snow.

"Teedie, you can go back to Harvard now."

I WAS AS ROTTEN as my predecessors, alas. In my frustration and despair, I hurled books at the lonely boy I had inherited. That's how hungry I was for news from West Fifty-seventh Street. I didn't even fathom my own cruelty at first.

"I'm sorry, Scout, I really am."

He rubbed his knuckles. "Understand, Mr. Ted. Your Papa's groanin'."

I had a shandygaff with him at one of the local grogshops. And then a telegram arrived on February 9.

TEEDIE COME HOME.

I took the boat train from Boston, climbed off the cars, and onto one of the palace steamers at the Fall River wharf. I'd booked passage on the *Priscilla*, grand princess of the Fall River Line; she luxuriated in her own gleaming white decks. The *Priscilla* could sleep and feed a thousand passengers with all the comfort of a floating palace. She was the preferred steamer of Presidents, aristocrats, and Wall Street tycoons. Her dining salon had gilded balconies and the thickest carpets between Boston and the Battery. But I wasn't trying to rub elbows with the *Priscilla*'s royal guests. I could have eaten at the captain's table with industrial barons and debutantes from Beacon Hill. I dined alone in my cabin. I could not bear a long evening of banter about women's bonnets and the etiquette of spittoons on board the *Priscilla* when I knew that Father was gravely ill, else I wouldn't have been summoned so curtly.

I stood out on the deck all night, as the *Priscilla* steamed around the perfidious mouth of Point Judith, with all its legends of mermaids who might lure men into the sea—there wasn't a mermaid alive that could have enticed me in my black mood.

I felt stuck in some strange, bloated eternity until the *Priscilla* arrived at her Hudson River pier. I rode uptown in a hired car. The coachman swayed from side to side as he dodged pedestrians, trucks, and other hired cars. His route was roundabout and frivolous. I had to change carriages in midstream as his horse began to hobble.

Finally we got to Papa's mansion near Little Dakota. There was an ominous vigil in front of the house; a hundred newsboys stood waiting in the slush and snow, cap in hand, like a choir robbed of song. With them was their watchman, Quentin Moss, sobbing softly to himself, his powerful body hunched over like a man with a broken back. For an instant he could not locate where he was. His eyes darted about. It was the newsboys who nudged the watchman and settled him. They were each clutching a candle, every one. The flames flickered in the wind and revealed their unwashed faces with a crooked glow. Their pockets were loaded with coins, I could tell. They'd come right from their routes to Papa's vigil with penny candles. They didn't cry, like Quent. The newsies swayed with their candles that burnt down to a nub. I cursed their devotion to Papa. It frightened me. But I could hear their silent chorus.

Too late, Teedie, you've come too late.

The servants were all sobbing. Mama wandered about in her white muslin wrap, like a ghost ship lost at sea. I couldn't dislodge her from her slow dance. It was a widow's dream.

"Mama, I'm here."

She continued to drift.

Couldn't find Corinne, and Bamie, our Fearless General, mumbled to herself. Her corset must have been undone. Her spine was all curled. Her sad eyes sank deeper into her skull. I'm not certain she recognized me. It was Ellie who seemed in charge. I hadn't realized how alike we looked. He was my taller, sturdier twin, without the side-whiskers.

"Teedie, it was terrible. . . . Papa had such fear in his eyes. I'd never seen him like that."

We went into the morning room where Papa still lay on the chaise, with crumpled linen and spilled basins all about. His lion's mane had gone all gray, with streaks of white. He was gaunt under his gray beard. I kissed him on the forehead and could not help my childish thoughts, the belief that I could wish Father back to life with a sincere song.

"Brave Heart," I uttered.

Bamie burst through her chrysalis, went outside to the news-boys in a shawl, fed them bits of cake. "Missy," said one of the boys, "can we see the Master?"

My big sister allowed them to clump up the stairs, several at a time; they stood near the door, curtsied, and went back down. And it was only then that I recognized the enormity of their loss. They'd had one lone champion. Another philanthropist might sup with them, but wouldn't arrive in evening clothes and share their meal with Father's gusto. He'd entwined himself into their lives. They mattered to him almost as much as we did.

That night I had a terrifying dream, the same dream that had haunted my childhood. A wolf-man with blood on his whiskers was waiting at the foot of my bed, prepared to pounce and gobble me up. It was Father who always woke me in the nick of time.

"Teedie, I'm here."

Yet *this* dream was more terrifying. The wolf-man had Papa's china-blue eyes, and its rusty fingernails were gone. It had supple hands and a groomed beard, without a trace of blood. I'd resurrected Papa in my own nightmare, without the totem of a single word. I was still mightily afraid of this wolf-man.

Mittie entered my room in a muslin gown.

"You were screaming, dear," she said. She looked like some bird-child out of the forest.

"I dreamt of Papa. . . . I'm all right. Go back to bed."

"Was he kind in your dream, dear?"

"Yes, Mama."

And she disappeared again. I was the boy scientist of Harvard Yard. I didn't believe in omens. Still, I did believe that Papa had visited my bed in the guise of a werewolf, his admonitions reverberating in my skull like a magnificent drum.

I FEAR FOR YOUR FUTURE, TEEDIE.

So did I.

CHAPTER 2

THE CYCLONE
ASSEMBLYMAN

1881–1883

NO OTHER ROOSEVELT HAD EVER ENTERED MORTON HALL, a barn-like maze above a saloon near Fifth Avenue and the corner of Fifty-ninth. It was the headquarters and "shop" of the Twenty-first District Republican Club, filled with cobwebs and brass spittoons, and run by a gang of rowdies who were little better than the hooligans of Tammany Hall. They looked at me with grave suspicion, as if a burglar in evening clothes had happened upon their premises by chance, with mischief on his mind. I was a twenty-three-year-old rube with red side-whiskers. I caught the eye of a man who sat hunched behind the barn's only table. He was Humble Jake Hess, Morton Hall's legendary district leader, who'd risen out of the streets and cracked many a skull on his way up. Disappointed by the Democrats, he'd bolted to the Republican Party years ago. A brute with big hands, a melodious voice, and a rare sense of political strategy, he'd lost one of his earlobes at Gettysburg to a lead bullet and also had to limp around with a silver kneecap. He wondered why a rube from the "solid element" had wandered into a hall of saloonkeepers and horsecar conductors.

"What is it are ye after, Johnny boy? And be quick about it."

"I'd like to become a member of Morton Hall," I said.

"And why would a lad like you be interested in such an unlikely miracle?"

His brethren laughed and winked, and I was able to catch them off guard.

"Because," I said, "I'm going to be the next Assemblyman from this district."

Humble Jake was silent for a moment. He didn't like the brashness of my remark. And he was cautious with me.

"Are you married?"

"Yes," I told him.

"Good. I don't like bachelors in our little arena. They're not reliable."

I'd disturbed Humble Jake, aroused his curiosity, obliged him to think like a district leader within the comfort of his own club.

"Do you have a profession, laddie?"

"I'm a law student."

Humble Jake seemed suspicious. He didn't admire lawyers, I imagine. I didn't let him know that I was a slacker at Columbia. My classes were filled with details that were like fancy swordplay and had little to do with fairness. I couldn't find much social justice in the law.

"And what's your name, perchance?"

"Roosevelt," I said.

The hooligans stared at Humble Jake. Something was awry. Their leader had benefited from all the boodle of Republican politics. Roscoe Conkling had helped appoint him Manhattan's Commissioner of Charities and Corrections, and Humble Jake couldn't have been ignorant of the gent who had started the Children's Aid Society. Father must have locked horns with Humble once upon a time, rescued little boys from the nightmare of Charities and Corrections. Humble Jake would have respected Papa's persistence. His narrow eyes lit.

"And am I speaking to the son of the late, highly regarded Theodore?"

"You are."

Suddenly it didn't seem to matter that Roscoe Conkling had ruined Papa. Humble Jake had a Roosevelt in his barn. I was given a badge to wear that differentiated me from every other hooligan. I have it yet—a metallic button with a dull sheen and the number "21" painted on it to mark Humble Jake's district. There was no more mention of my being a candidate for the State Assembly, but I'd planted the seed. I had to go through all the rites of initiation, to feel the rough-and-tumble of politics at the barn. I visited local bars on Second Avenue with Humble Jake and got into fistfights with saloonkeepers, who wanted their liquor licenses lowered, while I wanted the licenses raised.

"Ah," Humble said, "you're our resident teetotaler. I like that."

Members of my own clan considered me a maniac who deserved to be locked up on Blackwell's Island. Roosevelts didn't romp around in the mud of machine politics. Mother was horror-stricken.

"Your grandmamma would crawl in her grave if she was ever notified that you were mingling with the riffraff. Such crude men—*politicos*."

I didn't have to hide my mission from Bamie, like some heart-sore Count of Monte Cristo. Bamie understood. "You're attacking from inside their tent. Papa would be proud, Teedie."

But I did feel like a turncoat—Humble had taken me under his wing and put down any rebellion among the ranks. And I had no intention of following the rough politics of Morton Hall. I was a reformer, like Brave Heart, and had always been.

"The little lord is one of us," he said and bowed with a bit of mockery. "We're related, did ya know that?"

Had Humble ever worked at Roosevelt & Son, carried plate glass on his back? No, it was nothing like that.

"My nephew, Martin Hess, a plumber's apprentice he was, served as your father's paid substitute, during the late war."

"That's impossible," I said. "Father's substitute was an Irish mechanic named Carter."

Humble rolled his eyes. "This Carter never served. He was a swindler. He sold your father's ticket to another man. It was Martin who served."

"Did he survive?" I asked.

"He did not. He fell at Antietam. Lost both his legs to a cannonball and bled out right on the battlefield. Nobody could find him at first. His carcass—what was left of it—disappeared."

"Don't understand," I muttered.

Humble's brow wrinkled. "Disappeared, I said. We had to hire our own ghoul."

I was lost, utterly adrift, among the artifacts of Humble's language.

"Ghoul, what ghoul?"

"A corpse finder. There were dozens of them. It was once a lucrative profession. He finagled with the War Department on our behalf and dug up Martin's remains with a bunch of other ghouls. We buried him proper, we did, buried what was left of Martin."

My plans to smash the Republican machine had melted down with the death and dismemberment of Martin Hess. I felt like a fraud.

"Humble, I'm here to hurt your benefactor, Boss Roscoe Conkling."

"Aw, I knew that," Jake said. "I could read the larceny in your face the moment you arrived. I says to myself, what's an aristocratic pup doing at Morton Hall? Truth is Boss Roscoe's a son of a bitch. I'd like to maim him myself."

I was a far cry from the Count of Monte Cristo. "Then I have no business being here, Humble. I've betrayed your trust. Should I return my badge and resign from the club?"

"Not at all," he said, as his hand hovered over that missing earlobe, his souvenir from Gettysburg. "Roosevelt, you aren't ashamed of us, are you? Why haven't ye brung your missus to the barn?"

—

I HAD COURTED HER as if I were courting a cougar. That's how persistent I was. I wanted Alice, and I had to pursue her until she wanted me. It's a simple tale. I fell in love with Miss Alice Lee of Chestnut Hill during my junior year at Harvard, nine months after Papa passed. She had honey-blond hair and pale blue eyes, and she was a very tall girl at seventeen. Her hands and feet were already bigger than mine. It was excruciating. Alice had the long, gliding step of an athlete. She was already an expert archer, and no matter how many targets I went after and how many bows I strung, I couldn't compete with her bull's-eyes.

"Teddy, you are the most impatient boy I have ever seen."

I'd met Alice through a classmate of mine, Dickie Saltonstall, who came from an endless line of Harvard graduates—the Saltonstalls were the most Brahmin of Boston Brahmins. Dick advised me to be more temperate in my pursuit of Alice.

"Roosevelt, you'll frighten her away with that damn ardor of yours. *Doucement*, old boy. You'd break Lightfoot's legs at such a pace."

I'd had Lightfoot delivered to Boston with my dogcart, so I could visit Chestnut Hill at a gallop. I'd ride that horse through the roughest terrain. I had to conquer Chestnut Hill. I did have two ambassadors—Mama and Bamie. Bamie could read her own fate in the looking glass—a spinster with a crooked back. Her eyes withdrew deeper into her skull, but she and Mama rode up to Chestnut Hill to reconnoiter with Mr. and Mrs. Lee. Mr. Lee was a banker whose firm had invented the idea of a safe-deposit box in an underground vault. Whatever valuables you had would always be secure in one of Lee's vaults. He wasn't stern, and he didn't undervalue me and my clan, but he thought that his pale princess was too young to be a bride.

"We value Theodore," said this master of the underground vault. "But where's the rush?"

Mittie was the clever one. While Bamie blustered, Mama

spooned her vanilla trifle and never mentioned marriage. "Oh," she said, "when it's ripe and all, Teedie and Alice can come and live with us on West Fifty-seventh Street. We will surely have an apartment prepared. I have reserved an entire floor. It will be waiting, Mr. Lee."

That was the clincher. Lee couldn't resist the exotic charm of Mother's moonlight complexion and the seductive softness of her voice. The nuptials were arranged right in the middle of that vanilla trifle. I did hide something, however. I'd had a rough patch with Dr. Dudley Sargent, the college physician. He said that countless attacks of asthma and years of heavy exercise had weakened the walls of my heart. He was very firm in his prognosis. Even running up a flight of stairs might put a strain on my heart. I had to be as sedentary as a monk, or I wouldn't have much longer to live. I should have talked to Bamie about it, confessed to Alice, but it would have cursed my future, left me a chronic invalid. So I lied. I hadn't lost my vigor, and I wouldn't be damned by Dr. Dudley. I bought Alice a sapphire engagement ring and announced our wedding plans on Valentine's Day, and what a Valentine it was. The teetotaler drank champagne. I wasn't surly as I had often been after one of my rare benders with classmates at the Porcellian Club. I drank in Alice's honey-blond hair, as her pale eyes glowed in the lamplight.

"To my Valentine of Valentines, whom no other man on earth will ever know as I do."

My champagne glass shattered with the sudden force of my movements, but Mr. Lee didn't mind the spots on his silk cravat, while Mrs. Lee wept with a farrago of feelings that I could never hope to summon up. She caressed my sleeve, a scintilla of champagne in her eyes.

"Dear, dear boy, you will look after our little girl, won't you?"

We were married at Chestnut Hill on my twenty-second birthday, and spent our honeymoon at Tranquillity, Papa's retreat on Oyster Bay. We had the whole house to ourselves, with servants and horses. Alice rarely left my sight. We sat on the same verandah that had reminded Mama of her father's old plantation and we watched the palace steamers of the Fall River Line ply across the Sound with their booming whistles and great abundance of lights, and I thought of my own voyage on the *Priscilla* two years ago, when I arrived from Boston on the night boat too late to catch Brave Heart's last breaths. I didn't want to engulf Alice in my moment of melancholy. I missed Father yet, missed him more and more, even in the dreamland of my delight. The hunter had his sweet prey. . . .

I did bring Alice to Morton Hall. The hooligans were suspicious at first. Females seldom appeared at the club, except for an occasional floozy. And these lads were at a loss how to relate to Alice. They hid their own huge paws under the table. Half of them had broken hands from all the electioneering they did. But Alice soon won them over. They were hypnotized by her perfume and the long strides of her rhythmic gait. My wife must have reminded them of some ideal filly in a race that was never run.

Humble had ordered lemonade and tea biscuits from Delmonico's. He'd put on a wrinkled cravat for the occasion.

"Ah, Mrs. Ted, your husband has captured our hearts."

Alice caught Humble at his own hyperbole. "Not as much as he has captured mine, Mr. Hess."

I could feel the weave of pleasure on his face. "You'd honor me, ma'am, if you called me Humble—that is my moniker at Morton Hall."

"And I'll be your Alice," she said.

Humble preened in front of his hooligans. "I can tell you're a lady—from your accent, ma'am. But it's not Manhattan gilt. You're countrified."

"And what about you?" Alice asked.

"I'm also countrified. I was born in Little Bavaria, near the Bowery. That was a lifetime ago, and the accent has rubbed off."

"But you haven't lost your gilt," Alice said, delivering her own salvo.

My darling made the rounds, and every hooligan in the barn revealed a gnarled paw to let Alice have a good shake of the hand. She wasn't shy or remote with that crowd. I'd misjudged my pink little wife. She had an inborn sense of politics, or perhaps she understood my own longings to be part of the mix.

Humble had been undecided about my fate until this moment. The Party stalwarts were against having an interloper speak for them in the State Capitol. But Humble pushed back.

"Miss Alice, we'd like to run your husband as our man from the Twenty-first. He'd represent our district in Albany."

Alice had him purring now. "And what appeal would he have for the voters?"

"What could be better than a Dutchman in Dutch New York? Fifth Avenue is within our bailiwick. And isn't Mr. Ted one of the swells?"

I hadn't rehearsed Alice, hadn't coached her in the least. But she startled Humble and his cohorts. Bamie must have scouted the district with Alice, run with her to catch a horsecar, peeked into the window grille of a local saloon.

"And will the saloonkeepers side with him?" she asked with an ambiguous smile.

Humble seemed in command again. "Certainly, Miss Alice, if I say so."

"But my husband's allegiance is different," she said. "He will vote with his heart's command, and not with the Party's own symbols. That might cause you some pain."

"Not at all," Humble said with his own ambiguous smile. "Mr. Ted is what we call a 'Nightingale' in Republican parlance. Each Party can afford one, and only one."

Like the king's jester, I thought.

"Humble, I won't be Conkling's fool—that's too high a price."

"Ah, Conkling ain't much at Morton Hall. He's a ghost."

I was bewildered. "A ghost who still breathes?"

"The red beard has retired, and we have our Nightingale," Humble said, seizing Alice and waltzing her across the barn with the tempestuous sounds of a tuba exploding from his cheeks while his stalwarts laughed and stamped their feet with all the madness and joy of men from the Twenty-first District of Manhattan.

———

THERE WASN'T MUCH ROOM for a Nightingale in that dear old dull Dutch town of Albany, with a wind that howled off the Hudson and cold fronts that chilled you to the quick. I was Mr. Jane-Dandy, the Manhattan rube, the youngest lad in the State Assembly. I wore my red side-whiskers, a pince-nez with a gold tassel, and a peacoat from my Harvard days. The veterans at the Capitol mocked me and called my peacoat "an ass-buster," because the wind crept up my cylindrical trousers from Savile Row. They were a venal lot, looking to line their pockets. This "Black Horse Cavalry" was corrupt beyond measure, allied to Party bosses whose one allegiance was to the little corridors of power they had cobbled together from their various districts.

I meant nothing to the Black Horse Cavalry. I was a hindrance, who interrupted the humdrum proceedings with my calls of "Mr. Speak-ah," in my high-pitched voice. They couldn't doze comfortably in their cushions as I hustled about, trying to rip into yet another bill that would fleece the public treasure. They'd have to get rid of that downstate pup from the Silk Stocking District—"a Fifth Avenue fellah." And they summoned Long John McManus, their enforcer in the Assembly, who was one of Tammany's proudest lieutenants.

I might have been bushwhacked if Humble hadn't been waiting for me at my hotel on North Pearl, near the riverfront. He'd arrived on the night train and was in a grim mood.

"Humble, what's wrong? Have I betrayed your trust?"

"Not at all," he said, crushing the crown of his bowler with his big hands. "You're a Nightingale after my own heart. But they mean to toss you in a blanket. It's their way of humiliating you, Mr. Ted. McManus is their instrument. He's tossed many a lad, obliged them to leave Albany in disgrace. And I can't interfere. I've been sworn to silence."

"Where are they now?" I asked.

"At the Delavan."

The Delavan House was a dusty temperance hotel right across from the railroad yards. Liquor wasn't allowed in the rooms or in the lobby, but you could find whiskey everywhere, in canisters, flasks, and canteens, in teapots, coffee cups, and milk bottles. The Delavan was where bosses from both Parties conspired when they weren't attacking one another in the cavernous chambers of the Capitol, jumping out of some closet with an Indian war cry. The Delavan was their haven, their private retreat, and as good a spot as any to hide a strumpet or to trap an unsuspecting rube.

And so I played my part, walking into the Delavan in my pea-coat and cylindrical trousers. McManus, with his apelike appearance, was convening in a corner with other members of the Black Horse Cavalry. He had his run of the Delavan, drinking whiskey out of a teapot. I tapped him on the shoulder. He didn't respond. I tapped his shoulder again. He sniffed the foul air of the Delavan with his enormous nostrils—Albany was overrun with breweries, and the entire town stank of stale beer and the rot of coal tar in the river from the chemical works.

That great din of Albany barons and their vassals turned to a polite rumble. They could sense the massacre. Their gray eyes seemed swollen in the weak light.

"What's this?" McManus asked with another long sniff. "Do I smell a Harvard brat? His Royal Majesty Mr. Nightingale?"

McManus was showing off to the Democratic and Republican chieftains. I had realized within a week or two that there was little difference between the Parties: judges, lawyers, bankers, business tycoons, and political bosses divvied up the power among themselves. Humble must have realized that, and he exiled himself to Morton Hall. He'd come to Dutch Land to warn me about McManus, but he wasn't a loyal Dutchman; he wasn't Dutch at all; he fled Albany as soon as he could and returned to his fiefdom in the Twenty-first.

I watched Long John wink to his lackeys. I read behind his ruse. A number of cavalrymen rose from their table. They didn't even attempt to hide the horse blanket that was rolled up under the table.

While a pair of cavalrymen stooped over to unfurl the blanket, several others approached me with wild-eyed grins. They meant to grab my arms and hold me in place for McManus. I socked the first one and sent him sailing into the other cavalrymen. And then I socked the second.

McManus didn't like this sudden twist in his own parlor. "Roseyvelt, that's downright rude."

"Long John, I hear you mean to toss me," I said.

McManus still had his audience, the barons and members of the Black Horse Cavalry, who smirked into their fists.

"Toss you? Why the hell would I do that to a fine fellah like you?"

They were all tittering, and I had to put a stop to that or they'd go on razzing me in the halls of the State Capitol for the rest of my stay.

I tapped Long John's shoulder a third time.

"Don't you ever try to toss me, Mr. McManus. If you ever try, I'll kick you in the balls."

McManus had murder on his mind. His jaw twitched. By Godfrey, I would have to kick him in the balls. But he couldn't get a simple nod from a single baron. They had expected entertainment, a novice Assemblyman who had made a nuisance of himself tossed into the fetid air at the Delavan to the delight of their vassals, and McManus had made a mess of things, had bungled it all. They didn't want a spill of blood, not mine or his. So Long John had to pretend that he was still the master.

"I'll break you," he muttered under his breath, and then he bowed extravagantly to satisfy the barons. "You've had your fun, Mr. Nightingale. Go about your business." He hoped to mock me by whistling the nightingale's song. But McManus was utterly off-key. He sounded like a whiskey salesman. I had to warble the miraculous *chip-chip-chip* of the nightingale. I warbled every variation, every twitter.

Despite themselves, the barons and their Black Horse Cavalry were enthralled. They clung to every little splash of melody. Nothing in their own cynical lives had prepared them for that prolonged plangent cry. I completed my nightingale's song and marched out of the Delavan, with two of the cavalrymen sitting in a daze on the beer-soaked floor.

I ROSE LIKE A ROCKET after my encounter with McManus. More and more Assemblymen abandoned the stalwarts and joined my little clique of Nightingales. We couldn't outgun the Black Horsemen, but we could annoy the barons, who did not want their duplicity revealed. I began talking to the press about various bills the barons had smothered in the Assembly.

The Cigar Makers' Union had introduced a bill to ban the manufacture of cigars in tenements. And I was put on a committee to examine the merit of such a bill. We'd never been near a tenement, not one of us. What aroused my suspicion was that the manufacturers themselves owned many of the tenements, and thus served as landlords to the myriad cigar makers they employed. So I went on my own inspection tour of tenement land.

The cigar makers lived in damp, sunless hovels on Rivington Street, often five or six to a room, children and women working deep into the night, with tobacco leaves piled everywhere, and breathing in that raw, red tobacco dust.

I saw children of six crouched over their workbenches, some of them as humpbacked as Bamie, tobacco leaves stored behind them in towers of moist blankets. Not one of them would ever see the inside of a schoolroom. I wasn't some wizard of the courts but a freshman legislator on a fact-finding mission. I had no right to reprimand their mothers and fathers, or whoever else was in charge of these tenement factories, but reprimand them I did.

My rebukes fell into a mountain of tobacco leaves. These Hebrew cigar makers and their families rarely understood a word of English, or else played mum. Finally the foreman of one such factory did speak up. He was the uncle of an entire crew, sixteen adults and children in three rooms. He had his cutting knife, but he didn't menace me. This fellow had been run out of some hovel in Prague for trying to organize the cigar makers into a little army and he rode right past the immigration officers at Castle Garden with a false set of papers. He was never an anarchist, he insisted, more like a Bohemian Robin Hood. God knows what his real name was. The others at his shop called him Kapitán. His English was impeccable. He could rattle on without a flaw.

I smoked a cigar with him to be polite. I shivered at first, because the very act of biting into one of the Captain's cigars summoned up the rich aromas of my childhood. Father had taught me how to inhale precious air with the help of a fine Havana during my worst asthma attacks.

I didn't mollycoddle this cigar maker.

"Captain, do ye know who I am?"

He didn't hesitate. "You, sir, are the Cyclone Assemblyman."

That's what they called me inside the Capitol. I was everywhere at once, the great meddler, poking into other Assemblymen's affairs. How else could I get anything done? I had to meddle.

I perused that tenement shop with its tobacco towers and the soft, disheartening scratch of women and children as they sheared tobacco leaves with knives shaped like crooked crescents.

"And you, sir, have children sitting there mummified on a bench."

"*Mummified?*" he said. "I have them exercise in the back yard. We all go out for lunch—hard-boiled eggs and root beer."

"And how many hours do they work a day?"

"Fifteen," the Captain said.

"That's inhuman," I told him.

But he wasn't perturbed. "How else could we survive? Who would benefit if I had to close the shop? The landlord would bring in another cadre of cigar makers. It would also fail—fifteen hours. That's the formula of success, Mr. Roosevelt."

"And how would you define success?"

His mask of a face shimmered in the dusty light. "By becoming a landlord, sir. You have to own five or six tenements and have a multitude of factories and shops. Isn't that what they call laissez-faire capitalism? Well, I'm a capitalist."

I couldn't argue with this rogue Robin Hood. I went back to Albany, determined to steer the Cigar Bill out of committee and onto the Chamber floor.

"Mr. Speak-ah, we are perpetuating a system of child slavery. We must break up this coterie of landlords and their poisonous arsenal of tenement shops. We cannot sit idle while children cough themselves into an early grave with tobacco dust in their lungs."

I pounded into the barons and their Black Horse Cavalry. I courted every journalist I could. We Nightingales attacked. The stalwarts stumbled, and the bill sailed through the Assembly. But there was a bit of intrigue in the Chamber. Some jackal stole the final draft of the bill and it never arrived on the Senate floor. We'd been outflanked by the barons. I planned to reintroduce the bill next year, but first I had to persuade my constituents to bring back their Cyclone Assemblyman.

McManus swaggered into the Kenmore, where I kept a little flat. He was gloating with spittle on his tongue. "Albany isn't for you, boy-o. You shouldn't have mocked me at the Delavan. I'll find you in a dark corner of the Capitol one day, and you'll wish you were dead."

And that's when he saw Alice gliding down the stairs of the Kenmore in a green dress. Most Assemblymen didn't bring their wives with them to this dank Dutch village with its foul effluvia riding right off the river. But I didn't relish being apart from Alice. She endured the isolation and biting wind so that we could have quiet dinners and quiet nights at the Kenmore.

McManus had a crazy gleam in his eyes. I didn't like how he ogled Alice. "Ah, you're a picture of perfection, Mrs. Roseyvelt."

Alice appraised him with her pale eyes. She must have sensed some deep splinter beneath his cruel streak, like the staggered cry of the nightingale.

"I hope you will sup with us one evening, Mr. McManus, and tell me all about yourself."

"I'd love to, ma'am. I'm your husband's peer—and his rival. We do wonders together. He's kind of a miracle man, the little saint of cigar rollers. What would we do without him?"

And he loped out of the Kenmore with a triumphant grin.

I WAS NO BETTER than a robber baron.

I had to steal a honeymoon for Alice and myself every other weekend at West Fifty-seventh Street, even while Mother grew more and more mysterious and morose. She donned a white chenille net to keep the dust and grime out of her hair and wore this white net at dinner parties. She also kept up the ritual of two daily baths—the first to suds herself, and the second to rinse off the thick crust of soap, with a maid constantly beside her, as if Mother were Marie Antoinette. "Darlings, I cannot find another method to fight all the filth of Manhattan."

Bamie was the loyal clerk who kept track of Mama's bills. Mama always overspent, leaving a wild trail of purchases, while Bamie was right behind her with Papa's old, worn, leather-bound passbook from the Chemical Bank, handed down to Bamie herself like some musty amulet. Thank heaven my wife was freed of such money matters, since she had an allowance from the Lees of Chestnut Hill. Mama and Alice were *famous* together, almost as famous as sisters, one very tall and the other very short; both were country girls who loved to wear white, and neither of them had much use for the relentless pace of Manhattan.

"Alice, dear, people move so fast and talk so fast, I'm always a few steps behind. I'd wager that not a single soul ever runs to catch a horsecar in Boston and Chestnut Hill."

She'd never seen the cars in Cambridge, with Harvard lads like myself hanging from every available rail and limb. But I wouldn't contradict her. Besides, Mother was manageable until Elliott returned after sixteen months from a hunting trip to India, Singapore, and Saigon, with a small fortune of elephant tusks and tiger skins. Little brother had game bags galore. I envied him, have to admit. I must have inherited Mama's mad flamboyance, the residue of Bulloch Hall. I hunted Bengal tigers in my dreams, even while I marched from tenement to tenement in the Hebrew quarter, inquiring about errant cigar makers and children covered in red dust.

I congratulated Ellie on his great success—he'd dined with maharajahs, stared into the bloodshot eyes of man-eating tigers, raced after rogue elephants—but he couldn't seem to settle in. He was like a vagabond with a royal address.

"I don't have Teedie's fanatical grit," he told Alice. "I'm a different animal." He couldn't stay sober. He would start to drink at breakfast time, appear at the table with gin on his breath. He was having seizures, would black out from time to time, and attack me in his delirium.

"I'll slit your throat one day, I will. Look at me. I'm that werewolf you dreamt about as a child. But this werewolf is made of flesh and bone."

I could not consider my own little brother a maniac, but I still locked our bedroom door at night. And I'd find Ellie outside the door when we awoke.

"Forgive me, Teedie. I am not myself."

I'd escort him to his bedroom and put him under the covers, like Brave Heart might have done when Ellie was a little boy. I sat with him until he fell asleep. Mother wandered in and seized me around the shoulders, this birdlike woman with her white hairnet. "Teedie, I am lost without your father—lost. Didn't he appeal to you on his deathbed?"

She'd forgotten that I missed Papa's agony altogether; I was on the night boat from Boston, breathing in the moon on the main deck of the *Priscilla*, that maharajah of the Fall River Line, when Brave Heart made his last request, according to Mother.

"Darling, didn't he whisper, *Watch over Ellie, watch over Ellie!* I was right there."

I couldn't discount Mother's conversation with a ghost. Father might have whispered *something*.

—

ONE NIGHT, AFTER ATTENDING a lecture at the Century, a haven for artists, poets, editors, and bon vivants, I stumbled upon an altercation on a side street. The lamps were very shallow. But three men, ruffians really, were annoying a young woman in the finest clothes. It mystified me why this elegant young lady did not have an escort. She could have been a pigeon put there for my benefit, as part of some entrapment. Still, I could not abandon her. It was not in my nature to do so.

I tapped one of the ruffians with my stick. "You, young fellow, stop pestering that girl."

He smiled at me, this jackal, who was wearing a gaudy silk scarf. "And you, sir, should not interfere in what is not your business. Tell him, Nan."

The young woman seemed at a loss. She did not encourage me to stay, did not smile or wink. She had a bit of blood on her mouth. She was tall and had pale eyes, like my Alice.

"You are very kind, sir, but . . ."

"That's not good enough, Nan," said the young jackal. "Tell him to scatter."

He shoved her with his filthy hands. She tottered for a moment, like a child's top. And that's when I thrashed him with my stick. The two other jackals leered at me like Halloween lanterns from the Irish quarter near Third Avenue. I thrashed them, too. I didn't even realize the temper I had. The rooster in me had been aroused. And I was beyond caring whether this Nan was a pigeon or not.

The jackals ran off with their swag—Nan's parasol, pocket handkerchief, and purse. She seemed utterly bereft, but she did not seek my counsel. I was bewildered and a bit rash. I wiped the blood from her mouth with my handkerchief. She couldn't have been a chambermaid or a thief's companion. She had the strict carriage and soft, melodious voice of a duchess—or a songbird. I had to query her.

"Miss Nan, are you related to those rough boys?"

"No," she answered in the same melodious voice. It was even more of a riddle. I could have given her some hard cash and hailed down a cab. But I had a fanatical grit, as Ellie said. I couldn't rest until I got to the bottom of things.

"Yet they knew your name."

Her lip trembled. She didn't have one coarse feature. I took her hand.

"I'll help you."

"You can't," she cried. "You can't. You had better go." And the duchess removed her hand from my pigskin glove with a slow, silky glide, as if we'd just been pirouetting at Windsor Palace.

"Where do you live?"

"Not far," she said, avoiding that inquisitive steel in my eyes. But it was difficult for her to play at some sham. She'd given me as many clues as she could; I still followed her across the street. We arrived at a brownstone with a narrow stoop. My duchess had lost her composure and the delicate flow of her carriage—she'd been rehearsed at a local charm school.

I followed her up the stairs. I wondered if we'd come to a *maison close*. Women in silk gowns and gaudy satin corsets were parading on the stairs with their cadets, who wore derbies at a devilish angle. These cadets bowed like counterfeit courtiers. None of them had a touch of grace.

"Ah, what a handsome prince."

"He's mine," the duchess said, knocking off their derbies and scattering the women in their silk extravaganzas. Soon there wasn't a soul.

The duchess turned to me in her duress—I wasn't a stranger she'd found on the street. She'd lost her bearings, her sense of purpose, and she panicked. "Mr. Roosevelt, they'll crucify you if you go up one more flight. A whole arsenal is waiting."

"Shh," I said. "It's too late."

I gathered the duchess up in my arms like a renegade bride, stepped onto a landing of oilcloth, and rushed through a door that was slightly ajar. I wasn't surprised by the reception committee—

photographers with their flash pans, a police captain with all his ribbons on display, burly detectives from Mulberry Street with shields pinned to their vests, and Long John McManus. I stared into the flash pans and their crackles of light with my signature smile, a toothy Roosevelt grin. I still had the duchess cradled in my arms.

"Well," said McManus, "if it isn't the people's champion, trafficking in white slavery. Captain Striker, accompany the pup to your precinct."

Striker hadn't expected me to smile in front of the flash pans. I was a popular Assemblyman, with half the papers in Manhattan writing about my holy war with the barons. He could be exiled to a precinct in the cow pastures of the Bronx with one false move.

"Your Honor, why the hell are you in a house full of whores?"

McManus groaned. "What's wrong with you, Denny? Take him away. This squirt will swear that he was helping a damsel in distress."

I put the duchess down and let her spin on her own two feet. She didn't belong in a *maison close*.

"Speak up," I said. "I won't hurt you."

The duchess squeezed her eyes shut and stood there blindly, wagging her head, while Alice walked in with another policeman. McManus and his cronies meant to cripple me in their private cul-de-sac with oilcloth on the floor.

They shouldn't have brought my wife.

McManus bowed to her, doffing his black derby. He must have been so, so sure of himself to take such a big gamble. He'd sent for Alice long before I arrived.

"Sorry to involve you in this mess, ma'am. But we didn't summon you on a whim. Your husband is in the white slavery racket."

There wasn't any fear in Alice's pale eyes, just flecks of fire.

"Why did you have a policeman knock at this late hour, Mr. McManus? You frightened my mother-in-law. I was half asleep."

McManus doffed his hat again. "Ah, but we thought you might want to know about your husband's liaison with another gal."

I'd kept Alice away from every bit of sordidness I encountered as an Assemblyman. But she had an archer's agility, as if she could conjure up McManus and dismantle him in the same fall of an arrow.

"Long John," she said, "the only liaison my husband has ever had is with me."

"That's not true," McManus said. "That's not true."

I hit him. It wasn't out of malice, but to break his stride and end his streak of insufferable lies. I might have broken a knuckle. He could have swatted me with one of his gigantic paws. Yet he didn't. He displayed the medallion of blood on his mouth as a war trophy and presented himself as a victim of the Manhattan rube.

"Mrs. Roseyvelt, ma'am, I did not lay a finger on your husband, not once. And please listen to Nancy."

My duchess was a songbird of a different kind. All her veneer rubbed off. Her features hardened, and that soft, pliable face turned into a snarl. The duchess's diction was much more rarefied.

"He is a very cruel man, your husband. He kept me on a leash. He has disgusting habits. I had to perform monstrous tricks."

Alice wavered for a moment; that's how skilled was the duchess, who tossed out details like time bombs.

"My buttocks are raw from all his biting, Mrs. Roseyvelt. I can show you the marks."

Alice removed a pocket watch of solid silver from her purse, stared at the dials, said, "That's not my Ted," and proceeded to wind the watch. I heard a heavy padding in the hall, and then Humble Jake Hess appeared. I wasn't surprised. Jake had informers everywhere in his district. Someone must have summoned him from Morton Hall.

Humble sniffed about. He had his own sense of drama. He kissed Alice's hand with his native gallantry, ignored McManus, and lit into Captain Striker. "You shouldn't have become Long John's linchpin, Dennis, a lad like you from my district. Couldn't you tell that this little party wasn't kosher?"

"Humble," the captain said, "I—"

"Shut up. You cannot pick on *my* Assemblyman."

He slapped Nan, and I didn't like it at all. Her arms flailed and she fell to the floor. I didn't care how she had flimflammed me.

"Humble," I said, "we do not hit women."

"Oh, yes, we do, Mr. Ted. And please do not meddle. This gang was out to ruin your career. Mrs. Nancy Fowler is the best bunco artist in Manhattan. She was once part of your social set."

"A real duchess," I murmured to myself.

Humble did a kind of entrechat and plucked Mrs. Fowler off the floor. He was very light on his feet, as he told me all about the duchess.

No one had neglected her, tossed Nan into the street. She preferred the *Life*, as petty criminals loved to call their own little craft. She was, according to Humble, a natural steerer and a dip. That's how she met McManus. He was a pickpocket and a prizefighter—before he moved into politics and stole elections for Tammany Hall.

"Ain't that so, Long John?"

"Aw, Humble," McManus said. "We were only having a little fun with the rube."

Humble seized McManus' derby and stomped on it. "Captain Striker, since when do you allow confidence men and their molls to operate in your back yard?"

"Jake," the captain muttered, "have a heart. Long John has all the barons on his side."

Humble smoothed the ribbons on the captain's chest.

"Arrest him, or I'll smash your skull. And take the dip—she goes down with him."

He chased out all the detectives and the photographers with their flash pans.

I felt sorry for the duchess after Humble told me her tale. She abandoned her brownstone on Union Square, left her banker husband and two children, with servants, draperies, and silver, to satisfy her wanderlust in the Manhattan underworld. She'd traded in her identity for the identity of a dip. Yet I was riveted to her, as if her own fanciful tale had come out of the stories I'd heard

from Mittie as a boy—with every sort of monster and enchantress. Mother, you see, had had her own slave companion at Bulloch
Hall, a ragged little girl called Toy, who dressed in Mother's hand-
me-downs and slept on a straw mattress near her bed. Toy was the
bold one, who risked the wrath of the Bullochs. She would gambol
on the rooftop of Bulloch Hall and swipe sweet potato pie from
the cookhouse. Toy and Mittie were both cognizant of a diabolic
queen—Deirdre—who floated above the roofs and gobbled little
girls. This queen had once been the bride of a local manor lord, a
lazy, boisterous lout who could not manage his own plantation—or
his bride. She fled the manor in nothing but her nightgown and
declared herself queen of the countryside, with the right to pillage.

And one night, in the midst of a storm that bent every tree
within a mile of Bulloch Hall, the renegade queen appeared outside
Mittie's window with silver eyelashes and a puddle of blue paint on
her cheeks. "Come, my little ones," she beckoned in a birdlike song
that was hard to resist. Mittie might have gone with Deirdre into
the dark wind, but it was Toy who held her back, Toy who noticed
that wild sense of despair and destruction beneath the puddle of
blue. Mrs. Fowler was the same sort of enchantress, the same renegade queen, resurrected right out of Mother's tale. I admired her
pluck, that perfect stride she had—it frightened and exhilarated
me, as if I were one step away from the void. Perhaps we all were.

CHAPTER 3

LEEHOLM

1884

THE WIND RATTLED THE PANES, AND THE SNOW PILED up like pyramids, blocking all the carriages to Broadway, yet Alice, my Alice, dreamt of a sleigh ride through the park. "Oh, Teddy, it will be our own grand little adventure." She was a country gal who would not give in to the unwieldy cavalcade of city life. So I summoned our man, and he rescued Father's sleigh from some hidden perch. We wrapped ourselves in bearskins and blankets, and ventured across the park, into the Badlands of the West Side. Little Dakota had been built up bit by bit since my sleigh rides with Papa during the war. The river rats were all gone, driven out of the territory by the police and several citizens' brigades. The Bloomingdale Asylum and the orphanages were still there, and we passed many a shantytown as we rode from hill to hill. The impoverished souls of Manhattan had no other avenues to possess near the park; we discovered our own route among the human wreckage, as we zigzagged along.

My wife often stopped to feed a child from our lunch pail. She felt a sudden kinship with such hilltop tykes, with their bulging scarecrow eyes and clothes that were about to unravel.

"Aren't they part of your district, Teddy?"

"No," I said. "Not this far north."

"Humble's the Commissioner of Charities. Couldn't he do *something?*"

And I had to explain the peculiar tick of government to my wife.

"If the other Commissioners come by, they'll round up the children and take them to Blackwell's Island. They'll starve, Alicy, or vanish in the fog. Their lives won't be worth more than a pinch of salt. They're better off in the Badlands with whatever little family they have left."

We brought six or seven lunch pails on our next ride.

"Teddy, dear, couldn't we take some of these children on a picnic to Leeholm?"

I'd bought a splendid parcel of land out on Oyster Bay that spread across forest and field, with an unhindered view of the Sound. There we planned to build our own hilltop manor, with a wraparound porch and plenty of fireplaces. "Leeholm," as I called it in honor of Alice, would have ten bedrooms, at least ten, where we could raise our own brood. I hired an architect, planned the stables—a pony for each member of the tribe. While the architect's sketches still sat in the parlor of our new home on West Forty-fifth Street, Alice was thinking of the ill-fed scarecrows from the Badlands she would invite to Leeholm.

"Alice, what if their parents object? We can't just kidnap these tykes."

"Pooh-pooh," she said. "We'll invite the children *and* their parents."

I didn't argue. It would be years before Leeholm was ever built. And she'd have her own little bunnies to care about by then.

I HAD TO RETURN to the Capitol. I was prince of the Nightingales now. I shaved off my side-whiskers. The barons and their minions reviled me in the papers that their masters owned, financiers like Jay Gould, who dipped into the public treasure as often as he could. For the *New York World* and its Democratic Party faithful, I was an aristocratic snob in tight trousers and a pince-nez with a gold tassel. Still, most of the journalists favored me. And while the barons hid in the shadows, I attacked Jay Gould in front of the Assembly. I didn't have much of a choice—it was attack or die.

I was startled to see McManus here. I could have sworn that Humble had Long John locked away for good. Some judge in Jay Gould's pocket must have freed him from the Tombs. He was Gould's personal bagman, and I caught him whispering with several Nightingales, my very own precinct captains. So I had to act.

"Mr. Speak-ah, Jay Gould and his associates have done all possible harm to this establishment. They are common thieves, and they belong to that most dangerous of all classes, the wealthy criminal class."

I could picture Jay, the cavalier pirate, with his velvet collar and patriarchal beard and the nimble patter of his priceless pigskin shoes. I liked nothing about the man. I accused him of corrupting this very House with his bribes. My fellow Assemblymen said that their little Manhattan rooster had gone too far. By Godfrey, I hadn't gone far enough!

I had to worry about other matters. Alice had a siege of morning sickness, and I didn't want to leave her stranded in our little cove on West Forty-fifth Street, at the mercy of strangers. So we moved back in with Mama and Bamie. Now Alice wouldn't be alone when I was in Dutch town. I was chairman of a special committee to investigate corruption in the City and County of New York, and I was not beholden to the barons and their little tricks.

Hearings were held in the once-opulent ballroom of the Metropolitan Hotel at Broadway and Prince. Papa's firm, Roosevelt & Son, had supplied the ballroom's plate-glass mirrors. But that was many years ago. There were now cracks in the plate glass, and a blue crust across the edges of each mirror. The Metropolitan had thrived into the 1850s. It was one of the few hotels in Manhattan that allowed the slaves of its Southern clientele to live right on the premises. It fell into disrepair after the Civil War. Mary Lincoln loved to stay at the Metropolitan. The President's widow would wander through its halls with bags of jewelry to help pay for her lavish lifestyle at this ragged and run-down hotel. The clerks told me tales of how she often dressed for dinner in torn skirts, would hide a chicken wing in her napkin, and nibble on it all night. She'd accost strangers in the hall and declare how she had once lived in the President's mansion. She'd forget her own room number, and a bellboy had to escort her, with the house key. He didn't want her pennies. But she'd wink at him. "Keep the cash. You'll get rich."

She was one more member of the Metropolitan's menagerie.

Still, the hotel did have a cut rate. That's why the Committee on Corruption rented the ballroom, despite its creaky chairs and tables with crooked legs. There wasn't an empty seat at this desolate palace. I was maestro of my very own opera and amusement park. I tore into witnesses, all the loyal hacks in local government who had been appointed by Party patronage and fell asleep in their sinecures. I dubbed each and every one Rip Van Winkle. The press was dee-lighted.

ROOSEVELT ON
THE RAMPAGE

My own great dee-light was that Bamie and Alice were at the hearings. Alice sat on a gigantic pillow. Her face was puffy and she had a slight rash, but her doctor told us not to be alarmed—it was all benign, he said, indications of her advanced pregnancy. I was alarmed to see that yellowish tint and her swollen fingers, but I did not want to worry my wife.

My star witness was the county sheriff, a mean little cuss who milked his office and ran rampant over everyone under his charge— prisoners, various deputies, and luckless tenants who lost the ability to pay their rent. He was the tool of landlords, bankers, and Party bosses. His name was Archibald Towne. He had a waxed mustache and a cat's green eyes. I couldn't do much about the tribute he collected from his deputies, or the cash he took to keep Republicans from the polls, and all his loot from the landlords. None of this appeared on any ledger. But I could torment him over his transportation bills. He sat in his seat, under a swaying chandelier, and winked at the city's own counsel, Samuel Bratt, a shyster from Tammany Hall.

"Mr. Roseyvelt," declaimed the sheriff to an audience of Democrats, sent from the Wigwam—Tammany headquarters—to flood the ballroom with Party loyalists. "You are going astray, sir, prying into a gentleman's personal affairs."

"Tell him, Townie," sang the loyalists. "Tell the rube where he belongs."

"Quiet," I said, pounding the committeemen's table with a pepper grinder from Mama's kitchen that served as a gavel.

"Mr. Towne, your private carriage is your own affair. But we have the right to know the cost of your sheriff's van."

The sheriff mocked me with his murderous eyes. *He was a murderer*, having starved a dozen prisoners half to death at the Ludlow Street Jail.

"It's a pity, Mr. Roseyvelt, but the ledger for that particular item has been lost—in a fire. It was an act of God."

The sheriff didn't realize that my own team of detectives had discovered his "lost" ledger in a warehouse that was considered a dumping ground and a graveyard.

"Ah," I said, producing the ledger. "This is also an act of God." I didn't care how many hidden bank accounts the sheriff had. The ledger was perfectly clear. He was charging the City of New York five hundred dollars a day, which would have been enough to hire a whole fleet of sheriff's vans. I asked him if the ledger was genuine. He didn't even glance at it once.

"It's genuine enough," he said.

"Then how can you explain this outlandish expense?"

"I cannot," he said. "It could have been a bookkeeper's error. I didn't make the entries, Mr. Roseyvelt."

He could afford to exult in his chair. He lived in a modest house on Water Street. His fortune must have been invested under a fictitious name, perhaps by Jay Gould or another financier. I could poke at him with some imaginary lance, but I was nothing more than a minor nuisance. And the sheriff's own shyster decided to embarrass the Corruption Committee.

"Mr. Chairman, we would like to assist you in your inquiry and have the Honorable Humble Jake Hess appear in the witness box. Have you any objections, sir?"

"No," I hissed without hesitation. Humble was not on my list. But I had to call him or I would have been accused of nepotism.

My clerk shouted, "The Commonwealth of New York calls Jacob Hess, Commissioner of Charities."

Humble sauntered across the ballroom and occupied the sheriff's vacated seat. Sam Bratt grinned from ear to ear, like a mad pirate sniffing my destruction. I never hid the fact that I was Humble's protégé.

"Mr. Chairman, you seem a bit taciturn. Shall I question the Commissioner for you?"

I started to protest, but Humble signaled to me with the rapid beat of an eye.

"That's your privilege, Counselor," I said.

I'd gone to Columbia Law with this shyster—he'd been in one or two of my classes. He was some kind of a grub, who lapped up every word of our law professors. Bratt was in his glory now. He hovered over Humble's chair.

"Commissioner Hess, can you tell us how you happened upon your current employment?"

"Easily done. Senator Roscoe Conkling waved his magic wand." The shyster paused for a moment to punctuate the drama.

"Not the presidential hopeful and recently retired Republican Party boss?"

"The same," Humble said.

"Presto!" said the shyster, with a grin that could have swallowed up half his face. "You were appointed Commissioner, just like that. And what were your qualifications?"

"None."

All the Party loyalists laughed and stamped their feet, as the shyster moved closer and closer to Humble.

"And how did Roscoe Conkling acquire his thunder, his magic, his tricks?"

Humble stared into that audience of Democrats. "From the greatest thunderer of them all."

"And who is that?" the shyster asked.

"Your own boss, Honest John Kelly, Grand Sachem of Tammany Hall—himself soon to be retired."

The shyster's mouth swelled with spit. "Honest John is not my boss. I have none."

Humble sat like a soldier. "It's a pity, then. I was there the day you were appointed. I was in the Mayor's office with Mr. Conkling and Honest John. The Mayor was sound asleep. Honest John says to one and all, 'We'll need to bring a new lad onto the Corporation Counsel, some fellah who isn't too bright and won't get in our hair.' I nominated you."

"I won't listen," the shyster said. "This hearing is adjourned until further notice."

I pounded the table with Mama's pepper grinder. "You're not the chairman, Mr. Bratt. The witness stays where he is."

The shyster muttered to himself and fled the ballroom with Sheriff Towne and most of their Democratic lackeys. I'd never have called upon Humble, since neither of us swam in neutral waters. But here he was as a witness, and here I meant him to stay.

Humble unraveled the entire skein of misery and desolation, commencing with his department. His investigators couldn't prevent the bribery on Blackwell's Island. It didn't matter how many crusades he went on. The crusaders were often as corrupt as the guards, who sought sexual favors from female clerks and lads with longish hair, while older orphans preyed on younger ones. The island itself, with its public hospital, its penitentiary, its orphan and insane asylums, was one vast crime school, and its graduates returned to Manhattan as living, breathing carrion.

This was the future that Father had foretold, a city and a nation of troglodytes. And Humble had outlined it all in his little picture of Blackwell's Island.

"Then what is the solution, Commissioner Hess?"

"Only one," Humble said. "Send Blackwell's to the bottom of the sea."

"Ah, it will simply rise again as some other forlorn Atlantis with the very same asylums."

I didn't wait around with Humble. "Dismissed!" I growled with a knock of my pepper grinder, and I rushed home with Alice and Bamie to West Fifty-seventh Street in this *injurious* weather. A blinding fog had clung to Manhattan and most of the Northeast Corridor for the past week. The ferries had stopped running. There was a relentless drizzle and an endless delay on the rails, as signals suddenly disappeared between stations. The fog worsened. There was a green mist on most walls; elevated trains were becoming suicide rides as cars spilled off their tracks; the odor of dung and rotting produce wafted from street to street. We locked every window at the mansion, drew the curtains, and lived in a universe of lamplight, a yellow land as dense as the fog.

I'd almost forgotten Mama. I raced upstairs to her room. She wasn't asleep. She ruled from her bed with a lingering cold. That's why she hadn't come to the hearings.

"I'm so proud of you, Teedie—the Roosevelt name in every newspaper. And your father would be proud. Do you think Papa's ghost was at the hearings, guiding you?"

I did not believe in ghosts. "His presence, Mama, certainly. I had no other guiding hand but his."

She sat under the covers in her chiffon cap, like a philosopher, my Lady Voltaire, a blizzard of memories in her blue eyes.

"Teedie, Papa would like a word with you."

I pretended to listen, and there was so much eagerness on her moon-white face, so much unbridled passion for a message from Papa's ghost, I had to deliver something—a postal card from another world. I conjured as best I could, told how Father had been beside me at the committee table.

She shut her eyes, and her lids were as fine as the finest crêpe, with blue veins in them. "Teedie, did he tell you to attack or retreat?"

"Attack, Mother."

"Yes," she said, "that's him."

And her touch of panic was gone, as she sat like a prisoner in a royal bedroom filled with Father's relics, that beloved silver box of his with all its artifacts and trinkets—a watch fob with a frayed thread, a key chain of solid gold that once hooked into his belt, a pocketknife that was probably a Christmas gift or memento from Roosevelt & Son; how I could recall that handle of pure pearl and that blade with a British crown etched into the surface, like a mark of absolute fealty. He never picked at his nails with that knife, or cut the strings of a package. But he did reattach a renegade earpiece of my spectacles with the tightening of a screw, and cut the pages of a book that arrived from Harper & Brothers—there was no other sound on the planet like the musical scratch of Papa's knife against an uncut page, repeated again and again.

ALICY STILL HAD THAT yellowish cast under the yellow lamplight. Her doctor reassured me. He was in attendance now day and night, as he went from Alice to Mittie like some angel in silent, velveteen shoes. "You must not endanger your bill," Alice said. "You know how the barons love to bribe. They won't be as brazen with you in the House."

Humble must have taught Alice his own particular art. I had to nurse that damn "Roosevelt Bill" through the legislature, get all the Nightingales in line. But I couldn't rally my troops from a citadel in Manhattan.

I was restless, thinking of the Black Horse Cavalry and the harm they could do. I had that caged-wolf feeling while I wandered through the mansion. I went into Mother's room and borrowed the pearl-handled knife from Father's silver trinket box. I needed whatever talisman I could get to win against those Albany pirates.

There wasn't a cab to be found in this suicidal weather. I strode through the stinking miasma, where folks were invisible a few feet away, and arrived at Grand Central Depot, which looked like a tower of dripping yellow blood; the fog had crept inside the depot, and I had to skirt around a caravan of pickpockets. The train shed was an eerie spectacle of darkness at midday—the incredible illumination of its glass ceiling was gone forever, it seemed. I felt utterly abandoned in this vast tunnel of blanketed light. I lost my bearings for a moment. Suddenly I was part of Mama's landscape, a ghost among ghosts. Still, I managed to climb aboard the afternoon train to Dutch town.

A telegram from Alice was waiting for me when I arrived at my hotel.

MOTHER RALLYING. I AM FINE. GO BACK TO WAR.

But I didn't have the appetite for a cockfight at the Capitol.

And then Alice went into labor while I was rehearsing my Nightingales. A bellboy knocked on the door of our rallying room with a yellow slip from Ellie.

JOY ABOUNDS AT WEST 57.
DELICIOUS BABY DAUGHTER.

There wasn't much rancor at the Capitol on Wednesday morning—my enemies hailed me in the corridors; even McManus smiled. "Congratulations, Mr. Ted." Then a third telegram arrived while I was on the Assembly floor.

COME HOME.
ALICE AND MAMA IN TROUBLE.

EMBALMED IN A FUNNEL of black smoke, my train crept along the Hudson Valley into the deepening fog. The lamps in the car went out. I could not see the sky, or trees, or a bit of railroad track. I was the lone passenger, it seemed. No conductor appeared. Surely there were other passengers—a drummer, a Black Horse Cavalryman, a Nightingale or two? And then a man sat down next to me in the dark. He could have been a captain or a colonel, since he had a kind of military manner.

"What are you doing here, bub?"

"My wife and mother are ill," I said.

He laughed in the rudest sort of way. "This isn't the hospital car," he said.

The lights flickered for a moment. I caught the man's features. He looked like Jay Gould, but Gould had his own private line. Gould wouldn't have boarded a public car, not in a fog that squatted over Albany. We were stalled several times, waiting for some bell or whistle that never sounded once. And when we arrived at the depot that night near eleven, my rude companion was gone. . . .

Elliott met me at the door with such a shivering look of anguish, I had to shy away from my own brother, or run howling at an invisible moon.

"There's a curse on this house," he said.

Our bedroom was like an army barracks. Doctors and nurses fluttered about. I nearly knocked over a nurses' stand. I couldn't even tell if my baby daughter was in her bassinet. Bamie whispered in my ear. "Bright's disease. Alice's kidneys are failing."

I could not bear to look at the doctors who had misread Alice's swollen fingers and yellowish cast as marks of pregnancy. Alice was lying propped up on several pillows. She recognized me, recognized me not. Her blue eyes wandered. Her lips were cracked. Her nose was filled with bloody mucus.

I tore the nurses and doctors away from Alice, rocked her gently as I could.

"Mr. Roosevelt," said the chief quack, peering at me through his lorgnette. "Your wife must not be moved. She would shatter in your arms. She's frail, sir, frail as glass."

"Glass, you say? Dr. Peterson, I will move her to heaven or hell if I like."

But I held her tight now, as she trundled her head in alarm.

"The Black Horse . . . Cavalry," she muttered.

I stroked her, touched her hot flesh. "Darling, no damn cavalry could keep us apart."

I did not want all this clutter around us, invading the privacy of our bed. I glared at the doctors and the nurse patrol. "Out," I screamed, with the veins rippling on my forehead.

Bamie scattered them all and stood like a sentry near the door.

Alice laughed. I was convinced that I could cure her with my own electrical currents and the force in my arms. What did any of these quacks know? Dr. Dudley Sargent, Harvard's physician, had diagnosed my death, and here I was, leaping up the stairs and sparring with professional prizefighters in my rooms at the Kenmore, with no more punishment or fear of fatality than a blackened eye.

Alice laughed again. "Lee . . . holm," she said.

We'd built the stables and the foundation of our country manor, nothing more.

Her smile was petulant now. She did not mention our daughter. "Those children on the hill."

What hill?

She wasn't delirious.

"Promise to bring them from the Bad-lands."

"Yes," I said. "I promise."

I'd bring every last one of those rough-clad tykes to our deserted stables and feed them and their parents with a plunder of wine.

"We will have a carnival—on the lawn. I'll dance with the children."

"We both will," she said. "May a few of them come and live with us . . . for a little while? They'll be so happy."

I'd build them a stable of their own—not a stable, a small mansion next to ours.

"Teddy, dear, is the snow . . . hard or soft?"

That miasma had melted the snow. But my darling must have dreamt she was on a bed with runners and we were gliding across the Badlands on yet another honeymoon. I thought that if I could manufacture this sleigh bed in my own mind, I could keep her here, beyond the outposts of time. I shut my eyes and fell into the dream of our ride. But I was rudely awakened—by my own courier, Bamie, who had come to the door.

"Teddy, I need you."

"But I'm taking care of Alice, can't you tell?"

"If you want to see Mother while she's still alive, you must come now."

There was such force in my sister's sad, deep-set eyes, such rectitude, I could not contradict her. Bamie had to help me down one flight to Mother's floor. Damn those doctors and their medieval instruments. Mother's "cold" had masked acute typhoid fever. She lay under the quilts in that royal bed, wearing her chiffon coif. By Jupiter, she did not seem ill. She had that same ethereal, moonlit complexion. Her fists were clenched. "Teedie," she said in a trembling voice, "it's missing."

"What, Mother?"

"Your father's magnificent knife."

I cursed my own stupid hide. Mittie must have rummaged through Brave Heart's silver trinket box while I was with the Albany pirates.

"I'm the culprit, Mama."

I needed that knife. I wanted a piece of Papa in my pocket while I went after those renegades.

Mother didn't scold me. "Put it back, dear."

She had not forgotten a single object, could summon up the exact location of Papa's entire repertoire. I restored Papa's pearl-handled knife to his trinket box. Once Mama heard the familiar clink of the knife, she shut her eyes. But she did not lie still. A serpent seemed to run rampant through Mother's body and send her into a long, agonizing spasm, with a rattling sound in her throat.

"Brave Heart," she managed to mutter, still suffused with that moonlit glow, still within her secret estuary. That's where she resided since Papa's death, in some wild country of ghosts, enduring the grim colors of Manhattan for her children's sake. Yet we were well beyond Mother's estuary, had always been. And she abandoned us with one final rattle, frozen into that posture of pain.

Somehow, I returned to Alice's room with my own feeble grip on the banister rails. That liquid fever in Alice's eyes was gone. I stroked her, kissed her, as the light slowly left her limbs. I sat with Alice, as if I had had some umbilicus to her own interior. I couldn't let her go. I thwarted time, and could feel Alice and myself at Leeholm. Magically, the manor had been built, every shingle, every stone in place. It was packed with Roosevelts, sons and daughters galore. I couldn't recollect their names, my very own brood. We had ponies in the stables, air rifles for the urchins. We were hunting rabbit tails. The boys were all blond, the girls had weak eyes and royal red hair. The whole tribe wore spectacles. I didn't care about politics. Nothing mattered but Leeholm. Alice hadn't aged a bit. She danced with her weak-eyed children.

"Teddy, we do not have to dress for dinner, not ever again."

I was wearing a soiled dickey from one of Father's old dinner costumes. It scratched my neck. I heard a buzz in my ear.

"Teedie, she's gone."

I didn't listen. I had Leeholm.

There was a revolt in my brain. Leeholm unraveled a stitch at a time, as if the mansion had been manufactured on a spindle, with cotton rather than timber and stone. I had no anchors now, not Bamie, not Humble, not Morton Hall. I was bereft, a weak-eyed man without the will to linger in this world. And then Leeholm was back, not with my own brood, but with those tykes from Little Dakota. We danced around the stables, and I couldn't tell if I was in the midst of a carnival. A fiddler was there. Was I at a mock marriage, a charivari of sorts? One of the tykes, who couldn't have been older than ten, wore a wedding veil. I gazed under the veil. The little girl had a wizened, prunelike face.

"Will ya dance with me, Mr. Ted?"

I was contentious until I realized that I was the groom. We danced to the fiddler's tune. The pain of it was a whip away.

"Alicy," I called, but the echo rattled into the distance and died in the thunder of all those dancing feet.

CHAPTER 4

BLACK ICE

1884–1885

I SAID GOODBYE TO HUMBLE AT MORTON HALL.

"Ah, you will not be forgotten, Mr. Ted."

"Humble, I've already begun to vanish."

He was silent for a moment as he let my words sink in. "And what will be your next venture?"

"Ranchman in Dakota."

I'd visited the Badlands last year and felt the pull of that wild, barren terrain, its treeless plateaus, its buttes and battlements of many-colored clay. I was the only passenger to step off the Pullman car at Little Missouri, a former army cantonment that didn't even have a proper depot. I nearly landed in the cacti. But I fell in love with the underground fires that were fueled permanently in pits beneath clay and rock. That inferno had become my own glimpse of a strange new paradise. I acquired two ranches, the Elkhorn and the Maltese Cross.

"Will you go to the Badlands with your baby girl?" Humble asked, but he was quick to grasp my pain. "Ah, the Territory isn't the right venue for a child."

We hugged in front of his henchmen. He'd never profited from me. I was the one Nightingale he could afford in that pitiless parlor of politics.

I realized I might never see Humble again. He was the squire of Morton Hall. He had no interest in rising above his station. The Twenty-first was his mainstay and his coffin. Some ambitious roughneck among the ranks would mount a minor revolution and Humble would retire to a modest country estate. I couldn't tell if he had a wife and children—he was always at Morton Hall, presiding over the dust, the mousetraps, and the spittoons.

I had to settle accounts with Bamie before I left for the Badlands.

"I am heartless," I said, "a lawmaker who cannot even look after his own child."

"Teedie, you must heal yourself before you can attend to Little Alice."

"How?" I asked. "How?" Blondish she was, all blond, without a single root of red hair. Every glimpse of her summoned my departed wife. "I cannot abide to look at Baby Lee."

I had never seen such a furl of anger in my sister, whose lidded eyes were ablaze.

"I will not listen. Little Alice will not be the target of your grief."

We sold Mama's mansion on West Fifty-seventh Street, with its little reminders of Alicy—the bedclothes, the bric-a-brac, the sewing cushions, her archer's quiver, the footstool in her closet. And Bamie moved into a brownstone at 422 Madison—with Baby Lee.

That address would now be my Manhattan headquarters. But Bamie was swift in her reprisal. "This is your home away from home. I will raise Little Alice for you, become her devoted auntie, but I won't be your invisible wife."

Invisible wife.

I was furious at Bamie's bluntness. Yet she wasn't unfair. I had my own calling now. I would become a writer and a rancher out West.

I departed for the Badlands, furnished with silver stirrups, a tailored buckskin suit, and a Bowie knife from Tiffany's. I had to get outside my own country, leave the United States, to discover my own damn self in a Territory that was still uncharted and unknown. Dakota was full of desperadoes and other lost souls who needed to carve their fate in the alkali dust. The land around the Little Missouri River had been one of the last Indian hunting grounds in the West until ranchers and white trappers drove them off. So there was constant strife and bartering between the frontiersmen and the Cheyenne, the Sioux, and the Crow.

I was the first Knickerbocker the Little Missouri Cattlemen's Association had ever met. These cattlemen stared in wonder at my Bowie knife and buckskin suit, and welcomed me like a maharajah from Manhattan. "Roosevelt, you're the kind of pilgrim we could use in the Badlands." I was appointed a deputy sheriff to deal with all the strife. We had our share of vigilantes, or "Stranglers," who disposed of their victims with a piece of copper coil. They went after horse thieves and cattle rustlers, and wanted to go after the Cheyenne, attack their villages, and burn them out of the Territory. But I wouldn't give them that right. I didn't rile the Cheyenne, and allowed no one else to rile them. I'd string up the Stranglers if I had to, wipe them out to the last man. So the Stranglers behaved. And whatever skirmishes there were remained skirmishes. The Cheyenne tepees still stood. We didn't harm their women and children. And we maintained a fragile truce. There were Sioux war parties. Some young warriors might steal a horse and rob a lone mountain man. But we generally got that horse back, with the mountain man's belongings, after a little powwow with the local Sioux chiefs. I brought food in times of famine. I watched over the little ones with my medicine bag. I was considered royalty to the Sioux chiefs because of my fancy trousers and my red hair. The chiefs called me Prince Theodore. They loved to play poker. I'd never gambled in my life, not even at the Porcellian Club. But I gambled now, in the spirit lodge. The stakes were high. They eschewed poker chips and hard cash. They gambled for possessions, theirs and mine. I lost my sweetheart of a mare, old reliable Nell, in a poker game with the chiefs. The Sioux noticed how unsettled I was. "Prince Theodore, allow us to give you back the gift of your horse."

"But I lost Nell fair and square."

"No," they insisted in their own royal manner. "It would be a great unkindness. We would fear the ghost of your horse. We will take your repeater and your silver stirrups instead."

I still wasn't far from a tenderfoot, even with my deputy's badge. I couldn't handle a rope with the same flair as my cowpunchers, but I wasn't utterly useless on a cattle drive. Nell was as faithful as the North Star. I never got lost in some painted canyon while I was glued to that mare, even when I dozed in the saddle. . . .

I'd almost been caught in a snowdrift when I arrived that spring. We had the worst blow in years. It took days to dig out of the drifts, and left us with a mountain of black ice. That's the first sight I saw when I climbed down from the Northern Pacific car at Little Missouri—a world of black ice. The sudden freeze was so hard that the ice had become translucent, almost like a window onto the dark clay below. I had never once witnessed black ice in all my wanderings through Manhattan; it belonged in the Badlands, with its endless buttes of clay. Black ice was pernicious, because you could slide and slide and break your neck. If my own cowpunchers hadn't met me at the depot with an extra pair of hobnailed boots, I might not have made it back to the Elkhorn Ranch.

We trod softly in our spiked shoes and saved whatever cows we could. Then we dug out the white settlers. The mountain men, who lived in utter isolation, froze to death, sometimes in their tracks. That's how fast the blow had hit. And later, after we fed the horses and the cows, and drank our coffee over a fire in the barn, I assembled a search party—all volunteers from the Elkhorn—and we bit into the black ice with our boots until we arrived at the nearest Cheyenne village.

That village was buried in snow and black ice. The teepees had sunk into the hard, black morass, and the spirit lodge was invisible except for the clay roof. But there was something much more sinister than black ice. The Stranglers had arrived; they sat crouching on a butte above the village like a brace of jackals. Their leader was an ex–Army captain who had been an aide to General Grant and had also served with Custer in the Indian Wars. His name was Peter Albright, and he'd come to the Badlands five or six years ago.

He had his own ranch, but the Cattlemen's Association shunned him. He and his men displayed their Strangler's string, a copper coil attached to their belts. That coil was as fiendish as a wire snake; Albright would wrap it around some horse thief's gullet and choke the wind out of him. It was a terrible way to die, even for a horse thief.

"Hello, Four-Eyes," he said, wearing the gauntlets that General Custer had given him. He was as thick and ponderous as a barrel about to burst. I had no intention of tangling with him. He'd lost one nostril and part of his cheek to frostbite; the captain had even been scalped and survived. His face resembled a rough, indented map with eyes.

"Captain," I said, "you have no call to be here."

"I've as much call as you," he said, playing up to his Stranglers.

"We're here to rescue."

"So am I," he said. "We'll rescue these Injuns right to eternity."

But I knew his weaknesses. He'd graduated from West Point at the very bottom of his class. He'd always been a malingerer who wished for a fabulous military career. And his Stranglers were the residue of that lost career.

"Captain, you're begging for a fight on this damn ridge."

He smiled with his dented frying pan of a face. "Four-Eyes, you could waltz away on the black ice."

"What if I tell Ulysses?"

The sand had gone out of him. "You're on intimate terms with the general?"

I'd seen Grant at several soirees in Manhattan. I shook his hand once or twice. My *proximity* to Grant had unsettled the captain and dampened his designs on this village. He vanished into the clay with the Stranglers, like a snowman who was half asleep.

We climbed off the butte and chipped away at the black ice with our pickaxes until we dug out every tepee and tunneled right into the spirit lodge. We did not bury the dead. But we did feed the children corn mush, and warmed half-frozen women in buffalo robes. I cradled an infant in my arms, whistled a birdsong until his eyes grew alert, yet no matter how I toiled, I couldn't drive out my own demons. I'd always believed you could outrun sorrow and black care if your stride was long enough, but I couldn't shove past the image of Baby Lee in this land of black ice. Her blondness was like my own macabre Strangler's string.

BLACK ICE REMAINED EVEN after the second melt of the season, that March—it clung to the clay. And a cowpuncher of mine discovered a bald act of thievery that no rancher could abide. We had one of the rare scows on the river, a watertight blue flatboat, and it was gone. We'd tied it to a tree near the riverbank. That scow had ferried ponies and supplies across the stream. The culprits had left a red woolen mitten with a leather palm in a pack of snow, almost as a mark of defiance. I knew the owner of that glove. I'd seen him wear it many a time. He liked to flaunt it in a cowboy's face. He was a gunfighter and a bully, Red Finnegan, a giant of a man in a frayed buckskin shirt. He had a crop of red hair that reached to his shoulders. He gambled a lot. He came with a partner, an old German who was a little touched in the head. They lived together in a cabin about twenty miles upriver. Red Finnegan had been involved in several shooting scrapes. He was clever enough to evade the law, but he and his partner were under the constant scrutiny of the Stranglers. Red must have realized that the Finnegan gang didn't have much of a future in these parts. He'd have to disappear, go deeper into uncharted land of the Dakota Territory, where sheriffs and Stranglers couldn't follow. He'd never get there on his pony. A horse would break a leg on that black ice. And he couldn't get there on foot. Finnegan and I had the only flatboats on the Little Missouri, and he got it into his head to steal mine. His was rather leaky and couldn't have gotten him far in the unpredictable currents downriver. But larceny wasn't royal enough for Red Finnegan. He had to leave his rotten glove with that leather palm to get my gall.

I had to send a boy to town for a fresh bag of nails; the nails we

had were all rusted out. Upon his return, two of my cowpunchers, Sewall and Dennison, who'd been carpenters in Maine, built
a beauty of a boat with their hammers, chisels, a whipsaw, and our
brand-new nails. Dennison was a widower, like myself. He talked
ceaselessly about his dead wife. "Mr. Roosevelt, do ya think the
hurt will ever go away?"

He left off when I would not answer and returned to his hammer and chisel.

The culprits had six days on us. We packed our flat-bottom with
supplies and warm bedding. My two cowpunchers were quick as
cats, and I could rely on them in case of an ambush. But Red Finnegan was desperate now; he'd have shot out our eyes if he'd had
half a chance. That was his calling card—a bullet hole where an
eyeball had once been. But I had a feeling for the hunt; I meant to
capture Finnegan alive. We had our woolen socks and our Winchesters, and we couldn't have survived the cold currents without
a fur coat.

We shoved off downriver and took our seats, maneuvering with
paddles, oars, and iron-shod poles. We had to respond to the violent twists in the current with an artful distribution of our weight
and plunge after plunge of our poles, or we would have crashed into
the sandstone cliffs. And while we bobbed on the river, leaning in
one direction and then the other with all our might, we fell upon
a calamity; some tepees were burning on one of the buttes. It was
no deserted campsite—a Cheyenne village was on fire. The smoke
swirled dark and thick in the north wind. Attuned as I was to birdcalls, I listened to the slightest human cry, the muffled whimper of
a child. The fire crackled in its own deep silence.

"Sewall," I said to my steersman, "we have to stop."

Dennison answered for him. "The Stranglers wouldn't leave any
witnesses, sir. They kill *completely* by force of habit. And if we're
mired in the shoals, we'll never repair the scow in time to catch
Red Finnegan."

"We have to stop."

We escaped the shoals, and Sewall landed the flat-bottom near a solid wall of black ice. We scaled that wall with the help of our pickaxes and hobnailed boots. The sweet, sickly odor of burnt flesh was unbearable. We had to gird ourselves with neckerchief masks. We wore wet blankets to shield us from the relentless licks of fire as we wandered into the seared skeletal remains like ghoulish ragmen looking for some miraculous sign of life. The fire wasn't nearly as treacherous as the plumes of black smoke that bit right into our lungs.

"Mr. Roosevelt," Dennison muttered under his mask, "give it up, for God's sake, give it up, before we perish in this conflagration."

Just as I was about to quit this charred plateau, a white man ventured out of the fire—with feathers, beads, blue eyes, and blond hair. He'd camouflaged himself, of course. He had black dye on his scalp and a mask of war paint. But the fire had melted off the mask and the dye. He still kept up the pretense, whimpering to us in Cheyenne. I'd dealt with these flimflam artists before, and it made little difference whether they were hiding in Manhattan or Dakota.

"Son," I said, "you have thirty seconds to explain yourself, or you're going back into the fire, feet first."

His foolery ended right there. "That's rather harsh," he said in English as melodious as mine. "I thought you were with the Stranglers."

He referred to himself as Brother Bear, claimed he was married to the daughter of a Cheyenne chief, that he was as pious as a parson, and had been faithful to the tribe and his Cheyenne princess. But there was something too sly about that quilt of words he'd surrounded himself with.

"I didn't ask for your spirit name. Who are you?"

Dennison recognized him under the leaky war paint. He was Black Jack McGraw, a pistolero, backstabber, and cardsharp who had a bounty on his head and had been hiding out among the Cheyenne. The Stranglers had attacked the camp, he said, swooping down with their torches and their Winchesters. They forced themselves upon the women and obliged the warriors to watch. Then they herded the tribe into several tepees, set the tepees on fire, and as the Cheyenne came running out, they ripped them to pieces with their rifles.

I couldn't imagine carnage worse than that. I wanted to shake Black Jack to pieces.

"How did you manage to survive?"

Black Jack didn't flinch. He had the ice-cold blue eyes of a card-sharp. He was involved in the massacre. I was convinced of that. But I led him along on my own Strangler's string.

"Well?" I asked again.

"I was hiding—in a dugout."

"And the Stranglers pranced right over your head. . . . What were the Cheyenne doing here on this bluff—during a blizzard?"

"Where else could they winter, where else? They're not reservation Indians. They're hunters."

A hunter wouldn't let himself be herded into a tepee with his women and children, and bear witness to his own immolation—a hunter would have clawed back until his last breath.

"You son of a bitch, you steered Captain Albright to this camp."

"You can't call me that, sir," said this renegade white man. "That's lethal business."

Son of a bitch wasn't used lightly in the Badlands, not in a country of cows and horses, of thoroughbreds and half-breeds, of strict blood ties. Gunfighters had their own sense of gallantry, like half-mute knights with a poetics that belonged to them alone. But this outlaw had no claim to gallantry. He started to blubber.

"Albright made me do it—he threatened me, Colonel."

Black Jack liked to heap titles onto a deputy sheriff with a stolen scow.

"How much did he offer you to betray your own tribe?"

"Five dollars," said Black Jack. "But, hell, Colonel, I was biding my time, running from the law."

"And why didn't the captain take you with him?" Dennison asked.

"That's silly, sir. I can't run with the Stranglers. I got a price on my head."

We didn't quite know what to do with this renegade. As deputy sheriff, I had the legal right to dispatch him on the spot, but I was no damn executioner like Captain Albright. I couldn't murder Black Jack just like that, no matter what harm he had done.

"Mr. Roosevelt," Sewall said, "we can't bring Blackie with us. He'll slow us down. We'd have to watch him every minute. We'll never catch up with Red Finnegan. And this whole campaign will be an exercise in futility, sir."

"We could leave him where we found him," Dennison said.

I wasn't slow to answer. "He'll die."

We had to carry the renegade down that wall of black ice, hoist him from hand to hand, since he didn't have hobnailed boots, while we worried about falling blocks of ice and snow. We settled him in the scow, tied his hands and feet with leather strips, and poled downriver. The wind was fierce, and we had to navigate all the savage bends in the river, or spin out of control in a whirlpool of our creation. Blackie had a raucous laugh, as he mocked us, and it was hard to resist hurling him overboard. The poles would freeze near nightfall, and we had to make camp on some wooded point of land that wasn't canopied in black ice. Sewall was our cook and our steersman, and he prepared a feast of coffee and bacon and flatbread. Black Jack was eating into our provisions, and the flour and bacon wouldn't last. I didn't have to guess what my little posse was thinking: *Drown the son of a bitch, or leave him here on this spit of land.*

But I couldn't become like the Stranglers, who were a horde of killer wolves on the prowl. We packed the renegade into the scow and pushed on. But he could have loosened the leather strips on his hands, and we couldn't afford to stray, or he would steal our rifles and shoot us into the water. I hardly slept at all.

"You won't keep me here very long," he sang, rocking in the scow. "I'll catch you winking, I will."

But he never did. And on the sixth day of our journey, as we came around a precipitous bend, poling as hard as we could, we spotted my handsome blue boat, moored to the riverbank with Finnegan's own battered flat-bottom. I worried that Blackie might whistle or shout to the culprits, and I warned him. "One word, one peep, and I'll split you right down the middle like a pumpkin."

We tied my boat to the other two and slipped ashore. I could sniff the pungent odors of a campfire in the north wind. Then we heard a live crackle, and saw a wisp of smoke. I stripped off my fur coat and readied myself for battle with the Red Finnegan gang.

The old German half-wit was all by himself in the camp, with a Winchester nestled in his lap. His eyes went mean when he saw us. "I'll kill every last one of you," he cackled. He never had a chance to pull. I kicked the rifle off his lap with a hobnailed boot. He got down on his knees, in a bed of black ice.

"Don't hurt me, Sheriff. . . . 'T wasn't me who wanted the boat. I came downriver to catch some fish."

"Old man," Sewall said, "what kind of fish would you catch in this ice storm? A warm-weather whale?"

The half-wit nodded his head. He didn't have one particle of sense in his whiskey-raw eyes. He sat on a frozen log, playing cat's cradle with an imaginary string. The half-wit had stripped off his mittens; his fingers flew with amazing agility, as he went from fig-ure to figure, and for a moment I was caught in his spell.

"Old man," I barked in that biting cold, "put your mittens back on before your fingers fall off."

He obeyed, and sat there in meek resignation, his mittens idle now, dead objects in his lap. We didn't ask him about Finnegan. He wasn't capable of connecting one tale to another, and would only have lied. We heard the crack of a man singing, his voice like rifle shots in the glacial air, as he reveled in a bawdy song about bungholes, a harlot, and a cowpuncher with a live rattlesnake in his chaps.

Charlotte the harlot ran afoul of the law . . .

He was having such a good time, with his rifle slung on his shoulder and his bullet pouches bobbing up and down, that he walked right into camp, while we came out from behind a bank of black ice with our Winchesters cocked. "Hands up," I shouted in that high pitch of mine, while Red Finnegan was half crazed with the will to fight, his pink eyes daring us. Still, he dropped his Winchester in disgust.

"Hi ya, Blackie," he said to the renegade, "are you part of this bunch?"

"No, sir, Red, they corralled me while I was walking out of a fire."

"They're always corralling folks, these Elkhorn people."

"It's that damn colonel," Blackie said.

Red Finnegan did a white man's war dance, hopping along the black ice with his hands still in the air, but he had to be a bit cautious with his gestures and his words; we were in the wilderness after a blizzard, and I could have repeated his specialty and shot out his eyes. He knew that. I didn't have to bargain with him. He'd stolen a scow in the Badlands, and was as guilty as a horse thief. A deputy in the wild was also judge and executioner. So he berated Black Jack while he settled in with his hands in the air.

"Roosevelt ain't no colonel, you dummy," he said. "He's a literary fellah with a fat bankbook."

"Have ye read his *other* books?" Blackie asked.

"What's there to read? He writes about birds and battleships."

The bandits chuckled, but they weren't bitter about it, not with rifles close enough to caress their hides. A back wind rose up, and we couldn't break camp, not with three prisoners. Sewall and Dennison chopped away at some dead cottonwoods, while I stood guard with a duck gun that could have splattered all three of them in one pull, and pretty soon we had enough logs for a very long blaze. The cold was so sudden and so fierce, we couldn't tie up our charges, or risk having their limbs freeze off. That would have been a sight—capturing a bunch of legless men. We buttoned them down in their bedclothes, but first we had them shuck off their boots. They couldn't run very far in cactus country—the cactus spines would cripple them for life. We all had our beans and flatbread near the fire, sometimes sharing the same spoon. It was almost congenial. But Finnegan wouldn't let off bragging.

"If I'd had any show, Mr. Roosevelt, any show at all, you sure would have had a fight."

I wanted to keep him calm, so I nodded once, but Sewall was less kind.

"Finnegan, save that tale for Charlotte the harlot. I'd have cut your ears off with Mr. R's Bowie knife before you had a chance to pull on us."

"Hell," Finnegan said, roostering under the bedclothes, "that damn knife is a piece of Manhattan furniture."

"Furniture or not," Sewall told him, "it's still fine enough to reshape your ears into a trophy."

Finnegan fell asleep after that, and he snored like an engine plagued with asthma. I was familiar with that strangled, staccato music. I lay there in the howling wind, with coyotes attracted to our fire. It must have soothed them against the cold. Their eyes were as red as hot magnets. The fire had put them in a trance. I could have stroked each one with my gloves. I almost did. But when they tried to gnaw into a flour sack, I chased them with a stick. These coyotes would have torn our arms off at the socket.

We went back downriver in the morning, with the crazy old German and Blackie in Finnegan's flat-bottom, equipped with one paddle, while Finnegan stayed with us in my blue boat. They couldn't have gone far, couldn't have escaped, in that winding river. And neither could we; the river was all buckled up in black ice. We had to pitch camp and reconnoiter a bit, dragged down by prisoners who would have murdered us in our sleep. We were hunters who couldn't hunt; all the game was gone.

We stumbled upon the very last outpost of a downriver ranch that rose out of the wilderness like a castle baked in mud. This mud castle was run by a ragged plainsman who had a prairie schooner for hire and two ornery bronco mares. This plainsman was curious why I would risk my own carcass catering to rattlers like Red Finnegan and his lot.

"Hang them all," he said. "You have that privilege, Deputy." He squinted at me. "Tell me if you're an Easterner?" And when I nodded, he looked askance.

"That reduces the mystification of it. No deputy worth his salt would walk these skunks to jail. It's forty-five miles to Dickinson, sir, on a road of black ice. That schooner will tip, and your captives will overwhelm you. They'll roast you in their fire with a pinch of paprika—hang them, hang them now."

The prairie schooner came with a cowpoke who didn't satisfy me much. He was a cattle drover from a distant ranch. And he seemed to have some acquaintance with Red Finnegan. But I didn't have a choice—it was this drover, or none at all.

Red was the real danger. I couldn't trust him on a riverbed of black ice. He might drown us all in a mad rush to escape.

So I said goodbye to Sewell and Dennison, who took the renegade cardsharp—that fake Cheyenne—and the old German and went back to the boats. They'd ply their way downriver with their poles and pickaxes and wait for the big spring thaw, while I was stuck with the job of delivering Red to jail.

Dennison was suspicious of my whole enterprise. "Boss, that drover you have isn't much of a saint. He needs watching."

I elected not to ride in the prairie schooner with Red Finnegan. My drover kept whispering to Red. I told him to cut it out. I walked behind the schooner. I couldn't afford to sleep while standing in my hobnails, or I wouldn't have woken up. I kept the Winchester cradled in my arms. That river-road of black ice soon turned to sludge, and I was mired in the black earth and blacker mist. At times I had to push the wagon on my own, while the drover sat there humming to himself. The broncos stopped in their tracks, and I had to play up to these mares, coo at them, caress their forelocks, comb their withers with a metal brush, or I couldn't have gotten them to move out of that black mud.

Red sat inside the schooner, whispering to himself, his pink eyes juggling in his head, as if he were planning some magical event. Red was waiting until I grew drowsy, until my Winchester spilled into the mud. I had to educate that whoreson as quick as I could. Dickinson was the nearest town with an elected sheriff and a legitimate jail, and we had miles and miles to go.

"Red, I can kill you now—or later."

He guffawed with his rotten yellow teeth. "That ain't your style, Mr. Roosevelt. You're a gent who wears the Tiffany label."

I plowed a bullet into the prairie schooner. The rifle's report woke the stillness with a muffled clap that was akin to thunder. The broncos lurched, and the drover leapt high in his seat.

Red's toothy grin was gone. "You're loco, Mr. Roosevelt, you really are."

"Then sit tight, Finnegan, and stay put."

I had to feed the son of a bitch every six hours or so. I served him beans from the stock of that downriver ranch. The drover had some hardtack. I fed the mares, scooped some water out of the pail, and let them lap at it from the hollowed-out gourd of my hand. The drover slept in his seat, clutching the reins. I didn't sleep at all.

I marched in the rain, sloughing through sludge that ran to the ankle. I spotted the first barn sparrow after the frost, welcomed its piercing chatter, reveling in its song. I knew I was a little safer now. I wouldn't fall behind in my spiked shoes. Each birdcall would waken me out of my slumber.

I could swear that other renegades were right behind me.

—*Four-Eyes.*

It was Captain Albright and his Stranglers. I couldn't have been asleep, or I'd never have caught the crooked outline of his frying-pan face. That lunatic pressed his advantage. He was clutching Baby Lee.

I hadn't mentioned Little Alice once in my letters to Bamie. The Badlands had gobbled up her existence.

—*Captain*, I said, *you shouldn't have murdered those Cheyenne and set fire to their camp.*

I couldn't help noticing how comfortable he was with Baby Lee, how tender. She could have been the captain's daughter.

—*Pshaw*, he said, *serves those hostiles right for wintering here.*

I'd written Bamie about everything—the blizzard, Red Finnegan, the black ice, my blue boat, the Cheyenne fire, everything but Baby Lee. And here she was in Albright's arms, that lunatic with his missing nostril, his frostbitten cheek, the furrows in his crown where he'd been scalped. And then I realized that the baby in his arms didn't have blond hair. He was clutching a papoose, a little girl in her swaddling board that he must have plucked right out of the fire. Why that one papoose?

—*Four-Eyes*, he said, *I'd like to have a strangulation party right here. Give us Red Finnegan.*

I hadn't built me a boat and chased Red downriver just to surrender him to the Stranglers.

—*You'll have to kill me first.*

The Stranglers chortled and slapped their thighs. I looked into their broken mouths, filled with tobacco cud. This renegade captain had had his designs on me ever since I came to the Territory and started buying up ranches. I was a hindrance to him, a rich rubberneck in a tailored buckskin suit, carrying a rifle with my initials burnt into the stock in gold filigree. I'd never accept the Stranglers. And he knew it from the start—even if I was running from the United States, just like him.

—*Captain, I'm curious. Why'd you rescue that little girl and let all the others disappear in the fire?*

—*Because. I took a shine to her.*

That lunatic was no different from the rest of us. He had his rites of civilization. He'd killed men while riding for Custer and riding for General Grant, and strangled others for stealing a cow. He didn't harden to anything but the language of plunder.

He tossed that papoose up in the air—it waffled across the black sky. And then his Stranglers took turns shooting at the swaddling board. They ripped it to shreds, and the last piece of it floated into my arms. There was no little girl, alive or dead, nothing but a rag doll with a red mouth. Albright laughed at his own ruse.

Then the Stranglers fell back, and I slogged along in the mud. A second barn sparrow arrived, alighted on my shoulder, and chipped a night song. I didn't have a lantern. It was pretty dark in the prairie schooner. I could have been guarding an empty wagon. I heard the scrape of a match. I saw a flicker of light inside the canvas covers. Red Finnegan was cupping his hand against the bowl of a cherry-wood pipe. He was sucking hard on the short stem. That bowl of his was on fire.

I watched him with my own burning red eyes, watched him just as hard, with that sparrow still on my shoulder, delivering its night song.

PART TWO

CHAPTER 5

HER LITTLE LADYSHIP

1885

I GOT ME A ROCKING CHAIR AND A RUBBER BATHTUB THAT looked like a raft, had them delivered to the Badlands from St. Paul, and I'd sit out on the piazza of my ranch house and watch the river burst its banks or run dry as cow cake. Weather was a whispering word in the Territory. My ranch hands limped about with frostbite, veterans of an undeclared war; some were blinded in a sudden surge of ice dust; others went mad in the perpetual winter of a blue-black sky and ran naked into the wilderness, never to return.

Bamie took care of my bills.

I did not ask about live ghosts like Edith Carow. I damn forgot that she ever existed, that she'd once been a part of my life, and that I might have been in love with her a little, a long, long time ago. I'd buried her like a dead root. I was Mr. Four-Eyes, constant to a departed bride whose every relic I had rubbed raw. We Roosevelts did not marry a second time, no matter what the circumstance. I had a mourning band seared into my heart.

But Edith Carow was still on my mind. We called Miss Edith Her Little Ladyship because she had perfect posture. She's the only one of us who had attended Mrs. Dodsworth's School for Dancing and Deportment. She ran around with my sister Corinne and attended all our festivities. She devoured Balzac and Dickens before she was ten. She had darkly golden hair and the inquisitive blue eyes of a scientist or a great explorer. She could discuss Coleridge with my mother and Chester A. Arthur with my father. Brave Heart always found a rôle for Edie in the little plays he produced at home. She never botched a line, not once. She played Cleopatra with the exactitude of an Egyptian queen. It did not hurt to have a long, lyrical neck and a nose with flaring nostrils. She spent the summers with us at Tranquillity, when I was a young bobcat with spectacles and Edith a kitten with claws. There were reports that little Edie and I were engaged. She was just fourteen at the time, and I was about to begin my freshman year at Harvard.

Her family had not fared well. She belonged to a once-prosperous shipping empire, Kermit & Carow, with its fabled clippers berthed along the East River. But her beloved father, Charles, who had read *The Arabian Nights* to her when she was a girl of four, did not have half the shrewdness of Sinbad the Sailor. Edie's Sinbad was a drunkard who had squandered the Carow fortune. He'd fallen down the hold of a Kermit & Carow clipper, banged his head, lay unconscious for hours, and was never quite coherent after that. The Carows moved from one narrower house to another by the time Edith was six, and had to rely on the largesse of relatives. Perhaps that is what had touched Brave Heart so. He invited Edie *everywhere*. He knew her own papa had unraveled in front of her eyes. I cannot recall if Father contributed to Edith's upkeep. I suspect not. Her Little Ladyship would have been much too proud to appear in a beggar's wardrobe. But her summers with us at Tranquillity must have eased the burden on her family quite a bit.

We rowed together, walked in the fields, spent long hours in the icehouse, the coolest spot on the North Shore. It was like a great bricked-in cavern, ten or twelve feet deep, with the ice blocks covered in burlap, and the tiny windows painted black to filter out the glare of the sun; specks of light still poured through the chips in the paint and cast prisms on the walls in a panoply of colors. Edie and

I relished these shimmering rainbows—otherwise we would have been sentenced to sit in the dark.

But the icehouse was plagued with a tiny regimen of frogs that lived in the moss under the ice blocks. I'm not sure how they survived the cold. Edith and I had to wear sweaters and woolen socks. It was still our favorite haunt, where we had absolute privacy and could trace the swirling path of our own breath against the prisms of light. And when the frogs cut their racket, we shared a calm that could be found nowhere else at Tranquillity.

We kissed and fumbled in our layers of wool, but we didn't fumble very far. Edith, I remember, was in one of her black moods; they would come upon her like a sudden squall. And I was beginning to weaken in my own vows of celibacy. All the lambs' wool in the world couldn't hide her figure. Edith had a woman's share of flesh at fourteen.

Cleopatra.

I'd bought a few trinkets to celebrate our trysts in the icehouse: a brooch, a bracelet, and a silver ring—the gatherings of a boy who had a luxurious allowance.

"I suppose we're engaged," I said. "But it has to be a secret."

Her brow deepened in that cold, dark house with its flickers of magical light.

"Ted, it's common knowledge. We've been together the *entire* summer. Have I looked once at another boy, have I danced with your friends? And you know how much I love to dance."

It was in the days before Father took ill, when he was the master of Tranquillity with his broad shoulders and leonine looks. He was the impresario of all our games and diversions. I hunted wild geese with Brave Heart, collected seashells, while he joined us in our tableaux. He was more enthralled about Edith than he was about her family. I was at a loss how to tell her that. Father did not want me to entwine myself with the Carows. I was harsh, I fear. I recited my calumny like a kingfisher, with its strident call.

"Papa says your father's a dipsomaniac."

I'd cut her to the bone. Her quick blue eyes receded with a cruel intransigence. She could never have anticipated such a remark. She'd idolized my father since she was a child, had been the proudest accomplice in all his tableaux. Edith's perfect posture dissipated on the love seat Father had brought in from the garden; her shoulders sagged, and her breath turned blue in that temperature as she summoned every resource she had.

"*Dip-so-man-i-ac*, you say. Father banged his head. That's not a disease. But the Roosevelts, I hear, are inclined to scrofula. It's a scourge of the family."

The kingfisher struck back. I had little choice. Scrofula was a terrible disease that doomed the victim with burgeoning pockmarks and a chronically swollen neck.

"That's the baldest lie," I said. "Have you ever seen one scrofulous Roosevelt? Edie, feel my neck!"

"Theodore, I will do no such thing." And she began to rise up out of that love seat like a bitter swan in all the glory of Mrs. Davenport's posture classes. "My mother and sister would never invent a tale about the Roosevelts. They have their scruples— scrofula it is."

Her mother, Gertrude, was a hypochondriac who dreamt up maladies for herself and everyone around her, and her little sister, Emily, was a copycat who did not have Edith's bearing, beauty, or wit. Yet I shouldn't have maligned Charles Carow, not with Father's words. He really was a sad case. He'd lost his clippers, one by one. But it was a matter between Edith and myself. I preferred an *invisible* engagement, with the tiny token of a silver ring. I was attached to Edith, like a kind of twin. But I could still summon up the seal's skull I had gotten from the fishmongers at the Union Square market. I had presented that skull and other treasures of mine to the Museum of Natural History, as one of its first members, while it was still housed at the Armory in Central Park, and I was hailed as Manhattan's "teen" taxidermist. I meant to pursue a scientific career, and zoölogists were poor as mice, even with a stipend from Papa; few of them could mingle science and marriage. I professed that to Edith in the icehouse. It was the lame prattle of a nearsighted boy who couldn't see beyond the reach of his nose. Zoölogists weren't saints—some had wives, I trust.

Edith stared at me in the icehouse's dark well, her face half illumined in the irregular light, like a prehistoric mask. It was almost religious, looking at her.

"Theodore Roosevelt," she said, her lips moving in and out of multiple rainbows, "you are the fool of fools. I've loved you since I was a little girl, and now I'll have to mourn a love-lost friend."

She marched out of the icehouse with that magnificent sweep of hers and without ever returning the bracelet, the brooch, or the silver ring.

I went off to Harvard. There wasn't a lull in our correspondence. Her letters were lively and literate, as if the incident at the icehouse had never happened, and we fell back into the "deportment" of old comrades. She was a bridesmaid at my wedding, still unwed. But we lost touch, as I drifted toward the Badlands. And I instructed Bamie:

> *Rather not bump into Her Ladyship on my return trips.*
> *Please encourage her to visit your parlor whilst I'm not around.*

Bamie complied with my wishes, as I wandered between the Badlands and Madison Avenue. I felt less troubled around Baby Lee. She was Bamie's blond creature now. I was like a mysterious stranger whose visits from the wild were short enough to delight and confuse her. She loved to watch me shave, to hear the scratch-scratch of the razor against my skin. I'd acquired a roaring red mustache in the Badlands; my face and body had bronzed from chasing after heifers and riding in the saddle on nineteen-hour runs. I'd splash around in my rubber bathtub like a bad little boy and sit on my piazza, read in the dying light. I'd lost the habits of an Easterner. I hunted cougars, howled with the wolves.

I did not dream of Edith, did not dream at all. And I did not miss Delmonico's or the dance cotillions, the coming-out parties or the debutantes' balls. There was talk of appointing me Senator once the Territory was voted into the United States. But I was much more at ease as a deputy sheriff and the writer of Western tales about the wiles of ranching and the pursuit of desperadoes like Red Finnegan along the sinister black ice of the Little Missouri. I sought solitude, and was comforted by it.

Then that solitude was torn out of me. I returned to Manhattan to meet with my publisher, but hadn't advised Bamie beforehand of my exact calendar. I was clumping up the stairs of Bamie's brownstone with my satchel and my game bag when I spotted Her Little Ladyship on the landing. I froze for an instant, like a stag caught in the hypnotic blaze of a hunter's lantern. But it was Edith who reassembled me with her own hypnotic smile. She wasn't embarrassed one bit.

"Sinbad," she said, "my Sinbad the Sailor."

I knew what she meant. She hadn't given up her love of fairy tales. Sinbad must have reminded her of Kermit & Carow's clippers, of adventure per se. No matter what vessel he commanded, Sinbad was always shipwrecked on some remote island that could have been as desolate as the Badlands. And I had Sinbad's husky bronze look, with my red mustache and all.

I dropped my satchel and game bag, and leapt up to greet her on the landing. She was wearing a blue bodice and a ruffled petticoat. I traced the curve of her bodice with a hunter's keen eye. My hand touched hers, and our fingers entwined. It was no more complicated than that.

She laughed with a deep-throated warble that ripped right from her bodice.

"And why has Sinbad crept back to dry land?"

"To meet with his Cleopatra," I said.

She frowned and pretended to scold me. "Theodore, you cannot mix the fanciful and the real—Cleopatra lived!"

"And so does Sinbad."

Bamie must have heard our echoes from the parlor. She came out onto the landing with a quizzical glance and sensed the pure thunder of our meeting. I did not loosen my grip on Edith's hand.

We all returned to the parlor. A shiver went through Bamie, a tremor she couldn't control. Edith had had no coming-out party, no debutante's ball. Her father had collapsed and died of heart failure while I was still an Assemblyman with a young wife. The Carows had less and less to live on, and planned a move to Europe, a permanent move, where they could economize and not have to worry about the latest cotillions. I was confused about all this. But nothing could match the confusion on my sister's face. She was fond of Edith, had always been, yet the suddenness of the encounter on the landing had unsettled her—seems Sister would have to share the deputy sheriff with another living soul.

"I'M A WIDOWER," I chanted to myself.

Widowers must not remarry.

But another birdsong lingered somewhere inside me. I could have abandoned Leeholm, sold the property, and enriched myself overnight. But while I was away in the Badlands, I deputized Bamie, put her in charge—and my mansion rose on the crest of a wheat field, overlooking the bay. I rechristened it Sagamore Hill, after a warrior from a local tribe defeated in battle two hundred years earlier—the hill had once been his, and perhaps I wanted his presence and imprimatur, though I was not generally mindful of ghosts. Bamie outfitted the mansion with furniture from her brownstone and our former "palace" on West Fifty-seventh Street.

I wanted to fill those bedrooms on Sagamore Hill with a brood of my own. Yet decorum prevailed in my conduct with Her Little Ladyship. Still, our secret engagement at the icehouse ten years ago was finally consummated. I informed no one—not even Bamie—in that curtained-off Knickerbocker society of ours, where widowers had to mourn a minimum of two or three years. We had our trysts at the Carows' crumbling townhouse in Murray Hill, full of mousetraps and cobwebs on the chandeliers. I much preferred the icehouse at Tranquillity, with its abundance of frogs. And our private meetings were usually within earshot of Edith's mother and sister. We groped a little, but soon realized that this sordidness wouldn't do. I wanted marriage, not a back-parlor romance amid all the mice scuttling about. But Her Ladyship hadn't lost her good humor.

"Theodore, this house is a zoölogist's dream. Lord knows what spiders you will find in the attic."

"Or under our feet. But I've given up zoölogy. I'm now a rancher—and a lawman, too."

And she entertained me with that full-throated warble. "Well, ranching hasn't been a lucrative venture. How much do you earn for capturing desperadoes?"

"I'm entitled to fifty dollars a head."

She licked away with a pencil and a notepad. "That isn't much of a bounty in the long run. You might lose your own head to one of these outlaws, and I'd have to collect the reward."

The good humor was gone. She could tell what was troubling me. I'd delayed going back to the Badlands, because I was a deputy sheriff with a house on Oyster Bay and a sweetheart I had to hide from the Knickerbockers.

"Edie, I can keep my ranch or Sagamore Hill, but I can't maintain two households."

"Well," she whispered, "we could solve your money troubles and elope."

I knew what she was hinting at. Bamie was the real mistress of Sagamore Hill, and I was an absentee landlord, a sometime laird. But I planned to change that in a single stroke. I fell upon the perfect scheme to invite Edith out to Oyster Bay. I planned to hold the Meadowbrook Hunt Ball at Sagamore Hill on the eve of my twenty-seventh birthday. The Meadowbrook foxhounds had an almost mythical status. They had long muzzles, large hazel eyes, and bullet-like heads, and were notorious fox catchers, the best of their kind. These black and tan hounds were raised at the hunt club in private kennels. The hunt master was very secretive about his black-and-tans. I never even considered the damage they could do to a red fox with their lantern jaws. They were muscular and lazy, suspicious attackers taught to stun.

The hunt began that afternoon on my hill. I wore the colors of the club—a reddish pink coat and silvery black boots. It wasn't at all like running down wolves, or riding after herds of buffalo. The hunt had its own ritual, a maddening pace that was electric and slow. The hounds didn't even stir until the fox master blew his horn—that bleat ricocheted off the hill and seemed to last longer than any horn I had ever heard, like the ripples in a stream. The dogs leapt with their own design, and we followed them and the fox master, who contained the hunt with some invisible string. We didn't have magicians like that out West, only hunters who had their peculiar habits with animals in the wild. These hounds weren't wild. They were practiced executioners, and I was out on a run with them.

We had obstacle courses in the Badlands—buttes and sandbars and underground fires that could asphyxiate a man if he crept near enough. But these obstacles were man-made, administered by the maestro of the hunt himself—timber forts five feet high, fences with rough edges that could have ripped a horse's belly, situated five or six to the mile. I had my own jumper, a huge stallion called Lancelot. I urged him on with a cowboy's surefire yell.

YA-HA-HAW!

I was at the head of the pack, the maestro behind me with his fancy stirrups and his horn.

I didn't have much sympathy for the maestro's hounds. The target of the chase was much more appealing, with it fiery red coat, its ears like tiny antennae. That red fox was the one wild creature in this parade of costumes and killers. And I, in my pink uniform, watched it whirl past the dogs, avoiding every obstacle, while Lancelot went lame and couldn't keep up with those dancing dogs.

I should have quit the hunt, gone off with Lancelot and let the others chase after that red fox, yet I couldn't. I had to stay at the head of the pack—it wasn't courage. It was pure intransigence.

I allowed Lancelot to gallop on his lame leg. He was gallant for another three miles of marshland and hilly terrain, vaulting over every obstacle. Then he tripped over the jagged edge of a timber fort, and I landed under my own horse; my left arm hadn't fully knit after a fracture in the Dakota Territory, and it cracked near the elbow, while I cut my face on one of the fort's wooden rails. Lancelot rose out of the marsh, and I hoisted myself into the saddle, with one useless arm flapping at my side, and I rejoined the chase. But that damn red fox made fools of us all, with our banners and fancy riding habits. He led the master's hounds into a sand pit, and we had to call an end to the hunt.

The master cursed himself and his dogs; the more they yelped, the deeper they sank into the sand. These killer dogs were little better than delinquent pups. None of us could help the hounds or the master. He had to wade into the sand and mud in his riding boots and carry out creatures of solid muscle and bone, one by one.

His prize hounds returned to Sagamore Hill like drunken sentinels in a crooked line. I managed to get back to the stable, where Sister and Edith were waiting with Baby Lee, who looked at my bloody face and broken arm and hid behind Sister's skirts. I performed a ferocious hop-hop like I had done for the last chuck wagon jamboree to prove that I was all in one piece. Edith was horrified by the blood and my dangling arm, but my little daughter slowly peeked out from behind Bamie's skirts, and I grabbed her up in my one good arm. She'd come to accept me as her "sire," who appeared out of nowhere from time to time and was no threat to Auntie Bye, as she called Bamie. I was Papa Ted, nothing more.

I MUST HAVE LOOKED like a desperado from the buttes of Dakota masquerading in Eastern garb, with my left arm in a shoulder sling. We'd turned the main parlor into a ballroom, and we had our Hunt Ball at Sagamore Hill, with Bamie's plush cushions and purple settees sitting in the barn. I wasn't ignorant of Sister's gloom. She'd put Baby Lee to bed upstairs, sang her lullabies, and must have felt like an intruder with Edith in the house. Edith didn't have a crooked back, or wear a metal corset, while the mistress of Sagamore Hill had to sit on the sidelines and could not dance a single step. Edith was draped all in red, her pale skin burning under the lamps—it wasn't hard to notice. I danced with her as master of the ball.

"Theodore," she whispered, "you'll hurt yourself . . . if you keep dancing with your arm in a sling."

The great clock in the hall had struck midnight. And for a moment the chimes muffled the sweet sounds of the little orchestra near the window, borrowed from Delmonico's, like owls in bloom.

"It's my birthday," I said. "I'm twenty-seven, and I'll have me a wife."

"Shhh," she said. "You're a widower."

"Widower be damned. I'll have me a wife."

And I whirled Edie with utter abandon, in that little grasshopper step that defined my own peculiar art of dancing. It was the Roosevelt stuttering waltz. The other huntsmen and their wives looked at me with amazement—a widower with an unmarried woman in his arms. I did not care one dot of alkali dust. I would have worn my red bandanna had I been in cow country, not a starched collar and cuffs.

The ball didn't end until three. A carriage arrived for Edith— I'd booked a room for her at a local inn. I did not want her to leave my lair. But the widower had to maintain his widower's dance. I helped her into the carriage, with my right arm around her waist. We did not utter a word. My own weak eyes were bolted to hers. Then I signaled to the driver and off he went, while I returned to Sagamore Hill.

Bamie was sweeping up the debris. Her mind seemed scattered as she moved about; it was as if an army had descended upon us, not a hunter's ball, with a random boot, broken ostrich feathers, cigar ashes, and lost ribbons. The bodice she wore could not mask her broad, manly shoulders. Still, an aging heiress like Auntie Bye did not lack suitors. There was a multitude of poets, painters, and handsome drummers with blond hair who would have loved to solder themselves to Sister's fortune. She scoffed at every one. Sister was devoted to Baby Lee. She'd sculpted her existence around another man's child, and I was the real interloper.

"It won't change a thing," I said.

I felt ashamed to soothe my own sister with such a lie. She did not answer, but kept up her sweeping.

"I'm the stranger here," I said. "You have Baby Lee. I'm returning to the Badlands."

She looked up from that surfeit of lost ribbons and ostrich feathers.

"I felt the fool," she whispered. She was crying now; a shiver went up her swollen back. And I was frightened of her, as I had always been a little frightened of Father—of his goodness and the rage he could sometimes summon. I did not dare gather her in my arms.

"Teedie," she said, talking to the child I had once been and had remained, at least in her eyes. "All the huntsmen know more about your affairs than I do. Did you have to make such a public display of your affection?" She wasn't crying now, but her dark face was still fueled with a touch of Father's anger. "And did you have to sneak behind my back and carry on your assignations in Mrs. Carow's house?"

"I didn't. . . . There were no assignations."

"And you could not even tell me that you intend to marry Edith."

Here I played the cunning solicitor. "I promised myself to her in the icehouse at Tranquillity when she was fourteen—I gave her a silver ring."

Bamie's composure had come back; she smiled in the afterglow of the dimmed lantern light. "It was such a miraculous engagement that you married Miss Alice four years later. And what happened to your first betrothed?"

"We had an altercation . . . in the icehouse."

Sister peered at me with a marksman's blue eyes. "Your romantic conquests are far too subtle for me. How do you intend to deal with your own daughter?"

"Bamie, she's much better off with you."

I'd deeply angered her again—no, repelled her, I imagine. "She's a child, Theodore, not a rump of cattle from the Badlands. You cannot bequeath her—with or without a bill of sale. I will mind her for you, help you raise her until after your honeymoon."

I panicked. "I'm a widower. But I will have other children. Baby Lee is yours."

A kind of sorrow overwhelmed her. Perhaps she understood my own frailty and confusion. "Little brother, are you willing to start a war between Edith and myself? She will want the child, and I will be turned into an ogre—the evil, grasping aunt."

"No, no," I insisted. "We will start afresh."

"Then you have no idea of the woman you are marrying—good night."

CHAPTER 6

MAYHEM AT SAGAMORE HILL

1887–1888

Baby Lee was like a bolt of quicksilver, her blond hair helmeted in a little hat, while she clutched a bouquet of pink roses tall as a beanstalk, with Bamie right beside her.

"Say hello to your new mother, dear."

Baby Lee handed the bouquet to Edith. But she couldn't seem to pronounce *mother*. The word remained mottled in her mouth.

Sagamore Hill had been shuttered up for the winter while we were away, and until it could be replenished with Edith's furniture and a fresh coat of paint, we were installed as Sister's houseguests, at her palace on Madison, so that I could reacquaint myself with Little Alice before she came to live with us. Her Ladyship had been very clear on that subject, though she herself was pregnant with *our* child. Sister was brave about it. But I wasn't blind to the darkness that suddenly descended upon her. She and Little Alice had been inseparable for three years. Sister had raised her while I was in the Badlands and honeymooning on the Continent. I bought a Florentine sideboard and a hand-carved dining table for Sagamore Hill, even as my own finances sagged and I lost livestock in the worst blizzard the Badlands had ever known. Sister had sustained me through all my misfortunes, and now I was stealing the child I had *gifted* to her.

She did not scold. She was gentle with Edith, though Baby Lee was forever at Sister's side. We'd aroused her suspicion. *Mother* didn't mean much to that child. And one morning, while Bamie cracked the shell of her boiled egg with a tiny silver spoon, she declared, "I think I will go south for a while."

"What the devil for?" I asked over the breakfast table, with Baby Lee sitting on a cushioned chair.

"To visit some of our Georgia relatives," she said.

"But they're all gone."

"Oh, I might scare up one or two."

Edith nudged me under the table. And I was silent after that. Later, while we were alone, and I was getting into a sack suit, since tails and morning coats had gone out of fashion, my little wife said, "Theodore, for heaven's sake, your sister is bleeding blood and bile."

"What's she bleeding about?"

"Baby Lee."

"But we've given her plenty of notice," I said. "I warned her months ago that we were coming."

"That doesn't make the hurt any less. Theodore, *you* abandoned that child. And now we're claiming her."

"Isn't that what you want?"

Edith looked at me as if I were her very own child. "Yes, but she'd rather not witness the changing of the guard. Let her ramble and find a little peace, while I make my own peace with your little girl."

It felt like I was walking into a bear trap. "But we aren't at war with Baby Lee."

"We most certainly are," Edith said. "She has your stubborn ways. But I will win her over."

And Edith did, though it took a while. Even I felt a trail of emptiness, as if some living flesh had been cut out, once Bamie disappeared from her palace, with its venetian blinds and scalloped sconces.

Alice moped for a day in her pinafore and ringlets of blond hair. "Where's Auntie Bye?"

"Visiting," I said. "And now you're stuck with us."

She'd wait every morning in the front hall for Auntie Bye to come back. Then she'd shiver hard inside herself, and soon she stopped waiting. And who the hell was I, a Manhattan native with the Badlands in my blood, part cowpoke, part politician?

I was savagely irritated to read reports in the *Bad Lands Cowboy* of a certain deputy sheriff's recent marriage to a Montana cattle queen—it was a bundle of lies. And last year, the Albany barons swindled me into running for Mayor. I was "a pigeon," in their parlance. The Republicans and Democrats were frightened to death of a third-party candidate, Henry George, who ran on the United Labor ticket. So they figured that a reformer like me would siphon off some of the vote, and Mr. George, a decent little runt in a red goatee who liked to campaign in a horsecar, would never be elected. He talked about the greed of the industrial giants—the wealthy criminal class, as I had once called them—and how he was the "heartbeart" of the disinherited. By jingo, I might have voted for him myself if he hadn't also preached revolution. That's why the barons needed their pigeon. They would have lost their Manhattan privileges if that goatee man ever occupied City Hall.

I was dubbed "the Cowboy Candidate." I campaigned in buckskin and a red bandanna and had my own "fort" at the Fifth Avenue Hotel—my headquarters spilled over into several suites. We had bonfires every night, and rockets exploded outside my window.

Voters had an unbridled curiosity about the Badlands—they were more interested in the cowboy than the candidate. President Cleveland had catapulted the Dawes Act into existence. He believed that most Indians should get off the reservation and have their own plot of land, removed from their tribal chiefs. They might become citizens of the United States rather than remain wards of the government. Of course, there was a catch. White settlers were grabbing up parcel after parcel from every Indian who couldn't till the soil. And reporters from all the Eastern papers were eager to have my opinion of Cleveland's maneuvers.

"It depends on reform," I said. "If the Indian agents are crooked and unfair, then the white settlers will gobble up all there is to gobble."

They asked me what I would do if I were Secretary of the Interior.

"Boys, I'm Manhattan-bound, running for Mayor. I can't mix in. Besides, I'm all hobbled from the riding I did. My ranching days are over."

But I knew these Indian farmers didn't have much of a chance, no matter how well they tilled. Greed was rampant, greed was everywhere. The Secretary of the Interior was a snippet of a man, blind to that dance of chaos around him.

Still, I conducted a rattling good canvass. I rode up from Grand Central to Morrisania on a special car, climbed down from the observation cab at Tremont Station, in the bowels of the Bronx, and rushed to the local hall, where I had to don a floral horse-shoe and woo the ladies of the Twenty-fourth Ward. I promised to throttle the Tammany tiger and reduce its vast empire of patronage.

None of the barons visited my headquarters at the Fifth Avenue Hotel. But Henry George arrived in his red goatee, looking like a Confederate general rather than a raging radical. His hand shook while he drank a cup of Republican tea.

"Roosevelt," he said, in the mildest tone, "we ought to join forces, or we'll never win. We want the same thing—a fair deal for the working man."

"But you encourage class warfare, sir. You're a revolutionary."

"And so are you," he said, with a sip of Republican tea. "Haven't you talked of mounting an army of desperadoes to drive the Mexicans out of the borderlands?"

That wasn't revolution, I had to remind him. I had told the *Bad Lands Cowboy* and other gazettes that I would be willing to round up a regiment of desperadoes, cowboys, and Stranglers to safeguard our borders. "A pity, Roosevelt. We'll butt heads, and both of us will lose."

The barons may have abandoned "the Boy," as they liked to call me, but I continued to fight. I must have worried them, since they sent bruisers to break up my rallies. I leapt into the foray, and that's when caricatures began to appear in the press, with me in a bandanna and a cowboy hat. "Young socialite attacks the lawless," wrote the *Brooklyn Eagle,* and Brooklyn wasn't even in the race.

But that radical was right. I ran a dismal third to Tammany's man and Henry George. I returned to my fort at the Fifth Avenue next morning and found an empty shell—all our banners had been removed, all our desks and tallying sheets. My fort was occupied by scrubwomen. Less than a week later I snuck out of New York on the Cunard Line and sailed to England under a fictitious name, "Mr. Merrifield," to avoid the gossipmongers. And like two shady characters out of a dime detective novel, Edith and I were married at St. George's, Hanover Square, in a private ceremony, far from the curious, vindictive eyes of Manhattan's social set—the church was as dreary as a graveyard. I barely recognized Edith when she walked out of the mist. The church itself was laden with fog. We whispered our vows before the Anglican priest. We could very well have been at our very own wake.

HER LITTLE LADYSHIP WAS in perpetual motion, as she removed every trace of Sister from Sagamore Hill. Bamie's furniture was packed into the barn. The wallpaper was stripped, the shingles near the roof repainted in mustard-yellow, the wood paneling in the main hall varnished again and again, and the floor scraped to her liking. Mind you, she had to deal with *two* ghostly presences—Alice Lee and Auntie Bye. And she managed to expel both. She was also our chief clerk and chief mechanic. I could not handle money—it liquefied in my fist. Edith had to provide me with a daily allowance and warn that I could not overspend. She repaired the warped blades of the windmill that supplied the house with well water, took care of our orchards and acres of farmland and a household staff that included a cook, a nurse for Baby Lee, a laundress, and a furnaceman who was like a walking melody in a coal bin, but argued all the time about his wages.

And then there was Little Alice, who chattered like a magpie, imitating the snorts of the furnaceman and my very own snarls. My daughter was becoming addicted to Edith. They plotted together in the sun-drenched room Edith had appropriated as her parlor, with the pale flowery patterns of its armchairs and button-down sofas, together with its miniature writing desk, where she sat in the afternoon with Little Alice, who was careful not to spill Her Ladyship's red ink. When my first male heir—Little Ted—was born that September with his mottled hands and wrinkled red face, Baby Lee was his most attentive nurse, imitating Ted's cries and calling him "polly, polly parrot." She didn't seem to understand why Edith had to be wrapped in muslin bandages that pinned her to the bed like a mummy from a museum—that was the custom of the time, to *mummify* the new mother in a wealth of bandages, so she would have a miraculous healing and wouldn't harm her vitals. Edith lay there for two solid weeks under her doctor's orders, until finally the doctor himself unwrapped the bandages. She was transferred to her favorite sofa, where she had to sit in a corset with metal stops that resembled a medieval torture instrument. She fell into a profound gloom, sobbing all the time. She could not manage the household affairs, not even to bargain with the furnaceman.

Sagamore Hill required another chief clerk, but Bamie was reluctant to intervene. A delicate wire connected the former mistress of Sagamore Hill and the current one, and that wire could be untangled in a moment of duress. Bamie inherited her old bedroom on the second floor, and we took her furniture out of the barn— her chiffonier, her footstools, her four-poster, her lamps with the Chinese shades. And suddenly we had two women in iron corsets, though Sister's was permanent, and Edith's wasn't.

I sensed the confusion in Little Alice, as if the tiny planet she had constructed with Edith at Sagamore Hill had started to crumble. For a moment she could not locate herself and wondered aloud if she belonged to Auntie Bye or Edith, and I was somewhere in the middle—her older brother, perhaps, another sibling . . . with a mustache.

Baby Lee grew imperious—it must have been out of fright. "Auntie, you haven't combed my hair in ages."

And Sister's crooked back seemed to slump right into the sea outside Edith's window. She must have wanted to hug the little girl and bite her arms to death with love and devotion.

"Child," Sister said, just as imperious, "don't you have a nurse?"

"But Nurse doesn't know how to brush, not like *you*."

"Well, you have a papa."

And Little Alice stared at me with the subtlest of pinpricks in her blue eyes.

"Gracious, where is he, then?"

Little Alice owned the two of us, and she wasn't even four.

"Child," Sister said, "I have bills to pay. Do you want this house to collapse? You won't have butter with your bread."

It was Bamie who taught Little Alice how to converse with illustrious strangers and to cut a slice of bread into little truncheons, and butter each truncheon with a delicate stab of the butter knife. It didn't matter what Edith did, or how the two of them had conspired. Baby Lee was still Bysie's girl.

"I could help you," Alice said. "I'm good with figures. *Mother* taught me, you know."

Baby Lee was hurling barbs like a gunslinger. It wasn't Auntie alone who had given her so much poise. Edith had contributed to the education of that little monster. She sat with Auntie at Edith's desk, propped up on a kind of oversized pincushion. The entire staff at Sagamore Hill had to parade in front of this desk. They weren't equipped to deal with a humpbacked czar and a blue-eyed czarevna who guarded every banknote and silver coin.

"Are you satisfied with your employer?" Auntie Bye asked the furnaceman.

"Yes, mum."

"Then why do you come to us with coal on your chin? It's a sign of disrespect."

The furnaceman hopped about on one leg, like a stork with a fortune of black feathers.

"I'm down in the coal bin, mum. I have to breathe in all the coal dust."

"Don't you have a washbasin?"

"Most certainly, mum."

"Then wash," Auntie Bye said and ordered him out of her sight once Alice handed him his wages.

Now it was the czarevna's chance. No one was spared. She interrogated her own nursemaid.

"Nurse, why are you always so sad around me?"

"It's part of my profession, Little Mum. I'm not paid to smile. I have to keep track of your tricks."

"Then do so with a smile. Or you will be dismissed."

The nursemaid was cunning, of course. "You didn't hire me, Little Mum. Mistress did."

"Ah," Auntie said, "but Mistress is not herself at the moment. And *we* are her surrogates."

The nursemaid bristled. "I have seldom taken orders, mum, from a child who is in my own charge."

But Bamie was at her best. "Little Mum is under my supervision. And you can consider her my lieutenant. You may go now."

Those servants who had tried to take advantage of Edith's malaise soon discovered that they could not slacken for a moment—nor could I.

"You must go back into government service, Theodore. The nation is in dire need of you. There are spoilers, spoilers in every government post."

I was weary of Republicans and Democrats. They seemed to have the same barons and mischief-makers. "Did you forget my last campaign? The Cowboy Candidate couldn't even conquer City Hall."

"Yes," she said, "but that campaign will earn you dividends—in the future. You were the youngest candidate *ever*."

Indeed, she wanted me to return to the old heave-ho, but it wasn't politics that really chafed her.

"You have left me to drift, Theodore. I must pretend that Little Alice is mine again when the truth is I am barren. That child was my angel of mercy."

I started to speak, but I could sense her rancor—in the stiffening of her back. She loved me to distraction, but she had her own private well, and I could not breach the darkness of it.

"Brother, do not say another word, or I will scream. I will sit next to Edith in a sun mask. We will swallow this house in one great splash of silence."

Sister returned to her chores as interregnum mistress of Sagamore Hill and did not abandon the czarevna. I was at their mercy. It was Little Alice who delivered my daily allowance, coin by coin. She was already an heiress. Grandfather Lee had bequeathed her a yearly stipend that was far greater than mine. Edith guarded every cent for her, even during her little exile on the sofa.

Her collapse didn't last into the spring. One afternoon she removed the metal stops of her corset. Her face was no longer half frozen. She was back at her desk. The servants bowed to her with a look of conquest in their eyes. "Morning, mistress."

There wasn't a conflict of power. The two mistresses remained perfectly civil. Edith thanked my sister.

"We are forever grateful, Bysie."

It was the czarevna who had the most to lose. She went back to being a child. She had to stop giving commands to her own nurse. And I had my Edith again. She had not been a wife to me in months. I could play the big bad bear. "My darling," she said, "can you forgive me? It was like living in a cave." We could fire the wet nurse. Edith wandered around with my male heir in her arms, carried Little Prince Ted from room to room.

Bamie hired a cab and left in the middle of the night. She did not want a blizzardy goodbye. She left a note pinned to the scale in my dressing room.

*TEEDIE, YOU MUST FIND ANOTHER REPLACEMENT
DURING EDITH'S NEXT FIT.
I CAN NO LONGER PLAY THE PART.
I HOPE ALICE WILL NOT FORGET HER AUNTIE BYE.
YOUR DEVOTED BAMIE.*

Edith had her bedroom stripped; the furnaceman carried Sister's bedposts and footstools into the barn. I watched him from the piazza, as he crisscrossed the road with every article on his back, tottering under the weight of it all, while I had a clean view of the orchards and the woods and the wheat fields that dipped down into the swollen water.

CHAPTER 7

ELLIE

1891–1894

THE DARLINGS OF ALBANY CUTTHROATS THEY WERE,
reeking in perfume and rotten silk, Big Bill Howe, with all
his corpulence and diamond rings, and Little Abe Hummel, the
angelic one, with his fiddler's fists. They'd sent their runner, with a
personal note.

> *MUST SEE YOU.*
> *A MATTER OF LIFE AND DEATH.*
> *HOWE & HUMMEL.*

I scratched out their seal and scribbled, *Messrs. H & H, I have no
time for such mysteries. You're welcome to meet with my counselor.*
A second runner came, with *my* message crossed out.

> *BEST TO HAVE A HEART TO HEART.*
> *WOULDN'T WANT THIS TELEGRAPHED*
> *TO YOUR ATTORNEY, MR. R.*
> *YOU WILL LIVE*
> *TO REGRET.*

I'd just come back from a sojourn in North Dakota. I'd gone there of my own accord after an uprising of the Sioux on a reservation near the Little Missouri. They'd torn the settlement apart, set the commissary on fire. I saw a hill of ruins that belched gray smoke. These Sioux weren't strangers to me. I'd watched them ride their painted ponies across my ranch. Now they skulked in their moccasins, with whiskey eyes, like prisoners wandering in and out of the smoke. They'd become hostage to the local Indian agent, a chap called Curly Bell, who was a bounty hunter with pockmarks on his skull. Bell had been buying up parcels of Indian land and stealing grub, it seems. The Sioux didn't have a single say over their lives. Their children had no schools to speak of. This agent had been double-dealing at the post, selling alcohol under the counter. I fired him on the spot. He spat in my face.

"Commissioner, your word don't mean piss. I'm the President's man."

Indeed, he had Pinkertons as armed guards. I still intended to bring him up on charges before the Civil Service Commission. I wrote out my report to President Harrison, who had appointed me to the Commission, thinking it would be a sinecure, a political plum, like it was for the pair of louts who were my fellow Commissioners, but I had a job to do, and I would damn well do it. *Mr. President, the tribes had good reason to rebel. We need paid Indian judges and police, not Pinkertons. And we can't have schools without school teachers. Nor can we have agents who have no understanding of tribal justice. The Indian Bureau cannot sit wantonly outside the Civil Service. That is a prescription for disaster and despair.*

The next time I returned to Indian land, a Pink approached me with a Winchester cradled in his arms. He handed me a slip of paper. That was the oddment of it all. He hadn't come to do Curly's bidding and tussle with me. He was a mere messenger for those two Manhattan pirates.

IMPERATIVE.
HOWE & HUMMEL

They must have hired the Pinks to locate my whereabouts. But I hadn't informed a soul, not even my fellow Commissioners. I should have gone back to the District to file my report. I went to Manhattan instead, on a whim, to lick my wounds. The Dakota Sioux would have no respite from that lying Indian agent. They'd have to suck on clay and school themselves on the wind of their own words. Their rifles were locked inside the armory. They wouldn't rise up again. The Pinks weren't put there to patrol the reservation. The Indian Bureau had hired those damn detectives to scatter the Sioux, a clear violation of the Dawes Act. I couldn't rely on Harrison, that little gray man. So I sulked in Bamie's parlor. And I had to contend with the theatrics of Howe & Hummel.

"What is so urgent that you had to track me to a reservation in the middle of nowhere?"

Both of them had suspenders embroidered in gold. But Hummel had frayed cuffs. His collar was imperfect. He was trying to look like a slightly elegant hobo, but he still looked tatterdemalion to me.

"Commissioner," said Little Abe, "the Pinks are in our pocket. We can have them vanish from the Badlands at a moment's notice."

"But that's not why you're here," I said.

"No," said the fat man in the elegant sleeves. He had his own foyer at Delmonico's, filled with chorus girls, and that's where he mingled with politicians and members of the criminal class. He was known as Velvet Bill, because he could hypnotize a jury with the purr of his voice. He could also toss an occasional lightning bolt. He was irresistible in patent-leather shoes, as he performed his slick ballet. A banking scion might murder his mistress or his wife in front of half a dozen diners at Delmonico's, and Howe would have him declared insane. The banker would serve a month or two in the millionaires' ward on Blackwell's Island, and reclaim his throne at Chemical or Chase. And this wizard, Velvet Bill, had sent the Pinks to look for me in South Dakota.

"TR, it's a delicate subject. That's why we asked for a private rendezvous, not a visit to our offices, where the press might be involved.

We are not looking for scandal. We represent a certain Catherina Mann, otherwise known as Miss Katie."

I stared hard at these pirates through the gold rim of my pince-nez, but I could not get them to squirm.

"And what does your client have to do with me?"

"Very little," said Velvet Bill, "and quite a lot."

"She was your brother's mistress . . . and still is," said Abe Hummel, who had a habit of hurling Velvet Bill's darts and bolts. I'd dealt with Howe & Hummel at hearings in Albany and Manhattan, where they represented the usual riffraff summoned to testify before some oversight committee. Silent Abe would whisper into a ruffian's ear, and it was Abe's testimony we heard, Abe's non sequiturs. He had a talent for getting his clients to rumble and reveal nothing at all.

"Gentlemen, my brother's mistresses are not my concern."

"Ah," said Velvet Bill, his thumbs hooked into his waistcoat. "But Katie Mann is very much your concern. She was your brother's chambermaid, come all the way from Bavaria. He seduced Miss Katie, sir, had trysts with her in the attic. She carried *his* child. Your brother has abandoned her and moved to Europe with his family for the duration."

"He's taking the cure," I said. "He's currently at a sanitarium in Graz."

"But the damage has been done. Her reputation is at stake—and so is yours."

And now it was apparent why the Pinks had hunted me like a pack of hounds. These pirates were sniffing blood and money, Roosevelt blood and Roosevelt money.

"I won't be privy to blackmail," I said. "This chambermaid could have had a hundred suitors."

"Hardly," said Hummel. "The girl is pure. We have a locket inscribed to her and letters in Elliott's hand."

I knew about the mistresses. There had been other lawyers, other claims, other letters "in Elliott's hand." But I'd tossed those shysters out of my parlor. None of them had the ammunition and the audacity of Howe & Hummel, who could pick and choose their clients like the most brazen of killer vultures. Velvet Bill rarely lost a case in court. That's why the accused always settled with the injured party, however extravagant the claim. No one seemed to want Velvet Bill's corpulent shadow to linger very long.

"And what is the name of this wanton child, the unwanted one?" The pirates were humming to themselves.

"You mean the little bastard?" Velvet Bill asked in a silky voice, with a wink to his partner.

I scowled at him. "Yes, the little bastard."

"El-li-ott Roose-velt Mann," Hummel said, pronouncing every syllable like a sinister song. They expected me to strike back. But I had encountered their tricks in court.

"A Roosevelt, you say?"

They nodded in unison like a pair of thieves.

"And on the certificate of birth, what father is listed?"

"None," said Velvet Bill, "none so far. Born out of wedlock, that's what is inscribed."

"And the laundress will want a bit of relief?"

"Chambermaid, sir," said Hummel, "who had her own room in Mr. Elliott's Manhattan townhouse until a short while ago. . . . She couldn't survive on less than ten thousand dollars."

They could not see my anger—or my contempt. They were rogues of the law, who thrived on human carrion. There was little doubt in my mind that Elliott had dallied with Miss Catherina Mann. I had hoped he might change his habits after he fell in love, and it wasn't with a creature from the demimonde. He couldn't have found such an exquisite beauty at a brothel. Miss Anna Hall of Tivoli-on-the-Hudson could hurl any male into an absolute spell of devotion with her shapely figure and the rare blue eyes of a startled fawn. Later I would find out that she was frivolous, that she cared more about her own little pleasures than curbing Elliott's appetites and wild promenades. He ruined Bamie's parties with his drunken jaunts. I no longer invited him and Anna to Sagamore Hill. Ellie couldn't stop drinking. And he'd become addicted to morphine after a bad

spill on the Meadowbrook polo grounds. He had bloated cheeks
and sullen eyes. And Anna seemed to care about little else than
the social calendar. I felt sorry for their children. I was quite fond
of little Eleanor, a creature who had not inherited a pinch of her
mother's charm. She was the ugly duckling of the Roosevelt clan,
with a terrible overbite and no chin at all. And philanderer that he
was, Elliott still adored the duckling.

"I suppose you went to my little brother first for the ten thousand."
Silent Abe sucked me in with his solemn eyes.

"That we did, TR, we most certainly did. But he denied any
knowledge of the liaison, denied it most vehemently, even after we
read him portions of his own letters to Miss Katie."

It wouldn't have mattered. Elliott had used up most of his
inheritance, and he relied on Bamie for hard cash. He absconded
to France with his brood. Anna rented a house on a quiet street
in Neuilly, and she went on a binge, buying up hats at the Bon
Marché. In the end, it was Bamie who paid for the hats, Bamie who
went over Elliott's bills like an exchequer with a crooked back. But
Neuilly couldn't save my little brother. He fell into a deep gloom
and was carted off to Graz.

"The little boy, where can I find him?"

"Outside your door," said Silent Abe, with his angelic smile.

I was furious. "Has she been waiting all this time with the boy?"

"Miss Kate brought him in a bassinet," said Velvet Bill. "Shall I
invite her in?"

She was plump and blond, and had a slightly bovine look about
her, with shoulders as broad as Bamie's. She had the thickened
wrists of a mechanic. But her eyes weren't hard at all. She was wearing a locket, Elliott's, I assumed, in the shape of a golden heart. The
bassinet was huge, and she nearly tottered under the burden of it.

"Help her, for God's sake!"

Velvet Bill clutched the bassinet and plunked it on Bamie's
sideboard.

"Herr Roosevelt, I do not mean to bother," the chambermaid
chirped in a Bavarian accent.

"Ah," said Silent Abe, "you mustn't converse with Mr. Roosevelt on your own, my dear. We're your representatives. We have your *best* interests at heart. Mr. Hummel and I are your voice in all matters regarding Master Elliott."

She wasn't bovine at all. I'd misjudged her out of some idiotic sense of superiority. My own anger had blinded me. She was a Bavarian girl who had lived in Elliott's attic and meant to find a husband in America—she found my little brother instead, and was rewarded with a baby out of wedlock.

She clutched at the chain guarding her throat, as her body rocked back and forth with a rapid, irregular rhythm. Her anguish couldn't have been rehearsed, no matter how artful Hummel was in such manipulations.

"He promised to marry me . . . and I listen." And then she began to weep.

"Now, now," said Silent Abe, "mum's the word. We'll have our moment in court."

"The baby," I said.

And she reached into the bassinet with such a delicate swipe of her shoulders that I was immediately drawn to her. She was no hireling of Howe & Hummel. She held the little boy in her arms, while I had to endure a dizziness of shame. *Elliott Roosevelt Mann.* The boy had the crystalline glare of Ellie's eyes and the contours of his forehead.

"Might I see the woman alone?" I asked the two pirates.

"Can't be done, TR," said Velvet Bill. "It wouldn't be ethical."

He must have signaled somehow. Fräulein Katie curtsied and was gone—with the little boy in the bassinet.

"Well, what will it be?" asked Silent Abe. "Amicable or not? A poor chambermaid like Miss Katie could rip into a jury's heart . . . if we fed her a few significant phrases."

"Out," I said. "Get out."

The pirates knew they had won. They'd penetrated the Roosevelt castle, and they didn't have to rely on the firepower and brutal force of the Pinks. They had a buxom chambermaid, a bassinet, and a little boy cursed—or blessed—with Ellie's looks. I wired Sister, who'd gone to comfort Anna and the children in Neuilly. Elliott had fled the sanitarium in Graz and was on the prowl somewhere.

> *ELLIE UNSOUND.*
> *ANNA MUST RETURN WITH THE CHILDREN.*
> *HE AND ANNA MUST LIVE APART.*
> *I WILL NOT BE SWAYED ON THIS MATTER.*

Someone had to seize the reins. The moment Anna left for the States, Little Brother showed up in Neuilly, like some madcap magician in a purple cape. He was on morphine again. He'd attached himself to a drunken artiste, who was as depraved and besotted as he was. They had masquerade balls where men and women strutted about in the raw, and pissed on the garden wall like wild beasts. I tried to lure Ellie back home. I cut off all his funds. He got into a brawl with several firemen, and was hospitalized for a month. Even that didn't cure him. He took up with a band of clochards, lived like a beggar on the banks of the Seine. He stole scraps of food. He had a terrific row at the local gendarmerie. My little brother had become the wolf-man of Paris, with whiskers that covered his ears. Sensing his own precipitous decline, he had himself committed to the insane asylum at Suresnes. But he had no intention of remaining there. He maneuvered to have himself released.

Bamie returned with Anna, and she was much less sanguine about having Elliott declared a lunatic.

"Teedie, he loves Anna desperately."

"And fornicates behind her back."

Sister rose up on her beleaguered spine. She had to wear special shoes that lent a little violence to her movements, like a battering ram.

"You cannot instruct him in morals, you cannot. He does not have your gifts, Theodore."

"Have you seen the girl?" I asked Sister.

"What girl?"

"*Katie Mann.* You know, Anna's Bavarian chambermaid. He wrote her love letters, promised to marry her. And now Miss Katie is a mother."

Bamie squinted at me. One of her eyes was weaker than the other. "Her lawyers are Howe & Hummel, I imagine. You fell for their monkeyshines. They presented you with a boy in a bassinet. It's their bread and butter—paternity cases."

"The boy is real," I said. "The letters are real, and so is the locket."

Sister turned away from me. I could see the flare of her back, despite the corset she wore, with metal bands. "Ellie will be lost if we betray him now—you must go to that madhouse on the hill and reason with him. He loves you. He will listen."

THERE WAS A DONKEY CART waiting at the depot. I did not see another soul. I was the one and only passenger in the first-class carriages to get off the train in Suresnes. The conductor saluted, as if I were a general in a satin coat. I wouldn't wear a duster on such a short trip. I wasn't a cowboy in a sandstorm. I was a bereaved brother, searching for a solution to Elliott's nightmares. The driver of the cart arrived in a top hat and a slightly ragged cape. He thought it a miracle that I could chat with him in French. He did not have a high regard of Americans.

"They are all lazy, monsieur—and rich."

I wouldn't argue with such a lout.

We began to wind our way into the hills. I could see the Seine at a precipitous angle. In the sunlight, the river was a layer of burnished glass. I could not find a ripple. The birdcalls were deafening. I had to hum the different songs.

"Ah, you are a specialist, a professor of birds? They come here very often, the birdmen, with their notebooks and colored chalk. They belong in the *asile.*"

The donkey stopped moving on the steepest hill.

"We will have to walk, monsieur—she is a lazy girl."

I climbed down from the cart, approached the ass, and blew softly into her ear.

The driver was mystified, as the donkey continued her climb along the rocks. But I did not get back into the cart. The château suddenly appeared from behind a thicket of trees like a mirage rising out of a sudden scatter of birds—it gave the singular impression of a fortress with moist skin. The walls were white. The turrets clicked in my ear like castanets. . . .

I was startled at first. There were no wards at Suresnes, no knotted waistcoats to calm the violent ones, no tubs with electric currents to exorcise a demon or shock the morbidity out of some stranger. The lobby was as luxurious as any grand hotel inscribed in Baedeker's. The manager wore a monocle. The women paraded in petticoats and parasols. I did not see one maniac wandering about in a soiled nightshirt. But I did see a birdman carting a nightingale in a red cage. I wondered what he was doing here. Was he an inmate or an entertainer? I answered the nightingale's call with a long tweet of my own. And then the birdman and I had a duet. He was wearing slippers and a laboratory coat.

"Ah, you've come with the Audubon people."

"No, my brother is locked up in this hotel."

He peered at me from behind the bars of the red cage.

"We don't lock up people, monsieur. We are not savages in Suresnes. We comfort our patients. . . . Your brother must be the polo player with epileptic fits."

"Elliott doesn't have epilepsy. He's an alcoholic."

"And yet he faints from time to time. He blacks out, cannot recall who or where he is. He has seizures, monsieur. . . . You will find him upstairs."

The birdman bowed to me and went off with his nightingale. He was the chief quack of this clinic. A nurse led me to Elliott's quarters. My brother had a hand-carved armoire and a canopied bed. He did not seem glad to see me. His jaw was rippling. His mouth was full of spittle. His eyes had a vacant sheen. That boyish charm was gone, that air of lightness he once had, that pull of the born athlete. I could never compete with Elliott on a pony.

He was wearing a rumpled foulard and a flared shirt with torn elbows, like a deranged artist in some magnificent castle cage. He performed a pantomime in my presence, as if I were an invisible interloper, there and not quite there. He swiped a basket from the table, dug his fist inside, and began to distribute imaginary crumbs.

"Ellie, what on earth are you doing? Kiss me, for God's sake. I'm your brother."

Not a whisper of hello, or even a challenge about my right to invade his quarters. He kept distributing the crumbs.

"I'm parceling out pieces of cake," he said, "to all the urchins. You were with us, Teedie. The beggars were a frightful nuisance. And the odor was oppressive in that heat."

"Where?" I asked. "When?"

And suddenly my brother swelled out as if a bellows were hidden in his torn shirt. "Our guide got lost. We strayed into a back alley, and the urchins descended upon us; the little monsters overpowered Papa and clawed at our clothes. Papa broke free and acquired a basket of cakes . . . and we fed the little monsters, scattered all the crumbs."

I did recall our panic, the sea of faces and fists, and Brave Heart's resilience, his ingenuity in buying a basket of cakes.

"But why does this play on your mind? It was years and years ago—in some sour alley in Naples."

"Because," he said, "I can still hear the suck of their mouths as they gobbled the cake. Bamie was marvelous. She stood with Papa, toe to toe. . . . How was the crossing, old boy?"

I didn't quite know how to answer him. Specks of clarity had returned to his eyes. I tried to summon up the crossing for Ellie, the perpetual rocking of the *paquebot*, the wind that swept from cabin to cabin—it was much safer in second class—and finally overturned the captain's table, so that we sat with silverware and lamb stew in our laps.

"I was on my arse with a chatterbox, Ellie. She was on intimate terms with some lost cousin of ours. Frightful stuff—a black sheep who escaped our grasp. A regular Bluebeard. I had to listen while we were camping out. I told her that this cousin didn't concern us. We weren't the Roosevelts of Hyde Park. We were the North Shore clan, with plenty of Bluebeards of our own."

I couldn't entertain Ellie. All his bonhomie was gone again. I could not recognize my own brother—the dash, the vigor, the hearty appetite. He looked bloated and forlorn.

"Where's Bamie?" he asked. "Why isn't she here?"

Bamie had accompanied him to Graz. She swayed the masters of the asylum into allowing her to occupy the room next to his—it had never been done before, that a patient should have his own personal keeper. Sister remained in Graz as long as he did—until he ran away.

"Damn you," I said. "She's with your wife and children."

That didn't satisfy Elliott. "You cannot keep me in this dungeon," he said. "I won't allow it."

"Dungeon," I repeated, staring out past his balcony. The river glistened like a long, silver snake, and the songbirds flew from hill to hill like rockets with a feathery twist.

"You hate me," he said. "You resent me."

I did not know how to rekindle that love and bonhomie we once had, on the field and off. We'd been playmates together, rivals, and champions. We'd annihilated entire teams with Ellie's grace and my resilient right arm. "Why should I resent you, why?"

"That disaster at Oyster Bay," he said. "Edith lost her baby, and you cannot forgive me. You were sprawled on the grass like a dead man. You barely had a pulse."

It was the Challenge Cup. And I was master of the field. But I could not keep up with Elliott's litheness, with the singsong of his moves. His mallet had much more magic than mine. Brother rode me into the ground. Our ponies collided. I could see a great rip in the sky before I fell. Yes, I'd frightened Edie, and she had a miscarriage. And Meadowbrook won the cup—three years ago.

"That's how little you think of me," I said. "I'm vengeful and spiteful."

"Why else am I in this madhouse?"

He was in a château without one lock on its windows. He'd roamed the streets of Paris with an army of clochards, caused havoc wherever he went. Was I supposed to applaud?

"You sent my wife and babies back to the States, commanded them. It was like a court-martial. I was never even consulted about my own desperate fate."

I didn't want to stir up my brother, remind him of the widow he took up with after Anna left, of the bacchanals in the back garden, of the gendarmes who were called in, fisticuffs in the street with firemen, of whiskers that covered his ears during midnight rambles along the Seine.

He began to shiver, and he turned away from me. My little brother was sobbing. "I cannot bear it without Eleanor, not a moment, Teedie."

I had robbed Elliott of the one creature he loved the most, gangly little Eleanor, whose mother dressed her like a ragamuffin, in hand-me-downs. Anna couldn't be bothered to shop for her own daughter. And the little girl inherited half her wardrobe from Baby Lee, the other half from Edith, who shopped with her at Altman's, much to Anna's dismay.

Ellie must have brought one of Brave Heart's old cigar boxes to Suresnes. It still had its own curious perfume—or perhaps I imagined the aroma of Papa's tobacco leaves. Little Brother retrieved a batch of letters from the cigar box.

"She writes me every single day, and I do not have the heart to answer. . . ."

"Come," I said, removing the pencil box from my waistcoat. "I'll help you write to Eleanor."

I always kept a box of pencils somewhere on my person. I hoped to sketch that nightingale in the lobby.

Elliott laughed, though it was not the sound of a sane man—it did not have a seasoned timbre. He could have been a satanic little boy caught in an act of mischief. Perhaps a tub with electric current might have jolted my brother out of his sad display.

"You as my amanuensis? That's a clever card. What would you write to Eleanor on my behalf? That her father was a wolf-man who terrorized Paris and had to be locked away?" He paused, wiped the spittle from his tongue with a crumpled handkerchief, and his satanic smile returned. "I do recall a wolf-man with whiskers who visited your dreams—as a boy. Didn't I sleep with you in your bed during those visitations? Didn't I drive him off with a flap of my arms and a fierce yell, like one of your cowboys?"

"You did."

"Then where's the loyalty?" he asked.

"But I am loyal," I had to insist.

"And I'm the prodigal son. I disappointed Father. I did not have that strength you could summon up like a Sioux warrior, that clarity of purpose. You wrote your books, you had a ranch, and now you catch the foxes in the henhouse as our Civil Service Commissioner."

"And failed at all three," I said. "My books do not sell. I cannot bring my cattle to market—the blizzards have wiped me out. Elliott, there are more and more foxes in the henhouse. The Pinks are about to slaughter the Sioux, and I will not be able to stop their carnage. The President is blind to all my requests."

"And you will fail here, too," he said. "I will leave *this* henhouse. My lawyers are preparing a letter for my release. You cannot kidnap my wife and children." He clenched his fists. "I'll kill you first, Teedie, I swear I will." He was sobbing again. "I try to write Eleanor. The words won't come. . . . Why do you have such little faith in your own brother?"

"Katie Mann," I suddenly volunteered.

He was fumbling now, the polo player without his mallet and his pony.

"I am not aware of such a creature," he said. But he'd never learned how to dissemble. He'd gone to Morton Hall once or twice, and the riffraff nearly stole his pocketbook and his pants. His mouth was quivering. "Who is—Katie Mann?"

"Your mistress. You had no difficulty writing her dozens of letters. You gave her a golden locket—from Tiffany's, I trust. You talked to her of marriage. You used all the cunning of a safecracker. And when Howe & Hummel peppered you on her behalf, you fled the scene of the crime. . . . You did not have the ten thousand Hummel demanded."

For a moment his blue eyes were clear as crystal. "Twenty," he said. "They demanded twenty thousand."

"And what about Elliott Roosevelt Mann?"

I watched a mask form like a film of molten metal over his face.

"Don't believe a word. Hummel borrowed the brat from an orphanage. He's a bunco artist. Bamie must not give him a cent. He will hound her for additional payments for the rest of her life."

I stared at him now with the unbridled fury of a hunting hawk. "Ellie, I saw the little boy with my own eyes. He has your face and your carriage, he even winks like one of us. He is a Roosevelt, even if we deny it in court, and stave off Hummel and his army of Pinks. . . . Did you really tell the poor girl that you would marry her?"

"Yes."

"And the locket," I said, "was the sign and the cement of some insane clandestine romance?"

"But it wasn't from Tiffany's—I swear."

He'd *rotted* that poor girl, left her in a pinch with a boy who would never comprehend who he really was. And we had to eclipse the little boy and his mother—or we would be pulled into a royal scandal about the Roosevelt baby in the closet.

"I'll stay at Suresnes," he said. "I'll give up the family name if you like. I'll disappear."

It was pure Elliott, that fusillade, a bit of bravura, as if he were still in the saddle, riding across some polo grounds within his skull. No. Brother would return within a fortnight. I'd found him a little clinic in Illinois. He'd have to undergo a rigorous five-week cure. We'd enroll him as a certain Mr. Peters. Bamie took care of all the details, I told him.

"And after that?" he asked in a wavering voice.

Bamie was far more charitable. But I had to insist. "You will keep away from Anna and the children for two years."

His mouth was quivering. "Two years. That's monstrous."

It was monstrous, but I couldn't have him siring a litter of brats, like a champion horse on the prowl. "You are living on borrowed money, Elliott, and on borrowed time. You must prove your worth."

"And my redemption," he said, "to a heartless brother with the brave heart of an oak. . . . I must visit Eleanor, at least."

I had to deny him even that. But he'd brought himself to ruin, and I had to save Anna and the children at all cost.

"Brother, you're a brute, and you've always been one. I'll kiss you now."

Papa always kissed us. We'd hover around the great bear, and savor the silky scratch of his whiskers. It was our biggest treat, finer than peaches and ice cream on our summer porch. But there was a hint of malice in Ellie's kiss, like the hollow clack of a solitary soldier.

IT WAS THE LAST TIME I saw Ellie alive. I had been playing toy soldiers and toy kings with his life and mine. Perhaps he might not have faltered if the fates hadn't been so unkind. The solitary soldier did indeed go out to the clinic in Illinois, disguised as Mr. Peters, and took the cure. He kept his promise and did not seek Anna and the children. Little Brother resurfaced in the wild as a gentleman farmer, who managed an enormous estate near Abingdon, Virginia. The isolation seemed to suit Elliott. He prospered for a while, paid off his debts, a bronzed god in the burning sun. I hadn't reckoned that Anna could not survive without her solitary soldier. Their separation roiled her mightily, and she died of diphtheria, just like that—she was all of twenty-nine. Six months later, their older boy, Elliott Jr., succumbed to scarlet fever, and my brother broke. He abandoned his Virginia estate and fell out of sight.

He floundered somewhere, I suppose, and I must admit that I

was occupied with other matters. The woodlands were dying in the Far West during the irreversible march of settlement. So I formed an association of amateur riflemen, hunters all—the Boone & Crockett Club—and it was our sacred duty to preserve the forests and an abundance of forest creatures. I appeared before Congress as president of Boone & Crockett. I warned that Yellowstone was being overrun by every sort of commercial parasite and would soon become a wasteland. "Gentlemen, we cannot have a national park and wildlife preserve of mountains and rivers and rich dark soil while we have plunderers and wastrels marching about. Yellowstone Park will dissolve into an ocean of dead sand and sea where plants cannot grow and where the elk and bison cannot feed."

And when the Park Protection Act of 1894 was passed, giving sanctuary to every bird and beast in Yellowstone, certain Senators rose up to shake my hand. They weren't ignorant of all my other woes. As Civil Service Commissioner, I was at war with John Wanamaker, the department-store king, who had been named Postmaster General and heartily believed in the spoils system. The moment I went after some crooked postmaster in Indianapolis or Philadelphia, that hypocritical haberdasher had him shipped off to another venue or hid him where he couldn't be touched. And I had my old problems with the Indian Bureau. Local agents were relying on Pinkerton detectives to police their reservations. The Pinks weren't much better than the Stranglers. I had to fend them off as best I could. The Department of Interior wasn't much help—it was swollen with spoils like some lazy leviathan. I had to arrive unannounced at a reservation with my Winchester and fire the Indian agent in front of his own men. Of course, the folks at Interior wouldn't back me up. And sometimes I had to stare down an entire arsenal of Pinks. That's how it went on the Shoshone reservation in Wyoming. The Pinks caught me at dusk, a dozen of them. They all wore their derbies and waistcoats, with badges pinned to their chests in silver and gold. And they were carrying Colts.

"Mr. Roosevelt," said their leader, a Pinkerton lieutenant with a filthy collar and a dyed mustache. "Some might consider you a trespasser, sir, here to harm the general population with that rifle of yours."

I looked into the dull, dead light of his eyes.

"And others might consider you bandits, being reckless with Shoshone men and women."

He smiled his waxen smile and introduced himself as Detective Taggart, the Pink in charge of all Wyoming.

"Sir, we have the law on our side. Agent Adams invited us here. We're fully bonded. Would you care to have a look at my license?"

"I know how a license looks, Detective. But how many Shoshone have you killed?"

He calculated with those dead eyes peering out of his skull. "Four—so far. They drew on us. We didn't have much of a selection."

His bravos began to fidget in their waistcoats. They'd expected to bushwhack me without a bundle of words. The Indian agent was on their side, or else they wouldn't have acted. They could blame my death on a drunken Shoshone warrior. But I cut into their calculations with the scythe of an ex-lawman.

"I've written to your bosses in Chicago," I said. "And I keep a strict agenda. I like to account for every minute. I've told the people at Interior how disheartened I am with your waxed mustaches, your Winchesters, and your fancy Colts, how you should never have been allowed on Indian lands."

And while he was pondering, I happened to dig the barrel of my Winchester into the knuckle between his eyes. He lost that swagger of his. His fellow Pinks put down their Colts and vanished into the grayness.

"I'd find another locale if I were wearing your shoes, Detective Taggart."

I put Taggart into my report, and that tale must have reached his superiors. The Pinks were pulled from the Shoshone reservation. But I couldn't clean up every bit of Indian land. The Pinks were like their own nation. I returned to inspecting post offices. I wondered if Wanamaker and I would come to blows. And that's when I heard about Ellie. He was back in Manhattan, had leased a limestone house on West 102nd Street, leased it under the name of Mr. Eliot. He was cohabiting with a certain Mrs. Valentina Morris. I couldn't tell if Mrs. Morris was the same widow who had shared his house in Neuilly after Anna returned to America. She was an alcoholic, like my brother. That much I knew. Bamie had visited him behind my back. She'd come from London, where she found herself a beau, a naval man attached to the American Embassy. Perhaps she did not want to worry me about Elliott when I was feuding with Wanamaker, the Pinks, and various postmasters and Indian agents. She didn't think I could survive such an onslaught. But I did. It was Ellie who didn't survive. He was gulping down bottles of absinthe—nothing but green poison—with his paramour, and in a fit of delirium, he climbed out his parlor window and tottered on the sill like a crazed circus performer; it was Mrs. Morris and Elliott's valet who coaxed him back in. That night he had a series of convulsions and died right in his own bed.

I was in Washington, tilting against impossible windmills, when a telegram arrived from Sister next morning.

> *ELLIE GONE.*
> *COME HOME.*

HER FACE WAS UNDER A VEIL. But I caught the fineness of her features and the wistful, luminous longing of her brown eyes. Her fingers were also fine. She was dressed in the blackest weeds, like the most loyal of widows. She sat on a simple ladder-back chair beside my brother's bed, and I couldn't intrude upon her mourning, ask her to leave the very room she had shared with Ellie. Mrs. Morris was present by the laws and privileges of her private domain. I was glad Ellie hadn't spent his last days in a hovel, like his hobo boulevardiers of Paris. There were no bottles of brandy and green mint lying about. He had a picture of Anna and Eleanor on the mantel. He wasn't bloated now, didn't have that furrow of anger and grief I had encountered in Suresnes. That graceful brother of mine had always lived on a trampoline. Elliott was the handsome one, with the musical gait of a poet, while I could only mimic the music of birdcalls.

I kissed him on the cheek. It did not have the waxen feel of the dead. I went into the parlor. It was packed with mourners, whom Ellie must have acquired like a contagion at the local saloon. They reminded me of the rabble at Morton Hall. They'd been his drinking companions. They called me Mr. Eliot.

"He was a sport, your brother was. Never denied us a nip or a two-dollar bill."

I was troubled by their very presence in the parlor, by the sour perfume of their unwashed clothes. It irked me that Elliott had comported with such riffraff. At first I thought their devotion was feigned. I was wrong. They wanted something I could not give—camaraderie—but I couldn't sit there in silence. I drank from the same schooner of shandygaff. Alcohol had always made me aggressive, even at Harvard, where I would scrap with my Porcellian brothers after a sip of wine.

Bamie arrived. She had forgotten to wear her special shoes in the tempest of her own grief. She was hunched over, like someone who had been stricken, or had received a terrific stripe to the face. I should have asked her about London and her new beau, the naval attaché, but I did not seem to have that musical gift of speech, soused as I was with shandygaff.

"We will have to bury him, Theodore. He has a plot in Tivoli beside Anna."

"No," I said. "He belongs to us. We will bury him in Greenwood next to Brave Heart and Mittie . . . and Alice."

"But think of Eleanor and little Hall. They will want their mother and father in the same plot."

"He is my brother," I said. "He will lie down with us—in Greenwood. That is final."

She wouldn't contradict me in front of Elliott's drinking companions, even if they could hardly hear a word.

"And we must do something for poor Mrs. Morris."

"Why?" I asked. "They drank from the same bottle—his devil-ment is also hers."

"But she cared for him, Teedie. She paid his bills. And now she is heavily in debt. She cannot remain in this house."

"I will not indulge his concubine. She can remain here until the lease is up."

"Papa wouldn't have been so harsh," she said. And she looked at me out of that keen sadness she'd had, even as a child, when Papa was away at war as an Allotment Commissioner, and she had to run the household and deal with conniving servants before she was ten.

Bamie had never been unfair. She'd inherited Brave Heart's feel for charity, while fighting wicked postmasters and the Pinks had made me rambunctious.

"Teedie, we will talk another time . . . when you do not have such a bitter taste on your tongue."

She sat with the mourners for a little while, comforted Mrs. Morris, fondled Ellie's ear, and then she was gone. I went back into the bedroom. I was bitten with bile. I was still that deputy sheriff lost in a world of black ice. Mrs. Morris' shoulders began to heave in her ladder-back chair. I seized her up like a ruffian, took her in my arms. I could not treat her gently, but we did our own little war dance. She began to murmur.

"I loved him, Mr. Ted, I really did."

"I know."

I released her from that fierce grip, and she walked out of the room. I was all alone with the rumpled corpse of my baby brother. I could hear the hiss of the lamps, as the light seemed to lick his face like an ornament. And then he rose up, this dead brother of mine.

"Teedie, you are in big trouble."

I would not speak to the phantasm. He was growing whiskers, like that werewolf who had haunted me as a boy.

"Where is Granny?"

I was puzzled by that remark. He didn't mean Grandmamma Bulloch, who had died years ago. He didn't mean Grandma Mary,

Anna's mother. He meant Eleanor. Anna called the little girl Granny, because she had such a serious, solemn face. And Baby Lee picked up on that taunt, like a talisman.

—Father, when is Granny going to stay with us again? Do I have to look at my twin? She wears all my clothes.

Edie invited Eleanor to stay with us during the summers, when we were at Sagamore Hill. Her own mother couldn't seem to take care of that child. Eleanor became another one of my little bunnies. I didn't pamper her, but Edie did. Edie gave her a sewing kit, and they darned my socks with a fanciful stitch. She sat in the parlor, where Edie taught her penmanship with a personal flourish.

"Where is Granny?"

I started to cry, and my little brother fell back into his quietus. I was frightened to be with Ellie now. It was much of a muchness with John Wanamaker and the Indian Bureau. I'd never win no matter how many errant postmasters and agents I uncovered.

I could not seem to check my own tears.

Then Mrs. Morris returned, minus her veil. Her dark eyes had a startling gleam in the little penumbras of light.

"You shouldn't have banished him, Mr. Ted—taken his children away."

I was still besotted. "I will not be lectured to by his drinking partner—you deviled him, madame."

"Oh, I did much more than that," she said with a puckish smile.

"Should I have left him in Paris with his army of mendicants? He would have perished in the streets."

"That would have been better than banishment. He was lost without little Eleanor. Can you imagine for one moment the happiest day in his life? Your sister with the broken back brought Eleanor here to 102nd Street . . . like Cinderella in a glass carriage."

I was riddled with shame and doubt. "Bamie does not have a broken back."

"Your sister could see that Elliott was dying, but *you* could not. That visit revived him. Your sister was Elliott's secret agent. She had to bribe Eleanor's nanny and return her to Central Park—within the hour. They had ten, fifteen minutes together. It was their little paradise, without intruders."

"Stop! Not another sound."

She smiled again. "I will be as silent as the dead—and the damned."

She curtsied in her petticoats and was gone.

CHAPTER 8

POLICEMAN'S PARADISE

1896

THREE HUNDRED MULBERRY STREET. THERE WAS NOTH-ing of the purple in it but royal dust, grim and gray. I should have declared it a debacle, and had it ripped to the ground. It did have a stoop, where con men dallied, criminal lawyers mingled, and police reporters met. I had to bound up those steps or I would have been waylaid for an hour. My girl secretary, Minnie G. Kelly, had become a hit at headquarters. Previous Presidents of the Police Board had hired male assistants, but I couldn't have gotten by without Miss Minnie. She looked like a schoolmarm in her spectacles and black hair twisted into a bun. Still, she had that wild Irish streak. She flirted with every copper in the building, but she was territorial, wouldn't let a soul into my office without a fixed appointment. She saved every article that had ever been written about her boss, every caricature, and commented on them, too. She despised the newspapers that despised me—I had become the outcast of Manhattan because of the blue laws, teetotaler that I was.

"But they love you in Texas, Mr. T. You're a national figure. You could run for President—right from Mulberry Street."

"On what ticket? The Republicans dislike me almost as much as the Democrats."

I'd dug myself a graveyard downtown, a Dead Man's Alley, like the old Mulberry Bend. I'd instituted a bicycle squad that could catch pickpockets on the fly. I'd installed a pistol range at the Eighth Regiment Armory on Ninety-fourth and Park, where coppers could finally learn how to handle a weapon and wouldn't have it explode in the middle of some pursuit. But I couldn't control the endemic graft in the system. Boss Platt still hadn't forgiven me because I would not allow my election officers to rig the last election in favor of the Republicans. And Tammany had come roaring back into power.

Still, I didn't rein in my lads. I had them shut down every saloon that defied the Sunday prohibition. I even went after the "hotels" that hid behind the Raines Law, which declared that a saloon could sell liquor on Sundays if it had at least ten rooms to let. I accompanied my lads on their missions. The judges at police court exonerated every innkeeper. I didn't care. I went after the same fraudulent hotels. My fellow Commissioners reprimanded me. "Roosevelt, you're a madman." I ignored them and their outcries. I went around with a repeater tucked into my pants. I wore a poncho at headquarters. I even had my lads raid Senator Platt's little roost at the Fifth Avenue Hotel. I had warrants issued about illegal gambling on the premises. I closed down Platt's "Amen Corner," had his antique desk delivered to our property clerk. The court tossed out my warrants. I had to return the desk. But the Easy Boss was as quiet as a church mouse, while Mr. Joseph Pulitzer was relentless in his attacks on my presidency of the Police Board. He called me "that little runt of a man with the red mustache" who had failed as a Civil Service Commissioner and was now making a mess at 300 Mulberry Street. The *World* swore I was a despot, the czar of czars. I relished the fight, offered Pulitzer's photographers my best smile. Pulitzer couldn't stop talking about my teeth. "Roosevelt's satanic grin," the *World* said. "The Commissioner looks like a crazed colt."

Considered that a compliment.

Then the Social Reform Club invited Manhattan's reviled Police Commissioner to speak at its cramped headquarters on East Fourth

Street. The building was a firetrap. I could have had the fire marshals shut it down. But even the anarchists and the socialists had
to have their own little club. My talk had been advertised in all the
papers. The *Brooklyn Eagle* ripped at me. "Come across the river
and meet the buffoon who is both unwieldy and unwise." I arrived
with Edith, who had cautioned me against confronting the rabble. "Theodore, they will eat you up alive at their first chance. You
had best plot an escape route." Baby Lee had come along—as my
bodyguard.

The heat in that auditorium was decidedly hostile. I met nothing
but a sea of angry faces—the women in this workingman's parlor
were as ferocious as the men. And then there were the Democrats.
Boss Croker had his hirelings, vile lads trained to hoot and hiss—
they could drown the chant of any speaker. I had expected them.
This vituperative chorus followed me from engagement to engagement. There was also the Saloonkeepers' Association, with King
Callahan at the helm, here in all his glory. And there were hoteliers
I had locked out, with their lieutenants, and corrupt police captains
who hadn't survived the judicial decisions of my little court.

Accustomed to such enemies, I could have had my own phalanx of police. I wanted none. But I was startled by Boss Platt,
sitting in the audience, alone, without his flunkies, his nimble fingers surrounding the silk hat in his lap. He'd never graced any of
my other performances, but he'd come to this socialist den. My
mind wandered—no, it circled on to something else. I couldn't stop
thinking of Edith's lovely, aquiline nose, so startling in profile, like
an eagle with royal blood, and her deliciously dark hair, with Baby
Lee beside her, in all her blondness. The two potentates! Edith
hadn't wanted Baby Lee to come to this meeting hall, declared it
was unsafe for such a young girl. But Baby Lee said she would fill
Madison Avenue with smoke bombs if she couldn't be here to "protect" her father. They were always fighting, but they had a fondness
for one another, and their own reading club.

"Sissy," Edith said, "hold on to your father—there are ruffians
around."

"*Mother*," Sissy said, "I can take care of us all."

She'd brought a candlestick in her coat pocket as proof of her wisdom and her worth. She could have been a creature born in the Badlands—my little lady outlaw. But I had all this venom to deal with. The auditorium seated four hundred, and it was packed with a thousand souls, many with a grievance against me. They stood in the aisles, some like acrobats on other men's shoulders. They nuzzled into the armrests of certain chairs, occupied the window ledges. It really was a tinderbox, a fire hazard in derbies and petticoats.

The chairman of the club, a loathsome little rascal named Ashbel Grief, quieted the assembly with a patrolman's cylinder-shaped whistle. The sound racked my ears, but it did its own shrill work.

"Ladies and gentlemen, we have with us today a man who has always been knee-deep in controversy. Theodore Roosevelt, son of the late philanthropist and banker who did so much to help the disadvantaged, who was known as Brave Heart, and who built hospitals and lodging houses. There isn't a newsboy among us, past or present, who doesn't owe a debt of gratitude to Brave Heart. But Theodore Jr. is our Police Commissioner rather than a philanthropist. He comes to us from the Civil Service, where he slept for six years. But now we have him on our doorstep. And what a blunder it has been. He's denied workingmen their Sunday ambrosia, banished some of our very best Irish captains to 'Goatsville,' all the way in the Bronx, and ripped the gold bars off the sleeves of others. He was a sheriff in the Badlands, some say, captured vicious men. But does Manhattan desire a cowboy king? Is he not our tin czar, as Mr. Pulitzer says, the man who dictates terms at Police Headquarters? . . . Ladies and gentlemen, without further ado, please welcome Commissioner Roosevelt, the cowboy king."

I rose up from my chair, could glimpse the terror that Edie wanted so much to hide. She clasped my hand for a second, to comfort me in this assembly of knaves. The jeers resounded off my back. Baby Lee would have accompanied her father to the platform had I not signaled to her. The jeering didn't stop. Spittle flew around me as I climbed onto the platform. That runt, Ashbel Grief, was gloating. We'd sat on committees together, had settled grievances between cigar makers and their tyrannical bosses.

"Ash," I whispered in his ear, "I'm grateful for the introduction, but you shouldn't have riled this cowboy king. You'll find yourself a master without his domain—tattooed with summonses from head to toe. You'll have to vacate within a month."

Ashbel was still pleased with himself. The din grew to a disheartening roar. The female firebrands in the audience tossed knotted handkerchiefs filled with crumbling bits of masonry gathered from tenement rooftops. The handkerchiefs exploded near my head, and soon my scalp and shoulders were covered in a patina of gray powder. The roaring wouldn't stop until Senator Platt finally twirled his cane in the air and shouted perhaps for the only time in his life.

"Enough! You invited the man. Let him speak."

Senator Platt seemed to have some sway among the socialists and saloonkeepers.

I stood there with that dust on my shoulders. "I am your sheriff. That's a fact. I have rooted out some of the rotten policemen in my department. Others still thrive. I'm not an infallible judge. I have been appointed to uphold the law. That is my mandate. I have no other. If you want your Sunday pail of beer, start your own crusade. Shake the lapels of your Assemblymen until the Sunday laws are banished from the books."

"It's not *our* Assemblymen who are at fault," shouted one of the female firebrands. "It's the lads from upstate with their own private gospel. You're Albany's tool, you are."

"Madam, I assure you. I am not in Albany's pocket. Whether I have failed or not, I have tried to reform the police."

"Yeah," shouted King Callahan, "we now have a bicycle squad with nautical caps and yellow stripes on their pantaloons. Sublime they are, and admirable, sir, in the way they can peek under a woman's petticoats. They are no better than Peeping Toms on the prowl."

There was a roar of laughter from Callahan's compatriots, laughter at my expense.

"*King,*" I said, demanding an immediate intimacy with this lord of the saloonkeepers, "we must live in different towns. I have heard nothing but good reports about the flying squad. They have retrieved an ample number of women's purses and men's wallets. These lads have been making war on pickpockets. And they have broken up many a riot."

"So you say," answered the King, with his hands on his hips. "But Mulberry Street is a disconnected fortress—deaf, dumb, and blind. The bicycle squad is worse than Clubber Williams with their billies."

Clubber Williams was a notorious deputy inspector who had beaten vagrants half to death in the cellars at Mulberry Street. I "encouraged" him to resign during my first month in office.

"Well, now, King," I said, "if there are clubbers among the flying squad, why don't you report them?"

"We are not informers," shouted one of the King's kin, "we are not rats, kind sir."

And again there was that cruel roar of laughter.

"Mr. Roseyvelt," said the King, "never mind those lads—they're a trifle. We can deal with them and their fancy pants. It's my saloon that concerns me. You deny workingmen their Sunday pail, and you call that criminal justice. But the gentle folks like yourself sip Sunday aperitifs at their own saloons, and not a single one of them has been touched. I call that gross negligence."

I was cautious now among the riffraff. "Mr. Callahan, I am not aware of such saloons."

Callahan put on his spectacles and read from a crumpled slip of paper. "I have their handles, sir. The Jolly Corner, the Vestibule, Hatters' Alley, Ambassadors' Lane. . . . Should I read on, Mr. Roseyvelt?"

"But these are private clubs," I said, and I began to feel that I was standing on a precipice rather than the speaker's platform at the Social Reform Club.

"Private clubs, indeed," said Callahan, playing with that infinite charm to all his cousins and fellow saloonkeepers. "They are public enough to the polo crowd—we're the ones who are turned away at the door, the common folks."

And King Callahan had his chorus of chanters. "Hatters' Alley, Hatters' Alley, Hatters' Alley . . ."

I had lost the duel, and I couldn't regain any ground. We did not really protect the weak, and our laws existed at the workingman's expense. It was Tammany that reigned, with Boss Platt on his own bit of turf, and I was like a window dresser at Stern's. I had *prettified* the police. I was stuck on this platform, as the crowd bolted from their seats and surged toward me.

. . . *Hatters' Alley, Hatters' Alley, Hatters' Alley!*

I was prepared to wrestle the whole lot, but I did not want my wife and daughter trampled by these hooligans.

"Edie," I cried in a falsetto that seemed to strangle my windpipe in moments of crisis. "Edie! Alice!"

I was buffeted about. I looked for the feather on Edie's hat, that white flash of egret. But all I found was Ashbel Grief, who could not have planned this mêlée. He was a socialist with a private inheritance, who lived among the swells on Washington Square.

"Ash," I muttered, "are you satisfied?"

But there was little mirth in that little man's eyes. He'd been looking for the occasion to humiliate me in public, and had brought the Badlands into his den—sheer disquietude.

A brick glanced off the side of my head. I saw a swirl of colors, and then I could hear that familiar whistle of the flying squad. I wondered if Boss Platt had been far shrewder than I and had telephoned the bicycle boys *before* my dialogue with the saloonkeepers began. They worked in a kind of wonderment with their billies. It was a marvel to behold, the dexterity and the selection. They did not attack any of the female firebrands, just led them aside with the lightest touch. They went after the Tammany thugs who had sandbags in their fists, hitting them with lightning speed. They appeared and disappeared in a whirl of nautical caps. They weren't out to crush a man's skull. They didn't want the ambulance brigade. I caught the yellow stripes on their pantaloons, and the wide arc of their matador capes, as their billies struck the shoulders, backs, and thighs of assorted hooligans.

"Stop," I said, but no one listened once that dance of billy clubs began. There might have been one or two bloodied heads, almost by accident, in the backlash of a billy. I was able to walk among the casualties, had to step over a few. I found Edith all in a froth. My wife stood there wild-eyed and bewildered. "Theodore," she whispered, when she noticed specks of blood on my forehead—the work of that brick. "You must lie down—we'll locate an ambulance."

"Darling, I'm fit as a fiddler." And that's when I saw Baby Lee, who was having the time of her life with that candlestick of hers.

"Father, isn't this grand? I've been taking care of Mother as much as I could."

Boss Platt must have fled the auditorium. He wouldn't have relished this fight.

The lad in charge of the flying squad came up to me in his nautical cap. He couldn't have been more than twenty-five or twenty-six.

"Commissioner, the wagons will be here any minute. Should we arrest the whole crew, male and female?"

"No arrests," I had to tell him. "We don't want to create an incident. Have one of our doctors attend to the wounded. And if anyone can't walk, ride with him to Bellevue. What's your name, son?"

"Raddison, sir, Sergeant Raddison."

He looked as if he'd stepped from the moon with his broad shoulders and slim waist.

"And who summoned you here?"

"No one, sir. I read the newspaper articles. And I figured there would be trouble."

I put this adventurous sergeant in charge of the whole misadventure at the Social Reform Club and told him to right whatever had gone wrong. And then I saw the King sitting in his chair, abandoned by all his kinsmen who must have fallen afoul of the flying squad and lay groaning somewhere like scattered bits of debris.

The King had a glassy look, but still recognized me.

"I did not want this, Mr. Roseyvelt. I wanted a true debate. But the lads were overeager . . . and then the bicycle boys."

"They aren't here at my pleasure," I told him, and Callahan wagged his head.

I put my arm around Edith and limped out of this unfortunate club with her and Baby Lee, glowing like a lioness after a magnificent escapade.

CHAPTER 9

POLICEMAN'S PARADISE, PART TWO

1897

SHE WAS PULITZER'S STAR, THE FIRST FEMALE ON HIS little fleet of crime reporters who was permitted a byline. Pulitzer himself had redeemed her, rescued her from a life of crime, taught her to write the terse copy he admired. Having gone undercover, she slipped into Blackwell's Island, mingled with the lunatics, and exposed the island's utter rot—the bribes, the barbarism, the sexual plunder. She was the only one on Pulitzer's staff at the *World* who didn't attack me outright, and it was a mystery until I read her byline and realized she was the same Nancy Fowler who had once been Manhattan's most notorious bunco artist. Her previous intimacy with the underworld had given her an advantage over Pulitzer's other star reporters. None of them could compete with Nan. And it wasn't much of a miracle that she had her own distinct style—her "bite," as crime reporters liked to say. With a little push from Pulitzer, Nan Fowler had developed a flair for the piquant.

And while Pulitzer's other crime reporters were relentless in their attack on my stewardship at Mulberry Street, Nan softened her bite marks. She asked to accompany me on one of my midnight rambles, and I knew she might roast me alive, but I took the risk.

Her troubling height and pale blue eyes conjured up an image of my dead wife—I'd met Nan while Alice Lee was still alive. She had Alice's winsome beauty, even if she was much older now and wrinkles had surfaced at the edge of her mouth.

"I don't intend to flatter you, Roosevelt. I'm here to learn." And then she smiled. "But how could I forget the Cyclone Assembly-man? You knew that Long John McManus had hired me to rub your nose in the dirt, and you still walked right into his den."

"I couldn't relinquish a damsel in distress."

Her eyes fluttered with a disturbing intelligence. "I was hardly a damsel. I was paid a handsome sum to lead you into a trap. But I had never met a man as willful as you. It destroyed my equilibrium and my notion of a rube. . . . I'm glad you agreed to this ramble."

Pulitzer had plucked her right out of the demimonde. But I wondered about Nan's earlier incarnation as a banker's wife with a brownstone and two tots, a boy and a girl. I was reluctant to meddle, but meddle I did. Here was a sad tale, more than sad, since her husband wouldn't permit her to see her own children, who were still under his custody.

"But you have Pulitzer on your side. He can shake the whole court system. And I'm not powerless."

Her face hardened, and she was the duchess I recalled from our first encounter in that *maison close*.

"I abandoned them," she said. "I left them in their cribs, with the little toys and the wallpaper I had picked out at Lord & Taylor. I walked away. I was a madwoman looking for a madwoman's delights, and I created my own circus of hell. But we are not here to discuss my domestic situation, Roosevelt. It's your probity I'm after, not mine."

She'd shunned the hydraulic elevator, recently installed, and climbed two flights to my office. I went into the armoire, pulled out a black sombrero and a red sash with tassels, and put them on. I must have amused her.

"I never realized that Mulberry Street was near the Badlands." And she let out a full-throated roar. "Commissioner, you look like a Dakota cowboy who got lost in a snowdrift."

I stared into her pale eyes, one bunco artist to another. "Well, isn't that the whole point of a disguise? To create confusion and ample camouflage."

"Mr. Roseyvelt," she mumbled, mimicking my own roundsmen, "you are a Manhattan miracle."

We marched down the stairs, almost like a bride and groom.

The roundsmen and stragglers from the Detective Bureau ogled us both. "Evenin', Miss Nan, evenin', Commissioner Ted."

We walked east, into the darkness, the corner lamps a distant glow. But I wasn't the Lighting Commissioner, at least not yet. I couldn't control the eerie sense of danger that lurked after dark. Lower Manhattan had become a land of shadows. It wasn't like the electric panorama along Fifth Avenue, with its constant carriage trade. Down here, we had thieves who masqueraded as roundsmen, and roundsmen who had their own little company of pickpockets. Policing was a "business" rather than a code of honor, rife with corruption and all the privileges of patronage. Corruption flourished, even under "the Reign of Terror," as Democratic and Republican reporters dubbed my tactics. I'd barely made a dent. But I continued my midnight rambles, and I continued harrowing the other Commissioners. I had a dual purpose. As President of the Police Board, I also sat on the Board of Health. I could write summonses and shut down tenements that had turned into firetraps. The landlords feared me more than my own inspectors did. I was everywhere at once, as I went into the doss-houses and storefront distilleries with Nan, looking for coppers who were on the "coop," snoring away amid the bedlam around them. We uncovered a dozen, and woke them out of their stupor. I gave each lad a summons to appear before my tribunal, while Nan scribbled her notes.

The corner lamps were like a blind man's beacon. The fire in the globes had turned a pale winter blue, as we went into more doss-houses and distilleries. Roundsmen arrived out of nowhere and saluted me. Suddenly Lower Manhattan was brimming with as many coppers as cockroaches.

"Commissioner," Nan said, "it's a travesty. The roundsmen have rung the alarm. They know you're out on a ramble. We have to try the right saloon if we want to catch a copper."

I surveyed her under my pince-nez. Nan was right about the saloons. The ones with ties to Tammany never bothered to close. Roundsmen used these watering holes as their neighborhood nests, and completely forgot about errant patrolmen. So I decided on the most delinquent saloon in the district, the King's Table, owned by King Callahan himself.

He had the grandest emporium on Third Avenue, a prince of a place, with gold spittoons and hammered silver on the walls. His zinc bar, the pride of Callahan's saloon, was shipped over from a Dublin hotel. His clientele was predominantly German and Irish, with some uptown natives who preferred the raucous fun and flights of peril that might erupt any moment at the King's Table. King was an ox of a man. He'd been a deputy inspector who made his fortune on Mulberry Street and poured it into the saloon.

I didn't enter Callahan's through the side door with Nan. I barreled into the front hall in my black sombrero. I'd been disingenuous with Pulitzer's star reporter. I wasn't wearing a disguise. I wanted Callahan's lowlifes to recognize their pirate of a Police Commissioner. The six roundsmen who slept at the corner tables suddenly grew alert. A bully boy who must have been a recent recruit said, "King, should I dust this feller in the fancy hat?"

"Hush, now," said King Callahan. "It's His Nibs."

"Then why is he bringing a chippie into a decent establishment, and him not using the ladies' door? That's a criminal act."

Callahan knocked the bully boy off his barstool. "Pardon, Commissioner Ted. This imbecile failed to notice that the 'chippie' belongs to Mr. Pulitzer, but I remember when she was a thief, remember her well."

"Stuff it, King," Nan snarled, "or I'll have His Nibs arrest the whole lot of you, with all your rotten deals under the table."

Callahan bowed to her. "Didn't mean to offend Your Highness."
He was having a rip of a time with the one man who was out to ruin
him. "I rang the night bell, Commissioner, but it takes a while to
clear the King's Table of every lout."

"King, I'm not interested in your clientele. You're harboring
roundsmen."

"And that's my shame," he muttered. "I've been derelict, sir, in
my duty." And he growled at the six officers. They adjusted their
tunics, put on their helmets, and paraded past me. I could have
noted their badge numbers, chided them in public, demoted them
to desk jobs at Mulberry Street, but that would have meant waging
war with the other Commissioners. So I let them catch a glimpse
of my ire—my disappointment in their dereliction. And that deep
frown was enough to sear through their brass buttons and burn a
hole in their collective hearts. These lads would not be caught coop-
ing again at the King's Table. I seldom had to warn a roundsman
twice, even those under the sway of King Callahan.

I couldn't even bask in the little glories I still had as Police Commissioner. I recognized a man with stark white hair who sat at one
of the tables, and I realized that my forage into the saloon would
not end well. Whitey Whitman he was, a deputy inspector I had
forced to retire. Whitey once strode across Manhattan like a colos-
sus; he ran prostitutes and a galaxy of pimps, protected gamblers
from police raids, yet what irked me the most was that he preyed
upon newsboys, ripped their pockets right out from under them. I
reprimanded him at headquarters, or, as Sissy might say, I *shriveled*
him in front of his own men. And here he was, with that splendid mane of white hair. He'd gone into the construction business,
with the help of Tammany Hall and our own Republican bosses.
His finances hadn't suffered. He was far richer than any Roosevelt.
Yet I had stolen what was essential to him—his hierarchy at headquarters. Mulberry Street had been his roost. He'd strut about in
his braided sleeves with a certain majesty, cracking the skulls of
boisterous men and boys, who'd been assigned to our cellar jail.
But what troubled me about Whitman was that he had the angelic

face of a choirboy. He was never loud. His voice was soft and silky, and that's where his menace lay. He was the poet of violence. I'd never met another feller remotely like Whitey Whitman, not in the Badlands, with all its desperadoes. The Dakota man had some kind of a *draw*, a telltale delivery—a nervous tic, a sneer, a demonic laugh—but Whitey had none.

"Hello, Mr. Roseyvelt," he said, in a voice that echoed the lazy Harvard drawl; his boots were propped up, and they had a brilliant sheen. "I'm going to scatter your brains in front of Pulitzer's pet. Then I'll treat her to a shandy."

"Now, now, Whitey," said King Callahan. "You can't threaten the Police Commissioner."

"Shut up," Whitey said with that silken cord of his. "I'd like to hear from Madam—ah, I mean Miss Nan."

"Mr. Whitman," she said, "I will not drink your shandy."

Whitey grinned. "Roseyvelt, I propose to marry her. You could perform the ceremony as our chief constable—while you can still hold a pen."

He couldn't have known that Miss Nan had once been a bride with two babies and a brownstone on Union Square.

"Up with your dukes, Whitey," I growled like a grizzly, "and a little less of your gab."

"*Dukes*," he said, and Callahan's white-haired angel turned waspish with one twist of his tongue. "I'm strictly an elbows man."

The lads at the King's Table understood his lingo. Whitey was a barroom brawler. It wouldn't have mattered one atom to him that I had nearly won the lightweight cup at Harvard. I had boxed with fellow students in a ring, and brawled with politicians, who might have been ex-prizefighters, but I'd never tangled with a defrocked deputy inspector. Whitey Whitman had no rules. He was a reckless machine. He'd chewed off a man's ear once, blinded others, and had beaten felons into a crippling insanity inside the Tombs.

He gulped down a shandygaff, wiped his lips with the back of his hand, and with his tongue untwisted, he turned into an angel again. He was a head taller than Commissioner Ted, and had a much greater wingspan, so I had to crouch against his assault. I was tempted to wear my pince-nez, but he would have blinded me with the first whack of his elbow.

Callahan made one last appeal, as I took off my sombrero. "He's an appointed official, Ted is, and if you murder him, boy-o, there'll be no appeal from a sweet-talking attorney like Hummel or Howe. You'll sit in Sing Sing until you're catatonic."

Whitey scoffed at him. "It's a small matter. He humiliated me in front of my men."

For a big lad he had the dainty feet of a dancer, and dance they did. He could have been the Harvard boy, and I the barroom brawler. I felt unmanned. I forgot all the lessons I ever had from "General" Lister, my boxing master at Harvard, who taught me how to hit as hard as I could and to waltz away from a blow.

Whitey bowed to Miss Nan like her knight-errant and moved in for the kill. I could barely keep up with his dancing gait. I wondered if he'd had his own "General" Lister to teach him a few tricks. But he had no need of a boxing master. He didn't box. He pummeled me with his elbows while he maintained a whirlwind defense. I couldn't get near enough to jab at him. Blood and spittle flew from my mouth in long, merciless strings that were like the melody of my own doom. I lost a molar somewhere. Whitey hopped about, expecting to dust me. But I wouldn't fall. He seemed agitated; puckers appeared in his face, like self-inflicted wounds. And then I must have tripped against the leg of a chair.

Suddenly I was lying in the sawdust with a ball of blood in my mouth. I looked up at the darkening crystal of the chandeliers.

"Stay down, old Ted," King Callahan buzzed in my ear. "Whitey's been an orphan-maker many a time."

And then I could hear Miss Nan over the roar of Whitey's partisans at the King's Table. "Keep your own counsel, Callahan. We have no need of an orphan-maker. . . . Roosevelt, get up. Right now."

And I did. I spat that ball of blood into my cuff. I begged the Lord *and* my father's ghost that I wouldn't have an asthma attack or

the Roosevelt colic in the middle of my bout. I couldn't have counterattacked while wading in a bundle of my own filth. I couldn't have
counterattacked under any condition. It was Miss Nan who devised
a strategy of combat that confused Whitey and hampered his gait.
She smiled at him like some barroom sweetheart and blinked with
her blue eyes. Whitey missed a step, mesmerized by that bunco artist turned crime reporter, in her own imagined brothel. I landed a
right and a short left between his elbows, and it was as if I had the
"General" right behind me. *Give him a fistful of arrows in the solar
plexus, Roosevelt.* My combinations were like lightning in a velvet
bottle. He had nothing to answer with once he dropped his guard.
His elbows lumbered like detached limbs.

King Callahan stopped the bout. "I won't have bloody murder
in my saloon."

But I still had an urge to do him bodily harm. I was a cru-
sader despised in my own town, Manhattan's Oliver Cromwell,
who tried to shut every damn saloon on the Sabbath. To Callahan's
credit, he didn't advertise himself as an innkeeper, didn't turn his
beer hall into a lodgers' den, where prostitutes could parade in their
petticoats or a Mother Hubbard and have their own little paradise.
He was a saloon man, through and through, the King was, and he
didn't involve himself in that rascality of the Raines Law.

Whitey was another matter. Whitey found profit in those
fraudulent hotels, with his own corral of prostitutes. And Whitey
had a gamblers' association, enforced by crooked roundsmen. He
mocked my efforts to transform the police into genuine civil servants. A policeman's badge meant a whole lot of boodle. Even after
I had ousted him, Whitey held his own demonic dominion over
Mulberry Street—I couldn't root out all his rot. So I smashed at
him instead. His partisans couldn't help him now. They couldn't
rein in my blows. I hit him with a hook, gyrating like a bull with
spectacular horns.

"Commissioner Ted," he cried, "I succored your brother, I saved
his life, more than once—on 102nd Street."

I hooked him again.

Nan didn't know enough about Elliott. I was the orphan-maker, not Whitey. I was the one who exiled Elliott from his children. I wouldn't even let Ellie lie down in the sod with his wife.

Whitey clutched me with his claws. "I was kind to him, Commissioner Ted. I watched over the boy."

"He wasn't a boy," I hissed. I put my sombrero back on and adjusted my pince-nez, while Nan wiped the blood from my mouth. That missing molar ached like the devil.

"Roosevelt," she said, "I believe we're finished here."

OUR FINAL LANDING WAS at the headquarters of Senator Thomas Collier Platt, who held court at the Fifth Avenue when he wasn't in Washington. Known as the "Easy Boss," he wasn't like his Democratic shadow, Dick Croker, the grandest of Grand Sachems, who rose up from the whimsical mayhem of his own street gang. Croker didn't care for music or poetry and art. He was a mixer who may have clubbed many a man to death at the polls. He ruled Manhattan's precincts, but he didn't have Senator Platt's wide appeal. Platt seldom spoke above a whisper. Platt had the sweet, soft hands of a violinist. Platt had even attended Yale College once upon a time. He read poetry to his children. But he was murderous in his own way. He could wreck the career of a Governor with one of his whispers. Presidents would arrive for a Sunday chat at the Fifth Avenue Hotel, sit in one of the mandarin corridors off the main lobby until the Senator was prepared to greet you in his Amen Corner—Platt had been a theology student at Yale. He slumped behind his mahogany desk, an heirloom of some sort, and looked like a cadaver in a gray suit. Senator Platt was a sallow man. He had the complexion of a spent candle. But his lips were always moist, and he stared out at you from the deep hollows of his eyes. Nothing got past the Senator's gaze. And at the moment his gaze fell upon Nan. He didn't care for crime reporters, any reporters at all. But he hadn't objected to my bringing her here. And then I realized he had known Nan before she was baptized by Pulitzer. Perhaps he'd used her as a "swallow," to entrap Republican Assemblymen he couldn't keep in line. We were both escorted by one of his lackeys to the Amen Corner. You weren't allowed to sit in his exalted presence, not at first. But he found a chair for Nan, an heirloom like his own, with a velvet-covered cushion.

"You're a clever lad, Roosevelt, to bring Pulitzer's little girl with you. What's her name?"

He said all this in a menacing whisper, without gazing at me once.

"You know my name, Senator," she said. "I've sat on your lap many a time."

And the cadaver livened considerably.

"But that was in the old days. . . . Can you guess why the Commissioner dragged you here in the middle of the night?"

I could feel myself sliding down into some abyss. But Nan was as much a pol as Senator Platt.

"I suppose it was to eat your heart out," she said. "To overwhelm you with my wit."

"And your loveliness," he said. "Don't forget that."

But Nan was immune to the Easy Boss's accolades. "I'm practically a grandma, Senator. My thighs are full of ripples."

"Ripples an old man might admire," he said before that sallow ice of his returned. "But you know the rules. You will not repeat a word you hear at this table. Or there will be damage. Mr. Ted wants a favor I cannot grant—to pluck him out of a big black hole at Police Headquarters."

That big black hole was caused by a brand-new charter. Manhattan and the Bronx would marry Brooklyn, Queens, and Staten Island next year—1898—and become a Goliath known as Greater New York. The current Police Board would be out of business. "I have no future here, Senator Platt."

I campaigned for Mr. McKinley, visited him in Canton, Ohio, right after the last election. I wanted a bit of the spoils, I suppose. I was an expert on America's Navy, had analyzed the War of 1812 better than any man alive. I knew that we had to protect our sea lanes, "upholster" our antiquated warships. And as quietly as I could I petitioned for the post of Undersecretary of the Navy. Platt wasn't unfamiliar with my desires. Yet he was out to make me bleed as much as he could, and turn me into a beggar man.

Finally he swiveled around and peered at me from the hollows of his eyes. The cadaver grinned. My sombrero and velvet sash must have beguiled him. He clapped those violinist's hands with their long tapering fingers. "Roosevelt, is that what you like to wear on your midnight rambles?"

"Sometimes, Senator."

"It's no wonder the roundsmen draw pictures of you in their washroom—Mulberry Street's very own cowboy at the helm."

I was jolted a bit. I'd never seen his bald pate in the washroom at headquarters. Did he wander above the rooftops in his spare time? "And how are you privy to that piece of information, Senator?"

"Spies," he said. "I have many, and you have none. You canceled the contracts of every police stool pigeon. And no decent detective can survive without his squeal. Any copper knows that."

"But it's immoral to hire professional thieves," I said.

"Roosevelt," he whispered, "I think *you* should have been the divinity student at Yale, not me. A cowboy clergyman!" He bent over his antique desk. "I'm not without resources. I spoke to McKinley. The President doesn't trust your belligerent attitude. He thinks you'll have us at Spain's throat within six weeks. The people in the War Department are wary of you. Didn't you write to the Governor about raising up a regiment of cowboy desperadoes to fight alongside the Cuban revolutionaries? Revolutions lead to other revolutions. It's a bad habit. We have our own anarchists. I hear you've been receiving letter bombs."

I wouldn't whet his curiosity. "With matchsticks inside, sir, and cartridges filled with sand."

He was no philosopher, this spent candle. Yes, I did try to mount a regiment of my own. We had to get Spain out of Cuba and the Philippines, had to get rid of her European rot. The Spanish fleet was in American waters, interfering with our own destiny.

"No, no," he said. "We cannot have a warmonger sitting at such a sensitive desk."

"And you mean to dissolve the Police Board."

"If I can. . . . You were never a real Republican, Roosevelt. Go back to the Badlands. There you can crusade for whatever you want, and lead a revolution against some ranch. You can have your own colors in the Dakotas. Haven't you noticed? You're political poison. You should not have behaved like a Manhattan cowboy with the saloonkeepers. The lads love their Sunday shandygaffs."

"I was upholding the law," I said.

"*Law, law, law.* But Pulitzer's little girl knows better than a rough-riding Police Commissioner, don't you, Miss Nan?"

And I wondered if *two* pols were now ganging up against me. I'd have to fight against a new alliance—Boss Platt and Pulitzer's pet.

She warbled like a sparrow. Perhaps it was a signal to the man who was a master of birdsongs.

"Senator Platt," she sang, "I'm sure of one thing. I've been on this midnight ramble, and I have yet to taste a shandygaff."

She made the cadaver laugh. He whispered to his errand boy, who returned with a shandy on a silver platter from the Fifth Avenue's bar, which should have been shuttered at this hour.

The Senator was *dee*-lighted with himself. He watched Nan devour her beer and ginger ale in two gulps.

And now the cadaver turned into an elf, played the hapless politician. "I suppose the Commissioner will arrest me for serving alcohol at such a late hour."

I was bellicose, I admit, bullheaded and harum-scarum. Perhaps it was because Papa had been such a peaceful man.

"Senator," I said, "I'm in no mood to arrest you."

"You couldn't," he said, winking to Nan. "Police Commissioners used to wear shiny gold badges encrusted with jewels. A badge like that inspired confidence. And what does my Manhattan cowboy wear? A silver badge that has all the patina and glory of tin."

"Well, sir," I said, "the old badges cost four hundred smackers apiece. Mine costs fifteen. I'll take that as a sign of confidence. . . . Good morning, Senator."

I bowed to His Majesty. I couldn't battle it out with him. I'd have to retreat a little.

We withdrew from the Amen Corner, with pols huddled in every corridor, waiting for a nibble from Senator Platt. Why had he invited Nan into his inner sanctum, where he had allowed no other reporter? Her rise from the criminal class couldn't have intrigued him. She was as wellborn as the Easy Boss himself. Perhaps he wanted her to bear witness to his autonomy over me. I was nothing but dust in his domain—we all were. He ruled like a doge, without mercy or reprieve.

We arrived in the hotel lobby and happened upon an altercation. The house detective was bickering with a lady in a fur coat and a feathered hat. He was very rude to her, this detective was. And he had a superior air, though he utterly lacked her breeding. She didn't wear lip rouge. She wasn't dollied up. I could perceive the situation. She was a guest at the Fifth Avenue who had run up considerable charges and didn't have the means to pay her bill.

The detective pawed at her. "Out, I say. You'll collect your things when you have the cash."

He wouldn't have strutted like that in broad daylight. No manager would have tolerated it. But the detective could make a fuss at five a.m. while there were no other guests around, just a ragged line of political hacks skulking in the corridors.

"Roosevelt," Nan insisted, "you must stop that horrible creature, or I'm gonna break a flowerpot over his head."

But I was paralyzed, as if I had suffered an attack of the colic, or a sulfurous wound. I could barely breathe. I recognized that lady in the feathered hat. She was Mrs. Morris, Elliott's former mistress.

It was Nan who declared war on the house detective. "Sir, do you know who this gentleman is?"

"Santa himself," said the hotel detective, who was having a bully good time in the Fifth Avenue's cavernous lobby, with chandeliers that could have covered a battlefield. His laughter echoed right off the crystal teardrops. "But Santa's a little too late for Christmas."

I could have bitten off this houseman's head. He was as ferocious as a toy grizzly bear. But I was all twisted up at the sight of Mrs. Morris. My bowels churned.

It was Nan who rescued me. "Sir, have you not seen his badge?"

The house detective had a moment of panic. He looked at my red mustache, as if he were appraising a stallion at his own private stable.

"Mr. Roseyvelt? I'm the innocent party here. This vulturous female is a vagrant. She belongs in the workhouse at Blackwell's Island. She's registered here under false pretenses, living off the fat of the land, but the Fifth Avenue Hotel ain't a charity ward, I'll have you know. Her credit is worthless. She signed fake notes."

"I will vouch for her credit. Have the manager call Police Headquarters."

The detective stroked his mustache. "Well, that's a bird of a different feather. And I will apologize to all parties involved."

He didn't apologize. He pulled his derby over one eye and disappeared into that vastness, searching for some other transgression. And I was left with Mrs. Morris and her feathered hat.

"I did not ask for your help, Mr. Roosevelt," she said in a musical voice, with a touch of acid.

Nan must have sensed something familiar in Mrs. Morris' mysterious manner—another lady who had been bitten too hard. "Roosevelt, you have not introduced us."

It seems Mrs. Morris had followed Nan's articles in the *World*—her exposés of Manhattan rookeries.

"Nan," I said, with a catch in my throat, "meet Mrs. Valentina Morris. She was a friend of my late little brother."

"More than a friend," said Mrs. M.

"That will suffice," I answered as direct as I could. "Mrs. Fowler does not have to know your business. You can return to your room."

But she was harder on me than she'd been with the house

detective. "I will not accept your chivalry, Mr. Roosevelt. You are Elliott's hangman brother."

Ellie's hangman.

The colic was gone. I was filled with fury.

"Madam, this conversation is over. *Return to your room at once.*"

But Mrs. Morris would not move. Her face was quivering. She was barely under control. I didn't want to send for the wagon from Bellevue. She could never have gone back to the Fifth Avenue, not as a guest. Her belongings would have been bundled up and delivered to the madhouse.

"Madam," I said in a neutral tone, "my brother deserted his children and his wife—for you."

My words riled her even more—I was like Buffalo Bill shooting candles in the dark. I must have hit the mark.

"Mr. Roosevelt, I never kept Elliott from his children. He was a devoted father. But he did not enjoy your matrimonial bliss. *His* marriage was not blissful."

My temples were pounding. "I will not listen."

She crumpled up in front of Nan, sobbing in the Fifth Avenue's hollow foyer. The chandeliers had their own strange, silent music that seemed to fill the cavern like a sinister balloon. I took Mrs. M. in my arms, shielding her from that eerie silence. Was it to soothe her, or rescue my soul from damnation? I was like some whiskey judge in the Badlands. I'd condemned my brother, stolen him from the daughter he loved—lanky little Eleanor. Indeed, I was the orphan-maker.

"Madam, I beg you, return to your room."

I could feel the heartbeat through her winter robes. It thumped like some great primitive bird. I watched Mrs. M. shuffle toward the passenger cars with a shambling gait. Had I been ripped of all humankind in the Badlands, become as relentless as the cougar?

"Roosevelt," Nan said, "you must show a *little* mercy to that poor woman. It does seem that she did love your late brother."

"She was his paramour," I said, prim as a deacon.

Nan pounced on that word. "*Paramour.*"

"I'd rather end this conversation right now," I said, playing the deacon again.

"No one can hear us," she said, her nostrils flaring with anger. "We are all alone in the lobby of a hotel where your rival reigns like an emperor behind a desk that belongs in a dollhouse."

"The Senator isn't my rival."

"What is he, then?" she asked.

"A son of a bitch."

She laughed. But it did not embolden me. I was not my father's son. I did not have his Brave Heart. Papa could produce the impossible, make my asthma disappear—in our carriage rides through the cold winter, on his own version of the midnight ramble. I could breathe like a brand-new boy as we sped through the deserted streets, with one lantern after the other glowing like a lopped-off head. It was a ride that resembled no other ride, right after the war, when discharged soldiers in random uniforms sometimes haunted the avenues.

Father always stopped for such a soldier, gave him a few coins and asked where he had fought. Perhaps he had helped this very lad during his own days as an Allotment Commissioner. There wasn't another soul who had Papa's sense of service. We'd return after an hour, Papa exhausted, his eyes sinking fast, his beard disfigured in the wind, and I utterly refreshed, reborn on this ramble. . . .

WE STOOD UNDER THE great awning on Madison Square, and stared at the hotel's grandiloquent clock tower, its numerals etched in gold, yet it was not nearly as tall as Edison's arc lamps that lit Broadway with a nocturnal sunrise. I could imagine my own Antarctic moon in the middle of Manhattan—whiter than white. I wasn't done with our ramble. I didn't have to seek out slackers in the tenement district, or worry about some relic from the old Swamp Angels wandering from sewer to sewer after a significant swipe of jewelry or hard cash. There were no Swamp Angels this far uptown.

So I accompanied Nan. Carriages stopped for us on Madison

Avenue, even at this hour, but I waved them on. And then a wagon that resembled a railroad car came to a sudden halt with its team of six horses. The coachman never bothered to look at us.

A door opened. "Get in," a voice barked at us from the interior. We climbed onto the wagon's metal lip and hopped aboard. Pierpont Morgan sat in the cushions with his ruinous nose. He suffered from a rare skin disease that wasn't curable, even with Morgan's millions. And he preferred to sit in the dark, even with his fellow bankers. His nose swelled up like a pocked pear with oozing pores—a wound on his face. Morgan was a singular man. He'd filled this enormous vault with medieval manuscripts and paintings of the Dutch masters—it was his museum on wheels. He had a palazzo on Madison, but the banker didn't like to sleep. He went on his own midnight rambles in this ironclad car.

I had a strange affinity with the robber baron. He'd also lost his first wife, Amelia, who died in his arms, died of tuberculosis. Amelia had walked around in a veil to cover up her gauntness. She was so thin and frail in the end that she couldn't stand up, and Pierpont had to carry her from place to place. He never quite recovered from that marriage. He had a new wife, but she was a blue blood who didn't share his mania for art treasures and suffered from a chronic depression. Morgan had many mistresses. And I didn't approve of the way he trampled upon the marriage bed. But he was as much of a philanthropist as my father, and a grand patron of the Metropolitan Museum of Art. And there was a rumor that he had subsidized a lying-in hospital to provide for his own progeny of illegitimate children. He had melancholic fits where he took to mumbling for weeks at a time. He sat there in the dark, his banker's eyes like burning coals.

Nan introduced herself. "I'm Fowler of the *World*."

"Ah," the banker mumbled, "the famous Mrs. Fowler." We had to strain to catch every word. "Did you not call me a criminal a few days ago?"

"I did, sir."

"You said I do not pay my workers a living wage. But I keep this damn city humming with the men and women I employ. Are you a socialist, Mrs. Fowler?"

"No," she whispered. "But you are a tyrant, sir."

There was a long silence in this rocking carriage.

"TR," Morgan suddenly said out of the darkness, "you must resign. You're massacring the police. The very best detectives have retired rather than face one of your inquisitions. They were dependable. I could count on them."

"Yes, you hired them as your sheriffs," I said. He was the most powerful banker in the world. The President was a dwarf compared to Pierpont Morgan, who served as banker to the United States. But he had short shrift at 300 Mulberry Street. My roundsmen and captains were not beholden to him, and neither was I. He could comfort the Mayor with his millions and promise Boss Platt a palazzo for the Republican Party. I desired none of that swag.

His ire rose up. I could not recognize the Dutch masters in their gilded frames. The pirate with his pulsing blue nose was angry with me. "A man has want of a sheriff in this town, TR. My messengers are being attacked in broad daylight."

"I haven't seen a formal complaint. And you have your own guards," I said.

His eyes blazed out at me. It was the rare man who could stare back at Pierpont Morgan, but I did try. He could bring down empires with a look, and here he sat in his dark carriage, rambling across Manhattan until it was time to appear on Wall Street, or perhaps he wouldn't appear at all, and he would wander in this wagon until the end of his days.

"It would be a mark of weakness," he muttered, "to have messengers from J. P. Morgan accompanied by armed guards."

He had little interest in me now that I wouldn't do what he demanded. And he looked at Nan, who must have reminded him of some lost mistress. "Child, it's impolite *not* to stare at my nose."

The tycoon couldn't intimidate Nan. "I'm not a child," she said.

"Nevertheless, there's still my nose—it oozes. It's septic without a septic tank. Have you read *Cyrano*?"

"Of course," she snapped.

"Well, Cyrano would have frightened the audience out of their seats with a nose like mine."

Nan returned his gaze with her own blue darts. "But he would not have frightened me, Mr. Morgan."

Pierpont Morgan knocked his fists together like a Gaelic chieftain. "TR, I like this little socialist of yours."

His carriage lurched to a halt. The coachman pounded from the roof. We'd arrived at Bysie's brownstone. Pierpont Morgan had already gone on to other matters. We no longer existed in that banker's brain of his. There was a stab of sunlight on the carriage door. We hopped down from the metal lip, with Pulitzer's girl reporter clutching my hand. The horses neighed, and that impossible railroad car hurtled along. I had my own fit of melancholy on Madison Avenue.

Two philanthropists, Father and that financial pirate. They'd founded hospitals and museums and charity wards. I summoned up the image of Papa's beard and broad shoulders, that quiet vitality of his. He didn't have Morgan's thirst for empire. I loved him, and I would have shriveled at the first sign of his wrath.

Oh, Father, you should have survived those damned politicians. You would have made a marvelous Customs Collector.

I could feel a tug at my sleeve.

Sissy had come out onto the sidewalk with her latest companion, Eleanor, my little niece, who wore Sissy's discards and resembled a rag doll with a weak chin.

Sissy bowed to Nan. "I'm his firstborn. Who are you?"

I introduced one and all, while Sissy displayed her badge that the tinsmith had fashioned at headquarters.

"Gawd," Nan said, "a second Commissioner Roosevelt. And is Eleanor your deputy?"

"She will be. I have yet to swear her in." Then Sissy turned to me. "TR, Mother has the ague. And she is not in the mood to countenance any outsiders. But Cook is making biscuits, and Mrs. Fowler must stay."

Nan seemed reluctant to enter Bamie's winter palace. Perhaps my "firstborn" reminded her of the tots she had tossed aside during her long career as a bunco artist. But Baby Lee was hard to resist. She led Nan under the stone steps and into the kitchen. Cook was delighted. Cook followed all of Mrs. Fowler's undercover exposés, her descent into the demimonde without so much as a pocket pistol.

"Do ya wear disguises, mum?"

"There isn't much artistry in a disguise," she said, winking at my red sash. "I prefer a lighter touch."

"But your face, mum. It must be known by now."

Nan shifted expressions, went from a harpy to a young girl. Eleanor and Sissy were entranced. Cook grew hysterical and nearly spoiled the scones.

We all sat around the rugged wooden table, while Cook poured coffee and China tea, with milk and cream and maple syrup.

"Mum, what was your hardest case to crack?"

"I don't have cases," Nan said. "I'm not a Pinkerton. I do not have the power—or the will—to make an arrest. I simply write about what I see."

Cook was bewildered. She'd never talked so much since we had hired her. "There were arrests, mum, after your last encounter."

"Yes, sometimes there's a tiny crack in the underworld."

But she could have been a Pink. She had an acute picture of her surroundings. She sensed the sadness in Eleanor's narrow shoulders, a sadness I did not want to see. I had blinded myself, blotted out my brother's little girl. I played bear with her and the bunnies, let her accompany us on our summer strolls, treated her to ice cream, as if Elliott had never existed and Anna Roosevelt had never lived or died. But it was Nan who whispered to Eleanor, buttered a scone for her, braided her hair. And then she began to shiver. She could have been possessed, riven by some lightning bolt.

"TR," Sissy asked, "does Mrs. Fowler have the ague?"

"I doubt it."

Sissy would not be sidetracked.

"Mrs. Fowler, do you have children of your own?"

Nan broke out of her electric dream. "Yes, Sissy, I'm afraid I do. A girl and a boy. They're both a little older than you and Eleanor."

"What are their names?" asked Sissy, bold as ever.

Nan paused, as if to dredge up her past, like some devilish accountant. "Melody . . . and Paul."

"Melody," my daughter said, "is a most unusual name."

"Mrs. Fowler, Mrs. Fowler," Eleanor asked, jumping up and down with more vigor than I had ever seen, "can they come and play with us?"

"Dearest," Nan said, stroking Eleanor, "that is quite impossible."

Nan clutched her fists, got up from the table, thanked Cook, said goodbye to the girls, and ran out like a waif. She was a waif, and it did not matter how Pulitzer had anointed her, or how many followers she had.

She stopped for a moment to stare at me. "You must not desert that child—Eleanor."

"She's my niece," I said. "I have not deserted her."

"Yet she wears the high socks and short skirts of an orphanage."

I could have had Whitey Whitman's elbows in my face. "She lives with her Grandmamma—in Tivoli-on-the-Hudson," I said. "And half her clothes come from Sissy's closet."

"I am talking about the other half," Nan said. And then Pulitzer's waif wandered into the wind with that haunted look of hers.

I felt like a sea captain who had to face the wreckage he had just helped administer—on land, rather than at sea. This midnight ramble, I fear, had caused more pain than I had ever imagined. I was no Caliban, part monster, part magician. I could not bring back Melody and Paul, whereas little Eleanor, with her hand-me-downs, was almost a picture of Nan's very own grief. No wonder Nan had clung to her—both were members of the same orphanage, an icehouse frozen in time, both were waifs. I doubt Nan would visit me again.

CHAPTER 10

POLICEMAN'S PARADISE, PART THREE

1897

HOUSE OF MORGAN DECLARES
WAR ON MULBERRY STREET
CALLS TEDDY MANHATTAN'S
LITTLE TIN CZAR

THE PAPERS HAD A HOPPING GOOD TIME SCRAPING MY feet to the fire while Pierpont introduced a police commissioner all his own. That damn Pink, Detective Taggart, had been put in charge of the New York office—only he was Major Taggart now, and with a military swagger, too. He'd developed a drag-foot since the last time I saw him. He had the same dyed mustache, but his collar was clean—and starched—in Manhattan. He hadn't lost his Wyoming luster and flair. Taggart and his team of detectives went around in a wagon plated with metal—a gift from the old pirate, I presume. They did whatever mischief they could for Piermont and his cabal of financiers. Quietly, rampantly, they'd become a rival police force, with their own badges, billies, and silver-backed Colts.

Taggart was as cruel and calculating as he had been in the Far West. The Pinks broke up strikes, loaned themselves to landlords affiliated with Morgan, tossing out tenants who were behind in their rent, dragging them down the stairs, two at a time, leaving them in a bundle out on the sidewalk, like so much carrion to be collected. These victims had little recourse. Taggart was willing to take on my Mulberry Street men who got in his way. He would flash his silver badge and claim that local jurisdiction meant a sack of piss to him. He belonged to the "federals," he said. Pinkertons had been the bodyguards of Presidents, and certain Senators on Capitol Hill. But he hadn't counted on the flying squad. My bicycle patrol kept pace with his war wagon, and even the best of the Pinks couldn't outmaneuver Sergeant Raddison. They battled billy to billy in front of the Hester Street stalls, while shirts and ladies' underpants went flying onto the fire escapes, like a tatter of pale flags. Storekeepers and shoppers were caught in the mêlée. But Raddison himself watched over the civilians, while his lads bloodied the Pinks, who were no match for cops in striped trousers and nautical caps.

The Pinks filed a civil complaint. Harassment, they said. And of course they hired Howe & Hummel, with their silky touch and sour perfume. Hummel himself arrived at headquarters with the Major, while Sergeant Raddison stood at my side. He had become one of my aides in his spare time. He was wearing a nautical cap, as if he'd risen out of the East River like a demigod.

"TR," said Silent Abe, looking as rumpled as ever, "you mustn't feud with the Pinks. The Major and you are on the same side."

"And what side is that?" I asked.

"Law—and order."

"Mr. Hummel," I said, "the Major's idea of law and order is much different from mine. He works for Pierpont Morgan, keeps Morgan's enemies in check, and does favors for his friends."

"Now, now," said Silent Abe, "that's a touch unfair. Not one bank messenger has been waylaid since the Pinks arrived."

"Yes, they're busy lads. The Pinks have tossed tenants into the gutter . . . and broken the backs of innocent cigar makers."

"Innocent?" Taggart said with a smirk. "They're all rabble.

They've been inciting riots. They spend whatever time they have manufacturing diabolic stink bombs and tossing them at their own bosses. . . . Commissioner, you are reviled in your own town, while we are cheered wherever we go."

"That's not how I recall it," said Sergeant Raddison. "I had to save one of your own lads from the mob."

"That's a laugh," said Silent Abe. "Does the mob dictate law and order, TR? Then we might as well surrender to savages."

My girl secretary, Miss Minnie, with her coquettish eyes and brilliant black hair, brought around biscuits and cups of hot coffee, pampering the Major with marmalade and spoons of sugar.

"Thank you, Minnie, dear," said Silent Abe Hummel with a biscuit crumbling in his mouth, while the Major stood aloof. He'd posed with his war wagon in several gazettes, and was much too fine for Mulberry Street.

"We will win, Roosevelt, we always do," said the Major. "Even McKinley is on our side. And so is the Mayor. Your midnight rambles haven't changed a bloody thing. Roundsmen still gamble during their tours and enjoy a pail of beer. My men never drink. We aren't open to bribes. Headquarters will be cluttered with ghosts in another six months. Mark my word. . . . Come, come," he said to his lawyer in the pink shirt. "We will get no satisfaction here."

"Ah, but reasonable men have to be reasonable," said Silent Abe, nibbling on a biscuit like a rodent. "Surely we can arrive at an agreement. . . . We'll divide the turf. Major Taggart will have his little kingdom, TR, and you will have yours."

Hummel stared right through my pince-nez and saw that he couldn't arrange a truce between Taggart and Mulberry Street. Silent Abe was certain of his own powers, but not of a Pinkerton with dead eyes. Taggart was a bit sinister, wearing a mustache that hid a face full of scars.

Hummel sighed, sensing his own defeat. Yet Howe & Hummel never deserted a client. "Ah, a compromise, right here. Miss Minnie, will you put down the biscuits, please, and supply us with a steel-tipped pen and a bottle of ink?"

Taggart wasn't buying any of Silent Abe's silk. He had faith in his war wagon and the fealty of his detectives.

"Hummel, can't you tell that the little tin czar is on the way out? We don't require compromises with TR's detectives."

"Then why did you offer to come?" asked Silent Abe.

"To count the cobwebs on the wall."

And he left with his drag-foot, winking once at Miss Minnie.

"Then it will be civil war and a long, long stretch in the courts," said Silent Abe, as he trundled out, looking for Taggart.

Meanwhile, Miss Minnie did her best to hide her affection for the Major out of loyalty to me. His cruelty didn't seem to frighten her at all. Perhaps she was on a holiday of sorts, drawn to macabre detectives with a covenant to kill. It was a dream marriage, and I did not disabuse Minnie of her phantom love affair. Taggart had sized her up for another reason. He wanted to occupy my chair, seize Mulberry Street for himself.

TAGGART MARCHED WITH THE Fenians, scraping along with his drag-foot, had lunch with the Mayor, and was the lion of Newspaper Row. Reporters and photographers flocked to Taggart, followed him and his war wagon from place to place. It didn't seem to matter much that the Pinks trampled upon innocent grocers who were in arrears, smashed their windows, tossed their produce into the streets, and posed with each and every culprit on a pile of foodstuff turned to flotsam on dry land. The Pinks also had their own supply of stool pigeons and made spectacular arrests. They appointed themselves civilian sheriffs, and the courts upheld their right to do so. They captured pickpockets and highwaymen who had come from crime schools in Chicago and Baltimore, plucked them right off the ferry docks and train depots, men in homburgs and fur hats, like bankers wearing handcuffs. They swooped down on a team of burglars in the midst of a prodigious robbery, while my lads at Mulberry Street looked like bunglers and no-accounts—I was the Commissioner of nothing, nothing at all.

Yet I wasn't idle. Manhattan now had twelve exchanges and fifty thousand telephones, and I made sure that headquarters was connected to every precinct, every municipal department, including the Mayor's office, every merchandise mart, and every significant family, the only ones that could afford the subscription price of five hundred dollars. Thus we had our own umbilical cord to certain select souls. We could steer the flying squad into riot areas in a matter of minutes. But my wheelers never seemed to get there first. The Pinks arrived before Sergeant Raddison did. They had an uncanny gift to be at a riot or the scene of a crime.

The Major was either a magisterial detective, or he was privy to information that shouldn't have been in his pocket. He had a source *inside* Mulberry Street. I wondered if that source was my celebrated secretary. Was Taggart romancing Miss Minnie on the sly? I had Sergeant Raddison follow her, I'm ashamed to admit. He went wherever Minnie went. He waited outside the stoop of her Brooklyn tenement, rambled behind her at market stalls, even bumped into Minnie once.

"Why, Sergeant, what are you doing here? Are you in training?"

"Indeed," he said. "I like to track beautiful girls."

The vigil ended right there.

"Sir," the Sergeant said, "it's not your Minnie—unless she and that killer have an unbreakable code."

There was only one other source—the telephone dispatcher at Mulberry Street who directed calls to the precincts. We had a look at his bankbook. Sergeant Fleischer, a former roundsman, was suddenly awash in cash. I did not sit in judgment, relieve him of his pension or his rank. I had to be as wily as the Pinks.

I sat Fleischer down in my office and shut the door.

"When did Taggart first approach you?"

I'd frightened the poor fellow out of his wits. His eyes seemed to recede into his skull, and I could see nothing but two bloodshot balls. "Your silence condemns you, Fleischer. Speak!"

He patted his lips with a crumpled handkerchief, and his mouth opened like a raucous melody.

"It was on the very day the Pinkerton visited headquarters, sir. He slipped an envelope under my seat."

"Laden with cash," I said. That was Taggart's motive in coming here. It wasn't about any mythical truce. He meant to bribe as many coppers as he could.

My former roundsman wasn't a fool. "I think I will need representation, sir—Howe & Hummel."

"Fine," I said. "Have your Hummel. But you'll step into my Commissioner's court and I'll fleece you of everything you own. Hummel is not that fond of paupers."

So Sergeant Fleischer began to sing like a Mulberry Street canary, and thus we had our little ruse. But there was a complication, alas—a fog had settled in and refused to burn off, even in brilliant patches of sunlight. Our bicycle cops banged into civilians and members of their own illustrious unit, but I couldn't permit the fog to let the Pinks slip into their own camouflaged oblivion.

Here I was, sworn to protect the populace as Police Commissioner, and I faked a robbery—at a bridal shop on Grand. I had my dispatcher call this fake crime in to the Pinks. His voice was trembling, but he gave no other signal to Taggart.

"The Major will murder me," Fleischer said.

"He will not. A crime was reported, and you dispatched it to the nearest precinct."

I couldn't be bothered with Taggart's spies, crime reporters from the *World*, who had their cubbyholes across the street from headquarters. What could they discern with their binoculars in such ruinous weather? I'd never catch Taggart on my own. I had to join Raddison and his flying squad as an undercover agent. I borrowed a bicycle, the squad's striped trousers, a woolen cape, and a nautical cap. And we vanished into the fog. We all had our whistles, and our billies tucked under our belts. We had our lamps on; the meager glow didn't do much good in that miasma. Our bicycles were equipped with bells, but the piercing peal was swallowed up by the fog. Our whistles worked. Their shrill bleat seemed to carve a path into the descending dark. Wagons lurched out of our way, as we raced along Mulberry Street. A pushcart went flying—soggy sausages floated in the still air. We avoided pedestrians by Sergeant Raddison's own strange aeronautics. He rose up on his rear wheel like a bronco and was a pinch more visible than the rest of us. And so he was our guide and our compass needle. He had an uncanny gift to locate where we were.

"Mr. Roosevelt, sir, a little to your left, or you'll crash into that horse cart."

Yet we managed to arrive on Grand without a single collision. Grand Street was still Lower Manhattan's great shopping district. The Williamsburg ferry brought a flurry of passengers from Brooklyn in search of bargains and exotic merchandise. They were like a bunch of prowlers, with money in their pockets. They seldom smiled; shopping, it seems, was almost a crime.

We'd come to the land of bridal shops, with an explosion of veils and gowns in window after window. I had selected the Glass Slipper, at Orchard and Grand, as the site of our fictitious crime, because it was the Cinderella of bridal shops. It had an assortment of mannequins that reared up out of the fog like living creatures in their bridal veils.

I dared not dwell too long, not while I wore a billy and was with the flying squad. We hadn't notified the clerks at the Glass Slipper of the little communion with the Pinks that was about to take place. These clerks might have warned the Major. And so they were mystified at the sight of wheelers in front of their mannequins.

"Raddison, what if Taggart doesn't show?'

"He will, Mr. Roosevelt. He wouldn't miss this for the world."

I doubted Raddison for a moment. And then I heard the distant rumble of Taggart's war wagon—it cut through the fog like an ironclad turtle, an amphibious creature that might prosper both on land and on sea. Taggart was the first to leap down, even with his limp. His agents followed right behind him. He'd brought a battery of reporters and photographers to re-enact his arrest of bridal veil thieves, as he imagined a robbery in progress at the Glass Slipper. He dangled half a dozen handcuffs like exotic pieces of jewelry. And he did a curious dance with his drag-foot, a stuttering cakewalk.

He stopped right in the middle of his dance when he saw my wheelers. We should never have arrived first. He couldn't believe that he had been outmaneuvered by a bunch of bicycle boys. But he was nimble enough to shift gears.

He clapped his hands in that infernal weather and looked me in the eye. "You staged this whole affair," he said. "I should have figured—a bridal shop on Grand Street."

And he had to decide how much his private police force was worth. He had his coterie with him. But reporters seemed much more interested in my nautical cap than in a monstrous turtle on wheels and a little lord with a drag-foot. He scattered the reporters and squinted hard at Raddison's broad shoulders. He couldn't risk a battle on Grand Street, with clerks floating about and wax brides in the window.

He returned to his war wagon.

"Roosevelt," he said, "you wasted the city's resources. You'll suffer for that."

And suffer I did.

There were no immediate squabbles with the Mayor's office. But I was summoned to Senator Platt's headquarters. I'd given my bicycle back to the flying squad, and I couldn't race to the Fifth Avenue Hotel in this dense, sepulchral shroud. I stumbled along and arrived on Fifth Avenue by some mysterious fate—it was like wandering into a wet wall, with my lungs a paper windlass about to collapse.

Boss Platt had no petitioners this afternoon. I found him in his Amen Corner, dining on trout almondine and glazed carrots, while he guzzled champagne.

"Will you join me in a glass? Ah, I forgot. You're a teetotaler."

I had to outmaneuver him, if only this once. "Senator, I'll have a sip."

"Boy!" the Easy Boss rumbled with a forkful of carrots and fish in his mouth.

A bellboy in his fifties, wearing a soiled maroon jacket, arrived with a slight case of the trembles. He must have been a lost cousin of Platt's. "Will you bring the Commissioner a flute of the bubbly, for Christ's sake?"

The bellboy disappeared and returned with a flute of champagne. We drank a toast, the Senator and I. "To peace and war!"

Platt winked. "To our peace and other men's war!"

He took another forkful of trout, while the champagne drummed inside my skull. "Bravo," the Senator said, clapping his exquisite, half-female hands. "Roosevelt, you're on the wrong track. Mulberry Street is not for you. You're too visible in the worst sense—staging robberies in downtown bridal shops to undermine the Pinkertons. That won't stick. We have to put you where you can do less damage. I just talked to the President. He agrees. He doesn't want to look at any more cartoons of you in a cowboy hat, lassoing some poor devil of a Republican. You will have another outpost—the State, War, and Navy Building. Congratulations. You're the new Undersecretary of the Navy."

I did not feel enlightened. "And I'm the last to learn?"

Platt had been ten moves ahead of me all along. "That's politics, son. Remember—if you start a war in your first six weeks, you can expect the guillotine."

But he wasn't finished with me, not yet. "You're an infant, Roosevelt. The presidency has nothing to do with reform. It's a paradise of patronage. And don't you forget that. We're kicking you out of Manhattan."

The Senator smiled warily, as much as a cadaver could, among his cortege of henchmen, hacks, and vigilantes—the Senator's Stranglers had silk wires; they got rid of you without much of a trace, sent you into political purgatory.

I swallowed his insults, his taunts. I would never have guessed it, but the muck-a-muck had given me a ticket out of Police Headquarters. I could reform the Navy. Perhaps he and President McKinley didn't care, as long as I was tucked away in the War Department's monolithic castle, kept out of sight.

One of the Stranglers now approached and whispered in his ear. The Senator nodded and picked up the telephone receiver on his desk. "Roosevelt, it's Mulberry Street."

A female corpse had been found floating in the East River. Normally it wouldn't have been my concern. I seldom visited the morgue at Bellevue. But this corpse had been carrying items that did relate to me—letters and a cigarette case from my departed brother. I could tell who it was without a glimpse of her bloated body. Mrs. Valentina Morris. I'd paid her bills religiously. She still had her suite at the Fifth Avenue Hotel, and she chose to take a swim. My own personal roundsman, who looked after me in police matters, asked if I wanted to claim whatever belongings she had of my brother's.

"Commissioner," said my roundsman, "she could be listed as a Jane Doe, and I could collect her stuff."

"No," I said into the mouthpiece of Boss Platt's silver phone. "She deserves better treatment than that. I won't have her shoveled into a paupers' grave at Hart Island."

I didn't lie. I told Senator Platt the sordid tale.

"An apparent suicide, sir. My brother left his wife for this Valentina woman. She loved him. I'm sure of that. She was residing at your hotel."

"Penniless, I suppose," Boss Platt said, stroking his chin with those splendid fingers.

"I took care of her without meddling too much."

I couldn't seem to placate him.

"That's all fine, Roosevelt, but we can't have our new Undersecretary associated with this very sad affair. Go to the morgue, son. Collect whatever you can. But she'll have to be buried as a Jane Doe."

MY ROUNDSMAN SUMMONED A patrol wagon to the Fifth Avenue, and we rode that car right into the heart of an hallucination that was like a blizzard in the Badlands, but without the ice dust that could freeze you in your tracks; we were lost for a while in the lurid atmosphere, a climate in which men and wagons seemed to float. We did arrive at those iron balconies near the East River, where madmen paraded until they were whisked by ferry to Blackwell's Island. Bellevue had its own labyrinth of pavilions. We went right to the morgue, which had a magnificent loggia and a skylight that could have been a dark lozenge in this mysterious patch of weather.

Mrs. M. was lying on a table with a lamp over her and a shower head. She was wrapped in a grubby silk blanket with a tiny part of her bosoms showing. She wore a locket around her neck, a silver locket with a silver chain. The morgue attendant, who wanted to please me, tried to rip the chain from her throat.

"Don't put your filthy paws on her," I shouted in that echo chamber, my voice booming off the walls.

My anger was misplaced, and I bowed to the morgue attendant. But I was much more interested in the chief coroner, who was wrapped in a wrinkled white muslin coat and had a pince-nez with a tassel, like my own. I'd grabbed him away from Philadelphia, offered him a princely sum, far beyond our budget. The Mayor didn't dare intervene. New York's Finest deserved the finest of pathologists. He'd cracked cases on his own, had uncovered significant clues. He lectured everywhere, trained young coroners about the lessons and quirks of *morbidity*. He'd become a myth among other coroners, this Dr. Ferdinand Jessup. His eyesight was almost as poor as mine, and his origins were obscure. He'd been a morgue attendant until he trained at a medical college. He didn't have a Harvard degree, and was no Porcellian brother of mine, but I liked Jessup. I always imagined him as one of my father's protégés, though I doubt he had ever lodged with newsboys.

I squinted at Mrs. M. on the slab, disturbed by her evanescent beauty; drowning hadn't disfigured her, not at all—her mouth had a vivid wetness; her nostrils were perfectly pink, and seemed to stir in the semidarkness. I couldn't help myself, as I imagined Elliott nuzzling her mouth.

"Jessup, was there any hint of foul play?"

I scrutinized his brittle mustache; the chief coroner was unkempt.

"None, Commissioner. Not one bruise or laceration or break in the skin. It was like fishing a mermaid out of the sea. But I fear she was a troubled creature, perhaps prone to severe neurasthenia."

His words hit like a procession of hammer blows. I didn't want to have the Roosevelt colic, not at this death house.

"Jessup, I see a dead woman with a blue sheen. Where are any signs of this damn neurasthenia business?"

"Look at the eyelids, Commissioner, how narrow they've become, how they've lost their elasticity. That's an indication of damage to the human spirit, a kind of rigor mortis of the soul."

I was growing savagely irritated at this unkempt cockatoo. "Jessup, are you some metaphysician now?"

He fondled the ragged ends his mustache. "Commissioner, I deal only in clinical reports."

I had half a mind to send him back to Philadelphia.

"You won't include her on the paupers' run to Hart. I want her buried at Greenwood. I'll provide the plot."

"Understood," he said. "Another Jane Doe from the deep."

I took Elliott's cigarette case and the cache of billets-doux, which Mrs. M. had bundled into a pigskin pouch. I never signed for them—that was the privilege of a Police Commissioner. Still, I felt remorse as I walked out of Bellevue. I'd violated that woman, stolen her love letters.

I gave my roundsman the leather pouch. I had no interest in reading about Elliott's romance. I would have burnt the letters in Bysie's fireplace, with the pouch.

"You tell Jessup, tell him now, that this item *must* not appear in any ledger. The pouch is to be buried in Jane Doe's box."

I waited, stood under the wrought-iron balconies, with the nagging odor of the East River in my nostrils. I could see the madmen perform on the balconies, in the wisps of light. They must have been actors of some kind, players who had lost their reason. I couldn't quite understand their garbled tongue. Perhaps they were speaking nonsense at Bellevue. Like dogcatchers bearing giant nets, their keepers chased them back into the hospital, but they would reappear at another balcony, as if they were irresistible somehow. I wanted to toss up some coins to them, but I didn't dare. I might have been the only spectator, an audience of one. And then the roundsman returned, with a curious light on his back—the noisome smells had abated, as the fog lifted for a moment. His hair was utter gold.

"You told Jessup? Nothing written. No ledger."

"That pouch never existed, sir."

The sun was gone, all gone, and we were back in that nocturnal gray.

I had emasculated Elliott, gutted him, like a trapper, in the name of Roosevelt morality. And I, who had boxed, wrestled, hunted, and remade my pathetic body with an iron will, fell victim to my own wild thoughts. I was on another kind of ramble, voyaging somewhere. By Jupiter, I could see Mrs. M. marching toward the river without her shoes, steadfast, alert—this was no suicide, no leap into the currents. The woman had her own iron will, a sweeping panorama of bliss. Monstrous, yes, but not without a touch of divinity. She'd loved Elliott beyond the point of madness—that, that was a gift. She had turned her own body into a sepulcher with letters she must have memorized and recited in her sleep. And she would have them under the riptides, under the rowers' oars to Hart Island, under all the suicide runs.

The patrol wagon, drawn by an old lame mare, had come through the fog. We climbed aloft, the roundsman and I, sat among nightsticks, battering rams, and other police paraphernalia at our feet.

The driver, a young sergeant in the horse patrol, bearing a handsome set of whiskers, asked in the gentlest voice, "Where to, sir?"

The Dakotas, I wanted to say.

"Ramble a bit."

And we did.

———

MISS MINNIE SERVED BISCUITS to one and all, biscuits she had baked herself in her tiny Brooklyn flat and had carried across the ferry like one of Morgan's own bank messengers. She couldn't stop sobbing.

"We will never learn to survive without you, Commissioner Ted."

She'd been my police "wife," who kept the ogres from my door. I waltzed her around my desk until her crying jags disappeared.

"You'll do fine," I said.

I did not believe in sentimental attachments. I walked where I had to walk like a whirlwind, and then ripped that whole panorama from my mind. I had been that way as a rancher in the Badlands, as deputy sheriff, or Civil Service Commissioner, and President of the Police Board.

I wasn't always fond of souvenirs. But it was Raddison who pierced my armor. I was loath to leave him and the flying squad. His wheelers had chipped in to buy their boss a parting gift, a nautical cap stitched in silver thread. I wore that cap with honor—and with ease. I'd never had a cop with Raddison's magnificent bearing, a swimmer's broad shoulders and the waist of a girl. I remember how we rode like banshees to that bridal shop in the fog and made a fool of Taggart, who had no one to arrest, not even mannequins in a window.

Still, I couldn't avoid Taggart and his beady-eyed detectives, who serenaded me from my own stoop at headquarters.

He's the lad who won our hearts
With his four eyes and white teeth
Terrible, Terrible Ted

I sauntered down the stairs and met Taggart on the stoop with his Pinks. He was smiling like a wicked jack-o'-lantern, wrapped in a silk scarf. "Ta, Mr. Ted."

I bowed to him as uncivilly as I could.

"You, sir, are Morgan's pet tiger. You will not grin the next time we meet. That is certain."

I had a departing Commissioner's final privilege, as I rode across to Long Island City on a police barge, filled with water cannons and firemen's hooks, the captain tooting his foghorn in my honor, while the river roiled beneath us and sprayed my prize nautical cap in foam. I took the rails to Oyster Bay, and pedaled from the station on my final lap as Police Commissioner, on the lookout for the familiar gray wisdom of Sagamore Hill and its slanting roofs.

LITTLE TED WAS THE FIRST of our bunnies to attend a public school, a little clapboard one-room affair at Cove Neck, with sunken floorboards and a potbelly stove. I'd had scant time until now to meet with Ted's classmates, the sons and daughters of local farmhands and silver polishers, several of whom worked at Sagamore Hill. Edith had been far more attentive than I. She'd gone to Bloomingdale's with Baby Lee and had bought out almost half the toy department. She told the clerks that these toys were for public school children at Glen Cove, none of whom had ever had a toy from Bloomingdale's; the clerks met for a moment and decided to chip into the bounty.

And my wife and daughter marched out of Bloomingdale's with a bulging sack of toys. Edith wouldn't distribute the treasure until I spoke to the children.

"The wilderness is all we will ever have," I said. "Animals are our future—and our friends. If you find a bird with a broken wing, you must mend it."

A blond boy, the son of a nearby farmer, raised his hand. "And foxes, kind sir, are they not our friends?"

This lad would become a lawyer, I could tell—another Velvet Bill in the making.

"I found a wounded fox, Mr. Roosevelt; he had escaped one of your hunting parties with a broken leg. I hid him in Father's barn, mended him with a splint. I did not want to return him to the forest—and the fox hunters. I kept him, sir. And he is my friend."

"Your pet," I told him with a certain shiver. I could not lecture to this boy about hunters and the hunted, how his red fox invaded chicken coops, devoured birds and squirrels. I could see the perverse pleasure on Edith's face. She did not admire my trophies, my *kills*. Neither did Baby Lee. Edith had never been mistress of the hunt. I was incoherent with this blond boy, babbling to him about game preserves, and farms where foxes were bred. It was his teacher, Mrs. Cummings, who came to the rescue and asked me about birdcalls. I warbled a duet between a male and female sparrow, the male's constant *chirrup, chirrup*, and the female's brusque, almost belligerent chatter. Even the blond boy lost a little of his glumness, as the children imitated my birdsongs.

That's when Edith opened her sack. She asked the children to shut their eyes, count to three, and express their own deepest desires.

"Skates," said the son of a silver polisher. And Sissy plucked a pair of roller skates out of the sack. The boy nearly *liquefied*.

"A sled," said the daughter of a carpenter. And Sissy pulled out a toy sled with a team of hand-crafted reindeer. Sissy had dolls and fire engines, cap pistols, and windup mice on wheels. . . .

"Mr. Roosevelt," asked the same blond boy with the red fox in his father's barn, "would you have something for my new companion? A toy, perhaps, that a red fox would relish."

I had not been to Bloomingdale's with Sissy and Edith. I had not ravaged the entire toy department.

"Oh, we have a perfect pet," Sissy sang. She dug in with both hands and pulled an article out of the sack's deep well. It was a silk spider on a string.

The blond boy was *dee*-lighted. "Thank you, sir. You are most gracious."

I was rattling off about myself when I had a vision of the rescued red fox bounding across the classroom. The fox had a bit of silver on its coat, a silver spot, like a healed wound. It had the wanton, moonstruck eyes of a hunter, and a slivering black tongue. This room could have been the fox's private henhouse.

But it did not harm the children. Its eyes were emblazoned on me alone. I waited, waited for it to leap. And then this renegade fox began to chirrup like a male sparrow, which was maddening enough, until it broke into human speech.

—*Teedie, you will go from hunter to being hunted*, it intoned.

I would not converse with this fox.

—*You will wear a wounded flag, and walk like a blind man without your specs.*

I could feel a tug at my arm. "Theodore," Edith whispered, "you've been staring at the wall."

The fox had fled. But I could not catapult myself back into this sunken classroom. I was lost, alone, in a land of chirruping children at Glen Cove.

PART THREE

Tank Point

CHAPTER II

SINBAD

1898

M Y LUCK WAS LEONARD WOOD. HE HAPPENED TO BE A Harvard man, with his ruddy color and bullish neck, a football player, *and* the President's personal physician. A veteran of the Indian Wars, he'd served with the Fourth Cavalry and helped capture Geronimo and his renegade band, running them aground while he was still a medical officer in Arizona, put in temporary command of turncoat Apache warriors—these warriors crouched among the high chaparral and tracked Geronimo the way no cavalryman ever could.

Leonard had bristling blue eyes and would often box my ears back in the basement gym at the State, War, and Navy Building. Sometimes I felt like Captain Wood's orphan child.

But he did have the President's ear.

"Well, Wood, have you and Roosevelt declared war yet?"

"We don't have the time, Mr. President," the Indian fighter answered with that golden smile of his. "We were waiting for you."

McKinley had the soft, sunken heart of a chocolate éclair, but he couldn't linger too long, not while the *Maine* sat like a broken relic in the mudflats of Havana Harbor, with 260 casualties to haunt its prior existence as a battleship. Edith had always said I was Sinbad the Sailor, who sallied forth from adventure to adventure, outwitting all his foes, and Sinbad I was. The Secretary of the Navy and the Secretary of War were no match for Sinbad. I requisitioned whatever war supplies I could. The Cuban *insurrectos* were growing stronger with the matériel we gave them. The Spanish regulars rounded up peasant farmers—*campesinos*—and their families in the hillside and herded them into towns that soon became prison camps without a drop of potable water. It was the start of a great famine, with the regulars seizing whatever produce they could find. The farmers lost their teeth. And when our chocolate éclair of a President complained to Madrid about the prison camps, the Spaniards decided to declare war.

It was plain to tell that our Army was in a pathetic grip. The damn generals had been asleep for years. So McKinley grasped at the simplest straw he could find. America would have to scramble for an Army of volunteers, and he settled upon three regiments of cowboy cavaliers—sharpshooters on horseback who could help the *insurrectos* hurl the Spaniards out of Cuba. I won't lie. The myth of the magic horseman had come from me. I had whispered the rewards of a cowboy cavalry as I wandered on the black-and-white tiles of the State, War, and Navy Building, that monolithic castle on Pennsylvania Avenue that looked like a monstrous stone and wrought-iron layer cake.

I was summoned to the offices of Russell Alger, Secretary of War. There he sat, a gigantic stuffed parrot with his committee of generals. "What's this, Roosevelt? You're going to abandon your roost in the Navy Department to command your own regiment of cowboys?" He paused for a moment and winked at the generals. "Well, we decided to give you that regiment."

Having never been a soldier, I did not have the combat readiness to train cowboy cavaliers. I'd have brought chaos and dust balls to my own regiment. That would have dee-lighted the War Department. "I'd prefer to be second in command, Mr. Secretary."

"That's downright insane," said Secretary Alger. "You won't get another offer like this again. The Navy says it's tantamount to an act of war, abandoning your own desk. The Department is in disrepair. . . . And who should command *your* regiment, Mr. Roosevelt?"

"Captain Leonard Wood."

The generals snickered and rolled their eyes. "He's the President's physician, for God's sake," said Secretary Alger.

"But he served in the field," I said. "He was awarded the Medal of Honor. Geronimo and his renegades are prisoners of war thanks to Captain Wood. He captured them using some of Geronimo's own stealth."

The generals snickered again. The fattest of them all, General Shafter, who suffered from the gout and had to sit with his swollen toe on a separate stool, had once served in the same desert with McKinley's current physician and wouldn't mock Leonard's pursuit of the Apaches. "But those savages aren't Spanish sharpshooters, son. We'll be in the tropics, with boa constrictors, mosquitoes, and elephant flies."

The generals squinted hard but saw that I wouldn't relent. "Wood it is," the Secretary said. "*Colonel* Wood, and you'll wear the rank of lieutenant colonel . . . in your cowboy regiment."

The Secretary was convinced that I'd stumble hard and fast and would be back at my desk in a matter of weeks. "You can't turn rough riders into a regiment. It's never been done."

Fightin' Joe Wheeler was the only one I respected among that whole lot. He was a little over five feet tall in his cavalryman's boots. He had a wizened beard with gray streaks, and he wore a pair of women's white gloves to hide his tiny hands. He'd fought on the Confederate side as cavalry master and the youngest general in the Army of Tennessee. General Joe knew how to dance on a horse, and here he was in his women's white gloves.

"Roosevelt," he said in his Southern lilt, "I suppose Wood will have you hike to Florida and pardon Geronimo's Apache warriors."

"Why in hell would he do that?" asked General Shafter, shaking his swollen big toe.

"Because," said that bantam rooster of a general, "Injuns make the best damn scouts."

The other generals barked in their tunics and brilliant white galluses, but Wheeler wasn't wrong. The regiment would have to rely
on Indian trackers and scouts.

"What about the colored cavalry?" the Secretary asked. "Ain't
you gonna enlist some Buffalo Soldiers?"

"Well," said General Shafter, "Injuns are one thing, but we
wouldn't want to mix colored and white."

"The Comanche feared the Buffalos," said Little Joe Wheeler.

Shafter kept wiggling his toe. "Still, they're with the Ninth and
Tenth Cavalries, and they'll stay there."

"Say," the Secretary said. "Weren't there black cowboys? Roosevelt, you must have met a few."

I did, indeed. They were among the finest ropers I had ever seen,
and they could have walked through a blizzard in their chaps.

Shafter stared the Secretary down. "You can't have black cowboys in a cowboy regiment. It won't do. We'd better leave our lieutenant colonel to his business."

And I was dismissed by Shafter with a wave of his hand. These
Army men had a club all their own, and I was an interloper, a stray
pigeon.

Our recruitment office was in the underground labyrinth of the
War Department's castle, cluttered with meandering passageways
and foyers, which also served as the recruitment office of Shafter's
Fifth Army, but *his* was a deserted pavilion. We had little else but
cardboard signs for the First United States Volunteer Cavalry Regiment. The War Department vilified us, announced that our regiment wouldn't last. The generals called us "a red ribbon of noise."
Yet candidates arrived from everywhere, one by one. Possible
recruits found a path to our little dungeon. Some were half blind;
others were octogenarians or were missing an arm or a leg. And I
had to turn them away without much of a remark. "We're looking
for cavalrymen."

"I can ride like the wind," said the man with a missing arm.

But we'd acquired a sudden fame, as we captured America's

fancy. There were articles about us in *Harper's* and the *Nation*, and in the jingo press. We were dubbed "Roosevelt's Rough Riders," even if it wasn't really my regiment, and some of the riders weren't rough at all. Reporters pecked at us like a pack of hens. I appeared in all the papers, and my lieutenant colonel's uniform hadn't even arrived from Brooks Brothers. I had to pose without my gauntlets and campaign hat, with the regiment's crossed sabers insignia. We were marginal at first, basement bums and bravos. But candidates kept coming out of nowhere, covered in dust. We had ten thousand volunteers in two weeks. I sat like a deacon behind my little desk, within a welter of rat holes and warrens that belonged to the Army regulars. I couldn't accept much more than one out of twenty volunteers. We had polo players from the finest clubs, quarterbacks from Harvard and Yale, five or six masters of the hounds, frontier marshals, mounted policemen from my bailiwick in Manhattan, cattle drovers, and cowboys.

"But it will take more than saddle tricks. And are you willing to learn?"

I wasn't squeamish. I had taught myself to measure a man, to gauge his heft and the weight of his words. But I had the devil of a time with critters who had worked with me in the Badlands and at 300 Mulberry Street, friends, acquaintances, rivals—and enemies. The easiest of all was Sergeant Raddison of the flying squad. He'd become the squire of a far more sophisticated bicycle patrol since I'd seen him last. He had half a precinct all to himself, with two hundred wheelers and a "stable" to house his bikes. There'd been songs written about Raddison and his wheelers. He could have run for Mayor. But he volunteered to join my pony boys.

"Raddison, I'll be clear. Can you ride a horse? You can't coast your way through the chaparral."

"Colonel, I've been taking lessons with the mounted patrol. I wouldn't shame ya, would I?"

I wanted to sign him up as a lieutenant in the First Volunteers and name him second in command of our "New York" contingent, which turned out to be Troop K. But Raddison wouldn't hear of it. He'd never been that fond of officers. A sergeant he was, and a sergeant he would remain.

I was disheartened by the next volunteer. I had promised that we wouldn't accept any desperadoes or Stranglers from Dakota, and here was Red Finnegan standing in front of my desk. Red had served twelve years of hard labor inside the State Pen at Bismarck. That crop of red hair had gone all gray. He seemed brittle. He had the same shivering hand, kind of hard for a gunman.

"Red, I can't bring an outlaw into the First Volunteers. The War Department wouldn't condone it."

"I served my time, Mr. Roseyvelt. I'm a solid citizen. I have a cattle ranch."

And the son of a bitch had letters of recommendation from ranchmen I remembered. He'd gone right back to the Badlands from Bismarck. He'd been on a posse or two, had broken up a band of rustlers.

"I've scratched out a living as best I can."

I asked Red how old he was. He said it was hard to say. He couldn't recollect much about his childhood. He was orphaned as a little boy. A one-eyed farmer had raised him in that desperate country, had beaten him with a strap. Red Finnegan ran from the farmer with nothing but his shirt. "You can call me fifty, Colonel, give or take a season."

I'd turned away volunteers more qualified than Red. But he had that warlike spirit I admired. And the curious honesty of men groomed in the wild. He stole my skiff, and left a glove as his signature. That was Red's style. I signed him up with alacrity.

"But you're on notice, Red Finnegan. One bad play, and you're out."

He started to blubber right near my recruitment officers. He wanted to kiss my hand.

"Jesus, Colonel, you're my second chance. I'll make the First Volunteers proud as hell."

I had to whisk him out of there, with all the volunteers waiting on a line that almost stretched to the President's palace on Pennsylvania Avenue. The Army regulars began to grumble. They didn't have a parade of volunteers to fight the Spaniards in Cuba. They hardly had a volunteer at all. And I was sending lads back out onto the street, lads who didn't make a perfect fit. But I was troubled when the man with iron whiskers appeared—Taggart, that paid killer, had come with two of his Pinks.

"You aren't welcome here, Major. I can have you and your cronies escorted from this place, or you can clear out on your own steam. I have nothing more to say. You pollute whatever venue you're in. I suppose Pierpont Morgan will reward me with a bundle if I enlist you in the First Volunteers."

I'd rattled him. I could see the chiseled marks on his face. "Wait a minute. That isn't fair, Four-Eyes."

Now I was the one who began to bristle. "You will address me as Lieutenant Colonel Roosevelt, while you're on military grounds."

I hadn't been commissioned yet, but he saluted me with a lightning whip of his hand. "You need fighters, Colonel, and I've been fightin' since I was fourteen."

"Why aren't you back with the Pinks?"

"That's the whole point," he said. "The Pinks are a civilian army. We've been taught—"

"To maim and kill, Major Taggart?"

His steel-blue eyes softened a bit. "Ain't that a soldier's misfortune? We've wandered across a hundred territories. You wouldn't have to train us. We're born pony boys."

But I was mean to the Major. "With that drag-foot of yours? We don't enlist cripples. It's against the law."

He smiled under that thick mustache. "I wouldn't drag my foot on the back of a pony, sir. And ask anyone at our national office. I'm a miracle to behold with a carbine or a Colt."

I could have had that killer under my command, my own private Pinkerton. I'd abuse him, like a baby deprived of toys. I wanted to strip him of his varnish, mustache and all. But I couldn't bear to have him in our ranks.

"Taggart, didn't I warn you on the steps of Police Headquarters that you wouldn't have another chance to grin? Get out of my sight."

The son of a bitch was used to having his way with most people. "I'll sit down with the President and Pierpont Morgan. Four-Eyes, we'll see who wins."

He'd come into our dungeon with carbines and campaign hats, and left without a slot in the First Volunteers. It wasn't his drag-foot. I'd sworn in one or two cowboys with a twisted leg. We had our own surgeons, our own doctors' reports. We didn't rely on the regulars.

Taggart and his two killers had unsettled me. I should have torn the roots out of their hair, robbed them of whatever dignity they had. Instead, I'd let them walk out in campaign hats they had no right to wear.

WE SHUTTERED SAGAMORE HILL, locked the icehouse, left the orchards bare, and moved with the bunnies to a little house across from the British Embassy. My wife had been feverish for months. An abscess was found in her abdomen and had to be removed, while I was still stuck in that damn cellar, enlisting volunteers. The surgeon's ether had made her delirious, and I had to rush from my palatial cavern to N Street several times a day. Colonel Wood was her physician as well as mine, but he had to leave for San Antonio—that was the training ground he had selected for the Rough Riders. So I was put in charge of all local recruits, the Cowboy Colonel with his Brooks Brothers tunic and a saber that caught between his legs.

"Sinbad the Sailor," Edie said, recovering from the ether, "my poor darling Sinbad."

She was pale as a ghost under her gown.

"I can tell Leonard to find himself another lieutenant colonel. . . . I'm not indispensable, you know."

"But Sinbads are scarce," she warbled, teasing me a little. "Dearest, I would *die* if you didn't go."

Bamie was in the dining room, her darkened face in the shadows. She'd married her beau, Lieutenant Commander William Sheffield Cowles, in 1895, and had come to stay with us while her husband was at sea. I didn't mind a bit of nepotism in behalf of my big sister and her husband. I'd abetted Commander Cowles' career, given him a lethal toy to play with, a cruiser rather than a gunboat. Bamie was beholden to me. She checked her sharp tongue, but there was a rift after Ellie's death that could not be mended no matter how hard I tried. She blamed herself as much as she blamed me. She should have been more of an advocate for Ellie, should have persisted, like those two charlatans Howe & Hummel. We did not talk about Ellie, not ever, not now.

"Edith is ill," I said.

"We will manage, Teedie—a war cannot wait."

"But I do not have to leave for San Antone. My troopers can exist without me."

Her face, a bit sallow, rose out of the shadows, with that crisp, biting smile. Father had trained her well. That corrosive willpower had been there, even as a little girl, when she had to fight servants and tradesmen, while Mittie had one of her punishing headaches and Father was "abroad," as Mr. Lincoln's Allotment Commissioner, wandering about in his winter cape.

"Teedie, *you* are the regiment. It is a sham without your services. So do not pretend. Modesty is not your strongest suit."

"So I'm a cardplayer now—a gambler," I said.

"As you have always been. You wrapped that poor Secretary of the Navy around your little finger. He did not have your sense of politics—Mr. Secretary Long."

"He preferred his garden," I said, "to his secretariat."

"And you encouraged him, lulled him to sleep."

She could have been my quarterback. She'd memorized all my maneuvers.

"That precious old dear," I said. "He couldn't really run the Navy."

"So you ran it behind his back, and while he was tinkering with his rosebushes, you had every warship painted battle-gray."

"Was I supposed to stand idle?"

She laughed with a bitter taste. "Men and their war toys," she whispered. "I would have gone to Cuba with a white flag. . . . Teedie, you'll miss your train."

She touched my cheek with a certain tenderness, yet she was not feeling tender today. She curtsied once, and went into Edith's room, shutting the door behind her. That was not the end of her little sojourn. She ventured out again, stood high on her special shoes, thrust her arms around me with a flailing gesture, and said, "Theodore, I'll kill you if you don't come back alive."

QUIETLY RAMPANT, WAITING FOR the real war to begin. We were a regiment without regimentals. We did not have enough drinking water, and we had to bathe in the silver quiet of the San Antonio River. The quartermaster general could not provide enough horses and uniforms for the Rough Riders. Worthless trinkets and bits of machinery arrived by express, and our rifles sat among the lost cargo in some forgotten freight train. But we did have a mascot, a six-month-old mountain lion named Josephine, who pawed at us like a princess. We fed her whatever scraps we could spare. She trained with us in the mesquite, running after the tails of our blue flannel shirts, swam with us, and when she disappeared at night, I figured that she slept in a far corner of the State Fair grounds—three miles from the heart of San Antonio and the Menger Hotel—that had become our headquarters and campsite. Without dog tents, my boys had to sleep in the Fair's abandoned exhibition hall and grandstand. But I'd had a wall tent delivered from Abercrombie & Fitch, and when the morning bugler woke me after my second night in camp, I found Josephine snuggled beside me on my cot, whisker to whisker. There was no confusion in her enormous gray eyes. The little mountain lion was in love with me. I could have had her banished from camp. But the bravos from Arizona who had arrived here with her would have been disheartened. I allowed her no other liberties than an occasional lick of my face . . . and the dead field mice she brought into our hearth. She was a huntress, after all.

Attrition was our problem, not Josephine, that relentless loss of bravos. Boys would sneak out of camp after taps, catch the electric trolley to San Antone, with its chocolate-colored roof, and some of them never came back. Half our boys were loners, after all, buckaroos, and might have enjoyed a cattle drive, but not the mortifying monotony of regimental drills. If they did return, it was after a squall in a downtown saloon, where they smashed half the mirrors and stripped the bar of all its zinc. A court-martial wouldn't have been appropriate. I would have had to abandon them to the guardhouse at Fort Sam Houston. And Fort Sam was filled with Army regulars and officers who couldn't have appreciated cowboy cavaliers. Some of these bravos I kept, and others I sent home with a ten-dollar bill from the Rough Riders' "treasury," meaning my own pocket.

Still, we were losing men at an alarming rate. They wanted to fight, not run along the riverbank, ride on a chocolate trolley, and bivouac in a converted State Fair. I worried that the regiment would drift away. Perhaps the Secretary of War and his generals were right, and cowboy cavaliers couldn't be broken in, like the wildest broncos. And that's when Major Taggart showed up with a cadre of Pinks, sporting the blue neckerchiefs with white polka dots that I had taken to wearing and had become the official Rough Rider rag.

"I didn't send for you, Major," I said in front of my own troopers, with blue ice in my voice. "You aren't welcome in this camp."

He had the demonic look of a Pinkerton home from a kill.

"But you need us now, Colonel."

"Did you hear that from a passing crow?"

"Yeah," he said, "a crow called the Secretary of War. . . . We're trained, sir. We won't desert you or let you down."

I was caught between a lovesick mountain lion and the damages I had to pay for the havoc my bravos had visited upon the saloons of San Antone. I weakened a bit. I was bleeding boys every day.

"One false move, and you're gone. You won't have your Pinkerton ranks, none of you. Is that clear, Private Taggart? You'll report to the regimental commander tomorrow, and be sworn in—but not until you pass your physical."

He saluted me with that same old arrogance of a Pink, and went off to find a billet in the exhibition hall.

And now Bellows, my body-servant, was acting up. He wore a sergeant's stripes on his sleeves. He'd been a Buffalo Soldier, had served in the old Ninth Cavalry, had decimated the Comanche in the Indian Wars. I'd come to rely on him, on his way with horses, on his judgment of men. I felt a little lost without him. He'd broken in my mount, Little Texas.

"Have I been unfair to you, Sergeant?"

"That's the thrust of it, sir. I'm not a proper sergeant. I'm your valet."

"But I haven't deprived you of your stripes," I said. "Your rank is secure."

He was a handsome devil, over six feet tall. "Your own officers *see* a valet. It don't matter what stripes I wear."

"But you'll fight beside me—in Cuba."

He laughed, and revealed the gold teeth that some wandering dentist had presented him with in Cheyenne country. "You mean, I'll carry your sword."

"Fight, fight," I said. "I do not require a sword carrier, Sergeant Bellows."

"But there's an opening in my former regiment, sir. And I'd rather go to Cuba with the Ninth."

I panicked, that's how dependent I'd become on Bellows. He instructed me how to behave like an officer with one or two bits of pantomime and a wink of the eye. He'd groomed Little Texas, sharpened my saber on the wheel.

"I'll stay, sir, until the regiment is battle-ready. But I'll require your signature—and your blessing—to rejoin the colored cavalry."

"And you shall have it," I insisted, slapping my own leg with a glove. And Bellows did serve as a kind of shadow drill master. He was a far better soldier than the bravos we had mustered in San Antone. He helped me shape the regiment, often with a whisper in my ear. "Don't relent, Colonel. And don't tug on your mustache. It distracts the men." He was beside me at every maneuver, at every rush of an imaginary foe. We seized every hill, created pandemonium and showers of sand. I was also startled by Taggart and his Pinks. They fell into line, answered every bugle call. I loved the sweat of it, with my bone-white galluses riding below my kneecaps. Finally we all had our mounts, and we rode in fours across the plains. I had a schooner of beer with some of my bravos, and was summoned to the commander's tent.

"TR," he said, "you are neither their confessor—nor their friend. If you cannot separate yourself, they will ride past and never follow you into battle. You will be left stranded on some forlorn hill, clutching your own flag."

I had never seen such anger in Leonard Wood; his jaws were quivering. These cowboy soldiers demanded a special kind of familiarity and trust, but I wouldn't disobey my commander, even if I had picked him myself.

I saluted Leonard. "Sir, it won't happen again. No more beer parties with my troopers. I'll give up the luxury of being comrades. They'll have to feel my thunder, Leonard."

Yet our rifles still hadn't arrived. And we had to trudge through the mesquite with broom handles, like trick soldiers out on a picnic. On one such excursion, with Troop L, we happened upon a company of scouts from Fort Sam—Army regulars in irregular costumes, who must have wandered off the mark, or they wouldn't have trespassed on our training ground. I did not like it. They wore Apache headbands, ponchos, bullet pouches, leggings made of rags, and they hopped about on bare feet. But they were equipped with carbines, and we were a bunch of hawkeyes with broom handles. Their captain was also dressed in tatters. You could barely see his eyes under the war paint.

"Well, if it ain't Roosevelt and his Rough Riders. You, sir, are supposed to be our savior. And you're nothing but a four-eyed runt with broken suspenders."

I was readying to rip him off at the neck. But Bellows stopped me in my tracks. "There's something poisonous about this chance meeting. They'd bury us, Colonel, if they could. They're itching for a fight."

"Tell that boy to quit buzzing in your ear," the captain said. "Roosevelt, are you our savior or are you not? I suggest that you all strip down and do a little war dance with your assholes in the air. Well, I'm waitin'. Show us some of that moral fiber that the Rough Riders are made of."

"Captain," I said, "we will not strip."

"That's dandy. Then let the boy do it."

Bellows smiled and tilted his slouch hat.

"That ain't satisfyin' at all," the captain said. He and his bravos cocked their carbines. And that's when Private Taggart and his Pinks pranced out of the wind and dust. They hadn't been assigned to a troop. And they must have followed us into the mesquite country along the riverbank. They hadn't surrendered their carbines to our munitions officer.

"Colonel, sir," Taggart said, "pay these mischief-makers no mind."

I clutched the captain by the collar of his leather jersey, and dragged him across the mesquite.

"Who sent you here to belittle us?"

"The generals," he said. "The generals—at Fort Sam."

Bellows cautioned me to reflect before I ruined us all.

I bathed bare-assed in the river, then returned to my tent with its portable writing desk, put on my parade colors from Brooks Brothers, and went into San Antone in a regimental supply wagon, with Josephine on a leash. My driver considered me a maniac. We arrived on Alamo Square in the middle of a wedding procession, and the bride, who wore a blue veil, couldn't take her eyes off our mascot.

"What's his name, Excellency?"

"She's a girl," I told her.

"Well, that's original," she said and nuzzled Josephine, who licked her hand and then trooped with me into the Menger, the most *rarefied* bar in Texas. Senoritas did not dance on the zinc. The bar was all done in cherrywood, with lanterns and mirrors that lent very meager light. Deals were made at the Menger bar— it thrived in darkness. It was the watering hole of cattlemen and senior officers at Fort Sam. I'd intruded upon the privilege of their utter privacy with a mountain lion on a leash. I sat Josephine at my heels and fed her the local draft from my schooner. She did not growl once.

An aide of the provost marshal at Fort Sam tapped me on the shoulder. "TR, have you really brought a wild beast into the Menger?"

"Josephine ain't wild," I riposted. "She's the regimental mascot. And I don't like generals at Fort Sam sending scouts into Rough Rider country to rile us up. I don't like it at all. Should it occur again, I'll consider it an act of war."

It was an act of war, but I didn't expect Colonel Wood to read it that way. I was prepared to resign my commission.

"I will not fight if I cannot protect my own men."

It was the first time I saw Leonard laugh in weeks.

"The staff officers resent us. We're in the news, and they're not. . . . But, damn you, Teddy, did you have to bring Josephine to the Menger Hotel?"

"That was better than an all-out attack on Fort Sam."

Leonard laughed again. "Count your lucky stars that there weren't any reporters snooping around. If Josephine had landed on the front page of the *San Antonio Express*, we'd have to disband the Rough Riders. And not a single one of us would ever get to Cuba."

Our rifles arrived in an Army ambulance. We trained in the

dunes with live ammunition that sputtered in the sky like defective firecrackers. Some of my bravos rode in the mesquite in flared leather flaps. Colonel Wood said that our cavaliers ought to have machetes in the Cuban chaparral rather than the sabers of traditional cavalrymen—sabers couldn't cut into tangled, snakelike roots. But the quartermaster general wouldn't listen, and our damn machetes never arrived. And then we got the call. The War Department said we had to pack up and leave for Tampa; took us twelve hours to assemble our gear. And we rode in cavalry formation, with our buglers and our guidons, to the railroad tracks. We must have looked like nothing but a mirage to the farmers and watermelon boys at the wayside, coming out of the dust as we did, near a thousand strong.

No ordinary depot could have handled such a load of horses, mules, fodder, and men. We had to rely on the Union Stock Yard, because our assemblage was more like a cattle run than a shipment of horse soldiers. There weren't enough cars to carry all the Rough Rider mounts. We waited at the tracks for other Southern Pacific cars and engines to arrive. Whatever cars came still couldn't support a regiment. And our boys were packed like cattle heading to some Chicago slaughterhouse, with the sting of manure in their nostrils. Colonel Wood and I were in an open-air caboose with Josephine, who nearly slipped on the gelatinous blood from earlier cattle runs. I carried buckets of water and tepid coffee to as many boys as I could, but my arms failed me after a couple of hours. And Sergeant Raddison, who was with H Troop now, grasped the buckets without a word and continued along the aisles; he moved with the same silent deliberation as the bicycle-riding cop who had started the flying squad.

We were mobbed at every station along the route. Folks welcomed us to their own little war parades. Half-mad women scribbled letters to Rough Riders they had never met and would never meet again. Some proposed outright marriage. A few of our bravos fancied a particular lady and disappeared from our caravan of seven trains. Leonard cursed their hides. But these bravos managed to find us at the next station, or the next after that. A horse died of heatstroke, but we didn't lose a bravo, not one. People would shout from the tracks, "Teddy, Teddy, Teddy," and I realized why the Army regulars hated us so. We had captured the imagination of blood and battle somehow—the Rough Riders represented the romance of war. We could have risen out of some biblical rapture. The Army couldn't compete with cowboy cavaliers.

OUR CARAVAN FINALLY ENDED at some siding on the pine flats, in the middle of nowhere. The railroad men refused to deliver us to the Tampa depot. I couldn't tell if it was out of spite, or on strict orders from the Fifth Army Corps—it might have been a bit of both. And so we had to muster in that lonely place, near a sinking pyramid of ashes, grab our belongings, and ride our mounts in the middle of the night to the Fifth Army campground, a tent city on a savannah of sand—it stretched for miles like some illusion, though the array of snoring and farting soldiers was real enough, like a battlefield where the dead jostled back to life. Still, there was no one to greet us, or point us to our own site. We had to find it ourselves, amid the panorama of tents. It was a pathetic space on a broad sand flat, a bald spot nestled within a scatter of pines, a mile from the Tampa Bay Hotel.

Tampa was beginning to lose its allure; it had become a tiny metropolis of cigar makers, retired jockeys, and panhandlers, who congregated on Twiggs Street; most of the tycoons absconded with their retinue of railroad cars to Palm Beach and avoided Tampa's meager one-line track. The hotel had shut down for the summer, but had to open again to accommodate General Shafter and his Fifth Army Corps. That monstrosity with its minarets had become the headquarters of our invasion force. It was like a Moorish nightmare with a park of screaming peacocks, walkways that stretched a mile, a cavalcade of keyhole arches, and a myriad of silver domes. You could get lost wandering from room to room, and grow dizzy looking at treasures plucked from every European capital. I sat on one of Napoleon Bonaparte's gilt chairs. It gave me little pleasure to do so.

I did have some pleasure in that castle with its priceless hall of mirrors. Officers, junior and senior alike, weren't allowed to bring their wives to Tampa Bay. But Leonard declared an exception to the rule. He prescribed appropriate "medicine" for my wife—a rest cure at Tampa Bay, and not even the Fifth Army's high command dared contradict the President's physician.

I'd been in contact with Edith as much as my regimental duties allowed. Sister wrote me every day about my wife's condition. I'd managed to talk to Edith on the telephone exchange at Fort Sam. And here she was in the lobby of the Tampa Bay Hotel, with its forest of palmettos and silver chandeliers.

"Sinbad," she said, half her face hidden in a flouncy white hat, "you've grown thin as a rail. Don't they feed lieutenant colonels in your part of the world?"

I let out a Rough Rider roar. Generals looked up from their field maps and newspapers. Journalists froze in the middle of a phrase.

Ya-ha-haw!

Edie looked right into my eyes like the twin beads of a shotgun. She wasn't shy around that rotunda of generals. "I missed you more than any woman has the right to miss a man."

I had to stifle a second war cry. "You're the one military wife allowed in this damn hotel."

"I'll need more purchase than that."

"You have a rival," I said.

She seemed to startle herself out of her skull, under the flounce of her hat. And then Edith smiled. "Sinbad, is she friend—or foe?"

"She's a cougar cub named Josephine."

Edith didn't pause a moment to parse her words. "Then I'll duel her to the death."

And we explored that lunatic asylum of a hotel, built on the sand flats, so that you stepped in sand on every floor. But the sand couldn't be swept away. It clung to the carpets and the windowsills, blew across the rotunda whenever a door was opened. It clung to your teeth like gristle. Edith wrapped a silk scarf around herself like an Arabian princess. Still, she constantly had to shield her eyes. And I wondered if sand rather than Spanish snipers and yellow fever would destroy our invasion fleet.

Famished as we were, we had supper in the dining room with several boys from Troop H, while regular officers at the other tables looked at us askance, as if we were consorting with the enemy. There was no point in trying to explain the Rough Rider morale. We were cowboys, not cadets.

A lieutenant colonel in the First Volunteers couldn't have much of a vacation with his own damn wife. I had to return to the Rough Riders at five a.m. for reveille. So I had a few lovely hours beside Edith in one of the castle's mountainous beds, watching the curl of her lip as she slept. And the next morning she rode into camp in a regimental bucket. She watched us drill in the dunes, one Troop resisting the cavalry charge of another in all that extravagant sand.

And then there was that fated meeting with Josephine. She was trotting along on the savannah when she espied me with my wife. She growled deep within her throat, but that mountain lion was amazing. She must have sensed that defying Edith wouldn't work. So she sauntered over, lay down in the sand with her paws in the air, and allowed Edith to rub her belly. There wasn't much a man could do with these felines.

The regiment had a dance in Edith's honor on that last night of her stay in Tampa town. We seized one of the ballrooms for ourselves and invited Generals Wheeler and Shafter of the Fifth Corps. Shafter was like a hippopotamus as Edith disappeared within the folds of his tunic. He wheezed and had to hop about on one foot, but the commander of the Fifth Corps didn't decline to dance. And Wheeler did the Virginia reel with Edith like a runt in gold epaulettes. He was the wiser of the two generals. And I would have trusted his instincts in battle. He had decimated the Union Cavalry in the late war. But Chickamauga wasn't the Cuban chaparral. . . .

I escaped reveille and accompanied Edith to the Tampa depot.

"The generals value you, Theodore," she said, with a nervous lisp.

"But they do not value our regiment. And I worry that Shafter will leave us behind, sentence us to a second or third run to Cuba. And we will miss the show."

"Ah, he might sentence you in his dreams. But he cannot fight a war without the Rough Riders," she said with a wan smile. "You, dearest, are the show. And that is what I fear most—that you and your men will *always* be in the line of fire."

I had trinkets for the bunnies—a saber for Alice, with a shark-skin hilt; a campaign hat for Ted; an old, disused pistol for Kermit; an Indian doll I had found for Ethel in the markets of San Antone; shell casings for Archie; and a rattle that Bellows had made with bits of wire, wood, and quilt for Baby Quent. And I'd strung together a necklace for Edith out of an old silver chain and Indian beads that were clear as crystal.

"My war trophy," she whispered, as I clasped the chain of beads around her neck.

"Edie, we ain't been to war. We're congregating in the sand."

I nuzzled her as hard and as long as I could. The coach started to move. And I had to hop off, in my campaign hat. It felt like a bad omen, that sudden leap. And the news hit like lightning bolts. The utter idea of a cavalry in Cuba had been abandoned by the Fifth Corps. There wasn't enough room on the transports for thousands of horses. Only senior officers could have their ponies. And Shafter couldn't fit all twelve of our Troops onto the first expedition force. We would have to leave four Troops behind. We were horsemen without horses, a makeshift infantry. I wondered if Shafter was doing this to punish the Rough Riders for our panache, for that wildness of spirit, for our ability to use a lariat and perform somersaults. I was prepared to march on headquarters.

"Don't," Leonard said. "TR, you'll ruin whatever little cachet we have left to get ourselves onto that first invasion fleet."

"Leonard, you're wrong. We have no cachet, none at all."

If we were pariahs among the military, we did have some pull with the journalists. Just before the invasion of Cuba that half-forgotten monstrosity in the sand had become the most famous hotel in the world. It was packed with journalists and foreign attachés. And I happened to be on familiar terms with William Winters-White, the deacon of war correspondents, who was still in his thirties and trotted wherever he could, with an umbrella, a sun hat, and a Colt. Will worked for the *New York Herald*, and readers were drawn to his poetic style. He talked about being "swallowed in sand at this perverse Alhambra by the sea." He was no friend of the Fifth Corps; Winters-White said Shafter and his generals were idiotic. Tampa was the worst possible embarkation point, since it had only one railroad track. Shafter's army of twenty thousand was "like a camel balancing on a pea pod. . . . It will arrive in Cuba in the midst of its own nightmare."

Will hadn't been much kinder to me when I was Police Commissioner. He excoriated the Department over the blue laws, said I had no right to deprive the workingman of his Sunday pail of beer. But he did admire ex-Sergeant Raddison of the flying squad. And now Will suddenly admired me. He rode on the train with us from Texas to Tampa, did articles on the Rough Riders and its Indian scouts, on the Pinks who served with us, on a reformed desperado like Red Finnegan—"Mr. Roosevelt will never deem a worthy man unworthy"—and all the Harvard football players and cowpunchers from the Badlands. He had lacquered us in solid gold, and turned every Rough Rider into a mythical creature, half man and half bull, like the Minotaur.

But he had his own astounding tale to tell. Winters-White was his nom de plume. His real moniker was Alfred McCann. He'd once been a tyke at the Newsboys' Lodging-House. He became a printer's devil at eleven, fashioned words in his own fist, broke down type and rebuilt it—hot lead had become his dictionary. He was a cub reporter by the time he was fifteen, and soon had his very own beat. He owed the life he now had to Papa, he once revealed after a drunken revel. Brave Heart had encouraged him, had sat with him during those long Sunday dinners at the lodging-house, and used his influence to find him that job as a printer's devil. . . .

I caught Will while he was scribbling an ode to the First Volunteers' mountain lion. Like the rest of us, he'd fallen under Josephine's sway.

DESERT QUEEN

INCAUTIOUS CAT . . .

He sat on the hotel's mile-long verandah in boots with spurs and an impeccable white coat. He had the wisp of a beard. Will was feline in his own way. He had long eyelashes. There was a lithe, yet lazy force under the regimental bandanna he liked to wear. He considered himself a Rough Rider. He didn't have to brandish his Colt.

"TR, why so glum?"

"I think Shafter intends to strand us."

"He wouldn't dare."

That's all it took. He didn't banter with me. Will wandered across the verandah, hobnobbed with the other war correspondents—that was the advantage of an ex-newsboy. He was much more brazen. And I was summoned posthaste into the commander's office on the second floor of the castle. General Shafter's aides fluttered around him with maps and charts of Cuba and ordnance reports. None of it made much sense. His aides had never been near the tropics, couldn't have known how rapidly ordnance could rust. But their general could no longer fit into a chair. He sat on some kind of a love seat, nursing his sick toe and wetting his walrus mustache with a finger.

"Amateurs," he said. "I'm surrounded by amateurs—like you. Roosevelt, did you have to complain to that serpent, Winters-White? I hear he's a fraud. No matter. I told Wheeler we couldn't trust you. 'Roosevelt's not a regular Army man. He's not even a good sport.' Didn't I dance with your wife while I was suffering from the gout? Of course you and your cowboys will have tickets on the first invasion fleet. You're the crown jewel of our arsenal, according to Winters-White. But this isn't football, Roosevelt—it's war."

I had never trusted the commander. His promises fell a little flat in my ear, like a broken birdsong. Yet I had to mollify the son of a bitch. We'd never get near Cuba without a nod from this hippo with the walrus mustache.

"General, we're soldiers now, loyal to the Fifth."

"Yes, yes, my loyal buccaneers. But keep away from Winters-White. He's common dirt, you know, born with ink on his thumbs. You'll be among the first to board—I promise."

I didn't heed a word of his. I bade goodbye to the four Troops we had to leave behind in Tampa. "Boys, you'll be on the second fleet." But shame on us all! I was repeating one of Shafter's damn lies. They would miss the show. Still, the other eight Troops had to pack their ponchos and blankets. And the journalists didn't cease pestering us.

"Gentlemen," I said, "we ain't a bunch of Buffalo Bills."

I'd brought twelve extra pairs of spectacles with me from San Antone—they all had steel rims and locked around my ears. I wouldn't have been able to lead a charge across the chaparral if I was half blind. Bellows sewed several pairs into my campaign hat, my saddlebags, my boots, and my denim shirts.

"Watch out for snakes, Colonel," he said. He kept another pair as a kind of insurance, and he trotted down the track to join the Buffalo Soldiers, who were already at the quay.

Meanwhile, the rest of the Rough Riders had assembled at a particular railroad siding, where a special train was supposed to pick us up. We parked ourselves under a gibbous moon, like men made of stone. We sat there until the sun rose, and realized that we'd remain there forever—forlorn soldiers abandoned by the Fifth. And finally a train did appear, a rusty wreck that must have been used to haul coal. We didn't malinger.

Colonel Wood and I seized that train. It just happened to be moving in the wrong direction. The engineer was adamant. "This is the coal run." But we convinced him at pistol point to ride in reverse. I was already half blind from the coal dust on my specs. We were all covered in coal. But we rocked along and arrived at the quay, where the other troopers were already assembled—Shafter's men and Wheeler's men in their haversacks. They squinted at us and must have thought that another black regiment had come down to the quays—Buffalo Soldiers.

And we didn't disillusion them.

A MYSTERIOUS ARMADA HAD materialized off the coast of Cuba, an armada without clear markings that could have sailed from the other end of the world, and Shafter would neither leave the quays nor have his men disembark. He had to be hoisted onto his bright red flagship, the *Segurança*, with the help of a winch. He sat there in a metal basket, like a bloated sun god, barking orders, while we were condemned to our stinking ship in the still waters of Tampa Bay. Our drinking water soon went sour, and our rations of Army beef rotted as we opened the cans, so we had to survive on hardtack, bitter coffee, and crumbling cubes of sugar.

I managed to smuggle Winters-White on board with his Colt; he and Josephine were the only bits of amusement we had during our "incarceration" on the *Yucatán*. Our pet cougar was listless without field mice and local tomcats to swipe at with her paw, while mules were dying of thirst in the hold, and they let out long bleats, lamentations that could gnaw at a man's soul. I did find several gallons of water for them that hadn't yet gone sour—I had to bribe a grocer onshore.

That ex newsie, Winters-White, performed magic tricks with packs of cards and Rough Rider neckerchiefs he plucked out of his various pockets and sleeves, bewitching us with an arsenal of colors and a cardsharp's sleight-of-hand. I was one of his victims, discovering an ace of spades behind my left ear, while several troopers endured the crackle of balloons exploding in their trouser pockets. Yet it wasn't magic that we craved. It was something else—a softness, a solidarity with the regiment, a moment of peace. And our mascot provided all that.

Josephine climbed onto the rail of the main deck, prowling like a queen with golden spots, as she moved with a feline swagger against a startling blue sea. That big cat, I know, shouldn't have been on board, and the Rough Riders couldn't have disembarked with *their* mountain lion. Shafter would have shaved our souls and abandoned us right on the shore. I'd arranged with the captain of the *Yucatán* to return Josephine to the four Troops we'd left behind in Tampa town. But I sensed that the Rough Riders would need Josephine for the crossing. We were volunteers, yes, a *virgin* regiment. We'd faced rustlers and Stranglers, but not entire batteries. And the mountain lion made us laugh, as she pawed a particular trooper beside the rail, growled at a seagull, and bumped me with that bullet she had for a head. I nearly tumbled overboard, as I fed her whatever scraps I could find—or steal. We all wanted to ride the trade winds to Cuba, and we were stuck in our berths at Tampa Bay.

When our cooks in their bright middies and waxed mustaches hoarded whatever little we had, trying to fatten their own pockets, I threatened to toss them out of the scullery and have them swab the decks. But they laughed in my face.

"This isn't your tub, Colonel. You lost your ticket with the Navy, sir. You're our guest, you and your irregulars. And you have a jaguar on board."

"Josephine isn't a jaguar," I said. "She's an oversized kitten."

I could have complained to the captain about these *irregular* cooks, but they would have been replaced by bigger thieves, so I haggled with them, and they swindled us less.

That mysterious armada spotted off the coast of Cuba turned out to be our own battleships. A novice naval officer hadn't recognized our colors. It was the usual blindness of war. And we paid a pretty price—six lost days. Still, I rationed well. We had a lick of water every three hours, counting Josephine and the mules.

Shafter, I was quick to ascertain, didn't have an admiral's grasp of the sea. He treated our convoy like a caravan that could proceed across some wet Sahara with its own random melody. The cruiser at the head of the pack kept signaling to Shafter's flagship to tighten its line, but the caravan still moved lazily along at six or seven knots. It was bewildering, you see, as our little armada of battleships, cruisers, and torpedo boats had to escort an invasion fleet of thirty-nine transports that might wander off somewhere into the unknown, at a general's mad whim. Luckily, the lead cruiser never lost sight of the *Segurança*'s bright red decks, or we could have ended up in *another* Caribbean, far, far from Cuba.

The *Yucatán*, with its enormous hold, was carrying several hundred pounds of nitroglycerin for a newfangled dynamite gun that could hurl explosive charges at the enemy. The pilot on the *Matteawan*, the ship right in front of us, must have fallen asleep at the wheel. We had to reduce our speed precipitously, or ram into its hull. Our captain stood on the bridge and wailed into his speaking trumpet, "Ahoy, ahoy. You lubbers are putting us all at risk." We managed to pull away from the *Matteawan*, or the crates of ammunition in the *Yucatán*'s bow would have become an inferno, and the flames might have spread from ship to ship with each bite of wind.

BY SOME MIRACLE OF navigation we managed to arrive off Cuba's southern coast with our full invasion fleet, though my Riders on board the *Yucatán* lived below in tiny berths akin to animal cages. Their drool had a curious green color. I fed them water out of a jar and dragged one and all up onto the main deck, where they could actually suck some air.

"Ah," said Sergeant Raddison, "it's glorious, sir."

The blue mountains rose right up above the shoreline with a relentless sweep that stole a couple of breaths from a lieutenant colonel who was also a huntsman and an explorer. But I was second in command and had no time to draw sketches of every nick in a mountain. Still, Winters-White could notch that feast in front of our eyes with all the magic of his black pen.

The sea was a burning blue, with the sun reflected in the water like a tantalizing mask.

We had to land at a dusty little fishing village called Daiquirí, with its rotting port, fifteen miles from Santiago. Our gunboats pounded Daiquirí. The port crumpled up and split like pellets of teeth. I had a solid hour of whistling in my ears, two hours— deafness would soon become a disease in the tropics. There was a smoking black fog from the relentless gunfire, and when the fog lifted, one patch at a time, it was apparent that Daiquirí was gone. Our guns had flattened the entire village; not a house was standing, not a hill. Fragments flew in the air. I followed the twisted rattan of someone's favorite seat as it was swept up in the hurricane of our cannons. I did not see one corpse floating in the harbor. The villagers must have fled to the mountains before the fusillade and the firestorm began.

Josephine sat between my legs during the destruction of Daiquirí. The cooks promised to feed her on the return trip to Tampa. I parted with her, soldier to soldier. "Goodbye, little girl. I'll send for you when we seize Santiago." She wasn't fooled. The big cat rubbed me with her whiskers and slinked off into the hold.

Whatever horses we had were pitched into the water and expected to swim ashore. I watched several of them drown, cursing the Fifth Corps and its maniacal maneuvers. The horses had been wild with fear after being half starved and living in the dark. I wouldn't have Little Texas meet a similar fate. I had the sailors on board the *Yucatán* deliver my prize cowpony—with a white star on his forehead—into the water harnessed to a winch. But something must have gone wrong with the sailors' boom, and Little Texas hung there in his tangled harness, above the burning blue.

That image of Little Texas hanging in midair went through me like a blinding razor, and I swore at the sailors—the range of my insults astonished me. "You cocksuckers, you spineless sons of bitches, if you hurt my horse, I'll hang you by your balls 'til they're hard as hickory nuts."

The sailors squinted at me. "Yes, Commodore, we'll look after the little dear."

These sailors managed to untangle Little Texas, release him from his harness, and I watched him plop into the water, break the surface of that blue and silver depth, and bob to Daquirí's vanished shoreline, while I mimicked every thrust of his flanks, every whip of his mane.

CHAPTER 12

KETTLE HILL

1898

W E HAD OUR DUPLICATES, OUR DOUBLES, REALLY, hawkeyes and cowboy cavaliers who seemed to have their own strange camaraderie. They wore ragged green uniforms—the clothes rotted off your back in the jungle—and were wise enough not to wear hats. Our spotters couldn't identify such sharpshooters; they hid in the palm trees, nestled there, never moved, and had their Mausers—rifles with smokeless powder that couldn't be discerned. They communicated by birdcalls. It took me a while to realize that the songs of tropical doves weren't songs at all, but the musical whisperings of wild men. No one, not even the *insurrectos* themselves, could figure out where these Spanish cavaliers came from. They didn't have the funny straw hats with conical crowns that the Spanish regulars wore, together with the pale blue and white uniforms. It was the conical crowns that got many of the regulars killed.

I'd made a fool of myself at first, tripping over the sword between my legs. But I had to learn in the lightning quick of battle, or not learn at all. I rode into danger like some D'Artagnan in white suspenders, a Musketeer with silver-leaf clasps and my blue flannel shirt. The steel spectacles were pinching my nose, and I should have been shot off Little Texas a hundred times, but we took the heights at Las Guásimas, and I'm still here.

Leonard Wood was given his own brigade early on, and command of the Rough Riders devolved upon my shoulders. But after our first charge we had to lay back a little—Shafter must have been planning a long siege of Santiago while he sat on his ass. I established our camp on the side of a hill, with the regimental field hospital in the rear. Still, something deeply vexed me. The faces had been ripped right off our dead, the eyes plucked out of their sockets, and I assumed it was the diabolical work of Spanish cavaliers, who sought to wipe off every trace of their foes. I should have known better—vultures the size of eagles wheeled over our heads, looking for their own special carrion. I couldn't go on a vulture hunt. Chasing after these buzzards would have revealed our position to the Spanish regulars and those pirates in green uniforms. So we buried the mutilated corpses as quickly as we could. But that had its own risk. Such secretive cowboys weren't satisfied shooting at soldiers—Rough Riders or regulars. They fired from their jungle posts in the palm trees at our padre in the middle of a funeral service.

As it turned out, the damn burial detail was just as dangerous as leading a charge. The cavaliers preyed on noncombatants. Those human buzzards murdered, wounded, and maimed doctors, mule drivers, and war correspondents—made no difference to them. And they did worse. They shot at child scavengers who collected bloody bandages and other debris. They even shot at nurses of the Army Nurse Corps, who lived in their own little compound. And they seemed to have a special affliction for the Red Cross brassard. Red Cross volunteers had to stop wearing such brassards, or they would have been picked off one by one.

"It just isn't civilized," I complained to Sergeant Raddison of Troop H. "Selecting Red Cross armbands as targets."

"Colonel," he said, "we ought to shake those bastards right out of their trees."

He'd been spectacular on our run up that razorback ridge, holding his men to the firing line, with foliage in front of his eyes, yelling like a cowboy from Mulberry Street, driving the Spaniards out of their trenches and rifle pits as if he were still with his bicycle boys. But we weren't dealing with regulars in conical crowns.

"Sergeant, we can't shake *every* tree in the province."

"Then how shall we dislodge them?"

I had to rely on that poet-correspondent from the *World*, the ex-newsie, William Winters-White. He'd been on the charge with us, had carried field glasses and a carbine, while all the other correspondents remained at the rear. He'd spotted the conical crowns with his glasses, and led us out of one brutal ambush after another. But his hands were shaking now. The poor fellow could not function without nicotine. And I had to find him contraband tobacco made from dry grass, tea leaves, and manure.

"Will," I said, "we nearly lost that ridge at Las Guásimas. An invisible enemy is one thing, but someone has to know their antecedents."

"Capture a general," he snapped, with his saturnine, tobacco-starved face.

"But the Spanish generals are all in Santiago, sitting in the Governor's palace."

He bit into a crumbling cigarette, went off to meet with his confreres in the press, and returned with a sinister smile.

"They're volunteers—just like you. Vaqueros. Some tended cattle in Morocco and on the Spanish plains. Others are pirates and convicts from the Azores."

"But why are they here?"

"Ah, Colonel, that remains a mystery."

Meanwhile, we were near starvation. Shafter had bungled everything. We seemed to have lost touch with the Commissary Department. *Nothing* arrived from the seacoast, not a single sack of rice or a bag of red beans. We had to plunder what we could from captured Spanish mule trains, and we didn't capture much. Shafter couldn't even ride in a sedan chair. His gout grew worse and worse. He lay groaning on a cot at headquarters. He developed a scalp disease in this tropical climate, and his aides and junior commanders had to devote themselves to scratching his head—that's how he conducted a war. So I borrowed several mules, since most of our mule drivers had disappeared, and started down to the sea on Little Texas, Private Taggart and his ex-Pinkertons as my scouts. The *insurrectos* were not always reliable; I didn't want them to steal whatever I might bring back from the coast. And the Vaqueros might come down from their trees and ambush us on El Camino Real, or shoot the eyes out of my head. Taggart, to his credit, did not seem to fear any snipers.

"We can avoid them, Colonel," he advised.

"How?"

"With our noses."

"But were not bloodhounds, Taggart."

"Still, they have to defecate from time to time. We will track them by their sweat—and the crap in their green pants. I know what I'm talking about. It's an old Cherokee trick."

I suddenly had a little more faith in this professional assassin and his fellow Pinks. I also listened to the birdcalls, and could not discern any signals from tree to tree. Yet I wondered if the Vaqueros had given me a special "pass" to the Commissary Department. We were living carrion to them, a kind of fodder.

Down we went through the foliage, with fronds scratching our faces and an army of red ants at our feet. I even had to climb off my saddle, and coax our mules with a clucking sound. They were restless, ornery beasts, and I didn't want them to make an idle run and injure themselves. But we arrived in one piece at the commissary near the coast, an abandoned rum distillery with rotting floorboards.

I had to wait in line for an hour to deal with the commissary clerk. He'd established a fiefdom for himself with a mountain of goods guarded by a little corps of factotums. My rank meant nothing to him.

"Colonel," he said with a sneer, "we don't deal with irregulars."

I had to resist the urge to reach across his little booth, pluck him by the ears, and bury him in one of his own pathetic sacks of beans. It would have meant a court-martial. I'd have to stand in front of

Shafter, while some poor rascal scratched away at the general's scalp until his fingers bled. I'd come too far to miss the rest of the show.

"Corporal, you may think whatever you like of me, but my men require seven hundred tins and bags of tobacco and eleven hundred pounds of beans."

That little potentate sniggered at me and winked at his fellow clerks. "Colonel, you must be blind. Tobacco's vanished from the market—Bull Durham is scarce as blue jade. And I have no beans for your cowboys."

I pointed to all the sacks behind his booth. "But your commissary is full."

He grabbed a worn bible of regulations from the counter and started to read the rules. "It's clear as day, sir. According to section C of the codebook, beans and such are strictly for officers and not for volunteers and enlisted men."

I took off my steel rims and stared right at him. "Then this whole damn commissary is an officer's club."

He nodded his head. "That's the gist of it, sir."

"Fine," I said. "I'll take all the grub you can spare for my officers' mess—and bags of Bull Durham."

But I couldn't daunt him no matter what I said. "Roosevelt, I'd still have to ship your request to Washington—and that would take a week."

I was prepared to pistol-whip the clerk, no matter what the consequences were. But Taggart leaned over and whispered into the corporal's collar. That potentate's eyes lit with palpable terror. He hopped about; he and his fellow clerks provided us with our requisite tobacco and beans, and we loaded the supplies onto the mules. But Taggart was suddenly tight-lipped.

"Trooper," I finally asked, "how did you get that clerk to go into Ali Baba's cave?"

"Colonel, he could tell I was a Pink. I told him I would come back and set him on fire with a bottle of kerosene."

I was bewildered. "But *how* did you convince him that you'd been with the Pinks?"

"Oh," he said, with a little wink. "It's the demeanor we have, sir."

That bladelike walk of an assassin.

I rode back into the hills with my supplies and my scouts. We had to protect our new treasure of beans and tobacco from red ants and land crabs that were as large as any helmet. Tarantulas whirled in front of our eyes with their porous black capes. I began to worry about the birdcalls—the melodies were a little too detailed. We didn't find Vaqueros on El Camino Real, but three men stood in our way with repeaters and Rough Rider neckerchiefs they had turned into masks. They pretended to be outlaws, but I could recognize their leader by his bowed legs. He couldn't really disguise his voice or his cowpuncher's walk.

"Colonel, the beans are your own good fortune, but we'll take the tobaccy."

I didn't pause, or reflect on what my unmasking of this trick outlaw might mean. "Red Finnegan, you swore an oath to the Rough Riders."

"That's a damn shame," he uttered as he took off his neckerchief. "I've grown fond of you and the Riders. I was planning to let you live. But now you'll tattle."

He must have requisitioned two of the *insurrectos*, gotten them drunk with the dream of what they could make with a stash of tobacco that was trading at fifty gringo dollars for a couple of ounces.

"And all that pilfering among the troopers—the gold watches and other missing items—was that you, Finnegan?"

His eyebrows quivered. "I guess I was born to it."

"But you were as gallant as any trooper in that first charge. I saw you myself. You helped us take the ridge."

"Oh, when it comes to fightin', I'm as fine as the next fellah. But I had tobaccy on my mind the minute we landed—red and brown gold. And what does Mr. Taggart have to say?"

Taggart was silent. He couldn't draw on that gunslinger. But the other Pinks stood a step or two to the side on that road of red ants.

They didn't want to interfere with Taggart's play. There was a terrific racket in the trees. A troop of monkeys was shadowing us; the troop chattered and yelped and hurled an arsenal of coconuts at us, their lean arms extending out of the fronds like hairy fulcrums. I ducked, or I would have left my brains on El Camino Real. I didn't want the mules to bolt. They would have vanished into the jungle and shed all our supplies in some obscure trap of tangled roots. I had to hug their reins and pull against the load on their backs.

Red Finnegan created his own folly with a maniacal laugh. He shot the monkeys out of the fronds with his Colt repeater. The monkeys dropped their coconuts, tumbled onto El Camino Real, clawing at the air until they expired. Finnegan couldn't seem to lose that wretched laugh.

"You had no cause to kill those damn monkeys," Taggart told him. "They were funnin' with you, Red."

"And I'm funnin' with you."

Taggart was no quick-draw artist. Red could have shot the eyes out of his skull; that was his signature move.

"I'll take the tobaccy, Colonel, and you can sing your prayers. Hallelujah to the Lord!"

That's when I heard the birdsongs again, the tweets doubling and tripling until it was a riot of songs, a roar, and I knew that the Vaqueros were following this escapade, like some kind of chorus. Their Mausers struck the trees over our heads, with little explosions that left splinters in the bark. They weren't aiming to kill. Finnegan turned his head a trifle, and Taggart shot him in the cheek with his Colt. Blood splattered onto my specs and the tarpaulins that held our supplies in place.

The two other men ran into the jungle. I had to wipe my specs with a cloth. There was no wind in Red at all.

"Colonel, I think we should bury the son of a bitch right here."

"I can't," I said. "There'll have to be an inquiry."

Taggart had the saturnine look of an old soldier lost in the fray. "You'll crush the regiment, sir. The provost-marshal will want his own inquiry. His advocates will swoop down on us from Washing-

ton, and meanwhile the Rough Riders will be in limbo. The advocates will wonder how many other renegade Rough Riders there
are—if your cowboys can be trusted at all—and we'll sit out the
rest of the war."

This damn assassin was as sharp as any advocate-general, so we
carried Red's corpse to our camp on the back of a mule. I had to
swallow my own bile. I blamed the bullet in Red's cheek on the
Vaqueros. We buried him in a grove, with the padre reading from
an Army Bible and worrying about the snipers in the trees. He was
shivering all the time in this heat, with a handkerchief over his
ears like a curtain. One padre had already been killed. Those tree-
huggers shot our field hospitals to pieces; their savagery multiplied
the more we sat in our camp.

I had Winters-White come to my tent. The ex-newsie's hands
no longer shook and his eyes didn't wander now that he had his
tobacco. I kept our tins and bags of Bull Durham in my tent, but
we donated half our tobacco to other regiments and the general
staff to avert a civil war. But spies, like vultures, lurked everywhere,
and the stash we still had was always kept under guard. Finnegan
wasn't shrewd enough to steal his own supply from the commissary
clerks, but he hadn't been wrong—tobaccy was better than gold.

"Will, you know all the correspondents and reporters. They treat
you like a deity. You've covered pogroms and forest fires. You've
traveled from conflict to conflict. You've met with the Czar in his
summer palace. I shouldn't need to remind you. The Vaqueros have
to have a leader—find him, even if he's a ghost."

"And what if I fail?" he averred, with tobacco stains on his teeth.

"You're a wonder, Will."

He left with an ounce of tobacco, which I measured with a
spoon and a little cup.

"Roosevelt, you're the deity," he said, "not I. And your father was
even a bigger deity. I'm only here because of Brave Heart."

I felt a bit abashed. "Papa was devoted to the newsies," I said.

"That's true, but you got here on your own cunning, Will."

He was quiet for a moment, summoning up the difficult days and nights of a newsie. "You cannot *possibly* imagine what it meant to have him there week after week in his tie and tails. . . ."

Will returned in an hour with his yellow slicker and his Colt. "Colonel, come with me. Don't forget your sword and your carbine and your cartridge belt . . . and a little gift of Bull Durham."

"Where are we going?" I had to ask, clutching my own slicker.

"To meet a ghost."

THEY INSISTED THAT I wear a blindfold. I had little choice. We wouldn't have a padre left in another week. We couldn't fight the Spanish regulars and these sinister cowboys in the trees.

I tried to mark the time, pace by pace, as we traveled through the jungle. I could feel the corded roots at my feet. "Damn you, Will, why do I have to wear a sword?"

"In case a boa attacks."

"But how can I fight a boa while I'm wearing a blindfold!" I had to insist.

"No matter. A colonel wouldn't be a colonel without his sword— this is Cuba."

I had clocked twenty minutes, like pulse beats in my temples. Winters-White kept me from plummeting into that gnarled jungle floor. He tapped me on the shoulder and removed the blindfold. We were in a slight clearing, a bald patch without a single root or tree. And in this clearing was a canvas chair that might have come from a general's tent. A man in a pince-nez and a cowboy neckerchief sat in that chair. I'd have guessed he was my age—a few months shy of forty. He had a jeweler's nimble hands. His mustache was almost as red as mine, and his eyes were probably just as weak. I couldn't imagine him as a sniper, shooting at children and nurses from the Army Nurse Corps. Yet here he was, in the green uniform of a Vaquero.

"We've met before," he said in a slight accent.

"Captain, or general, or whoever you are, I rarely forget a face."

"Well," he said, "it seems you have forgotten mine."

But I didn't forget, you see. I had to rip him right out of his jungle habitat before I could master that camouflage of his. He'd been in my class at Columbia Law. Rueben Martinez. His father had been a peasant who broke into the merchant class with a cigar factory in Santiago, and had sent his oldest son to Manhattan to study law.

"It was not amiable," he said. "The winters, and all the poverty and the wealth. I did not graduate. I caught double pneumonia . . . and nearly died in Bellevue. But we often chatted."

"I cannot recall a word. Forgive me—are you a general or not?"

He laughed and revealed his crooked teeth. His was the only chair. Will and I had to squat on our haunches.

"Teedie, there are no titles here, not even a rank. We don't use such nonsense in the jungle."

"Yet you are the chieftain of the Vaqueros."

"Perhaps," he said, "perhaps. I have followed both your careers in the papers. Mr. White is fond of traveling on a camel's back. He can describe the sunset in Arabia." The Vaquero shut his eyes and recited the correspondent's words like an incantation. "'The sky in Arabia is not red. It is bloodless, and bleaches the blood out of any man. The sun does not set—it dies in mid-sentence, and darkness hits like a hammer.' Have I misquoted you, Mr. White?"

"Not at all," said Will.

"Your beginnings were much more humble than mine, but I will not dwell on that. And Colonel, you cannot seem to outrun your own glory days. A sheriff in the Badlands, a Police Commissioner who got rid of corrupt captains, and now a colonel with his own regiment. What does your wife—your *second* wife—think of all this?"

I wasn't too fond of this fox with a jeweler's hands. "She calls me Sinbad," I said.

He twirled his mustache, just a bit. "Sinbad, yes. That is perfection. Sinbad has come across the sea with his cowboys to liberate us from the hidalgos."

He presided on his canvas throne in the wild and pontificated like a jungle poet.

"But the hidalgos have rounded up your own people and put them into camps. Why are you supporting them?"

"Because I am a businessman," he said, "in the business of war."

"I find that hard to believe, Don Rueben."

He snarled at me. "I'm nobody's *don*. You can call me *Coronel*. Finally, I do have a rank. It's the same as yours, Colonel Sinbad. The Spanish governor of Santiago pays me a small fortune to protect his province. And so I have my cowboys, too."

"But you cannot win. Your snipers shoot at little children and helpless nurses with armbands, not to mention a padre or two. That is not war. It is wanton cruelty."

"Anything," he said, "anything to slow you down. The hidalgos are like a tottering wall. The whole Spanish conquest will crumble—it is crumbling as we speak. The generals hide in Santiago with most of their army. And they leave a thousand regulars in a blockhouse on a hill. Colonel, I am more frightened of you than that idiot of a Governor in his palace."

"Why?" I asked. "Why?" I could see that Will was scribbling one of his dispatches—an interview in the raw, amid an army of red ants, with the elusive leader of the Vaqueros.

"Because," that other colonel said, "the Yankees have confused their own destiny with ours."

I wasn't amused by this Plato of the forest, who was a soldier of fortune and a philosopher. I dangled a bag of Bull Durham. All his ranting stopped. He plucked the Bull Durham out of my hand with his tiny talons.

"There is no tobacco here, Colonel—none. Couldn't you spare another bag?"

I did not have a second bag.

"Don Rueben, enjoy your Bull Durham. I doubt that we'll meet again. We will chase the Spaniards out of Cuba, erase their presence in the New World. The Governor will return to Madrid with half the wealth in the province."

"And we will have the Yankee invaders in our laps—no!"

We listened to a piercing birdcall, and he answered the call with a staccato tweet of his own. He collected his canvas chair, and without a word of warning he vanished into the foliage.

THERE WAS ANOTHER MATTER, not as urgent, but still a regimental folly, the kind a novice colonel could never expect in war. Sergeant Raddison came into my tent with Corporal Anton Little Feather of Troop H. The corporal was our standard-bearer. And he'd clubbed a few of the Spanish regulars with the Rough Rider flag. I'd inherited him from a school in the Indian Territory. He'd come to our recruitment counter with the highest letters of recommendation from his teachers, and his physical exam in hand, signed and sealed. I took great pride in the corporal—not a bravo among us had trained so hard.

"We have a problem, sir," Raddison said. "He is a *she*."

"Raddison, you're talking riddles."

"Well, let me unriddle it. I caught him undressing, and the corporal has, ya know, female genitals."

"That's preposterous," I said. "Trooper, is that a lie—or a fact?"

"A fact, sir," Anton Little Feather said in a husky voice. He didn't have one female feature, at least one that I could surmise. While he didn't wear a mustache, his shoulders were as broad as mine.

"What's your real name, Corporal?"

"Antonia Little Feather, sir."

I should have known. Little Feather was the name of a princess, not a Sioux warrior. But that had completely skipped my mind because of her corded neck and the sweep of her shoulders. Antonia had indeed been a pupil at a school in the Indian Territory. Her letters of recommendation were genuine. She was applying for the Army Nurse Corps. And she had passed the physical, too. But she craftily altered both documents. She had wanted so much to be a Rough Rider—she could shoot in the saddle and ride the roughest bronco. We'd climbed that razorback together at Las Guásimas, with her holding the colors while she fended off Spanish regulars. And she had guarded Little Texas after I got down from my chestnut cowpony. I tripped once on my own sword. And it was Antonia who pulled me back into the fray—the corporal was everywhere at once.

"Sergeant," I said, "I'm damned whatever I do; if I notify the provost, we'll be laughed right out of the war."

"Then it might be best to notify no one," Raddison volunteered.

"And what if another bravo uncovers her female charms?"

"That's unlikely, sir."

"Doesn't she use the latrine and the shower stalls?"

"I shower after midnight," the trooper insisted. "And the jungle is my private latrine."

I'd been duped. She'd lied and cheated and falsified legal documents to become a Rough Rider. But it meant as much to her as it meant to me. I'd created the Riders out of my own phantasm, an unbridled wish. The Riders were my Aladdin's lamp, and perhaps Antonia was its genie—perhaps, perhaps.

SHAFTER'S TOE MUST HAVE risen out of its burlap bag like an oracle. Finally, the order came to advance upon San Juan Heights, a pair of ridges actually, one lower than the other. The lower one we dubbed Kettle Hill, because it was a ruined ranch with a great iron kettle, which had once been used for sugar refining, I suppose. It was a deadly place, since it had its own red-tile blockhouse that commanded the hill. But right across the ravine was the upper crest, San Juan Hill, a hacienda with an infernal line of rifle pits and a red-tile blockhouse that was a regular fort, located on the cusp of El Camino Real, our only route to Santiago, mud and all.

We were told to seize the Heights from two separate points, like a pincer. Our big guns were practically useless. Their black powder left a dark residue of smoke that gave the enemy a chance to punish us with their own big guns. Our Gatlings were another story. These hand-cranked guns on their swivel mounts raked the enemy with a relentless precision all along our lines of fire. We couldn't have advanced without the Gatlings, couldn't have scaled the Heights, but our dynamite gun did not have the same wallop. It was difficult to operate, yet its shells of nitroglycerin could rip into a rifle pit or explode in front of some abandoned blockhouse.

Our orders arrived at four a.m. by a courier in a campaign hat with a missing crown—a bunch of us had to charge Kettle Hill. I do not remember much after that. I heard the bugle's call, like the patchwork of a dream. I was caught up pell-mell in a brigade of Buffalo Soldiers and Rough Riders, horseless horsemen on the run, in the hurly-burly of war. The Spaniards had called our black bravos "smoked Yankees," and considered them ghost warriors, who could rise up from the dead and reassemble all their body parts. The regulars ran from their rifle pits once the smoked Yankees arrived.

I led the charge from my saddle. I had tucked my blue bandanna under the floppy brim of my campaign hat, so that it could protect the back of my neck from the bite of the morning sun, and it must have looked strange to my boys, like the headdress of a sheikh. Thus I rode Little Texas into battle. Still, our Gatlings couldn't rake every damn royal palm in the hills. The Vaqueros shot troopers on both sides of Little Texas. Yet there I was on my warhorse, escaping bullets with an invincible flair.

Sinbad.

I went up and down our lines, waving my hat with its blue tail. "Forward, boys, we have to take that hill."

But there were ranges of barbed wire strewn like the devil's own instrument across our path. And I didn't want to catch Little Texas' flanks on a piece of that wire. So I climbed off my saddle and shooed that chestnut cowpony back to our camp with a swat of my hat. "Go on, now."

Little Texas galloped unharmed across a hail of bullets. And I continued my charge. I must have been caught in the tremor of an exploding shell. I tumbled to the ground, scraped my knee and smashed my specs; the steel frames were gone. I knew I had another pair in my hat, but I couldn't seem to reach them somehow, as if my hands belonged to a marionette. All my preparations had gone awry. I had to push and grope into battle half blind. I'd lost that powerful compass in my head. I panicked, because I could have been slogging in the wrong direction.

And then I tripped. A hand reached out and grabbed mine. A smoked Yankee had wandered out of the haze. It was Bellows, my former body-servant. "Colonel, what is a white man doing on his hands and knees?"

"Looking for my specs, Bellows, why else? I got thrown into the wake of a shell."

"Well, ain't that a catastrophe?" he said with a smile, as I caught a glimpse of his gold teeth.

Thank the Lord he still had an extra pair that he kept for me in his pocket. I put them on, my hands shivering over the earpieces. I barely had time to salute Bellows. A bullet slapped him in the shoulder, spun him around. I cradled him in my arms. His eyes had that vacant, bleeding look.

"Sergeant Bellows, do you know who I am?"

He blinked once. "Teddy Roosevelt, sir, of the Riders."

"Well, I'm sending you back down to the field hospital. I'll find an orderly."

But Bellows twisted right out of my grasp. "And miss my chance to take Kettle Hill with the Buffalos? I didn't come here to have beetles and tarantulas bite my ass."

He took his neckerchief, knotted it into a sling around his wounded shoulder, and went back into the haze. I had my specs now. I saw Trooper Antonia with our flag, a dozen boys behind her. Antonia's flag must have blinded the Spanish regulars. We arrived at that mammoth cast-iron kettle that must have been used for sugaring once upon a time at this hilltop hacienda. More troopers congregated behind that kettle. The snipers couldn't get to us from this iron mass. We weren't scarecrows, straw men. We kept hearing loud, metallic pings. The Spanish regulars were shooting at us from their stronghold in the red-tile fort of the hacienda. But all they could catch was their own damn kettle—on Kettle Hill. Then the whole hacienda began to shiver, and there was a groundswell under our feet, like a minor earthquake. A nitroglycerin shell from our dynamite gun must have landed on the hacienda; the red tiles began to crumble.

We charged the red-tile fort, with Trooper Antonia grimacing while she clutched our flag. We screamed until our throats were raw.

YA-HA-HAW!

The sheer ferocity of the Rough Riders' cowboy call must have frightened the Spanish regulars, who didn't want another shell from the dynamite gun to burst on top of their skulls. They dropped their rifles and fled. They left wine bottles in their wake. Their trenches were filled with corpses, splayed like tatterdemalions and rag dolls. Through the mist and wavelike ribbons of heat, we caught glimpses of Santiago emerging from its own mirage, with a shimmering rattle of red tiles and white, white streets, as if the Yankees had never come to Cuba. . . .

Yet the Spanish regulars were firing at us from the blockhouse and rifle pits on that hill across the ravine, six or seven hundred yards from the sanctuary of our kettle. They had their own big guns and sharpshooters. A Spanish regular had been creeping near the kettle in his blue and white coat. He had a bad case of battle fright, I imagine. I shot at the son of a bitch. I'm not sure what happened next. Suddenly the Spaniard crumpled up and crashed to the ground. My own orderly, Bardshar, winked at me through the feathers of smoke and little sparks of gunpowder.

"Nice shot, Colonel."

Our own regulars were attacking the blockhouse on San Juan Hill and getting shot to pieces, so I decided to lead a charge down that ravine. But I let out a rip that was lost in all that smoke and thunder. I had to run back up Kettle Hill to collect Rough Riders and stray Buffalos here and there. The constant drum of the Gatlings had created a deafening roar that diminished every other sound. I felt like an idiot, leading a charge where no one came. I found Bardshar wandering about, with blood everywhere. A shell had exploded near him, and two Rough Riders had been hit by the fragments—it was their blood that covered his face and his clothes. He seemed like a random dummy as I shouted at him. He did a pantomime and pointed to his ears.

"Colonel, I'm a little deaf."

I did my own pantomime and pointed to the San Juan blockhouse.

"We're gonna enfilade that cozy little nest of theirs."

We were a crazy mix of Rough Riders, smoked Yankees, and white regulars. A bullet cut down one of my boys in the cross-fire. "Medic," I cried, but there were no hospital orderlies on this charge. The Vaqueros were still in their royal palms, and the orderlies wouldn't go near a battlefield. We could not seem to make that final charge to the San Juan blockhouse. The Vaqueros had pinned us down.

"Sir, it's a suicide run," Raddison said.

"Maybe so. But we'll have to risk it. We can't shake the sons of bitches out of their trees."

We ran into a blistering storm of bullets. Ripped to shreds, Trooper Antonia's standard still flew like a regimental rag. But she never stopped once, never faltered. She used that flag as a lance, stabbing into arms and legs as she ripped up Spanish regulars and cried—*Ya-ha-haw!*—with a demonic grin that sent those regulars as far as they could from San Juan Hill.

Sergeant Raddison lost a finger in the skirmish, but that couldn't even break his stride. One of the Pinks fell, and then another. The Vaqueros fired at us from their royal palms with impunity—those damn bullets of theirs landed like plops of soft silk in the rustle of leaves. Still, our Gatlings ripped across the blockhouse. And once our black and white warriors arrived at the crest of the hill, some with torn shoulders, others with missing pockets and welts on their backs from all the flying metal, the Spanish regulars abandoned the blockhouse for the safety of Santiago. Their officers had left big iron kettles on the stoves filled with beef stew and boiled rice; there were decanters and demijohns of rum—rum, a river of rum.

THE GENERALS IN SANTIAGO, who hadn't taken part in a single skirmish, hadn't raised or lowered a flag, wouldn't surrender the city unless we fired upon them—it was a matter of honor, they said; and their demands were as surreal as the war itself. Shafter didn't want to maim women and children with cannonballs. But civilians began to flee Santiago in anticipation of some big surprise attack. We did not have enough grub to feed them—our rations were running low, while the Spanish generals had shuttered all the markets and warehoused whatever food there was in their garrisons. We worried about a scourge of yellow fever—"the black vomit," clotted with blood. The negotiations continued. More refugees arrived, dragging wobbly piles of furniture in little three-wheeled carts, with a grandma or two at the very top of the pile like some reigning queen in a ripped mantilla.

Shafter, in desperation, had Santiago shelled for three days and nights. He did not want it to become a city without roofs and without water, with bits of red tile in the roads—he'd have had to send in nurses to care for cases of yellow fever, and gravediggers to bury the dead, or the city itself would have become one vast graveyard. So he bombarded Santiago *above* the rooftops—it was the madness of a general laid up with gout. He still left a lot of debris. Meanwhile, the Spanish generals vanished with a mule train of gold. I broke into the garrisons and fed as many people as I could—all I could provide was rotting potatoes and blackened cobs of corn. I reopened every hospital, every clinic, often with Antonia Little Feather at my side, and her rumpled flag.

Raddison warned me not to enter Santiago alone. "We'll be your honor guard, Colonel."

"Nonsense," I said. "There isn't a Spanish regular within miles."

"And what about the snipers, sir?"

"Sergeant, what would they do in a provincial town? They've hired themselves out to other generals, for the next war."

And so I wandered into that dusty old town in my yellow suspenders and blue denim shirt—a colonel without the least sign of my rank. I marched through the narrow, winding streets, passing little shops with empty windows, squat little houses of stained stucco, with fanciful wrought-iron balconies, and arrived at a plaza with a white cathedral and a watering hole called the Café Venus, with plaster chips on its awning. I knew the fates had brought me here, like Philoctetes stranded on the rocky isle of Lesbos, but this island café was full of wild men, Vaqueros, and I had a misshapen knuckle rather than a festering foot, from the shrapnel I'd caught in the crossfire, charging San Juan Hill.

He was sitting there at the center table, still wearing his green uniform, guzzling rum, while the walls and little narrow bar of the Café Venus were decorated with souvenirs and relics, *our* souvenirs, it seems—Red Cross brassards, ripped campaign hats, and Rough Rider neckerchiefs with the distinctive polka dot.

"Don Rueben, I have the right to arrest you. You're a criminal. You've murdered my men with your Mausers."

He laughed. "And you come into my headquarters in your suspenders and your red mustache, without an escort."

"Is the Café Venus really your headquarters, señor?"

"Yes. Do you think I live in trees, Colonel? We should go into business together. You will never leave this town. Don't you understand the business of war? The generals in Washington will say that you have mingled with the locals and have become infected with the black vomit. And Santiago will become your charnel house. You will spend your days roaming among the red tiles."

"I could still arrest you, Don Rueben."

"Not likely," he said, surrounded by Vaqueros in the Venus Café.

I no longer knew what to believe. Shafter must have had grave news from the War Department. Even with his gout, he summoned us to Santiago for a council of officers, and I went back into those winding streets. We met in the governor's mansion, a rambling little palace with boarded windows, across from the white cathedral. Shafter had a funereal look. A buckboard had to carry him from his headquarters in an abandoned sugar factory to a palace full of floating white dust. We were all sentenced to the black vomit, it seems. Shafter was whimpering now. I could see the sores in his scalp, red pockmarks that looked like little swollen mouths.

"We must either stay here, in Santiago, or move into the mountains," he mumbled. I had to strain to catch his words. "Lads, the Army will not release us. We have become worse than vultures. We are not considered safe."

As the one maverick and irregular at the council, I was enlisted to write a letter to General Shafter that could be circulated among ourselves and used later as live ammunition.

"Make it pungent," Shafter said. "Make it wise—and very dire."

I did have help from Winters-White, whose pen had all the craft of a poisonous snake.

General Shafter:

Our clothes are in ribbons and rags. My officers do not possess a decent pair of socks. Our boys sit idly in their dog-tents, with nothing to do. Each day the torrential rains and blistering sun sap our energy. There's no quinine—nothing. No supplies. Our Gatlings have gone to rust. The Red Cross nurses have vanished with all their medical kits and hospital cots. The last padre has left. We will not survive Santiago. . . .

The letter was leaked to the press, of course. And within three days our invasion force of regulars, Buffalos, and Rough Riders was ordered to assemble and sail for home. We'd gone from saviors to stumblebums in less than a month.

CHAPTER 13

MONTAUK POINT

1898

REPORTERS GRABBED AT THE ROUGH RIDERS, GAUNT AS they were. And they grabbed at me.

"How are you, Colonel?"

"Disgracefully well."

I'd thrived in the tropics.

"Will you be our next Governor?"

I knew that Boss Platt and his cronies were desperate for a white knight to stave off a Democratic landslide in November. They had none. And I wasn't in the mood to banter. I had to wait until the *Miami*'s decks were cleared, and I walked a mile and a half with my boys to the "detention camp," and a detention camp it was, with guards at the gate. I'd asked my wife not to come with the bunnies to meet the *Miami*; I wasn't certain when we would dock. And I didn't want her near all the brouhaha about politics and war atrocities—what we did to the Spanish regulars, and what the regulars in their conical hats did to us.

Nothing pleased me more than the fact that the Rough Riders had their own "street" at the camp, a ragged carousel of tents, but there was little to chew on at the mess hall, as if we were still somewhere in the Cuban jungle. I had to order eggs, milk, and oranges from a local market. And then I had to wheedle a bit to get around this ridiculous quarantine. I was able to convince a young officer to place a cryptic call to the druggist at Oyster Bay—we didn't have a telephone at Sagamore Hill.

"He's to have his boy bicycle up the hill to Mrs. Roosevelt and tell her the coast is clear."

And this same kind lieutenant, who might have been jeopardizing his own future, met Edith at the gate the very next morning and smuggled me out of camp in one of his raincoats. There was a Red Cross hut across the road, with a little lunchroom. And that's where we had our secret rendezvous, in plain sight of the Red Cross. She wore a veil of white tulle. I didn't know whether the veil was in remembrance of her soldier husband, or the boys we lost in Cuba. I clasped her hand. She was trembling.

"I wasn't certain I would ever see you again. . . . "

"But I'm your Sinbad. And Sinbad is a survivor."

She unclasped her hand with a slightly violent gesture and put it to my mouth. "Don't say that, darling. We cannot always reside in a fairy tale."

We had so little time. The lieutenant had granted us a reprieve of half an hour. Then he would be replaced by another duty officer. And I would be denounced as a deserter.

"How are the bunnies?"

"As lonely for you as I am. I did not dare break down—or that terrible suspense would sweep over me and I would have been helpless against it. I am helpless now."

I undid her veil. She clasped it again. She did not want me to remember her with puffy eyes.

"Talk to me," my wife said with a whimper. "I so love the sound of your voice."

I prattled on about my grievances. "Shafter has recommended me for the Medal of Honor. I'll never get it. I'm persona non grata at the War Department. That's why we're all here in this bloody camp. There is no yellow fever epidemic among the troops, and there never was."

"And your Rough Riders?"

"Bitten to the bone. Half of them are like skeletons, Edie, and the other half . . . I worry what will happen after they're mustered out. There's been so much attention, so much press. They can't all be—"

"Sinbad."

Cash was pouring in from wealthy friends at the Boone & Crockett Club. I intended to parcel it out with a fierce devotion—to Rough Rider widows, and to the Riders themselves, after the bravura of the regiment began to unravel, and they were cowpunchers again on some nondescript ranch, with tall tales to tell—everyone had a tall tale.

I had to return to the detention camp. But Edith clung to the Red Cross, and volunteered as a nurses' assistant at the camp hospital for the next four days. I did not have to worry about her quarters. She slept with other nurses in a Red Cross hut. And even a quarantined colonel could visit his own wife at the hospital.

It was a dismal hugger-mugger of shacks and tents, with a shortage of cots, so that the sick and the wounded had to sleep on a "kit" of crumpled blankets. Pale as she was, Edith had to wipe each soldier's forehead with a damp cloth and feed him chicken broth. The head nurse had flaming red hair and freckles the size of walnuts.

"I cannot nourish these men—I cannot."

I probed her. "What do you need, Sister Nell?"

Her eyes lit with a kind of delirium. "Eggnogs," she said. "And we have no eggs or milk or cream—or bourbon."

"Well," says I, "there's always a simple solution."

And the next day an enormous tureen with a silver ladle arrived, and a hundred flutes packed in straw, with a note dangling from a piece of wire:

DELMONICO'S EGGNOG SUPREME
DIET TENT
MONTAUK

Nurse Nell, with her face full of freckles, basked in the glory of that tureen. She herself had a bit too much bourbon. And we had to plunk her down in a chair. I devoured the moments I had with Edie, wandering from blanket-bunk to blanket-bunk, with Rough Riders and Army regulars. They were all curious about Sagamore Hill.

"Do ya grow corn, Colonel?"

"Yes, it's a working farm."

"And do ya till the soil, Mrs. Colonel, ma'am?"

"Sometimes," Edie said. "In our garden. But we do have a resident farmer."

Our words seemed to comfort them in this rag-and-bone hospital. But I couldn't escape politics, not even in Sister Nell's Diet Tent.

"Don't disappoint us, hear? Run for Governor."

Edie wanted me to retire to Sagamore Hill and write my books. "You've had enough of Boss Platt for one lifetime."

"And he's had enough of me. I don't intend to make a pilgrimage to his Amen Corner when the quarantine is over."

My wife had to get back to our bunnies. We hadn't spent a single night in my tent. I couldn't even burgle a kiss.

"Darling," she said, "it's like Tranquillity. When you courted me in the icehouse."

"And got walloped for all my efforts."

"Shame on you—you didn't have the mind or the willpower to engage yourself to a girl."

"You were fourteen," I said.

"And no less a woman than I am now."

An Army wagon then drove her to the railroad station. And I marched back across this madness that the War Department had designed for us—a Sahara of tents. I shared my own wall tent with Winters-White. Yes, he was here, too. Will had to remain in quarantine, as if he'd been one of the troops—he had been our spotter and had fired his gun. And, wouldn't you know, the War Department treated him with the same contempt. But we weren't alone in our exile. I had a mysterious guest—Senator Thomas Collier Platt, resplendent in a white summer suit. It didn't startle me that he had enough sway to walk into a quarantined camp, but the real miracle was that he'd left his Amen Corner. He glared at Will, who excused himself. I wasn't going to rescue the Easy Boss. Finally he spat out his venom.

"Roosevelt, you are a perfect bull in a china shop—everything around you crumbles."

He hadn't lost his old bravura, that sense of dash.

"Then why are you here? I haven't asked for this interview, Senator."

He stroked the silk of his beard. "I'm not here. What you have, son, is my emanation."

"Then I'll profit from it. What does the Easy Boss's emanation want?"

He rubbed the yellow moons of his fingernails. "Damn you, Theodore, you can have the nomination."

I dug into his flesh with a phantom stick. "I did not seek it, Senator."

"Republicans will rally around the hero of San Juan Hill. I can end this quarantine in a minute, declare war on the War Department."

"Senator, I can fight my own battles. Besides, I'm beginning to enjoy this monk's retreat. I might take over Montauk with my Rough Riders."

He purred like a night owl. "I've visited their tents. Theodore, they're all skin and bone."

I stared into his pale, watery eyes. He knew I couldn't retire to Sagamore Hill. Republicans of every stripe would badger me to run, but I did not relish returning to that old Dutch town with its deep chill off the Hudson, and he could tell.

"I take all the risks, and you take none," he said. "You'll rile up Albany, and send me packing."

"And what if I will?"

He started to roar in my tent. "I'm satisfied."

"But I haven't accepted the nomination," I said.

And he disappeared from the tent without another word. I had to puzzle it out with Winters-White, who was palpably excited as he trod across the tent. "What a victory! The Easy Boss leaves his shrine at the Fifth Avenue and comes crawling. It's a first. He's never done that before. He's desperate. His precinct captains must be in open rebellion."

"He played me," I said, "like a country fiddle."

And he had. The grand overture of a visit to Montauk. The political prince had anointed me with a touch of his hand. I would not have to bargain with him. He'd plucked a winner out of the hurricane. But I could not concern myself with November, not now. I had to nourish my troopers, those who hadn't died on Cuban soil. New York's Mayor, a Tammany man, wanted to honor the Rough Riders with a parade up Fifth Avenue.

They are America's uncrowned royalty, masters of the moment— Indians, cowpokes, miners, tennis champions, stockbrokers, and Harvard oars, who charged up that nefarious hill with Mr. Roosevelt, he wrote to the War Department and barely got a reply. Ordnance couldn't release the guns and the mounts for a parade, not while the regiment concerned was under quarantine.

These boys didn't merit such a slap. They could deny me the Medal of Honor, but the Riders deserved their royal trot from City Hall to Central Park. Niles, the commandant of this camp on the dunes, was sympathetic to our plight. He was a young captain who had been caught in a compromising act with another officer's wife, and was exiled to the edge of Long Island—he existed in a state of permanent truancy at Montauk Point. The War Department had forgotten who he was and why he was here. But he kept his rank and could still sign his name on a chit. He had the Rough Rider mounts delivered from several military stables in Tampa and San Antone. And then a crate arrived pocked with air holes. Inside the crate was Josephine, our cougar cub. I couldn't tell how she would react to my battle-worn red whiskers. But our regimental lion made a heartbreaking yawp and leapt into my arms. I fell into the sand dunes, with Josephine licking my face.

My cougar had grown since I saw her last. She could cover my pate with a single paw. Her own whiskers were as wild and unkempt as a plantation. And when she stretched on the sand, she was like her own transport ship with yellow spots. There was nothing savage, nothing rough, about our girl. She insisted on sleeping in my wall tent, and we had scarce enough room for Winters-White and his belongings. She'd climb onto my lap while I was at my desk, and the desk would totter as I flopped onto the floor. She would lick my face and purr like the gigantic she-cat that she was. There was no denying Josephine. I was, it seems, second in command.

Out of a terrible ennui and anger at the War Department, the Rough Riders galloped along the shore, our guidons rattling in the wind, Josephine keeping pace with her near-perfect strides. It was a double reunion—Little Texas and a lovesick mountain lion. Captain Niles often rode with us, lost in a reverie that was impossible to unriddle.

"You should leave the service," I said.

"And what would I do? I was bred into the military from the time I was a pup. I went to the Point—I was second in my class. I cannot conceive of another life."

"But they will leave you here until you rot. That's how vindictive they are."

I began to scheme while I was in the saddle. I would ask Will to write up a portrait of the captain in the *Herald*. The War Department could not bear unfavorable publicity. But the general staff might wound Niles even worse out of pure spite.

This quarantine could not last forever—yet Secretary Alger must have wanted it to seem that way. It was Will who rescued us. He smuggled out a series of dispatches to his editors at the *Herald*. He was wickedly shrewd. He never criticized the quarantine. He simply wrote about the troopers and their curious nicknames. Taggart was "Mr. Pink," of course. But he was also known as "the

Padre." Trooper Anton-Antonia was "the Angel," and she really was. We couldn't have survived the charge up San Juan Hill without Antonia and her bloodied flag. Pollock the Pawnee, who never smiled, was "Boisterous Bob." Henshaw, the blacksmith, who had hurled rock after rock at the Spaniards from our trenches, was "Professor Rockpicker." Neiman, our regimental surgeon, became "Bloodless Bill." Norfolk, his stretcher bearer, who didn't even carry a gun, was "Billy the Kid." Schoenfeld, the Jewish merchant who checked our payroll stubs, and tried to keep kosher in the jungle, was "Ham & Eggs." Henderson, the trumpeter of Troop L, was known as "Noiseless."

Winters-White also listed the renegades who ran away and each Rough Rider who fell in battle:

> Brown, John, Private, Dropped from rolls as deserted,
> June 3.
> Hendriks, Milo A., Mortally wounded at battle of San Juan,
> July 1.
> Crosley, Henry S., Private, Dropped from rolls as deserted,
> July 8.
> Green, Henry C., Killed in action, July 1, near Santiago de
> Cuba . . .

We were mustered out within a week and the First United States Volunteer Cavalry regiment ceased to exist—as if we'd been a chimera these past four months. The ordnance clerks collected our guns, our uniforms, and our mounts. Our ponies were sold at auction and we could not have our parade. Little Texas was mine, of course, and I also kept Josephine—the Riders from Arizona had given our regimental mascot outright to me.

We were horseless horsemen in civilian rags. But not even our fiercest enemies on the general staff could have realized how we would enter the nation's myth. Entire circuses, I was told, would be constructed around our charge up San Juan Hill. The battle would be rehearsed and reconstrued in every schoolhouse across the land, even in the Indian Territory, because of the Riders' sensational scouts. But on our last day at Montauk Point, I was summoned out of my tent by an orderly, and had to confront a very bizarre configuration—a hollowed-out square of Rough Riders, Buffalo Soldiers, and civilians; not one of them uttered a word. And in truth, I thought I was among the living and the dead, that the casualties in Cuba had risen out of their graves to accuse their colonel of some terrible slight.

"Trooper Green, is that you, son?"

The trooper didn't answer me. He'd died on the run up Kettle Hill. And then Private Will Murphy, the quiet one, of Troop M—alive he was—stepped in front of my path and guided me to a crooked table on which some object was covered with a horse blanket. I'm not sure why Will Murphy was chosen to represent the Rough Riders. He didn't have Abe Hummel's silver tongue. He hardly had a tongue at all. His face twisted into a knot and finally he said, "A gift, sir, a gift—a minuscule token of admiration from the First Volunteers to their commanding officer, who led them through thick and thin. . . . In conclusion, let me say that one and all will carry in his heart a memory of your kindness, sir, and your fairness that is so uncommon in war."

Poor Will Murphy must have practiced for a month. He put me to shame. He removed the horse blanket, and there on the table sat a bronze statuette of a bronco buster, with Fred Remington's unmistakable mark; no one else could have captured the furious décor of horse and rider, welded into one.

And I, the master of sounds and birdsongs, was struck dumb. This gift hadn't come from Fred's own friends in the regiment, but from the cowpokes and bronco busters themselves. "Boys, you gave me your hardtack and your blankets when I had none."

"Aw," said one of my ruffians, "you robbed the commissary clerks blind for our sake."

"Colonel," said another, "you busted the generals' balls."

"Never once were you outside the firing line."

"Except when I could not find my specs," I shouted with a hoarseness in my throat.

"Hurrah, hurrah for the next Governor of New York!"

I could not part with them like that, knowing that I might never see my Rough Riders again, with their bandannas and sunburnt smiles.

"Come," I said, "I want to look you in the eye and shake every hand. I insist—indulge me, boys. It will be your commander's last command."

The ranks formed, and my ruffians—one by one—passed before me in single file. I was not dreaming, I swear. I did talk to an occasional dead man. There was no fuss, no furor. Trooper Green's hand wasn't gray from the rotting soil. I did not hold on to him. I let the man go.

I fell upon Bellows, my former body-servant, who was again with the Buffalos—his shoulder wound had healed.

"Bellows, I would have crawled to Hades if it hadn't been for you. I was blind, man, blind without my specs."

"Colonel, I had sewn a pair into every one of your garments."

"But the Mausers would have shaved me clean."

"Poppycock. You were immortal on that line."

And he was gone, every last one, paid their $77 by the clerk and signed their discharge slips. I went back to my tent, like some lost plainsman, with my bronze horse and rider, the wind blowing off the dunes with a constant roar, and I could still see their silent ponies pounding the shores, the rip of a regiment, the trumpeter's call.

PART FOUR

CHAPTER 14

JOSEPHINE

1899

MANY OF MY BOYS COULDN'T ADJUST TO CIVILIAN LIFE. I'm not talking about the stockbrokers and bankers and tennis champions from the East, of course. They doubled their good fortune on the Rough Rider legend. And I did hire a few of the cowpokes as my companions and bodyguards on the campaign trail. The Republicans would have lost without the Riders—Boss Platt was indeed a pariah with all his greedy barons. The Riders accompanied me to every whistle-stop. They hardly uttered a word, but it really didn't matter much. We had Josephine, who raced along the roof of every car, her long tail curling in the wind; that cougar loved to show off and play to a crowd, as the yellow spots were beginning to vanish on her sand-colored coat. Her blue-gray eyes had turned brown since Montauk, but her muzzle was as white as it had ever been. She leapt onto my shoulder and sat there like a sentinel, while I swayed a bit under her seventy pounds of muscle and bone. And her constant caterwaul—that cougar serenade—was enough to enlist an entire town. Big as she was, she licked every Rough Rider on board.

We prevailed with our regimental mascot and the sheer force of our charge up San Juan Hill, encrusted with memory and myth that sent the Tammany Tiger into a dizzying spin. But sutlers and other charlatans took advantage of my boys, even after I was elected Governor. A number of the Riders couldn't read or write. And they signed away their life stories to some quack publisher for a pittance. I had to hire lawyers to get them out of these contracts. Others worked in Wild West shows, some for Buffalo Bill himself. I did receive a letter dictated by ex-Trooper Abel Martinson to one of the stagehands at Madison Square Garden.

> *Colonel, I am in the doghouse with Buffalo Bill. I will owe & owe & owe for the rest of my life. I miss Wyoming, sir. I miss my mare.*
> *Forgive me. I am ashamed to write.*
> *One of your devoted boys,*
> *Otherwise known as Abel.*

It ripped at me, that damn letter. I could hear Abel's slow, saturnine drawl behind the words he dictated. He'd been my ace of spades with a long gun. He left more casualties with holes in their heads than any of my other sharpshooters. But he couldn't stand up to Cody. So I abandoned my morning séance with reporters at the Capitol and took the train down to Grand Central. . . .

I crossed the road to that terra-cotta Moorish castle on East Twenty-sixth with its three-hundred-foot tower—Madison Square Garden. Its arcades were covered with painted cloths of Buffalo Bill in his spangled buckskin suit. I didn't fancy *Buffalo Bill's Wild West* as a nativist dream against all outliers—white, red, or black. It had a different melody in Manhattan, summoning up a frontier that was all but gone. Cody had transformed the amphitheater at the Garden into a vast forest, with painted murals and backdrops that could reveal mountains, rivers, and a Pawnee reservation. Cowboys, Indians, or the Seventh Cavalry could come riding out of a flap in a mural and disappear into another flap. Nothing was ever stable except Buffalo Bill himself. He was the only constant in a shifting narrative tale. But I wasn't here out of any nostalgia for the Badlands. I'd come for Buffalo Bill.

The *Wild West* began with a curious race between a Pawnee on foot and a Cheyenne on a spotted pony. The runner was no stranger to me—it was Young-Man-Afraid-of-the-Sound-of-His-Own-Voice. I'd recruited him last year in the basement of the War Department in Washington. He'd gone with me to San Antone, to the sandy streets of Tampa, and to the hills surrounding Santiago, and had been one of my best scouts, though he never uttered a word. He had a fever in his hands. He communicated with a simple sign language that was akin to smoke signals. And here he was, racing a spotted pony in his moccasins. I wouldn't have given him a chance in a million. But he must have had Cody's wind machine in his rump. Perhaps the problem was with the pony, or the Cheyenne on its back. The pony galloped across the arena with a whinny that was fierce as any war cry. Its nostrils flared. Yet the strides of the Pawnee scout in his moccasins were faster than the human eye could behold, much faster. And he beat the spotted pony to the far edge of the arena by the length of a moccasin.

Buffalo Bill stood there stunned in his spangled buckskin suit, his long hair as fine as a lady's. His sharpshooter's hand shook. He could barely put his lips to his speaking trumpet. I suspect that Young-Man-Afraid-of-the-Sound-of-His Own-Voice, or any other runner in Cody's camp, had never won this race before. The Pawnee couldn't have known I was in the house—it was much too dark in the stands. But he must have intuited it, like some miraculous smoke signal.

So I didn't have to worry about this Pawnee. It was the others who concerned me now. Boys like Abel Martinson, who had his present and his future held in Cody's pocket. He was quite apologetic.

"Couldn't help myself, Colonel. I drank and drank and signed little chits. 'T ain't Cody's fault. I could have sucked on another nipple."

I went with Abel into Buffalo Bill's headquarters—it was a wide tent, like the one I'd had at Montauk Point, only much grander. It was equipped with a telephone and a telegraph machine, a desk with brass handles, a sofa, a bed, hurricane lamps, a hardwood table, several plush chairs, and pictures on one of the canvas walls of Custer and Wild Bill Hickok.

Cody eyed me and Abel up and down. He didn't wear buckskin in his tent. He had yellow trousers and a coat with silk lapels.

"Governor, I would have gladly given you a free ticket to the show. But I must insist that this Rider of yours leave. He is forbidden to enter my quarters. And rules are rules, sir."

I nodded to Abel, and he left.

"General," I said, plastering him with his rank in the militia, "your sutlers have been plying my boys with alcohol. Half of them are grown children. I'm susceptible to this. My father had to fight off sutlers during the late war."

Cody stepped out from behind his desk. "We do not employ sutlers of any kind at *Buffalo Bill's Wild West*, Colonel."

His long white hair was gorgeous, and he would not wear it in a knot. He was tall, with broad shoulders and the waist of an asp. He must have adored Hickok, genuinely adored him. Away from his customers, he wore a long black coat, like Wild Bill, with a belt rather than a holster. He employed more Indians than there were on some reservations. General Cody was a fitting title. He had to travel from terrain to terrain with an army of performers, mechanics, and cooks, plus stage props, horses, buffalo, and half-tame bears. He had to stage prairie fires without burning down the Garden and hire artists to paint his scenery. He couldn't make a move without renting three dozen railroad cars. The logistics of it all would have ruined a lesser man.

"There's a more pressing matter than ex-Trooper Abel," Buffalo Bill said, grooming his mustache and beard with a silver comb. "That big cat of yours. What's her name?"

I was shivering, I admit. I didn't want Buffalo Bill near my cougar cub. "Josephine," I finally said. "And she doesn't concern what's happening here."

"She sure does. She'd be a great attraction at my *Wild West*.

What other big cat went off to a foreign war? *Riveting*. I could offer you five thousand—in gold—and a percentage of the gate."

"Josephine's not a circus animal," I said. "I do not want her mentioned again."

"Well," he said, as if I had suddenly exhausted him and whatever interest he had in me. "I gave you my best offer. . . . Now, it's not a question of whiskey, sir. Your heroes have been stealing from us. That's why I have had to garnish their salaries."

I was annoyed with his truculent air. "That's difficult to comprehend," I said. "Abel Martinson is a sharpshooter, not a thief."

"But this isn't Cuba, with war and the distractions of war. This is a civilization of tents and arenas. With whiskey, yes, and women. Martinson's a celebrity. That's the real problem. And it comes with a price he can't afford. I've warned him. I won't again."

"It's still hard to fathom," I said. "How much does he owe?"

Buffalo Bill stroked his long hair with one of his beautiful hands. He didn't need a gunman's glove inside his tent. And he didn't need to inspect his books. "Nine hundred dollars and ten cents."

I took out my checkbook and scribbled a check for that amount. I'd surprised this son of a bitch. He couldn't quite grasp my devotion to the boys. "His debt is erased, Colonel. But that won't solve the problem. Martinson has nowhere else to go."

"You're wrong," I said. "He has a ranch in Wyoming. He's been dyin' to return there."

Cody laughed. It wasn't savage or bitter. "And get caught in the middle of a range war, where his celebrity will be uncertain. He's in the show business, and he'll stay with my tents. . . . But I have a resentment, Colonel. *Rough Riders*. You stole that appellation from me. I had my own Congress of Rough Riders ever since my European tours—gauchos, Vaqueros, Cossacks, Mexican cowboys."

The press had pinned that title on my cowboy regiment, and the title clung.

"Cody," I said, "you'll have to sue every publisher in America if you want that title back, and you still won't get it."

He brooded for a moment. He wasn't a showman in his heart of hearts. He was a man-killer, another Wild Bill, in a world where man-killers had become fossilized. And so he dreamt of Hickok, while he curated the *Wild West*. That's why he was so successful. It wasn't his strengths as an impresario. It was the dream of violence that lay embedded in every one of his acts. A two-gun man hovered under his tents—Hickok's ghost.

"Colonel, I'll still give you five thousand for the cougar," he said.

I walked away from Cody and his lavish tent without a single word of goodbye.

I PLANNED TO HOUSE Josephine at Sagamore Hill, have her roam the forest and the seashore. I hired a special warden from the Boone & Crockett Club to watch after her while I was away with Edith and the bunnies at the Governor's Mansion in Albany. But she broke into the chicken coop, plunderer that she was, and also ran down every woodchuck and rabbit in our little preserve. The warden had to have her caged. It was a calamity, holding her like that. Josephine couldn't prosper without human company. She was used to my lads, used to me.

I couldn't keep a mountain lion at the Governor's Mansion, but I did. I let Josephine have the observatory as her lair, and she prowled on the banisters, sniffed every corner she could, battled spiderwebs. The bunnies adored her. Edie was less felicitous about her former *rival* from Tampa Bay. My wife was adamant when Josephine curled up under the quilts, near my legs.

"Dearest, I will not sleep with a lion in our bed. You will have to choose your mate."

"But she's still a child," I groaned, "a baby girl."

Edith glared at me. "Quite a baby! She's six feet long."

"Five and a half," I insisted.

"*Theodore.*"

I had to lock Josephine out of the bedroom. She crouched there, whimpered half the night, scratching on the door. Edith relented—

a little, or none of us would have slept. Our handyman built a crate for her, and that was her nighttime residence, near the foot of our four-poster.

After breakfast, I marched along Eagle Street with Josephine at my side, past the mansions of Dutch town's wealthy merchants, who had little love for me and my pet cougar. Arriving at the Capitol, with its red-capped twin towers, we bounded up the marble stairs to the Governor's Office on the second floor, as legislators and hucksters panicked at my sudden appearance and bolted out of our way.

"The Boy Governor," one of these lads shouted within earshot, "with his celebrated carnivore."

I paid these rascals no mind—they were bought and sold by the local barons and Black Horse Cavalry. The Legislature hadn't evolved since my time as the Cyclone Assemblyman—it had slipped back into the antediluvian mud, with the assistance of Senator Platt. Hence, I wasn't surprised when Platt himself appeared as my first appointment of the morning.

"Senator, I'm *dee*-lighted. What are you doing in Dutch town?"

The Easy Boss didn't answer right away. I'd had my antique Commissioner's desk from Mulberry Street delivered to the Capitol. And Josephine lay sprawled across the top in all her feline glory.

"I'm attending an undertaker's convention," Platt said. "Governor, you ran a corking campaign!"

I let him imbibe his own beliefs and then I rattled him. "I did not. We won by the skin of our teeth. Tammany would have stolen the State if my Rough Riders—and Josephine—hadn't rescued your stinking ship. You've let the corporations prosper, while you hurt the little man."

"The little man," he said with contempt. "Are you now some kind of a socialist?"

I bowed to the Easy Boss. "No, Senator Tom. I'm the Boy Governor. Isn't that what your barons call me?"

"Because you behave like a boy," he said. "Who else but a man with a boy's desires and delights would let a lion run rampant in the State Capitol?"

"She isn't rampant at all. You should be kinder to Josephine. This *lion* won the election for us."

"She did not," snarled Senator Tom. "It was all decoration. You wouldn't be here without the corporate chiefs you despise so much."

"That's a lie," I said, as Josephine began to grow restless with Boss Platt in the room. She growled—it was a grating noise, full of anger and mistrust.

The Easy Boss paid scant attention to my cat and her growls.

"Well, Governor, go and ask Pierpont Morgan. We had to borrow ten thousand from him at the last minute, so we could secure additional troops in questionable precincts."

Pierpont. Then I really was in a fool's paradise.

"If you keep attacking the corporate trusts," Platt said, "you'll not have a single donor. And there won't be a second term."

"I'll still have Josephine."

"Sonny," he said, "I ain't so sure."

He doffed his hat to my pet cougar and was gone—but his *imprint* remained. There was a knock on the door, and Little Haynes, who'd been the cloakroom attendant ever since I could recall, entered without his eternal air of humility.

"Haynes," I growled, "what the devil do you want?"

"Ah, Governor, you will have to address me as Commissioner Haynes."

"Commissioner of what?" I had to ask that simpleminded man.

"Health, Governor. It's what is called a pocket appointment in local parlance, sir. Senator Platt appointed me with a scratch of his pen."

The Senator and his cronies had been imbibing Haynes with every sort of *illegality.* "Haynes, he does not have the power to appoint you, not even to the cloakroom."

"Ah, but he will get the Legislature's approval, Governor. And meanwhile, I have both badge and title. And you are strictly forbidden to bring that lion to the Capitol."

I threw this fraudulent Commissioner out of my office. But

I couldn't battle Senator Tom, the State Legislature, *and* Edith. And so I found a solution, sad as it was. The Boone & Crockett Club had created its own preserve, the Bronx Zoölogical Gardens, on 261 acres of abandoned farmland near Fordham Road— it was the largest zoo in the world, without a rival to its Beaux Arts pavilions and massive wrought-iron gates. I'd been to the London Zoo, with its two-headed turtle and other freakish attractions. I'd visited Berlin, with its little battalion of six-legged deer. Even Prague, with its pink lioness. *All* the animals were kept in tiny cages. Gone was their natural habitat. These zoölogical parks weren't parks at all—they were seductive prisons. That's not what I had planned for the Bronx. We had granite ridges, forests, meadows, and plains we often had to sculpt with our own hands. We intended to breed buffalo in the Bronx and then return *our* buffalo to the Great Plains. We had an Antelope House and a Lion House—enormous pavilions—to entertain *and* educate our visitors, but these animals could also wander in our local wilderness, with its own river, lake, and streams. My brothers at Boone & Crockett convinced me that *this* Noah's Ark on dry land would be the perfect habitat for Josephine. She would have a pavilion all her own, with a pair of keepers, who would wander across the Bronx plains with her at will. And I, as Chief Executive of New York and founding member of Boone & Crockett, could visit Josephine at any hour—even if the gates were shut—and as often as I wished.

I had a companion, too. Miss Nan Fowler, Pulitzer's undercover agent and prize reporter. Pulitzer had wanted to send her to Cuba to cover the conflict, but the War Department knew of her affiliation with me and wouldn't accredit her as a correspondent. "TR has enough attention for *two* lifetimes," said the generals. So Nan sat out the war. She looked haggard upon my return from Cuba, with a certain dullness in her eyes. She could have unmasked the corruption of Senator Tom and Boss Croker of Tammany Hall, but she didn't write a word about the election, not a word. Nor did she visit me in Dutch town. And without warning, Nan sent me a wire from Pulitzer's headquarters on Newspaper Row.

MUST INTERVIEW MISS JOSEPHINE.
DEMAND AN EXCLUSIVE WITH THE CAT.

I couldn't even tell if Nan had gone mad. There she was at the Fordham Gate, her hair all awry, her lipstick smeared in a crooked line. She hadn't prospered while I had been away; I did read her undercover tales from time to time, but her usual flair was gone; she wrote as if she had just come out of a static dream.

She curtsied and clapped her hands. I wanted to shake some sense into her.

"Miss Nan," I asked, "why the sudden interest in our regimental mascot?"

"Mascot, Governor? You're not the kind of man who would keep souvenirs of a war. She must mean a great deal to you."

"She does, dammit," I said.

Now Nan smiled. Her teeth were crooked. I should have noticed.

"Yet you donate her to a zoo for others to gawk at."

"It's a scientific haven," I said. "I helped build this zoo—we all did, at Boone & Crockett."

Dr. Martin Faraday, the head zookeeper, met us at the gate. He'd overheard our conversation.

"Mrs. Fowler, you mustn't chide Governor Ted. He made the right decision, a difficult one. Yes, Josephine is still a cub—her spots haven't completely disappeared. But she's also a predator. She's devoured chicken hawks, I believe, broken their necks. Female cats are quite possessive. She might rip off the arm of any unfamiliar person who comes close to the Governor."

"I'll take my chances," Nan said.

We marched across the gravel path. Construction was still going on at a furious pace—there were ditches everywhere, potholes, and piles of dirt. We passed a lone ostrich behind a wire fence—looking both fierce and defenseless—and arrived at Josephine's pavilion; it had an enormous gallery for visitors and a cage where the cougar could roam. A pair of young wardens were playing with Josephine outside her cage, feeding her scraps of meat; otherwise the pavilion was empty. It looked like a well-lit cave stuffed with sand and straw.

Josephine kept grabbing at the meat, even after she noticed me. She'd been rolling around in the straw. I wasn't coy with her, or shy. And I didn't really care how Miss Nan described this meeting in Pulitzer's rag.

"Jo," I whispered. My sweetheart of a cub didn't even purr, not once, or caterwaul, to reveal some sign of displeasure at my sudden disappearance from her life. She stopped chewing, and glanced at Nan out of the corner of her eye. Still, she stood there, like a huntress—no, a predator, as Dr. Faraday had predicted. And then she yawped—it was near a human cry. She did a somersault, much faster than any man could behold. She swatted at me with one paw, but that swat was as soft as a kiss. She had no shame. She stood on her hind legs, not lazily, like a dancing bear, but with the swiftness of a cougar, grabbed my shoulders with both paws, and licked my face in front of Faraday, Nan, and her two feeders.

"Aw, Jo," I said, and her purring was louder than the croak of a frog in an icehouse.

I asked Faraday and the wardens to leave. The younger warden glanced at me.

"But that's breaking the rules, Governor—one of us has to be present at all times if we have a visitor."

Faraday shook him off with a nod. "Take you time, Governor. We'll be outside the pavilion."

I hadn't come unprepared to the Fordham Gate. I put on my colonel's gauntlets and wrestled with my cub. We rolled around in the straw and dust; she attacked my gauntlets with mock savagery, while I serenaded her in the thick of battle. "Josephine, my Jo."

I rolled over once and espied Nan, who studied us both with a quizzical look.

"Well, Mrs. Fowler, I thought you came here to interview my pup."

"Governor, believe me, that is my intent. But Josephine can't growl her retorts."

"Maybe I can," I said. And she laughed for the first time, again revealing her crooked teeth.

"What future does this animal have—in a cage?"

"A cage within her own pavilion," I said. "Like a princess."

"Look at her, Mr. Ted. Miss Josephine is a wounded cat."

I put down my gauntlets for a moment. "Wounded cat? What does that mean?"

"She's in love with you—that, sir, is mortal business."

I didn't know how to answer Nan. "I can't keep her—I've tried. And I can't give her back to the Riders from Arizona who gave her to the regiment. Both of them are currently behind bars. I'm one of the founders of this zoo. We collected a fortune to have a deluxe domain for wildlife, a habitat. These animals will live much longer under our dominion, Nan."

"Yes, yes, but how often will you visit Josephine?"

"Jumping Jesus, as often as I can."

I WAITED FOR THIS PHANTOM interview to appear in the *World*. Nan didn't disappoint me. She rarely did. She called it "The Roughest of Rough Riders." And she didn't rely on the luck of a photographer's flash pan. She'd drawn her own sketch of Josephine, whiskers and all. And she endowed Josephine with the gift of speech. My big cat answered Nan's questions like a veteran trooper.

You can call me Josephine, or Jo. I didn't get to see Cuba, Ma'am. Mascots weren't allowed in the tropics. But I trained with the Colonel, accompanied him and the Riders on their regimental runs near San Antonio, on the plains outside Tampa, and along the dunes at Montauk Point. I also sat with the Colonel at the bar of the Menger Hotel, in order to eat the heart out of those generals at Fort Sam who tried to cause havoc in our regiment. But the Riders are not Regular Army and had to disband. A regimental

*mascot can't exist once a regiment is gone. Now I live in the wilds
near Fordham Road, with my own palace. Come visit if you can.*

The interview was a sensation, of course, and it drew endless
lines outside Josephine's pavilion, lines that stretched right to Fordham Road and beyond. Suddenly Josephine had become the Bronx
Zoo's star attraction. I didn't like it. I thought of Cody. Wasn't this
a version of *Cody's Wild West* on the plains near Fordham Road? I
received a note from Nan.

> FORGIVE ME, GOVERNOR.
> I DID NOT MEAN TO CREATE SUCH A STIR.
> I WANTED TO PUNISH YOU, I SUPPOSE,
> AND ALL I DID WAS PUNISH JOSEPHINE.

Our experiment with the Bronx buffalo failed. They could not
feed on fake prairie grass. The local wardens had to feed them genuine grass from the Great Plains. And still they grew spindly, one
by one. Several died. We could not reproduce their natural habitat
in the Bronx. The *Brooklyn Eagle* lambasted us, called us amateurs
and wild experimenters, even said Boone & Crockett was filled
with charlatans and racketeers.

Nan never attacked me once.

I visited Josephine again, among that furl of people. I waited
until the pavilion emptied out. I wrestled with my little girl, rolled
around in the straw. But her shoulder blades seemed kind of thin
to me, not packed with muscle. She licked me a-plenty, purred, and
grew silent as I was about to leave, as if I had become one more
illusion in a land of illusions.

I voiced my concern to Dr. Faraday.

"Governor, I won't lie," he said. "She bonded with you, and it's a
real dilemma. We've given her playmates—other cougars—and all
she does is attack them with her paws, not to maim, just to declare
her own distance. My wardens sit with her for hours, and she's fond
of them, but they're not Rough Riders."

I was gripped with a grief I couldn't control. "I'll have to take her back," I said. "I'm not sure how to handle it, but I will."

"I understand," he said. "Still, I'm sorry to hear that. We'll just have to prosper without her."

But I stalled, you see. I was so damn occupied, battling the Easy Boss and his army of plutocrats. They broke the unions, swallowed up little manufacturers in their wake, until not a soul could compete with them. I fought back—like a lioness. I harangued the Legislature. "Gentlemen, you have become carrion that the Easy Boss serves up to his plutocrat friends. I will not abide that." I vetoed bill after bill. And Josephine vanished from my daily agenda until I got a call, not from Faraday, mind you, but from Nan.

"Governor, come quick."

NAN HAD BEEN TO SEE my little girl every day, had stood in line for hours. And when I arrived at the Fordham Gate, she got in front of Faraday, seized my hand, and we walked to Faraday's little palace, his own pavilion, with a tiny hospital, a study room for scholars, and a morgue. Josephine lay near a wheezing tiger, on the mattress of an enormous crib, in the hospital's surgical station. Her tongue was out, slaked with foam. Her brown eyes had gone blood-red. Faraday's entire little team of veterinary surgeons were there in their waxed mustaches and starched white coats. I couldn't get an answer out of them that made sense. Her heartbeats were too rapid—or too slow. They spat out the names of a few sedatives and tonics, powders they had concocted themselves.

"Governor," one of these surgeons said, "at first I thought she had bronchitis. She's had trouble breathing. . . ."

"Faraday," I said, "I've lived with this cat, nursed her through a bellyache and a fat fever, and it looks to me as if she's dying right in this room."

"It's more than possible," muttered the head zookeeper.

"And what can mend her?"

"I'm not sure," he said. "Perhaps a different locale. We're not Rough Riders."

And then another surgeon intervened. He was the youngest of the lot, a recent graduate of Harvard's veterinary college, who was considered the most brilliant animal doctor in the Bronx, I had been told by my brothers at Boone & Crockett. He had very thin nostrils and a high forehead. Unlike every other surgeon in the room, he did not fear me at all. He introduced himself as Dr. Lionel Trell.

"She's a lovelorn cat, TR. I have seen other such attachments. And they are pernicious. They do not end well—it's partly my fault. I thought we could retrain her."

"Lionel has worked miracles with other cats," Dr. Faraday said.

Trell mused a bit. "It was my own pride that failed me. There's not another animal in the world quite like a regimental cat. No matter how well we treat her, how hard we juggle and groom—and I've tried—we will always be strangers to her."

Trell let me have the zoo's own ambulance and driver. I lifted Jo in my arms, and all that redness went out of her eyes, as I carried her to the ambulance. Her breathing was less labored. My cat seemed calmer, while I was near to lunacy. Nan rode with us.

"I mean to take her to Sagamore Hill."

Nan could sense that wildness in me, that desperation. She rubbed Josephine's muzzle. "Governor, Jo might not survive that trip."

"I'll have to risk it—I don't have another plan."

We rode all the way downtown, while I fed Josephine water out of a nursing bottle. I hired a barge. The captain recognized our regimental lion and wouldn't take a nickel from me.

He had his foghorn bleat once—and every bit of barge and ferry traffic swerved out of our way, even the burial runs to Hart Island. I could see the little shops and stands on the Brooklyn shoreline, the half-sunk fishing schooners, and old, leathery fishermen on their little makeshift bridges.

I cradled Jo, listened to her heartbeat, trying to breathe to my cat's irregular rhythms. I sang her a Dutch nursery rhyme that Brave Heart's own father—Grandpa Cornelius, the family tycoon—had taught me.

Trippel trippel toonjes,
Kippen in de boontjes . . .

I couldn't have told you what the words meant, not then, not now. But they soothed Josephine—she didn't wheeze as much.

I could see all the shoppers on the Grand Street ferry, in their long stylish skirts and magnificent chapeaux that resembled an admiral's tricorn with feathers and bows—that must have been high fashion in 1899, a seafarer's hat and cape. I'd been like an ostrich at the Capitol, oblivious to fashion, high and low.

"Teddy, Teddy," they shouted, their handkerchiefs in the wind.

It was Nan who nodded for me.

A fireboat came near us, with its cavalcade of water cannons—captain and crew were curious to see a big cat in my arms, one paw dangling around my neck.

"Governor, can we help?"

I could not hear Jo's heart in that squall of water, and it was as if I had stopped breathing, too.

"Governor," Nan whispered, "she's gone."

We sat there, two mourners in a splintered barge, minding a cat with claws that had come so sudden and haphazard into our lives, giving us such gaiety for a little while, with one paw still dangling around my neck.

THE TRUMPETER FROM TROOP L had traveled all the way from Illinois. Fifty other troopers arrived—sixty, I'd say, with several Buffalo Soldiers and my former body-servant, Bellows, who'd frolicked on the sands of Montauk with Jo. Our bunnies had prepared pieces of cake. We had cups of apple cider, fermented right on the farm. Several of my brothers from Boone & Crockett were also there. We buried Josephine near the rabbit hutch, since she loved to chase rabbits so. Edie kept nudging me, with a silk rag against her nose.

"It's my fault. I shouldn't have hectored you. Josephine had a home on Eagle Street."

"Darling," I said, "we couldn't keep her locked up in a mansion. She would have gnawed every bit of woodwork—she's wild."

"Mrs. Theodore," Nan said, "she was a soldier who lost her place—like any other casualty of war."

And then Buffalo Bill arrived out of the blue with his long white hair. I hadn't invited the showman. He tipped his wide-brimmed hat to Edith.

"Forgive the intrusion, ma'am. I know it's a private ceremony. But I couldn't resist." Bill didn't berate me for not selling Josephine to him.

"TR," he said, "she was an astonishing gal."

"But you didn't meet her once."

"I heard about her from half a dozen people," Cody said. "Colonel, I think we ought to dance. . . . Abel Martinson, do you have your mouth harp?"

I'd bought Abel's freedom from Cody's circus. He didn't have to answer Buffalo Bill.

"I do, sir," Abel said.

"Well, son, why don't you play—"

"'The Devil's Dream'" I shouted. It's was Father's favorite ballad.

Forty days and forty nights
The Devil was a-dreaming
Around the bark, old Noah's Ark
The rain it was a-streaming . . .

He'd learnt that ballad as a boy; perhaps it was his lone act of rebellion, a lad who was apprenticed to his father, old Cornelius, before he was eleven, brought into the Roosevelts' shop of plate glass, and never really left. Papa would sing this ballad on our sleigh rides, sing it with a wicked pleasure.

Abel plucked out his dented silver mouth harp that he had picked up for pennies at a market square in San Antone and began to play Papa's ballad, accenting the rhythm with one of his boot-heels. Somehow, it seemed appropriate. Josephine had had her own infernal temper at times, just like Papa. And we all clutched hands and performed a jig around Josephine's grave site, like cavaliers hopping near a fire at the end of a roundup.

I was startled to see Dr. Lionel Trell, the zoo's master surgeon, at Josephine's wake.

"Governor, I fear I let you down—badly. I'm supposed to be a scientist. Yet nothing in my arsenal could cure her."

I touched his sleeve. I didn't bear Dr. Lionel any ill will. "But you were right. She suffered the fate of a regimental lion—and my neglect."

"Our neglect, sir."

And he joined the cotillion of dancers. . . .

Cody held on to Nan, and whirled her about with all the swagger of the *Wild West*. She laughed for the first time since both of us had accompanied my cat, alive and dead, to Sagamore Hill.

Suddenly I couldn't hold on to the beat of Abel's mouth harp. I was lost for a moment. It was like that crowded hour on the climb up Kettle Hill, with the polka dots fluttering at the back of my head, a flag at half mast, and me without my specs—a man caught in the hugger-mugger, a colonel no less, leading a charge without any knowledge of where to go. And here was Sergeant Bellows again, Bellows, who had brought me out of that morass with another pair of my own specs.

"She was a sweetheart, Colonel. I'll miss her sore."

"So will I, Sergeant, so will I."

Every damn day of my life.

PART FIVE

CHAPTER 15

THE COWBOY
CANDIDATE

1900

EDITH AND I STAYED AT THE REPUBLICAN PARTY CASTLE in Philadelphia, the Hotel Walton, with its roof of caplets and copper domes, like dour witches' hats. The Honorable Mark Hanna, lord and master of the convention, had done his own witchery, turning delegates toward his little tide of candidates. But Cabot broke through Hanna's malignant design. Delegates went from floor to floor of the castle, dressed as wounded Minutemen with bandaged skulls while they carried drums and fifes and shouted, "We want the Cowboy, Yah! Yah! Yah!"

That bedlam was hard to resist. And Cabot, with his white hair and hazel eyes, accompanied these delegates with a drum of his own, as one more wounded Minuteman prepared for battle; and battle it was, as they encountered some of Hanna's clique in the hallway and attacked with fife and drum. There had never been so many torn collars and split lips at Republican Party headquarters. House detectives had to be called in; Hanna's lads retreated to a lower floor. "Cabot's as cracked as Ted," their leader rasped. "Turned loony—overnight."

He was my oldest ally in politics. I trusted Cabot's instincts. Heir to a shipping fortune, he was a fellow Porcellian, who had supported my attack on the Indian Bureau when I was Civil Service Commissioner and had rallied Congress against rogue Indian agents. The two of us seemed woven out of the same sturdy cloth, without a single rip-line. Neither of us philandered—we adored our wives. Neither of us feared the tycoons and their influence. We were buccaneers of the Republican Party, at least I was, and Cabot was about to become one. He had a slow, deliberate majesty, and that's why Hanna's lackeys were bewildered. The Hamlet of Beacon Hill was Hotspur all of a sudden. They had never seen such truculence in Senator Henry Cabot Lodge, who was willing to take on the President and his Party chairman, Marcus Alonzo Hanna, at the Party's own castle on Locust Street.

"Children, we have to separate him from Ted."

Hanna had dubbed me a deputy sheriff with a saber who had charged up an obscure hill with a regiment of cowboy ruffians and basked in the glory of my own insane enterprise. I did not contradict him. He worshipped his "Major," as McKinley was often called. The President had been a supply sergeant during most of the Civil War, and was promoted to major at war's end. His wife was ill. Ida was subject to sudden seizures. And the Major was devoted to her. He did not abandon Ida to some closet in the White House. She sat next to him and crocheted in the midst of cabinet meetings. The Major was much too beholden to Republican bosses and entrepreneurs like his chubby counselor, Mark Hanna, the coal and iron baron who was many times a millionaire and had given up iron and coal to settle into a mansion across the road from the White House and become chair of this convention and the Republican National Committee. He was, he loved to say, the maker of kings. "But I have only one—the Major."

I happened to bump into Mark Hanna on the sun deck at the Walton, a pudgy little man with a cherubic face that belied his perpetual sneer. He had tiny fists and tinier feet.

"TR, you could have stayed in Albany. No one asked you to be a delegate—we certainly didn't."

"Ah, but I've had a miserable season, fighting Republican barons like yourself. And I wanted to catch a bit of your magic tricks."

"I have no tricks. I'm here to serve the President. And if you get in my way, TR, I'll crush you. This isn't Cuba, where you can dance with a sword."

He was about to boil over, and boil over he did, with hot froth on his tongue. "Cabot was *always* reliable. But you have led him astray. He runs around with his little band of Minutemen, beleaguering delegates, bullying them. He's become a Mugwump, like you, disloyal to his own Party." Hanna dabbed at the spittle with one of his cuffs. "Cabot has betrayed our king!"

I grabbed the President's little monkey by his silken lapels. "You are mistaken, Mr. Chairman. The Major is *your* king, not mine."

I released him, and off he went, that pudgy little man, with a handful of lieutenants.

I WAS SUMMONED TO PLATT'S suite in the hotel's highest tower. The Easy Boss lay abed with a broken rib. His complexion was as gray as ever. He'd caucused with his barons. And he delivered his edict with an air of finality. "Governor, you will accept the convention's call."

"What call? Cabot has his Minutemen whooping in the corridors. But Fat Marcus has the convention locked up. He considers me a maniac who might harm the country."

Platt pursed his lips. "Fat Marcus happens to be correct."

And there he lay in his infernal tower, with a pillow under his arse. "Then why did you summon me, sir?"

"Because," he said.

"That's not much of an answer, Senator Tom."

He could not sit up correctly. The brace he wore hindered his movements. "You are a menace to the Republican cause. But you're popular, far too popular. And you'll help the ticket—as McKinley's Vice President."

I did not like his reasoning. "You could have found a much simpler way to get rid of me."

"Governor, there is no simple way. If we hurl you out of Albany you'll only come back at us with a hammer blow."

"Senator Tom," I said, "you can never seem to make up your mind. You tried to bury me once in Washington and now you want to bury me again."

There was a twinge in his back, and he couldn't speak without a sip of water. "Bury you? You insinuated yourself right into the war."

"I volunteered."

"Yes, you ran the Navy and then abandoned your own desk—to fight alongside a bunch of renegade cowboys. Well, you can campaign with them, as McKinley's Cowboy Candidate."

"Madness and all," I muttered. "And you'll counter Fat Marcus, I suppose—your usual war with a knife. You always went for the gullet."

He smiled with his own murderous silk. "That won't be necessary. Mark Hanna is more isolated than you think. . . . I'm leaving this afternoon. I can't direct my soldiers from a bed."

His tactics were always curious to me. "Then you won't be at the convention for the big battle."

He looked away from me. "Governor, the battle's already won."

And his sycophants led me to the door. He was counting on me to chase Jennings Bryan. Bryan had the barrel chest and the basso of an opera singer. He was much younger than the Major, and was still considered the best orator of his era—I considered him an eloquent jackanapes who benefited from the collapse of silver. "You shall not crucify mankind on a cross of gold," he chanted to Democrats four years ago at their national convention, and bolted out of obscurity to become the youngest presidential candidate ever, at thirty-six. And he'd captured the Party again. "Cross of Gold," was his battle cry. The Easy Boss understood that I alone could match Bryan's vigor—with my much scratchier voice. I was the battler who could be buried at the same time.

—

THE EASY BOSS VANISHED from the hotel in a wheelchair. A private ambulance, owned by Pierpont Morgan, would carry him to Manhattan. But his presence clung to the Walton like a pungent perfume. . . .

I arrived at Exposition Hall with my wife on the final morning of the convention. The galleries were packed. Edith had her own pale beauty that couldn't have gone unnoticed. She wore a black hat and a black skirt that heightened her fierce alabaster look, like a lady gaucho. "Darling," she whispered, "don't be swayed by these straw men. They don't have your welfare at heart. They will use you and send you into exile." And she climbed upstairs to the women's gallery.

She shared a box with Cabot's glorious wife. Nannie had purple eyes and the chiseled profile of a princess. She ruled Washington society, and Edith happened to be a member of her court, whenever she wasn't in Albany or at Sagamore Hill. Both women would constantly conspire over some bewildering book. Cabot and I were helpless in their wake, since they were the royalty of our respective clans. How could a Republican convention compete with Nannie's purple eyes?

There was a curious aroma in the great hall, like a whiff of cough medicine—perhaps it was the mingling of so much human flesh with all the banners and balloons. I was wearing a black slouch hat. While I went to join New York's other delegates, there was a constant roar throughout the hall—"Teddy, Teddy, Teddy!" Cabot had met with delegation after delegation, my cunning Hamlet with his hazel eyes, whispering my name as McKinley's Vice Presidential candidate.

"Teddy, Teddy, Teddy!"

I wondered if Buffalo Bill was hiding behind a stanchion somewhere with his silver chin beard. This arena didn't have show Indians and Hebrew Cossacks, but it had much of the same hullabaloo—

trick horses, jugglers, men on stilts, and cowgirls carrying sign-boards that featured my ferocious grin.

"Teddy, Teddy, Teddy!"

Mark Hanna was at the podium. He couldn't curtail that roar and the constant stamping of feet. "Silence," he said, brandishing his gavel like a war club.

Streamers floated down from the galleries. For a moment Hanna was lost in a blinding glare of paper. It seemed like a conjurer's trick, as if the Easy Boss had arranged it all from his ambulance. But the convention itself was in a maddening haze. No one was really in charge, not the Major, who sat on his porch in Canton, Ohio, with his invalid of a wife, and not Mark Hanna, who couldn't stop the streamers and the repeated roar.

"Teddy, Teddy, Teddy!"

I wasn't blinded at all. I built a spyglass with my fingers and could catch the frozen pallor on Edith's face in her gallery box. She was mourning our future. She could manage our finances from that stolid mansion on Eagle Street, near the State Capitol. She'd gotten used to the icy winters. But we would become paupers in Washington, paupers without a proper home. Alice had to have a governess to control her wildness and her whims—and it was costly.

"Theodore," she had bemoaned, "we'll have to beg in the streets."

But it didn't seem to matter now, amid all the maddening fury—the pricked balloons and the stamping of feet. And neither of us could escape the chanting.

"Teddy, Teddy, Teddy!"

Fat Marcus had given up. He stopped pounding with his gavel. He stood there on the podium like a petulant child. He'd lost his chance to pick McKinley's running mate, to broker the convention. He was chairman, yes, chairman of cowgirls and balloons. The Major had given him no instructions. The Major had not expressed his will. "Silence," Hanna squealed one last time. But no one listened, no one heeded his call.

And I had a dream of such utter loneliness and despair that I could feel my head ride right off my shoulders and bounce across the convention hall like some monstrous gourd with a mustache and a pair of spectacles, as Hanna's delegates and their wives in the balcony hissed and heaped their venom upon me with balled handkerchiefs of spit. . . .

Senator Platt had been the shrewd one, sauntering away in his ambulance. It was, indeed, war with a knife. And I was both victim and winner in the same sordid blow. I would become McKinley's running mate—Cabot and his Minutemen had seen to that. And Fat Marcus could whimper that the maniac of San Juan Hill would soon be one heartbeat away from the presidency. A very long heartbeat it was, alas, much too long for the likes of me.

Yet in some inner recess, I was still that monstrosity, the dancing gourd. I must have encouraged Cabot, *without* encouraging him, encouraged Nannie, too, she with the purple eyes, who had more sway in Washington corridors than Cabot himself. Hanna was correct. I did not have to come to Philadelphia, sit with the New York delegation in my long-brimmed black hat, crouching like some candidate, a cougar prepared to kill.

I FOUND NANNIE IN the tea parlor back at the hotel, *almost* by accident. We sat like two conspirators, ordered a pot of China tea and a brace of buns. Every damn eye was on her. She was wearing a bodice of blue velvet and a military cape. She looked like a gorgeous Cossack in her Burgundy-colored boots.

"I'm selfish, Governor Ted. I spurred Cabot, led him on. I feel adrift without Edith sometimes."

"Well," I said, "I could have sat out the convention, stayed in Albany."

She laughed. "Senator Tom would have flayed you alive."

Delegates came up to her, knelt like acolytes. They all wanted to be part of her Washington salon. I might as well have been invisible.

"Oh, they're amusing," Nannie said. "They expected one of their own clique to suck up to the Major, and you got in the way."

Then the muck-a-muck himself, Mark Hanna, appeared on the

mezzanine, with its little sea of lamps and newspaper sticks, and asked Nannie if he might join us.

"Wouldn't want to intrude, Mrs. Cabot."

"Nonsense," Nannie said and signaled the waiter to bring another chair.

Hanna took out a crumpled slip of paper from his pocket—it was a telegram, not from the Major himself, but from Miss Ida.

> CONGRATULATIONS, GOVERNOR, FROM MY WILLIE.
> MAY GOD GRANT YOU BOTH A LONG, LONG LIFE.

Hanna smiled at the ploy. I did not merit a note from the Major himself, but from his half-mad missus. I returned the telegram. "Please thank Ida for me."

"Oh, I will thank her myself," Nannie said. "She belongs to my Thursday reading club."

Nannie was the clever one, the diplomat. She stroked Fat Marcus like a feathered bird. "We all want the same thing, Mr. Hanna. A smashing victory for the Major. Governor Roosevelt will do his part."

Hanna gobbled a bun and left the table like a fat cavalier, kissing Nannie's hand. She shut her eyes for moment; her eyelids wandered like a pair of stunned butterflies. "Oh, that awful man," she said. "We will give him the dagger one of these days. We will rip apart his loins."

Then all the savagery fled from her face as she patted her lips and poured both of us another cup of China tea.

CHAPTER 16

THE GHOSTS OF
SAN JUAN HILL

1901

BAMIE HAD A CHILD AT FORTY-THREE.

William Sheffield Cowles Jr., a ruddy ten-and-a-half-pound boy with a spine that was as perfect as a polished row of piano keys, was born three years ago, while I ran for Governor. It was the one campaign of mine that Bamie had to miss. And Sister grieved about it. "Theodore, you might have captured another fifty thousand votes had you canvassed with the rabbis on the Lower East Side."

"Bully," I said, "and Boss Croker would have dented their skulls."

Bamie's husband, Commander Cowles, was stationed in that grim, gray War Department castle near the President's palace, and Sister had rented a brick house on N Street that served as my home and headquarters while I was in Washington, as McKinley's man. It was a very short interlude. I presided over the Senate until it went into recess, after four days.

"I'm done. Hanna doesn't want me around. He says I might start another war."

Bamie perused me with a pinched face. My little niece, Eleanor, was in London at the moment, where she attended a finishing school that Bamie herself had selected.

"Teedie, it doesn't matter one bean what Hanna says. You will conquer them all."

She watched me mope about. "The Major's kind enough," I said. "I had cake and wine in the Red Room with him and Ida. But I'm not allowed near the cabinet. I ought to wear a sign: 'Part-Time President. All Speaking Engagements Welcome.' . . . How is Dear Little Eleanor? Does she ask about her uncle?"

That hump on Bamie's back she hid so well bristled under her shawl.

"I do not like to touch upon that topic, Theodore. She is confused about the relationship you had with her father. And I'm loath to discuss it."

"Why?" I asked, like a little boy waiting to be slapped, though Sister had never slapped me once, not even when I put my pet salamander in the maid's blouse and caused a panic in the parlor.

"I will not revisit what cannot be revisited," she said. "I prefer to talk about your future."

"I have none," I said.

She saw how somber I was, and she didn't laugh. "They fear you, Theodore, and they cannot survive without you. The Major is a porch politician. You're the one who had to duel that tin Jesus, Jennings Bryan."

"Bamie," I said, "I did not duel Bryan. We never debated once."

"But you followed his tracks," she said like a huntress, "and outmaneuvered him wherever he went."

That had been my strategy—to *outdeliver* Bryan—but I cannot measure how well I succeeded. The Major had all the money in the world behind him, with a hurricane of pamphlets and advertisements in the press, as biographers created one myth after the other about McKinley and TR, both bloodied in battle.

"Sister," I said, "I think I saw Ellie."

Her brow deepened and she slumped inside her corset of metal and bone. "Where?"

"I'm not sure. . . . On the battlefield."

She neither barked nor laughed.

"In Cuba," I insisted, "while I was charging up San Juan Hill. Ellie's ghost just might have been there—might, I say, among the other troopers. I did not converse with him."

She would not succor me. "Brother, you have never believed in ghosts—you dreamt of Ellie. Perhaps you will dream of him again."

She kissed my forehead—it felt like an affectionate bee sting— and left her Teedie to build his own battlefields. . . .

THE SENATE WITHDREW FOR six months, and I returned to Sagamore Hill with Edith, Alice, and the bunnies. I had books to write—still, I'd never been so idle. I chopped wood, kept in touch with Riders in distress, but I had to hire the Pinks to locate some of my lost cavaliers, with ex-Trooper Taggart at my side. He still had his vitals in Chicago and the Far West. And he used his agency like a vast sweeping net that you might have once found on a whaler; he trolled for Rough Riders who had loosened their grip and did not have a targetable address. I expected as much of cowpunchers who wandered from rodeo to rodeo, ranch to ranch. Taggart had his affiliates track such rovers and keep a strict tally of each man's whereabouts. We found every last one, those who were incarcerated, or had become a local nuisance. I spent weeks riding the rails with Taggart.

"I owe it to the regiment, sir. And it's my great honor to travel with you."

For the first time I could cash in on the title I had to wear. "Vice President" had a bit of prestige in the cattle towns of Montana and Wyoming. We were able to get five cavaliers out of the calaboose. And the Boone & Crockett Club paid for their upkeep at a rest home in Nevada.

They all blubbered in my presence. That was the hardest part of rescuing them from their private hell.

"We damn let you down, Colonel. We disgraced the regiment."

"You did not," I said. "We trained you to fight and then pitched you aside."

I gave them pocket money. I'd turned warriors into beggars, and it made me livid.

The worst of it was when we had to enter Indian Territory. Trooper Antonia Little Feather had been unmasked again. A certain prosecutor was holding her at the hall of justice in a pretentious little town called Hallelujah Springs. It was crammed with white settlers who hoped to make a killing once the Territory was admitted into statehood. They'd hurled most of the Indians out of this potential paradise. And Antonia Little Feather lost her luck. She fell afoul of the law in a barroom brawl. Antonia bashed a few skulls before the sheriff of Hallelujah Springs and his deputies arrested her and obliged her to strip. They discovered her discharge papers from the First Volunteers and handed her over to the town prosecutor, who wanted to build his reputation in the West. It was strictly illegal in the Territories for a woman to impersonate a man and was punishable with a hefty fine and three years in prison.

So we met with the prosecutor at the hall of justice, Bryson Carterett, and he couldn't have been more than thirty-five. Taggart did a little digging, and he discovered that Carterett owned half the town—the saloons, the barbershop, the dusty hotel, and the land that the hall of justice was built on.

He had a wicked, dancing smile, as if he'd just caught me by the seat of my pants. He was clutching Antonia's discharge papers.

"Mr. Vice President, the First Volunteers, that's another name for the Rough Riders, is it not?"

"It is," I said to this despicable land baron.

"We wouldn't want word to get out that the Rough Riders sheltered a female volunteer, and that Princess Little Feather fought in your ranks."

"What are you proposing?" I asked.

"Well, that's a good question. Colonel, someone like you might do miracles for this town. You could reside here for a month, break bread with us. You could talk up Hallelujah Springs in the corridors of Congress, and support our petition for statehood."

I wished for one moment that I'd been a Strangler, with a Strangler's copper coil.

"And what would that do for Little Feather?"

"Wonders," said Carterett. "I'd release her outright in your custody, erase her very existence from our books."

Taggart grabbed the back of my coat. "We'd like to have a glimpse of Little Feather before we conclude any deal."

The young prosecutor stared at Taggart. "And who is this gentleman with the drag-foot, Mr. Vice President?"

"I'm a Pinkerton," Taggart said.

Carterett smiled like a potentate. "You won't find any Pinks in this town."

"We'd still like to see Little Feather."

A deputy brought her upstairs in some kind of sackcloth, the town's own hair shirt. The sons of bitches had shaved her skull. She had bruises and bumps on her temples. Her nose was bleeding. She was all buckled up in chains, and Antonia could barely walk.

I didn't want to ruin her exit from Hallelujah Springs with too much emotion. I signaled to her with my eyes. She didn't meet my gaze. I had the damn indigos. I'd trained these troopers, and then abandoned them to dust.

Carterett surveyed the room, feasting on his success.

"Well, Mr. Vice President, do we have a deal?"

Taggart nudged me. "We'll ponder a bit, and tell you tomorrow."

"Meanwhile," I said, "I'd like Little Feather released on a bond. You have my word of honor, Mr. Carterett. We won't run."

"Of course," he said. "Then you'd all be fugitives. But I'm not releasing Little Feather until we have a deal. The trooper stays with me."

Taggart went down to the telegraph office, and after that we had breaded lamb chops for dinner at the land baron's hotel. Taggart ate my portion. He gobbled up all the mashed potatoes and peas. He hummed throughout the meal. All I could remember was Antonia's hair shirt.

I should have had more faith in Taggart. I went to bed in a sack-cloth made of silk and woke in the morning to a different town. A confused rumbling had nagged at me in my sleep. The hotel seemed to rise up from its foundation and drift about in a dream. Finally I looked out the window in my silk nightshirt. I'd forgotten all about the Pinks. They arrived in buckboards, wearing dusters and wide-brimmed hats, with Winchesters cradled in their laps. I'd opposed them while I was Governor. They were mercenaries and strike-breakers at the beck and call of industrial barons. But they'd come here at Taggart's behest like an army of locusts. They broke into the saloons and served themselves shots of whiskey, then pranced into the breakfast room and seized all the tables except our own. "Morning, Mr. Vice President," they muttered, tipping the pointed brims of their felt hats, as they devoured every fried potato the kitchen could produce.

They were sinister in their thoroughness. They sent barbers and bank clerks off on a holiday, while the sheriff and his deputies were exiled within their own jailhouse. Carterett was a prince without his princelings inside the hall of justice. The Pinks devastated a dustbin like Hallelujah Springs through sheer attrition. Not a shot was fired. The Pinks preferred a bloodless coup whenever possible. They'd stripped the town and its prosecutor of all their privileges before noon.

Carterett wasn't the same fellow when we returned to the hall of justice. He had Little Feather in her street clothes, with a hat on her bald head. That dancing smile of his had disappeared.

"Mr. Vice President, I will not tell a soul about Little Feather's sexual secret, nor will I ever mention her name and the Rough Riders in a single sentence."

I was merciless, like a man composed of arrowheads. "Mr. Prosecutor, you will do much more than that. You will forget that she ever existed, or else the Pinks will break every bone in your body."

Antonia still had her bald head. I couldn't send her back to the reservation. She was used to mischief. She would have to carry some kind of a flag.

"I've troubled you, Colonel," she said. "And it will haunt my days. I should have joined the Army Nurse Corps."

"Trooper, I wouldn't have had it any other way. We took the hill. You were our standard-bearer. That charge wouldn't have been the same without you."

But no reminiscences could help her now. We'd all become victims of that one little hour of glory. It was Taggart who came up with a solution. He could ease her into his Manhattan office as an undercover agent, where she could be both Anton and Antonia. Pinkertons were used to masquerades.

"But if she's ever captured by some heartless gang . . ."

"Colonel, I won't let her out of my sight."

Yet I could never feel quite comfortable about Little Feather as a Pink. There was this nagging guilt. I had created my own little circus of war monsters. And no matter what I did, that circus wouldn't go away. Linger it would as long as I lived.

CHAPTER 17

THE
COWBOY KING

1901

I WAS ON A REMOTE ISLAND IN VERMONT WHEN THE President was shot.

He had two columns of soldiers in front of him, I believe, to funnel every visitor who wanted to shake his hand at the Expo. And I whispered to myself, the Pinks should have been there, or some of my Rough Riders. They would have spotted that peculiar boy with the golden curls, who clung to a handkerchief, a revolver hidden underneath. He could have been an angel or an anarchist. The Pinks would have wrestled him to the ground and carted him off. And the Major would still be alive. . . .

But I was Vice President on permanent recess. I had little to do with the Major and his wanderlust that summer. Our paths never crossed. I had no documents to sign. I saw none. I could have become prince of Saturn's seventh moon as far as the Major was concerned, and I would still have sat in the dark—official spokesman for an administration that made an invisibility of me. I was the Major's man at a Vermont fish and game luncheon on Isle La Motte, in Lake Champlain. I wouldn't wear a rose in my lapel, like the Major, who often awarded such a rose to some winsome bride visiting the White House. The water had an incredible purl, like tiny, moving cracks in a lake of solid green fire. A majordomo suddenly arrived with a very sour look. He whispered in my ear. A telephone call had come from the Secretary of State. The President had been hit, not once but twice, by a lunatic with a baby face inside the Temple of Music. One bullet managed to fall out before he was operated on at the Expo's tiny hospital; the other bullet couldn't be found. He was bundled across the half-lit streets of Buffalo by the hospital's lone ambulance, with a policeman on horseback marking the traffic, then was taken to the Milburn mansion on Delaware Avenue, with its scatter of chimneys and solid brick front, where he had been staying with his wife. And when I arrived in Buffalo, I couldn't get near the mansion in my carriage. My driver was forlorn. He had a holster at his side.

"We cannot move, Mr. Vice President. We might get killed in all the confusion. I recommend that we untangle ourselves the second we have a chance and return to the station."

"That's ridiculous," I said. "I'm here to see the Major, and see him I will."

The block had been roped off and was surrounded by a detachment of soldiers with bayonets. These soldiers did not take kindly to me.

"Who the hell are ye, son?" their sergeant growled. He must have recognized my spectacles and mustache. The Vice President meant as little to him as to the rest of the nation.

Cortelyou, the President's own assistant, with his pince-nez and trim mustache pocked with silver, had to come out of the mansion and fetch me. He didn't seem dee-lighted to have me on Delaware Avenue. The crisis had passed. The Major was on the mend. He would be back at work within weeks, Cortelyou predicted. I'd become kind of an embarrassment—a twilight creature who seemed to suggest something was out of joint at the Milburn mansion. Ida McKinley kept mumbling to herself. I couldn't understand a word. One side of her face was a bit sunken, and I tried to soothe her. She kept pinching her own arms.

"Miss Ida, it will all work out. You'll see."

She recovered her mental state for a moment and inspected me like a general. "Are you the boy who cleans the slop?"

"Sort of," I said.

She had a shrewdness in her eyes of the half insane. "You're not that boy. You're my husband's hangman. Where's your gloves?"

"I'm the Vice President, ma'am."

She inspected me again, from top to bottom. "Did you enter through the servants' door?"

Ida wasn't insane, not at all. "You'll be kind to my Willie, won't you? Tell him that he shouldn't forget his wife."

The cabinet had me under hook and wire. I wasn't permitted much of an audience with the Major. The sons of bitches kept me in the vestibule for an hour—confidential stuff, one of McKinley's ushers said. I wasn't entitled to share such urgent matters. And in the cabinet's eyes I didn't exist. I was like an alligator's extra tail. Finally the door opened to the President's suite. It had the unmistakable waft of chloroform. There were no doctors present, not even a damn nurse to wipe the Major's brow. His bedroom had been turned into the Ship of State.

McKinley wore a silk robe in bed, with satin pillows propped up behind him. His owlish eyebrows had been combed. A barber must have sneaked in before I arrived. There wasn't an idle hair to be had on his cleft chin. But no powder in the world could have hid his pale, waxy complexion.

I felt that I had fallen upon some rehearsed tableau. The Major had a pen in his fist. Cortelyou and the cabinet stood around him like a handful of hawks. He glanced up from the document he was signing.

"Roosevelt, how kind. . . . You'll make sure the assassin isn't harmed. Leon, isn't it? I can't pronounce his second name. I don't want him beaten."

There was no assassin, I wanted to say, not yet. But I would have had to inform the President that Leon Czolgosz was still alive.

"Pan America," he said. "We will own this new century, Roosevelt, and why shouldn't we celebrate this ownership with a fair?

Did you see the electric shower, delivered from Niagara Falls—an empire of light? We destroyed the darkness, killed it. I challenge you to find a single shadow at the world's fair."

The Major started to cough. One of his eyes wandered all over the place. The pen dropped out of his hand.

"Can I do anything?" I asked. "I mean, can I . . . ?"

"Not at all," said Cortelyou. I had no right to be in a mansion surrounded by bayonets.

I shook the President's vacant hand, clotted with black ink.

"Come visit us again, Roosevelt. I'll be your personal guide. We'll both take the Trip to the Moon. God knows what we'll find."

I'd gone to that pavilion at the Pan-American fair months ago, with Edith, Alice, and the bunnies. It was crammed with midgets who danced and sang and went around with baskets of green cheese; moonstruck, the midgets were half mad from all the wattage, that constant pounding of electric light.

Then I heard a soft sob from the vicinity of the bed, like the mewling of an animal in pain. "I've ruined the Expo, Cortelyou. How silly of me to go and get myself shot. People will shun the fair. I've slowed down the century and cost Buffalo a bundle."

"Nonsense," said Cortelyou. "The receipts have gone up after that unfortunate incident. . . . Customers are always curious."

I WASN'T ALLOWED ACCESS to him after that. They closed ranks, McKinley's loyal men. I had nothing to look at but John Hay's distinguished beard in the mansion's vestibule. I admired the Secretary of State. He'd been Lincoln's confidential secretary, had worked beside him when he was a very young man—that lent the Secretary an aura of angel dust. He had a peculiar method of pursing his lips, as if he were about to swallow his own tongue.

"Theodore, you've been a good soldier to come here from Vermont. All of us are humbled by your act. But it might give the wrong impression to have you with us in Buffalo . . . as if we were preparing for a presidential wake."

I left for the railroad station, in the President's own carriage with its pair of palominos and a luxurious silvered roof. There was still a bullet in the Major's body, lodged somewhere at the back of his stomach. The surgeon had sewn the wound with black silk, but the bullet remained. I was not as sanguine as Cortelyou or John Hay. The Major had that sour smell of a man who was not on the mend.

I knew they would have to call me back, and this time there would be a touch of panic, a flutter perhaps in Cortelyou's voice, or whoever else had to make the call. I was derelict while the Major was alive, the outcast of Sagamore Hill. But I would not allow a sickbed in Buffalo to interfere with my vacation plans. I'd been a hunter and a soldier in the field, even if my soldiering had been very short; and I could almost divine the day when gangrene would set in around a lost bullet.

Edith had chosen a cottage at the site of a former mining camp on Mount Marcy, in the Adirondacks. The mining camp had been turned into a posh resort and a haven for hunters and mountain climbers. The site was as rustic as ever, with deer licks and bird sanctuaries galore. It had a horse-watering station called the Lower Works. Alice insisted on exploring one of the abandoned mine shafts with Archie and Kermit, and a forest ranger accompanied them.

"It's dangerous," Edith said. "They might fall . . . and disappear."

The ranger tried to reassure her. He'd descended the shaft many times, and he had Alice and the two boys cinched to a harness connected to him. But Edith was restless until her bunnies returned.

"Mother," Alice said, with coal marks on her face, "it was pure dee-light. I could listen to the darkness breathe."

The next morning we left the bunnies in care of a governess, and Edith and I departed with a couple of rangers on a trip to Lake Colden, five or six miles from the campsite, with tiny ripples in the lake's surface, soft as wind-blown silk. There was a light drizzle, and Edith borrowed the yellow mackintosh I had worn in Cuba. We could not see Mount Marcy in all the mist. Edith had her boots from Abercrombie's, or she couldn't have accomplished the climb in that rugged terrain. Her fist was balled in mine.

"A young Pole, wasn't he? And an anarchist, the assassin. No one can pronounce his name. Wasn't he a disciple of Emma Goldman?"

"The crowd would have killed that boy, gobbled him up, Cortelyou said. But the Major had to beg for mercy . . . with a bullet in him."

Edith shivered under her mackintosh. "Then we should consider ourselves lucky that you weren't harmed on our own visit to the fair. I remember that tower of electric lights. And all the domes—it was like the City of God." She started to laugh. "I expected angels to descend."

"They did," I said. "Guides appeared from all the pavilions and followed Alicy around."

Edith scolded me. "It's your fault. You've turned your own daughter into a siren. She breaks the heart of every boy she meets."

I didn't want to dwell on that. Alice was sixteen and couldn't be controlled by a governess. She joined a gypsy camp once in the forest around Cove Neck, and I had to chase them off our property, or she might have eloped with the caravan and married the gypsy king. She lived within her own civility, and there was no way to barter with her. But she was kind to the bunnies, even if she confused them with her various rôles. Was she their sister, or Auntie Alice, who fell from the sky? Still, Edith had raised her as her own, despite their bickering. My wife never wavered once.

We arrived at Lake Colden, had a campfire feast, and slept in a cabin that smelled of mothballs. The drizzle still clung to us in the morning, but I decided to push on. Edith elected to return to the mining camp with one of the rangers. She had a quizzical look, as if I might get lost in some great unknown.

"It's a mountain, Edie, not heaven or hell."

That couldn't reassure her. "It has caverns, dear, and what if I never find you again?"

"You'll find me," I said. And we kissed in front of the two rangers. I recalled our senseless quarrel in the ice house at Tranquillity, almost thirty years ago, when I should have held tight to my fourteen-year-old Cleopatra, not let her slip from my grasp. I would have remained a drifter without her. I might have joined *Cody's Wild West*, or settled in as a deputy sheriff.

I climbed deeper into the mist with the second ranger. I nearly tripped once or twice, and could have tumbled into a ravine, but I was cinched to the ranger now. We climbed belt to belt. The fog lifted for a moment, and I could see a swirl of forest with no outline and no end. But the fog rolled back in, and the ranger said there was too much grayness surrounding us to arrive at the next peak. And so we climbed down from that treacherous terrain. We met other rangers at an outpost near a little lake called Tear-of-the-Clouds. They knew we were coming and had packed a hamper lunch for both of us. But we didn't stay long.

Another ranger ran up from the hollows with a telegram in his hand, like a tiny yellow banner in the wind. That banner was no flag of glory. I suspected what it was about. The President had suffered a relapse.

I returned to our cottage at Camp Tahawus in my wet clothes. I was too damn tired to take a sponge bath. We ate dinner in front of the fire. My wife made me put on my blue Rough Rider flannels and a pair of dry socks. The fire crackled a lot, and the sparks flew around us. I dreamt of Brave Heart, delivering the finest sheets of glass, long before I was ever born. I imagined him in a workman's blue bib, and with a boy's whiskers, not a full beard. Papa might have found a home for my lion had he still been alive. He wouldn't have pawned her off to a bushel of zookeepers in the Bronx, not even at the call of science. Papa knew how to take care of kittens, even if they were warlike. . . .

Alice had already picked out a ranger to marry. All that climbing must have made me giddy.

"We won't stop you," I said. "But you'll have to live in a hut for the rest of your life."

"Father, it couldn't be worse than that icy mansion on Eagle Street."

I was feeling demonic with my daughter. "Aren't you gonna introduce us to your beau?"

I had caught her off guard. She hadn't contemplated complete compliance on the part of an ogre.

"Father, he's frightened of you. William says you might get him fired."

"But you were cinched to him in a mine shaft. That's almost like a marriage."

It was Edith who put an end to our little war. She said I was tired, and Alice's marriage plans would have to wait.

I went to bed at nine. I slept with Edie in a narrow bunk, a kind of sleigh bed.

A ranger woke us a little before midnight—it was Alice's current *fiancé*. He handed me a telegram and left. It was from the Secretary of State.

> *PRESIDENT DYING.*
> *CABINET THINKS YOU SHOULD LOSE NO*
> *TIME COMING.*

Ah, why did I feel all in a twist? The Major's factotums needed me now—*lose no time coming*. They couldn't run the country with a corpse in the President's bed.

A buckboard was waiting outside the cottage. It was a seven-hour drive down the precipitous slopes to North Creek Station. There would be several relays; one team of horses couldn't make that descent. I was startled to see that my driver was the same young forester who had handed me the telegram—Alice's erstwhile fiancé. I did not utter a peep about Alice. Both of us were wearing mackintoshes. We were the victims of a summer sirocco—a wind and rain that blew dust into our eyes. My specs turned into blinders; I had to keep wiping them with my neckerchief from the Rough Rider campaign. That couldn't kill the dust, and I pulled my black slouch hat over my ears. I must have looked like a desperado on the run.

The driver was poor at the reins. I had to steady him, or we wouldn't have had much of a buckboard.

"You'll do fine, son," I said into the biting rain.

"Mr. Vice President, I didn't propose to your daughter. I can swear on that. Yes, our hands touched—once. That was the whole of it."

"Look at the road, son. I'm sure Alice will release you from any obligation."

I had to chuck pebbles at the horses' flanks, or we might never have arrived at Aiden Lair Lodge, halfway to North Creek. The landlord, Mike Cronin, was a seasoned whip. With his broad shoulders and his dark beard, he reminded me of Brave Heart. I thanked the young ranger. He could rest at the lodge that night. I didn't have much time to reassure him.

"Son, you should be careful about escorting young ladies into a miner's shaft. The real danger isn't the dark."

And I climbed into Cronin's buckboard in my Rough Rider mackintosh and desperado's hat. The young ranger had cost us half an hour.

"Cronin, you'll have to rush."

"This road ain't a picnic, Mr. Vice President. There are too many damn curves. We could miss a curve and fall a few hundred feet."

"Well, we'll have to risk it."

The landlord had two big black Morgans and an excellent rig. I did not fear the slopes. The Morgans seemed to have memorized every curve, like the bends in a river. One of those black beauties stumbled, but we didn't lose any ground. That's the kind of whip the landlord was. There was no visibility at all in the fog. I had to rise up on my haunches and shake the lantern. We had the devil of a time spotting boulders in the middle of the road. I worried about our weight on the log bridges—the logs rumbled beneath the horses' hooves like some hidden eternity. But the Morgans got us through that summer sirocco.

We passed swamps and a graveyard, and a tiny village that wasn't even on the map. It was the lantern that led us, and the land-lord's firm grip. Froth gathered at the horses' mouths like crooked plumes. "Landlord," I said, "damn this ride. We have to let the horses blow, or we'll slip into the next creek." The landlord leapt down from the buckboard and wiped the lather from the Morgans' coats with a red rag that he took from his pocket. He had a gentleness about him that was genuine.

"You were right, Mr. Roosevelt. The horses needed a blow."

We crossed a crooked little bridge into North Creek with a loud rattle. There was already a crowd on Main Street. They looked hypnotized, as if I were some gilded creature that rose out of the morning mist. "There he is! That's him." We arrived at the depot. There were several soldiers, a couple of bodyguards, detectives, and clerks, with a grimness about them—and a train with my own private carriage. One of the clerks handed me a telegram from John Hay.

THE PRESIDENT PASSED AT 2:15 THIS MORNING.

I must have been the last to learn. The soldiers looked at me with a strange awe.

"Mr. President," their captain said, saluting me.

"I'm in limbo, son," I said. "Neither here nor there. I haven't earned that title yet. You can call me Colonel Roosevelt . . . or Mr. Ted."

I climbed aboard. The soldiers had bayonets. The bodyguards wore holsters and black derbies. They were attached to some macabre presidential detail. I sat in a velvet seat on the handsomest locomotive of the Delaware & Hudson line. I commandeered one of the clerks and dictated a telegram to my wife.

DARLING, TAKE THE BUNNIES HOME.
MAKE SURE ALICE DOESN'T MARRY SOMEONE ON THE CLIMB DOWN.

I dictated another to John Hay.

EXPECT TO ARRIVE IN BUFFALO AT THE SOONEST.

And then I dismissed the clerks, the detectives, and the soldiers with the bayonets.

The captain was suspicious of my command. "Mr. Hay told us not to let you out of our sight, sir. We are to guard your life—to give up our own lives if necessary."

"Captain," I said, "Mr. Hay isn't here, and I am in charge of the nation. You can guard my life from the next car. But right now I want to be alone."

And so that's where they assembled, the entire little platoon.

This elite contraption had its own cook. I ordered sandwiches and cake for all my guardians and clerks, and had the porter bring me coffee in a silver pot like the ones at the Fifth Avenue Hotel. I drank out of the Delaware's own porcelain cup. I savored the biscuits and cucumber sandwiches, just as they served them at Brown's in London, where I had stayed as the mysterious stranger who married Edith Carow in a dark church. This Pullman belonged to the president of the line. It was a princely carriage. I believe it even had a compartment for his mistress. I did a bit of exploring. Her compartment wasn't locked. I could read an entire narrative in her nightgowns and vials of perfume. I felt like an interloper in another man's private affairs. Still, I needed a bit of diversion. I did not want to think of Buffalo and bullet wounds, of Ida weeping in her rumpled dress, and McKinley lying in state, his toenails under the covers.

So I sipped my coffee. But I did not have my little idyll before the crush of public office landed on my head. *President Roosevelt.* The carriage lurched forward with a terrific jolt. I went flying out of my seat with the porcelain cup in hand. I could not rescue the railroad's cup—it shattered into pieces. The coffee spilled onto the curtains. The entire platoon stumbled into my Pullman, bayonets aloft.

"It might be those damn anarchists," the young captain said. "A coordinated attack to bring down the presidency. There's too much at stake. We will have to squire you from now on."

The conductor arrived with a sullen look—it seems that the Delaware Executive Express had crashed into a handcar that had been left haphazardly along a route that was supposed to have been cleared all the way from North Creek to Buffalo; a couple of train-men and a soldier had suffered injuries in the caboose. A crew had to be called in to clear the debris; an ambulance arrived. I got out of the carriage with my bodyguards behind me and talked to the trainmen. I gripped the soldier's hand.

"Colonel, I was with you on the run up San Juan Hill."

I should have recognized him. I had that gift never to forget a face. "Which regiment, son?"

"The Ninth, sir."

I still couldn't recognize that face. It irritated me. "I hope you didn't watch me embarrass myself."

"No, sir. You charged like a windlass with a bandanna flying from your hat. It was edifying—better than having a trumpeter at your ear."

The boy hadn't seen me crawling on my knees without my specs. I was grateful for that.

I returned to my carriage. The porter brought me another one of the railroad president's porcelain cups. I watched Mount Marcy disappear into the distance with its desolate peak. My mind col-lected around details—the chips in the ceiling of the Red Room, the White House's ragged carpets that Edie would inherit. And then it all began to drift. I imagined myself in Buffalo Bill's circus. The whole caboodle: Edith wrapped in an unfamiliar coat, guard-ing a rifle as tall as she; Alice in the tulle of a high-wire acrobat, with Ted, Kermit, Ethel, Archie, and little Quentin as her assis-tants. And I was wearing a black wide-brimmed hat like the kind Custer favored. We had become the featured attraction of Cody's cavalcade—the Roosevelt Family of Sagamore Hill, sharpshooters, acrobats, and entertainers. Our likeness was on every handbill and appeared in painted colors on the canvas flaps of the master tent.

I'd abandoned politics and writing for the show business, in my phantasm. Edie didn't complain. She took control of our salary. Little Eleanor had come with her overbite and gawky limbs, a kind of ragged Cinderella. She helped us change our costumes and was part of Alice's performance, a minor acrobat. I didn't have much of a tussle with Buffalo Bill. He had his act and we had ours. But whenever we appeared, folks stood up and yelled, "The Cowboy, the Cowboy—and his Clan."

We were in a panorama of cowboys, and that still didn't seem to count. Cody's buckskin garb had become too familiar, like his silver beard and his waspish waist. He could have been cut from cardboard. But I was the gunfighter with stubby fingers and specs, and I had no ambition beyond that. I'd become the antithesis of everything Brave Heart had believed in. I didn't rescue stray kittens at *Cody's Wild West*, or provide lodging for newsboys. I was an entertainer now. I made my entrance on Little Texas, my cowpony, retrieved from Cuba and our barn at Sagamore Hill, with that white star on his forehead. I waved my black slouch hat.

"Ya-ha-haw!"

Then Alice did a somersault; diamond-shaped sequins had been sewn into her costume by little Eleanor, Alice's tailoress; the diamonds shimmered in the tent's darkening light. I went round and round with my Winchester, shooting bobbins out of the air—the bobbins exploded into little feathers of wood. Then Edith stood on a platform, wearing her fireman's leather coat. I shot off the clasps, the pockets, the metal tips of her collar, until the coat looked like a relic from a rag shop. I'd grazed her arm, and a splotch of blood appeared in the leather like an inkblot. Poor Edie was mummified with bandages from all my misfires. But that's what drew the crowds—the sense of danger that Cody himself couldn't provide. Alice dangling on the high wire without a net while Quentin drummed below and Kermit tooted on his tin trumpet, Ethel danced like Salome in a tutu and Archie watched with his mouth agape.

Then the bleat of the train broke through the *Wild West* like a grim warning, and a reminder of where I was, and we arrived at Exchange Street, with its barnlike roof. There were folks outside my window, men and women with wonder—and fright—on their faces, as if they were looking into the blue eyes of immortality. The soldiers and the bodyguards assembled—a phalanx formed like the funnel that couldn't seem to protect McKinley at the world's fair. I stepped out of the carriage with that toothy Roosevelt grin.

People jostled against that funnel of soldiers. Bayonets were drawn. I didn't want a riot in the middle of the station. "There could be blood," the young captain whispered in my ear. But I didn't see any anarchist angels with blond curls. I stepped into that roaring crowd of greeters—that was the Roosevelt way.

"Mr. President, Mr. President."

Men and women were itching to touch my sleeve. Soldiers crept between us, shoving whoever they could. I had to keep a lad from falling. "Stop that!" I shouted.

Babies were thrust at me. I wanted to rock them in my arms, reassure a mother or two, but I didn't dare in a field of bayonets that reminded me of monstrous porcupine quills. I could feel my freedom slip away with a sudden pull, like the silent shrug of a straitjacket. I didn't require bayonets, not at all. Deep within my throat, I let out the Rough Rider rip.

YA-HA-HAWWW

ACKNOWLEDGMENTS

THE AUTHOR WOULD LIKE TO THANK GEORGES BORCHARDT, Lenore Riegel, Marie Pantojan, Dave Cole, and also Robert Weil, the Captain Ahab of publishing, in his continual search for the blinding white whale of perfection.

ILLUSTRATION CREDITS

BITTER BRONX: THIRTEEN STORIES

"[Jerome Charyn] is to the Bronx what Saul Bellow, early in his career, was to Upper Broadway—bard, celebrant, mythologizer."
—Jonathan Yardley, *Washington Post*

I AM ABRAHAM: A NOVEL OF LINCOLN AND THE CIVIL WAR

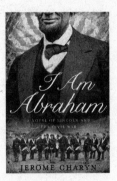

"*I Am Abraham* is not only the best novel about President Lincoln since Gore Vidal's *Lincoln* in 1984, but it is also twice as good to read."
—Gabor Boritt, author of *The Lincoln Enigma* and recipient of the National Humanities Medal

THE SECRET LIFE OF EMILY DICKINSON

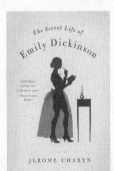

"In this brilliant and hilarious jailbreak of a novel, Charyn channels the genius poet and her great leaps of the imagination."
—Donna Seaman, *Booklist*, starred review

LIVERIGHT